War Cry

Also by Wilbur Smith

The Egyptian Series

River God
The Seventh Scroll
Warlock
The Quest
Desert God
Pharaoh

The Courtney Series

When the Lion Feeds
The Sound of Thunder
A Sparrow Falls
The Burning Shore
Power of The Sword
Rage
A Time to Die
Golden Fox
Birds of Prey
Monsoon
Blue Horizon
The Triumph of the Sun
Assegai
Golden Lion

The Ballantyne Series

A Falcon Flies
Men of Men
The Angels Weep
The Leopard Hunts In Darkness

Thrillers

The Dark of the Sun
Shout at the Devil
Gold Mine
The Diamond Hunters
The Sunbird
Eagle in the Sky
The Eye of the Tiger
Cry Wolf
Hungry as the Sea
Wild Justice (UK)
The Delta Decision (US)
Elephant Song
Those in Peril
Vicious Circle
Predator

WAR CRY

WILBUR SMITH

and David Churchill

WILLIAM MORROW
An Imprint of HarperCollinsPublishers

WAR CRY. Copyright © 2017 by Wilbur Smith. All rights reserved. Printed in the United States of America. No part of this book may be used or reproduced in any manner whatsoever without written permission except in the case of brief quotations embodied in critical articles and reviews. For information, address HarperCollins Publishers, 195 Broadway, New York, NY 10007.

HarperCollins books may be purchased for educational, business, or sales promotional use. For information, please email the Special Markets Department at SPsales@harpercollins.com.

FIRST EDITION

Library of Congress Cataloging-in-Publication Data has been applied for.

ISBN 978-0-06-227649-0 (hardcover)

ISBN 978-0-06-266319-1 (international edition)

17 18 19 20 21   LSC   10 9 8 7 6 5 4 3 2 1

I dedicate this book War Cry *to my wife, Mokhiniso,*
who has been my total joy and inspiration
over these last many decades of my life
and all those others yet to come.
I love you, my Fireball.

War Cry

WO MONTHS HAD PASSED since war had been declared and the autumn sun that shone down from the clear blue skies over Bavaria was so glorious that it seemed to cry out for beer to be drunk and songs to be sung in hearty, joyful voices. But the Oktoberfest had been cancelled and the Double Phaeton limousine proceeding up the short drive of the villa in Grünwald, just outside Munich, bore tidings that were anything but joyous.

The car pulled to a halt. Its chauffeur opened the passenger door to allow a distinguished gentleman in his late sixties to disembark and a uniformed butler admitted him into the house. A moment later, Athala, Countess of Meerburg, looked up as the family lawyer Viktor Solomons was shown into the drawing room. His hair and beard might now be silver and his stride was less vigorous than it had once been, but the impeccable tailoring of his suit, the gleaming white of his perfectly starched collar and the flawless shine of his shoes reflected a mind that was still as precise, as sharp and as insightful as ever.

Solomons stopped in front of Athala's chair, gave a respectful little nod of the head and said, "Good morning, Countess."

His mood seemed subdued, but that was only to be expected, Athala reminded herself. Solomons's beloved son Isidore was away at the front. No parent could ever be light-hearted knowing that their child's very survival now lay at the mercy of the gods of war.

"Good morning, Viktor, what an unexpected pleasure to see to you. Do please sit down." Athala extended a dainty hand toward the chair opposite her. Then she turned her attention toward the butler who had show the guest in and was now awaiting further instruction. "Some coffee, please Braun, for Herr *Rechtsanwalt* Solomons. Would you like some cake, Viktor? A little strudel, perhaps?"

"No thank you, Countess."

There was a somber tone to Solomons's voice, Athala realized, and he seemed uncharacteristically reluctant to look her in the eye. *He has bad news*, she thought. *Is it the boys? Has something happened to one of them?*

She told herself to remain calm. It would not do to betray one's fears, especially not while a servant was still in the room. "That will be all, Braun," she said.

The butler departed. Athala felt a sudden desire to postpone the bad tidings for just a few seconds. "Tell me, how is Isidore getting on? I hope he's safe and well."

"Oh yes, very well thank you, Countess," Viktor replied, with a distracted air, as though his mind was not fully engaged. But he took such pride in his beloved son that he could not resist adding, "You know, Isidore's division is commanded by Crown Prince Wilhelm himself. Imagine that! We received a letter from him just last week to say that he has already seen his first action. Apparently, his major declared that he conducted himself admirably under fire."

"I'm sure he did. Isidore is a fine young man. Now . . . what is it, Viktor, why are you here?"

Solomons hesitated a second to gather his thoughts and then

sighed, "I fear there is no other way of saying this, Countess. The War Office in Berlin informed me today that your husband, Graf Otto von Meerbach, is dead. General von Falkenhayn felt that it was better that you should hear the news from someone you knew, than simply receive a telegram message, or a visit from an unknown officer."

Athala slumped back against her chair, eyes closed, unable to say a word.

"I know this must be very distressing," Solomons went on, but distress was actually the last thing on her mind. Her overwhelming feeling was one of relief. Nothing had happened to her sons. And finally, after all these years, she was free. There was nothing that her husband could do to hurt her any more.

Athala controlled herself. She had been trained from her earliest girlhood to compose her fine, porcelain features into an image of calm, aristocratic elegance, no matter what the circumstances. It was now second nature to hide her true feelings behind that mask, just as the waters of a pond cover the constantly paddling feet that enable a swan to glide with such apparent ease across its glittering surface.

"How did he die?" she asked.

"In an air crash. I have been informed that His Excellency was engaged in a mission of the greatest importance to the German Empire. Its details are classified, but I am authorized to inform you that the crash occurred over British East Africa. The Count was flying aboard his magnificent new airship the *Assegai*. This was her maiden voyage."

"Did the British shoot him down, then?"

"I do not know. Our ambassador in Bern was informed by his British counterpart merely that the Count had died. This was a gesture of courtesy, in honor of your late husband's eminence. I gather, however, that the British do not have any Royal Flying Corps units in Africa, so we must assume that this was an accident of some kind. The gas used to elevate these "dirigibles" can, apparently, be very unstable."

Athala looked Solomons straight in the eye and very calmly said, "Was she on board the *Assegai* at the time?"

The lawyer did not need to be told who "she' was. Nor, for that matter, would anyone remotely acquainted with German high society. Count von Meerbach had long been a notorious philanderer, but in recent years he had become obsessed with one particular mistress, a ravishing beauty, with lustrous sable hair and violet-blue eyes called Eva von Wellberg. The Count had begged Athala to divorce him, so that he could make the Wellberg woman his wife, but she had refused. Her Catholic faith would not allow her to end her marriage. And so they had come to an arrangement. Countess Athala lived, with their two young sons, in her perfectly proportioned classical villa in the chic little town to the southwest of Munich where the smartest elements of Bavarian society could be found. Meanwhile, Count Otto had retained his family castle on the shores of the Bodensee. And there he kept his mistress, or as Athala thought of her, his whore, and saw his sons on the rare occasions he was able, or remotely willing to spare the time to attend to them.

"The *Assegai* was housed within the grounds of the Meerbach Motor Works," Solomons said, referring to the gigantic industrial complex on which the family fortune was based. "I am told by senior company officials who were present at the airship's departure that a woman was seen going aboard her. I was also informed by the War Office that the *Assegai* went down with all hands. No one survived."

Athala allowed a slight, bitter smile to cross her face. "I will not even pretend to be sorry that she is dead."

"Nor can I pretend to criticize you for that. I am well aware how much you have suffered on her account."

"Dear Viktor, you are always so kind, and so fair. You are . . ." She paused to correct herself, "You were my husband's lawyer, yet you have never done anything to hurt me."

"I am the family's lawyer, Countess," Solomons gently corrected her. "And as long as you were, and remain part of the von Meerbach family, then I will always consider you my client. Now, may I ask, are you ready to discuss any of the consequences of your husband's tragic demise?"

"Yes, yes I am," said Athala and then, for reasons she could not quite explain, she suddenly felt the loss to which she had been numb up to that point. For all that she had suffered, she had always prayed that one day her husband might see the error of his ways and devote himself to his family. Now all hope of that had gone. She began to cry and started rummaging through the bag at her feet, trying to find a handkerchief.

"May I?" asked Solomons, reaching into his pocket.

She waved him away, shaking her head, not trusting herself to speak. Finally she found what she was looking for, pressed the handkerchief to her eyes, dabbed her nose, took a deep breath and said, "Please forgive me."

"My dear Countess, you have just lost your husband. Whatever difficulties you may have faced, he was still the man you married, the father of your children."

She nodded and ruefully said, "It seems that I do not have a heart of stone after all."

"I, for one, never supposed that you did. Not for a single moment."

She gave him a nod of thanks and then said, "Please continue . . . I believe you were going to describe the consequences of . . ." She could not bring herself to use the word "death" and so just said, "Of what has occurred."

"Quite so. There cannot be a funeral, sadly, for if the body has been recovered, the British will by now have buried it."

"My husband died serving his country overseas," Athala said, straightening her back and resuming her air of poised composure. "That is to be expected."

"Indeed. But I think it would be entirely appropriate, indeed expected to have a service of remembrance, perhaps at the

Frauenkirche in Munich, or you may feel that either the family chapel at Schloss Meerbach, or even a service at the Motor Works would be more appropriate."

"The Frauenkirche," said Athala, without a moment's hesitation. "I don't think a factory is a suitable location at which to commemorate a Count of the German Empire and the chapel at the *schloss* is too small to accommodate the numbers of people who will wish to attend. Could someone from your firm liaise with the Archbishop's office, to secure a suitable date and assist with the administration of the event?"

"Of course, Countess, that would be no trouble. Might I suggest the Bayerischer Hof for the reception after the service? If you give the hotel manager your general requirements, the hotel staff will know exactly how best to provide exactly what you need."

"I'm afraid I can't even begin to think about that just now." Athala closed her eyes, trying to put the jumble of thoughts and emotions in her head in order and then asked, "What will become of my sons and I?"

"Well, the extent and variety of the Count's possessions mean that his will is unusually complex. But the essential facts are that the family estate here in Bavaria, and a majority share in the Motor Works all go to your eldest son, Konrad, along with the title of Graf von Meerbach. Your younger son, Gerhard, will have a smaller shareholding in the company. The various properties and the income they generate will be held in trust for each son until he is twenty-five. Prior to that point, they will each receive a generous allowance, plus the cost of their education, of course. Any additional expenditure will have to be approved by their trustees."

"And who will they be?"

"In the first instance, you and I, Countess."

"My God, fancy Otto allowing me such power."

"He was a traditionalist. He felt that a mother should take

charge of her children's upbringing. But you will note that I said "in the first instance". Once Konrad is twenty-five, and takes control of the family's affairs, he will also assume the role of trustee to his brother, who will then be eighteen years old."

"So for seven years, Gerhard will have to go cap in hand to Konrad if he ever needs anything?"

"Yes."

Athala frowned. "It worries me that one brother should have so much power over the other."

"His Excellency believed very strongly that a family, like a nation, required the strong leadership of a single man."

"Didn't he just . . . I take it that I am provided for."

"Oh yes, you need not worry on that score. You will retain your own family money, added to which you will keep all the property, jewellery, artworks and so on that you received during your marriage and receive a very generous annual allowance for the rest of your life. You will also have a place on the board."

"I don't care about the damn board," Athala said. "It's my boys that I worry about. Where are we meant to live?"

"It is entirely up to you, whether you wish to reside here in Grünwald, or at Schloss Meerbach, or both. His Excellency has set aside monies that are to be spent on the maintenance of the castle and its estate, and on employing all the staff required to maintain the standards he himself demanded. You will be the mistress of Schloss Meerbach once again, if you choose to be so."

"Until Konrad's twenty-fifth birthday . . ."

"Yes, he will be the master then."

* * *

When Solomons had gone, Athala went upstairs to the playroom where Gerhard was playing. She looked on him as a gift from God, an unexpected blessing whose birth had brought a rare moment of joy to a marriage long past rescuing. Gerhard had been conceived on the very last night that Athala and Otto had slept together. It had been a short, perfunctory coupling and he had been away with Fräulein von Wellberg on the night Gerhard was born. But that only made her baby all the more precious to Athala.

She wondered how she was going to explain to him that his father was dead. How did one tell a three-year-old that sort of thing? For now, she didn't have the heart to interrupt Gerhard while he played with the wooden building bricks that were his favourite toy.

Athala always found her son fascinating to observe as he arranged the brightly coloured bricks. He had an instinctive grasp of symmetry. If he placed one brick of a certain color or shape on one side of his latest castle, or house, or farm (Gerhard always knew exactly what he was building), then another, identical one had to go on the opposite side.

She leaned over and kissed his head. "My little architect," she murmured, and Gerhard beamed with pleasure, for that was his favourite of all her pet names for him.

I will tell him, Athala told herself, *but not yet*.

————

She gave the news to both her boys after Konrad had come home from school. He was only ten, but already regarded himself as the man of the house. As such, he made a point of not showing any sign of weakness when told that the father he took after so strongly was dead. Instead he wanted to know all the details of what had happened. Had his father been fighting the English? How many of them had he killed before they got him? When Athala had been unable to give him the answers he required, Konrad flew into a rage and said she was stupid.

"Father was quite right not to love you," he sneered. "You were never good enough for him."

On another day, Athala might have smacked him for that, but today she let it go. Then Konrad's fury abated as fast as it had risen and he asked, "If Father is dead, does that mean that I am the Count now?"

"Yes," said Athala. "You are Graf von Meerbach."

Konrad gave a whoop of joy. "I'm the Count! I'm the Count!" he chanted, marching around the playroom, like a stocky little red-headed guardsman. "I can do whatever I want and nobody can stop me!"

He came to a halt by Gerhard's building, which had risen, brick by brick, until it was almost as tall as its maker.

"Hey Gerdi, look at me!"

Gerhard looked up at his big brother, smiling innocently.

Konrad kicked Gerhard's wonderful construction, scattering its bricks across the playroom floor. Then he kicked it again, and again until it was completely obliterated, and nothing remained but the colourful rubble carpeting the room.

Gerhard's little face crumpled in despair and he ran sobbing to his mother.

As she wrapped her arms around her baby, she looked at the boy count now standing proudly over the destruction he had wreaked and she realized with bitter despair that she had been freed from her husband, only to be enslaved anew by her even more terrible son.

———

The skinny little girl wore a pair of jodhpurs that flapped around her thighs, for she lacked the flesh with which to fill them. Her short, black bobbed hair, which was normally unconstrained by bands or clips of any kind had been pinned into a little bun, to be worn beneath her riding hat. Her freckled face was tanned a golden brown and her eyes were the clear, pure blue of the African skies that had looked down upon every day of her life.

All around her the grassy hills, garlanded with sparkling streams, stretched away to the horizon as if the Highlands of Scotland had been transported to the Garden of Eden: a magical land of limitless fertility, incomprehensible scale and thrilling, untamed wildness. Here leopards lounged in the branches of trees that were also home to chattering monkeys and snakes, like the shimmering, iridescent green mamba, or the shy but fatally poisonous boomslang. The head-high grass hid lions sharp in fang and claw and, even deadlier still, the buffalo, whose horns could cut deep into a man's guts as easily as a sewing needle through fine linen.

The girl barely gave a thought to these hazards, for she knew no other world than this and besides, she had much more important things on her mind. She was stroking the velvet muzzle of her pony, a Somali-bred chestnut mare from which she had been inseparable ever since she had received it as her seventh-birthday present, eight months ago. The horse was called Kipipiri, which was both the Swahili word for "butterfly" and the name of the mountain that stood tall on the eastern horizon, shimmering in the heat haze like a mirage.

"Look, Kippy," the girl said, in a low, soothing murmur. "Look at all the nasty boys and their horrid stallions. Let's show them what we can do!"

She stepped around to the side of the pony and, waving away the offer of a leg-up from her groom, put one foot into the nearest stirrup, pushed off it and sprang up into the saddle as nimbly as a jockey on Derby Day. Then she leaned forward along Kipipiri's neck, stroking her mane and whispered in her ear, "Fly, my darling, fly!"

Possessed by an exhilarating swirl of emotions in which pride, anticipation and giddy excitement clashed against nervousness, apprehension and a desperate longing not to make a fool of herself, the girl told herself to calm down. She had long since learned that her beloved Kippy could sense her emotions and be affected by them and the very last thing she needed was a nervous, skittish, over-excited mount. So she took a long deep breath, just as her mother had taught her, before letting the air out slowly and smoothly until she felt the tension ease from her shoulders. Then she sat up straight and kicked the pony into a walk, stirring up the dust from the peppery red earth as they moved toward the starting gate of the show jumping ring that had been set up on one of the fields of the Wanjohi Valley Polo Club for its 1926 gymkhana.

The girl's eyes were fixed on the fences scattered at apparently random points around the ring. And a single thought filled her mind: *I am going to win!*

———

A loudspeaker had been slung from one of the wooden rafters that held up the corrugated iron awning over the clubhouse veranda. The harsh, tinny sound of a man's amplified voice burst from it, saying, "Now the final competitor in the twelve-and-under show jumping, Miss Saffron Courtney on Kipi-pipi-piri . . ." Silence fell for a second and then the voice continued, "Awfully sorry, few too many pips there, I fear."

"And a few too many pink gins, eh, Chalky!" a voice called out from among the spectators lounging on the wooden benches that were serving as spectator seating for the annual gymkhana the polo club laid on for its members' children.

"Too true, dear boy, too true," the announcer confessed, and then continued, "So far there's only been one clear round, by Percy Toynton on Hotspur, which means that Saffron's the only rider standing between him and victory. She's much the youngest competitor in this event, so let's give her a jolly big round of applause to send her on her way."

A ripple of limp clapping could be heard from the fifty or so white settlers who had come to watch their children compete in the gymkhana, or who were simply grasping any opportunity to leave their farms and businesses and socialize with one another. They were drowsy with the warmth of the early afternoon sun and the thin air, for the polo fields lay at an altitude of almost eight thousand feet, which seemed to exaggerate the effect of their heroic consumption of alcohol. A few particularly jaded, decadent souls were further numbed by opium, while those who were exhibiting overt signs of energy or agitation had quite likely sniffed some of the cocaine that had recently become as familiar to the more daring elements in Kenyan society as a cocktail before dinner.

Saffron's mother Eva Courtney, however, was entirely clear-headed. Seven months pregnant, having had two miscarriages since her daughter's birth, she had been forbidden anything stronger than the occasional glass of Guinness to build up her strength. She looked toward the jumps that had been set up on one of the polo fields, whispered, "Good luck, my sweet," under her breath, and squeezed her husband's hand.

"I just hope she doesn't have a fall," she said, her deep violet eyes heavy with maternal anxiety. "She's only a little girl and look at the size of some of those jumps."

Leon Courtney smiled at his wife. "Don't you worry, darling," he reassured her. "Saffron is your daughter. Which means she's as brave as a lioness, as pretty as a pink flamingo . . . and as tough as an old bull rhino. She will come through unscathed, you mark my words."

Eva Courtney smiled at Leon and let go of his hand so that he could get to his feet and walk down toward the polo field. *That's my Badger,* she thought. *He can't bear to sit and watch his girl from a distance. He has to get close to the action.*

Eva had given Leon the nickname Badger one morning a dozen years earlier, soon after they had met. They had ridden out as dawn broke over the Rift Valley and Eva had spotted a funny-looking creature about the size of a squat, sturdy, short-legged dog. It had black fur on its belly and lower body and white and pale gray on top, and was snuffling round in the grass like an old man searching for his reading glasses.

"What is it?" she had asked, to which Leon replied, "It's a honey badger." He told her that this unlikely beast was one of the most ferocious, fearless creatures in Africa. "Even the lion gives him a wide berth," Leon had said. "Interfere with him at your peril."

He could be talking about himself, Eva had thought. Leon had only been in his mid-twenties then, scraping a living as a safari guide. Now he was just a year shy of forty, the look of boyish eagerness that had once lit his eyes was replaced by the calmer assurance of a mature man in his prime, confident in his prowess as a hunter and fighting man. There was a deep groove between Leon's brows and lines around his eyes and mouth. With the frustration felt by women through the ages, to whom lines were an unwelcome sign that their youth and beauty were fading, Eva had to admit that on her man they suggested experience and authority and only made him all the more attractive. His body was a shade thicker through the trunk and his waist was not as slender as it had once been, but—another unfairness!—that only made him seem all the stronger and more powerful.

Eva looked around at the other men of the expatriate community gathered in this particular corner of Kenya. Her eyes came to rest on Josslyn Hay, the twenty-five-year-old heir to the Earl of Erroll, the hereditary Lord High Constable of Scotland. He was a tall, strongly built young man and he wore a kilt, as he often did in honor of his heritage, with a red-ochre Somali shawl slung over one shoulder. He was a handsome enough sight, with his swept-back, matinee-idol blond hair. His cool blue eyes looked at the world, and its female inhabitants in particular, with the lazy, heavy-lidded impudence of a predator eyeing its next meal. Hay had seduced half the white women in British East Africa, but Eva was too familiar with his type and too satisfied with her own alpha male to be remotely interested in adding to his conquests. Besides, he was far too young and inexperienced to interest her. As for the rest of the men there, they were a motley crew of aristocrats fleeing the new world of post-war Britain; remittance men putting on airs while praying for the next check from home; and adventurers enticed to Africa by the promise of a life they could never hope to match at home.

Leon Courtney, though, was different. His family had lived in Africa for two hundred and fifty years. He spoke Swahili as easily as English, conversed with the local Masai people in their own tongue and had excellent Arabic—an essential tool for a man whose father had founded a trading business that had been born of a single Nile steamer but now stretched from the gold mines of the Transvaal to the cotton fields of Egypt and the oil wells of Mesopotamia. Leon didn't play games. He didn't have to. He was man enough exactly as he was.

Yes, Badger, I am lucky, Eva thought. *Luckiest of all to love and be loved by you.*

————

Saffron steadied herself at the start of her course. *I've simply got to beat Percy!* she told herself.

It was Percy Toynton's thirteenth birthday in a week's time so he only just qualified for the event. Not only was he almost twice as old as Saffron, both he and his horse were far larger and stronger than she and Kipipiri. Percy was not a nice boy, in Saffron's view. He was boastful and liked to make himself look clever at other children's expense. Still, he had got round the course without making a mistake. So she absolutely had to match that and then beat him in the jump-off that would follow.

"Don't get ahead of yourself,' Daddy had told her over breakfast that morning. "This is a very important lesson in life. If you have a big, difficult job to do, don't fret about how hard it is. Break it down into smaller, easier jobs. Then steadily do them one by one and you'll find that in the end you've done the thing that seemed so hard. Do you understand?"

Saffron had screwed up her face and twisted her lips from side to side, thinking about what Daddy had said. "I think so," she'd replied, without much conviction.

"Well, take a clear round at show jumping. That's very difficult, isn't it?"

"Yes," Saffron nodded.

"But if you look at a jump, I bet you always think you can get over it."

"Always!" Saffron agreed.

"Very well then, don't think about how difficult it is to get a clear round. Think about one easy jump, then another, then another . . . and when you reach the end, if you jump over all the jumps, why, you'll have a clear round and it won't have seemed difficult at all."

"Oh, I understand!" she'd said, enthusiastically.

Now Saffron glanced at the ragged line of her fellow competitors and their parents that ran down one side of the ring and saw her father. He caught her eye and gave her a jaunty wave, accompanied by one of the broad smiles that always made her feel happy, for they were filled with optimism and confidence. She smiled back and then turned her attention to the first obstacle: a simple pair of crossed white rails forming a shallow X-shape lower in the middle than at the sides. *That's easy!* she thought and felt suddenly stronger and more confident. She urged Kipipiri forward and the little mare broke into a trot and then a canter and they passed through the starting gate and headed toward the jumps.

————

Leon Courtney had made sure not to convey a single iota of the tension he was feeling as Saffron began her round. His heart was bursting with pride. She could have entered the eight-and-under category, but the very idea of going over the baby jumps, the highest of which barely reached Leon's knee, had appalled her. She had therefore insisted on going up an age group and to most people that in itself was remarkable. The idea that she might actually win it was fanciful in the extreme. But Leon knew his daughter. She would not see it that way. She would want victory or nothing at all.

"Come on, Saffy," he whispered, not wanting to shout for fear of spooking her pony.

She cantered up to the first fence; steadied Kipipiri then darted forward and sailed right across the center of the jump, with masses of room to spare. Saffron smiled to herself. She and Kippy were both strong-willed, stubborn characters. As her mother used to say, "You two girls are both as bad as each other!"

On days when Saffron and her pony were at odds with one another, the results were invariably disastrous, but when they were united and pulling in the same direction, it felt as though they could take on the world. The energy with which Kippy had jumped, her perfect balance on take-off and landing, the rhythm of her strides, and the alert, eager way her ears were pricked gave Saffron hope that this could be one of the good days.

Now, however, the challenge became much harder. The next fence was a double: two railed fences with a single stride between them. "Good girl!" said Saffron as Kippy scraped over the first element of the pair, took her single stride perfectly then jumped the double rail too.

Now all the nerves had gone. Saffron was at one with the animal beneath her, controlling all the power that lay coiled up in the muscles bunched beneath Kippy's rich, dark, glossy coat.

She slowed the pony, turned her ninety degrees to the right and set out along the line of three fences that now presented themselves to her. The first was a plain white gate and she made easy work of it. Saffron had long legs for her age, even if they were as thin as a stork's, but she kept her stirrups short, all the better to rise out of the saddle as she jumped and drive her pony up and over the obstacle. Next came another single rail, although it was placed over bundles of flame-tree branches, still bedecked in their blazing red and yellow flowers: again it proved no match for Saffron and Kipipiri.

"I say, Courtney, that girl of yours is as light as a feather in the saddle," said one of the other spectators, a retired cavalry major called Brett, who also served as the local magistrate, as she tackled an oxer, comprised of two railed fences side-by-side. "Lovely touch on the reins, too. Good show."

"Thank you, Major," Leon said, as Saffron brought Kipipiri round again to tackle the next couple of fences strung diagonally across the ring: a wall and the water jump. "Mind you, I can't claim any credit. Saffron's absolutely her mother's daughter when it comes to riding. You wouldn't believe the hours that Eva's spent with her in the schooling ring, both as stubborn as each other, fighting like two cats in a bag, but by God it pays off." Leon smiled affectionately at the thought of the two most precious people in his life then said, "Excuse me a moment," as he switched his full attention back to the ring.

For some reason, his daughter's pony had a terrible habit of "dipping a toe in the water", as Leon liked to put it. She would leap over the highest, widest, scariest fences, but it was the devil's own job to persuade her that the water was an obstacle to be avoided, rather than a pool to be dived into.

As Saffron steadied herself before the challenge in front of her, Leon took a deep breath, trying to calm his racing pulse.

I don't know how Saffy feels jumping this course, he thought. *But I'm absolutely shattered watching it.*

———

"One fence at a time, one fence at a time," Saffron repeated to herself as she fixed her eyes on the wall. "Here we go, girl!" she said and urged Kippy on across the parched turf. The wall was high. They got over it without knocking any of the painted wooden tea-chests from which it had been improvised, but the pony stumbled on landing and it took all Saffron's skill to keep her upright, maintain their forward momentum and have her balanced and moving strongly again by the time they approached the water jump.

Saffron was absolutely determined she wouldn't make a mess of the water this time. She galloped at full pelt toward it, misjudged her pacing, had to take off miles away from the jump, but was going so fast that Kipipiri flew like a speeding dart over the rail, and the shallow pool of muddy brown water beyond. It was all Saffron could do to slow her down and turn her again—hard left this time—before they charged out of the ring.

Saffron was out of breath, but inwardly exultant. *No faults! Almost there!*

In front of her stood a low fence made of three striped poles one on top of the other. The polo club's gymkhana committee had decided to make this a particularly gentle challenge to the riders, for just beyond it stood the last and hardest jump: a vicious triple combination of a plain rail fence, another hay-bale and rail, and finally an oxer, each with just a single stride between them. Some competitors had scraped the first element of the triple, hit the second and simply crashed into the third, completely unable to manage another jump. None apart from Percy had managed to get through without at least one fence down.

Saffron had to clear it. She summoned every shred of energy she still had in her and rode along the side of the ring nearest to the spectators, her mind replaying the pattern of steps she would need to enter the triple combination at the perfect point, going at just the right speed. She barely even thought of the poles as Kipipiri jumped over them.

As the pony's hind hooves passed over the jump, Saffron thought she heard a bump behind her. She glanced back and saw that the top pole had been rattled but it seemed to still be in place, so she thought no more of it. She barely even saw the people flashing by beside her, nor did she hear the faint gasp they emitted as she approached the first element. She met it perfectly, jumped the rail, kept Kippy balanced through her next stride, made it across the second rail, kicked on and then pulled so hard on the reins that she more or less picked up her pony and hauled her over the oxer.

I did it! I did it! Saffron thought exultantly as she galloped toward the finishing line. She crossed it and slowed Kipipiri to a trot as they exited the ring. She saw her father running toward her, dodging in and out of the applauding spectators and gave him a great big wave. But he didn't wave back.

Saffron frowned. *Why isn't he smiling?*

And then she heard the loudspeaker and felt as though she had been kicked in the tummy by a horse's hoof as the announcer called out, "Oh, I say! What awfully bad luck for plucky Saffron Courtney, hitting the last-but-one fence when she was so close to a clear round. My goodness, that pole took an age to fall off! So that means the winner's rosette goes to Percy Toynton. Well played, young man!"

Saffron hardly knew what was happening as her groom took hold of Kipipiri's bridle. All she could think was, *How could I knock down that silly, stupid, simple little pole?* Her eyes had suddenly filled with tears and she could barely see her father Leon as he lifted her out of the saddle and hugged her to his chest, holding her tight before gently putting her down on the ground.

She leaned against him, wrapping her arms around his legs as he stroked her hair. "I'm better than Percy, I know I am," Saffron sobbed. And then she looked up, her face as furious as it was miserable and wailed. "I lost, Daddy, I lost! I can't believe it . . . I lost!"

———

Leon had long since learned that there was no point trying to reason with Saffron at times like this. Her temper was as fierce as an African storm, but cleared as quickly and then the sun came out in her just as it did over the savannah, and it shone just as brightly too.

She pulled herself away from him, tore her hat off her head and kicked it across the ground.

Leon heard a disapproving, "Harrumph!" behind him and turned to see Major Brett frowning at the display of juvenile female anger. "You should read that little madam some Kipling, Courtney."

"Because she's behaving like a monkey from *The Jungle Book*?" Leon asked.

The major did not spot the presence of humor, or perhaps

did not feel this was the time and place for frivolity. "Good God, man, of course not! I'm referring to that poem. You know, triumph and disaster, impostors, treat them both the same and so forth."

"Ah, but my daughter is a Courtney, and we've never been able to live up to such lofty ideals. Either we triumph, or it is a disaster."

"Well that's not a very British way of seeing things, I must say."

Leon smiled. "In many ways we're not very British. Besides, that poem you were quoting, 'If—' "

"Absolutely, that's the one."

"As I recall, Kipling wrote it for his son, who died in the war, poor lad."

"Believe he did, yes, rotten show."

"And the point of the whole thing is summed up in the final line which is, if memory serves, "And—which is more—you'll be a man, my son."

"Quite so, damned good advice, too."

"Yes, to a boy it is. But Saffron is my daughter. She's a little girl. And not even Rudyard Kipling is going to turn her into a man."

* * *

"Darling Leon, how good of you to come," said Lady Idina Hay.

"My pleasure," Leon replied. A select few members of the gymkhana crowd had been invited back to the Hays' house, Slains, which was named after Josslyn Hay's ancestral home, to have dinner and stay the night afterwards. Leon had thought twice before accepting the invitation. Idina, a short, slight woman with huge, captivating eyes, who matched her husband in his appetite and seductive power, had swiftly become as much of a source of scandal to Kenyan society as she had been in London. Now on her third marriage, with armies of lovers besides, she was apt to greet guests while lying naked in a green onyx bath; to entertain while wearing nothing but a flimsy cotton wrap, tied at the bust in the native style, with nothing underneath; and to hand guests a bowl filled with keys to the Slains' bedrooms, invite them to take one, inform them which room it opened and suggest that they slept with whomever they found within it.

"Apparently it's impossible for the servants," Eva had said, when she passed the gossip on to Leon. "They pick up all the dirty laundry off the floor, get it all cleaned and pressed but then have absolutely no idea whom to return it to."

Tonight, however, Idina was on her best behavior and was dressed as if for the smartest salons of Paris in an impossibly short, translucent but just about decent dress of fluttering, champagne-colored silk chiffon. Leon felt sure Eva would be able to identify it in an instant as being the work of some celebrated designer of whom he had never heard.

"So sorry to hear that Eva wasn't up to it," Idina said, as if reading his mind.

"Well, she gets jolly tired, lugging the baby around inside her," he replied. "She swears it must be a boy, says it's twice the size Saffy was at the same stage. So she's gone back to Lusima with Saffy and the pony."

"She's not driving, I hope!"

"She wanted to, you know. Absolutely determined to get behind the wheel. But I put my foot down and said absolutely not. So Loikot, my estate manager, is taking her back in the Rolls. He'll be back for me tomorrow."

Idina laughed. "You're the only man in Kenya who would even think of driving on the appalling, unmade roads in such a wildly extravagant car!"

"On the contrary, it's an extremely tough, practical machine. It was built as an armored car, spent the war charging around Arabia and Mesopotamia. When peace came the army had far more than they needed, so I bought one. I smartened it up a bit, but underneath it's still a military vehicle." Leon grinned at Idina, "If the balloon ever goes up again, I can weld on some armor plating, stick a gun turret over the passenger seats and drive straight off to war."

"Perhaps I should get one," Idina mused. "I have my Hispano–Suiza, of course and she's a wonderful thing."

"I'll say. At least as grand as my Roller, and that silver stork on the bonnet rivals the Spirit of Ecstasy for style."

"True, but she'd still rather be toddling around Mayfair than bumping about on the dirt tracks of Africa . . . Now I must get on and make sure dinner is being prepared properly," Idina concluded. "Just because one is a long way from home, that's no excuse for lowering one's standards."

Apart from swapping the room keys, thought Leon, heading off to get dressed for dinner. *Unless they do that in Mayfair, too.*

The guests had gathered for drinks before dinner and split along gender lines, with the men, all dressed in white tie and tails, engaged in one set of conversations and the ladies, like a flock of brilliantly plumaged hummingbirds, all gathered in another. Leon Courtney was cradling a whisky in his hand as he talked with a small group that included his host, Josslyn Hay. The two men stood out from the rest, both because they were taller than the others, but also because they were so obviously the dominant males in that particular pack: a pair of magnets for watching female eyes.

"I rather think I'm going to make a play for Leon Courtney," said the Honorable Amelia Cory-Porter, a well-dressed, brightly painted young divorcée with fashionably short, bobbed hair who had decided to lie low in Kenya until the fuss over her marriage, which had been ended by her adultery, died down. "He is quite utterly scrumptious, don't you think?"

"Darling, you'll be wasting your time," Idina Hay informed her. "Leon Courtney's the only man in the whole of Kenya who refuses to sleep with anyone other than his wife. He barely even eyes one up. It's quite disconcerting, actually. Makes me wonder if I'm losing my touch."

Amelia looked startled, as if confronted by an entirely new and unexpected aspect of human behavior. "Refuses sex? Really? That hardly seems natural, especially when his wife is in no condition to oblige him. You don't suppose he's secretly a queer, do you?"

"Heavens, no! I have it on good authority that in his younger days, he was quite the ladies' man. But the moment he clapped eyes on Eva, he fell head over heels in love and he's been besotted ever since."

"I suppose one can't blame him," said Amelia, though her air of disapproval was plain. "I saw her at the gymkhana and she's perfectly lovely. What is it they say in romantic novels— eyes like limpid pools? She has those, all right. But even so, she's enormously pregnant. No one expects these days a chap to live like a monk just because his wife's blown up like a barrage balloon."

"Well perhaps Leon Courtney's just an old-fashioned gentleman."

"Oh, don't be silly. You know as well as I do that there's never been any such thing. But anyway darling, do tell all about Eva. It's very strange. I thought I could detect a Northumbrian lilt in her voice—Daddy used to go shooting up there and we'd all go up with him, so I know the accent from the staff and gamekeepers and so forth. But I've heard that she's actually a German, is that so?"

"Well," said Idina as the two women moved fractionally closer together, like conspirators sharing a deadly secret, "the real British East Africa hands, like Florence Delamere, who've been here for years and years, can still remember the first time Eva pitched up in Nairobi, about a year or so before the war. Some ghastly German industrialist arrived in town on the most lavish safari anyone had ever seen, accompanied by a magnificent open motor car in which to go hunting, numerous lorries to cart all his baggage and two huge airplanes, made by his own company."

"Good lord, what an extraordinary show," Amelia said, clearly impressed by such a display of power and wealth.

"Absolutely," Idina agreed. "Of course, the whole town turned out to see the flying machines, but by the end of the day there was just as much talk about the ravishing creature who was parading around on the industrialist's arm, making no bones whatever about being his mistress and calling herself Eva von something-or-other."

"And that was the same Eva I saw today?"

"Indeed she was. And guess who was the white hunter acting as the Germans' guide?"

"Goodness, was it Leon Courtney?"

"The very same. Anyway, Eva and the industrialist—apparently he was the absolute picture of the bullying, bullet-headed Hun—went back to Germany, and that seemed to be that. But then, really very soon after the start of the war, she was mysteriously back in Kenya, having parachuted down to earth from a giant Zeppelin."

"Oh don't! That's just too extraordinary!" Amelia laughed.

"Well, that's the story and I've heard it from enough people who were here at the time to believe it. Apparently, the Zeppelin crash-landed deep in the heart of Masailand. And it was shot down by . . . ?" Idina paused, teasingly.

"No! Don't tell me! Not Leon again?"

"Absolutely . . . and out of the wreckage, looking as pretty as a picture and as fresh as a daisy, steps the lovely Eva and falls, swooning into his arms!"

"Lucky girl. I'd happily swoon into his arms right now, if he'd have me."

"Well, he won't, so you'll just have to find another man to swoon at!"

"Are you sure?" Amelia asked, wrinkling her porcelain brow with a little frown. "It really is too bad to give up without a fight. After all, Leon's rich as well as divinely handsome. Lusima must be one of the biggest estates in the country."

"He paid cash for the land, you know," Idina said. "Half a million pounds for a hundred and twenty thousand acres, didn't have to borrow a penny. I know that for an absolute fact because I heard it from the chap who conducted the sale."

"Half a million? Cash?" Amelia gasped.

"Absolutely. I once plucked up the courage to ask Leon where his money came from it, but he was very coy. First he described it as "war reparations" and then he said it was payment for various patents that had belonged to Eva's father."

"Perhaps he's a gangster and it's all the proceeds of his evil crimes!" said Amelia, excitedly. "I rather like the idea of being— what's the phrase?—a gangster's moll."

"I'm sure you do, duckie, but whatever else he might be, Leon Courtney's not a criminal. My guess is that it's something to do with the war." Idina's eyes suddenly sparkled with mischief. "I tell you what, darling, I shall set you a challenge. I'm going to change the placement I'd planned for the dinner table tonight and put you next to Leon. If you can find out where he got his gold by the time we retire to leave the men to their brandy and cigars I shall be very impressed indeed."

"Done!" said the Hon. Amelia. "And I'll seduce him, too, just you watch me, wife or no wife."

Idina arched an eyebrow and concluded their little chat: "Now, now, darling, let's not be greedy."

———

Thanks to the combined efforts of Idina Hay and her formidable housekeeper Marie, the kitchen staff at Slains had been trained to produce French cuisine that would not have shamed the dinner table of a château on the Loire. The wine, notoriously difficult to keep in good condition in the tropics, was of equally high standard. Leon had long ago learned to pace himself when drinking at altitude, but the woman sitting next to him, who introduced herself as Amelia Cory-Porter, seemed determined to force as much Premier Cru claret as possible down his throat. She was attractive enough, in an obvious, uninteresting way, and covered in far too much makeup for his taste. She was also very clearly determined to get something from him, but Leon was not yet sure quite what that might be.

At first he'd thought she was flirting, for everything he knew about women told him that if he made a pass at her she would very happily oblige. But as the starter of *confit* duck breasts served with a salad of vegetables from Slains' own gardens gave way to superb *entrecôte* steaks served in a pepper sauce, he realized that Amelia was not after his body—or not at this precise moment anyway—but was instead angling for information. It was, of course, good manners to show interest in one's dining companions and any woman with half a brain knew how to make a man feel as though he was the wisest, most fascinating and witty fellow she had ever met. But Amelia was not flattering, so much as cross-examining him, working her way through his life and becoming more intense in her questioning as she went on. His war service seemed to be of particular interest to her. Leon had done his best to fob her off by saying he never talked about the war, adding that in his experience any man who did was a bounder who was almost certainly lying. "Unless, of course, he's a poet," he'd added, hoping she might, like many an idealistic young woman, be distracted by thoughts of Wilfred Owen, Siegfried Sassoon and the other bards of war.

Amelia, however, wasn't distracted for a second. She was like a terrier with the scent of a particularly juicy rabbit in its nostrils. "I heard the most extraordinary story about how you'd shot down a giant Zeppelin, single-handed. Do tell, that sounds so brave, is it actually true?"

"That sounds pretty improbable to me," Leon said. "Damned hard thing to shoot down, a Zeppelin, just ask any pilot. Now, I've talked far too much. You must tell me everything that's happening in London, what's new and interesting and so forth. Eva will be thrilled if I can pass on any news of home."

Leon had been telling the truth, up to a point. It really was extremely hard to down a Zeppelin with machine-gun fire, which was one reason why he had never done any such thing. And Eva would indeed be keen to hear about the latest clothes, plays, novels and music that were captivating London society.

Amelia, however, was having none of it. "Oh, who cares about silly dresses and even sillier books? I want to hear about that Zeppelin."

Leon sighed. This was not a subject he had any intention of discussing, but how could he evade this woman's steely clutches without being unforgivably rude? He was just pondering his next move when he heard a man's voice, clearly somewhat the worse for wine, braying across the table.

"I say Courtney, is it true you have a Masai blood brother?"

The voice belonged to a newcomer to Kenya, who called himself Quentin de Lancey and affected the mannerisms of the upper-class, though his appearance was far from noble. He was overweight and prone to become both red-faced and very sweaty in the heat, which caused his thin, reddish-brown hair to lie in damp strings across his pale, flabby skin.

"Something of that sort," Leon replied, noncommittally. When he was a nineteen-year-old Second Lieutenant in the Third Battalion of the King's African Rifles his platoon sergeant had been a Masai called Manyoro. Leon had saved Manyoro's life in battle, and when Leon had then been court-martialed on trumped-up charges of cowardice and desertion it had been Manyoro's evidence that had saved his neck. There was no man on earth whose friendship he valued more highly.

"And a coon name? Bongo-something, was what I'd heard."

A few people smiled at that, one of the women tittered. "Bongo from Bongo-bongo-land, what?" de Lancey added, looking delighted by his own rapier wit.

"The name I received was M'Bogo," said Leon, and a wiser, or more sober man than de Lancey might have heard the note of suppressed anger in his voice.

"I say, what kind of name is that?" de Lancey persisted.

"It is the name of the great buffalo bull. It represents strength and fighting spirit. I count myself honored to have been given it."

Again, it took a fool not to heed the warning contained in the phrase "strength and fighting spirit", and again de Lancey was deaf to it. "Oh, come-come, Courtney," he said, as if he were the voice of reason and Leon the common fool. "It's all very well getting on with these people, I suppose, but let's not pretend that they are anything but a lesser race. A chap I know was up-country a few months ago, looking for a good spot to start farming. He hung a paraffin lamp by his tent when he stopped for the night. The next thing he knew there were half-a-dozen nig-nogs coming up out of the bush, absolutely stark bollock naked apart from those red cloak things they wear."

"It's called a *shuka*," said Leon.

Beside him, Amelia Cory-Porter's eyes had widened and she was breathing just a little more heavily as she sensed that the man beside her was readying himself to impose his authority, possibly by force.

"Yes, well, whatever it's called, the poor chap was absolutely terrified, real brown-trouser time," de Lancey said. "Turned out the niggers just wanted to sit by his tent, cocks swinging gently in the breeze, gawping at the light—my chum didn't know where to look! They'd never seen anything like it, thought it was a star trapped in a bottle."

Leon realized that he had clenched his napkin in his right fist and recognized the signs of an imminent explosion. *Control yourself,* he thought. *Count to ten. No point making an exhibition of yourself over one blithering idiot.*

He consciously relaxed his body, much to Amelia's disappointment as she felt her own gathering anticipation subside.

"It's true that the first sight of a white man and his possessions comes as a surprise," Leon said, as dully as possible, hoping to close the subject and move on.

"Of course it does," said de Lancey, who was equally keen to prolong the thrilling sensation of being the center of everyone's attention. "These people haven't developed anything that remotely passes for a civilization."

Leon gave an impatient sigh. *Damn! I'm just going to have to put this buffoon in his place.*

"The Masai have no skyscrapers, or airplanes, or telephones in their world, that is true. But they know things that we cannot begin to understand."

"Go on then, what sort of things?"

"Even a Masai child can track a stray animal for days across open country," Leon said. "They'll spot the faint outline of an elephant's footprint on a patch of rock-hard earth where you or I would see nothing but dirt and stones, and identify the precise animal to which the print belongs. If the Masai soldiers I once had the privilege to command came across the trail of an invading war-party from another tribe they would at once know the number of men in the party, the length of time since they had passed and the destination to which they were heading. And if you doubt the capacity of the African brain, de Lancey, answer me this: how many languages do you speak?"

"I've always found the King's English perfectly adequate, thank you, Courtney."

"Then you are two behind a great many Africans, who speak three languages as a matter of course: their tribal tongue; the lingua franca spoken by everyone in the nation of which their tribe is part; and the language of their colonial masters. So the

particular Masai who calls me M'Bogo grew up speaking Masai.
As a young man he joined the King's African Rifles where the
ranks spoke Kiswahili, which he swiftly mastered. In recent
years he has become fluent in English. These men are not niggers or coons, as you like to call them. They are a proud, noble,
warrior race who have grazed their cattle on these lands since
time immemorial and in their own environment they are every
bit our match and more."

"Well said," said a small man, with a bald pate and a scattering of silver hair, peering across the table through a pair of
steel-framed spectacles.

"Well, I still say that there is a reason why we are their
masters and they our servants," de Lancey insisted. "They're
just a bunch of bone-idle savages and we are their superiors in
both mind and body."

Having dismissed the option of beating de Lancey to a pulp,
Leon had been wondering how he could teach him the lesson
he so richly deserved, and now a stroke of inspiration came to
him. "Would you like to put that proposition to the test?" he
asked.

"Ooh . . ." purred Amelia. "This is going to be fun!"

"How so?" de Lancey asked, and for the first time a note of
caution entered his voice as it occurred to him he might just
have blundered into a trap.

Leon thought for a moment, working out a way to draw de
Lancey in, while still ensuring his ultimate humiliation. "I will
bet that one Masai from my Lusima estate can outrun any three
white men you put up against him."

"In a race, do you mean?"

"In a manner of speaking. What I have in mind is this . . ."
Leon leaned forward onto the table so that everyone could see
and hear him clearly. He wanted this to be public. "One week
from today, we will all meet up again at the polo field. String
a rope around all four sides of one of the fields. The competitors
will run around the field, outside that rope. D'you follow?"

"Yes, I believe so," said de Lancey. "They all run round the field and if a white man wins the race I win the wager, and if your darkie wins, you do?"

Leon smiled. "Actually, that would be too easy for the Masai. They would be insulted by the very idea and say that one of their young boys, or even a woman, could win."

"Listen here, old man, you sound like you hate your own race."

"I wouldn't say that. I just think that you're either a good man or you're not and skin color's got nothing whatever to do with it. The most appalling bully and bounder I ever met was a white man." Leon paused for a moment and looked around the table at the disapproving faces. Then he added, "Mind you, he was a German."

The frowns turned to smiles and laughs at that and someone called out, "I say, what happened to this horrible Hun?"

"His chest got in the way of a bullet from a .470 Nitro Express hunting rifle."

"Was that what passed for your war service?" asked de Lancey acidly. "Better than nothing I suppose."

The man in the steel-rimmed glasses cleared his throat. There was a philosophical, almost sad look in his eyes and a wry cast to his mouth, as if he were all too aware of the imperfections of man and the shortness of his life. Yet at once the table fell silent. This was the Right Honorable Hugh Cholmondeley, Third Baron Delamere and the unquestioned leader of Kenya's white population. He had been among the first British settlers in British East Africa, owned two huge estates and was famed for the fortune he had spent trying to establish cattle, sheep and grain farming on his farmland, while preserving the wildlife in the vast areas of country that he left untouched. There was a cane resting on the back of his chair, for he walked with a limp, the result of being mauled by a lion. Yet there was real strength behind those faraway eyes.

"Gentlemen, gentlemen, let's not have any unpleasantness,"

Delamere said. "I can testify to the fact that Courtney here served alongside me throughout the war, chasing that infuriating German rascal von Lettow back and forth across East Africa. It may also interest you to know that Mrs. Courtney assisted us as an aircraft navigator and pilot and was, at my particular request, awarded the Military Medal for her courage under fire. The Courtneys did their bit, you have my word on it."

Leon gave a little nod of gratitude. "Thank you, sir."

"Think nothing of it, dear boy. Now, pray finish telling us about your wager. As you know, I rather share your opinion of the Masai."

That, too, was something known to all the British in Kenya. Delamere even built his homes with the same mud and thatch that the Masai used for their huts. "Of course," he continued, "I maintain that our European civilization as a whole is more advanced than the native African. Still, the individual Masai is a fine man and I might even put a guinea or two into the pot, once I know what I'm betting on. Courtney?"

"Very well then," Leon began. The argument about the war had been entirely forgotten and there was a palpable air of growing excitement as he spoke. "I propose that the three white men run in a relay against the solitary Masai. One of them will start alongside him, the starter will fire his pistol and they will both set off around the field. The white man keeps running until he either gives up, or the Masai laps him."

"Is that really likely to happen, Courtney?" Josslyn Hay asked. "A polo field must be twice the size of a football pitch. It's a long way round."

"Possibly not," Leon replied. "I just don't want anyone to get away with walking. This has to be a race that is run."

"Fair point. But I take it your rules apply the other way around, as well. That is to say, you lose the wager if the Masai stops first or is lapped."

"Of course."

"I see, so then what?"

"Then the second man takes the first one's place, under the same conditions, then the third. My wager is very simple. I will bet you five thousand pounds de Lancey, that when the last of the three white men either stops or is lapped, the Masai will still be running."

The blood drained from de Lancey's face as all eyes were fixed on him. "I say Courtney, five thousand's a bit steep," he objected. "Rather beyond my means, what?"

"All right," said Leon. He took a thoughtful sip of his claret, trying to suppress a huge grin as inspiration struck him. "I suppose you don't want me taking the shirt off your back, eh?"

"I'd rather you didn't, old boy."

"But that's exactly what I'd like to take. Here's my wager. If I lose I won't give you five thousand pounds. I'll give you ten."

There was a gasp around the table. Idina Hay smiled to herself. Ten thousand pounds, given to her by her mother, had bought her car, Slains and the dresses she took such pride in receiving direct from the couturier Molyneux.

"And if you lose, de Lancey," Leon went on, "you will indeed give me the shirt off your back, and every other stitch of clothing that you are wearing, and you won't get them back until you've completed a lap of the polo field."

"What . . . run around the field? In my birthday suit?" de Lancey gasped, as the other diners each formed their own mental picture of him naked and on the run. Laughter began to spread around the table.

"As naked as God made you."

"He's got you there, de Lancey," said Joss Hay, grinning from ear to ear. "Ten thousand pounds against a trot round a field, you can't say no to that . . . What was that splendid phrase you came up with? Oh yes, with your cock swinging gently in the breeze. I'll bet every white woman in Kenya will be there, just to see the view."

De Lancey could see that his only hope now was to brazen it out. "Let me get this straight: you are betting me ten thousand pounds against a run round a field that one African native can beat three British gentlemen?"

"Absolutely."

"I see . . . oh, one last thing." De Lancey paused for a second and then asked, "Will your chap run naked too? Isn't that what the natives do?"

"I should imagine so," Leon replied. "Is that a problem?"

"Worried that the Masai might make you look small, de Lancey?" one man asked to more peals of laughter.

"No, of course not. Just thinking of the ladies. Don't want them getting upset."

As a number of the female diners glanced at one another with rolled eyes and little shakes of the head, Leon made an offer. "I'll tell you what, I will provide a pair of shorts for my chap to wear, how's that?"

De Lancey looked around the table, knowing that his name in the Colony depended on what he said next. Like a man jumping into an ice-cold pool he steeled himself, breathed deeply and took the plunge: "Then in that case Courtney, you've got a bet," he said as a cheer went up, more drinks were called for, and the night's festivities began in earnest.

———

Leon Courtney emerged from the Great War with a fortune even bigger than Amelia or Idina had imagined. Having once been close to destitution he found himself with the means to buy one of the finest estates in East Africa. He named it Lusima, in honor of Manyoro's mother, whose skills as a healer, counselor and mystical seer he had come to cherish deeply. Leon planned to follow the example of Lord Delamere who kept much of his land untouched, for use as a nature reserve, and gave over the rest to agriculture. When it came to setting up a safari business that would attract rich customers from Europe and the Americas, Leon was in his element, but the farming was a different matter. He could not help noticing how many British settlers lost everything they had trying to marry

European agricultural techniques with African land, weather and pestilence. He therefore decided to work with the grain of Kenyan life, rather than against it. So he made an agreement with Manyoro, by which he and his extended family could have the freedom of the entire Lusima estate, provided that they also herded and cared for Leon's cattle alongside their own. Since the Masai measured a man's worth not in money, but by the number of his cows and of his children, Leon paid his people in their preferred currency. For every ten calves born to Leon's cows, the Masai kept one for themselves.

This arrangement had a few teething problems. The Masai believed that every cow on earth belonged to them and, as a consequence, felt perfectly entitled to rustle from non-Masai. They also lived off their animals' blood and milk and so kept their cattle alive for as long as possible, rather than sending them to the slaughterhouse. The concept of keeping another man's cattle until such time as they were taken away to be sold and killed struck even Manyoro, accustomed as he was to British customs due to his time in the army, as bizarre.

On the other hand, the offer of huge areas of grazing and a guaranteed increase in his and his people's herds was too good to turn down. As the years had gone by, he had prospered mightily, particularly once he had seen how much money his cattle could fetch and how useful money could be in a world now run by white men. The arrangement had worked perfectly for Leon, too, since his herds did not suffer anything like the same rates of disease as those of his fellow farmers. His Masai herdsmen knew which ground was corrupted by plants that produced poisonous feed or insects that carried disease and so they kept to areas of safe, sweet grass. They guarded their animals and Leon's against lions and other predators and they lived well on the blood and milk that they took from the animals they were herding, a practice to which Leon turned a blind eye once he realized that it did the cattle no harm whatsoever.

In time Manyoro had handed over the day-to-day running

of the estate and its buildings to his kinsman Loikot, whom Leon had watched grow from an impish boy to a young man worthy of his trust and respect. Manyoro now lived in the village where his mother had raised him. It stood atop Lonsonyo Mountain, a mighty tower of rock that rose from the plains by the eastern escarpment of the Great Rift Valley, at one corner of the Lusima estate. Two days after the dinner at Slains, Leon drove out to the mountain. He left the Rolls at its foot, guarded by two of his men (their job was to deter curious animals, rather than larcenous humans, for no man who valued his life would touch M'Bogo's property and thereby risk Manyoro's wrath). Then he set off up the footpath that zigzagged back and forth across the steep slope, recalling, as he always did whenever he visited, the first time he had made the journey. He had been half-starved and parched with thirst, his feet bloody and blistered, the skin flayed from his heels, the wounds so severe and the pain so great that he had managed no more than a couple of hundred feet up the climb before he had collapsed and been carried the rest of the way on a *mushila*, or litter, borne on four men's shoulders.

That had been twenty years ago, yet the memories of that time and his first encounter with Lusima were as vivid as if mere days, not decades had elapsed. He remembered too the times he had spent with Eva in this, their secret shelter from the outside world, the love they had made and the times they had swum in Sheba's Pool, a crystalline sanctuary nestled beneath a waterfall that fell from the mountain summit. He smiled as he recalled the sight of her, dashing down the path toward him, heedless of the precipitous drop that fell away beside her, then throwing herself into his arms. He felt himself harden and it was not the climb that made his heart beat faster and his breathing deepen as he thought of her naked body, so lithe and graceful in the water, her legs locked around his waist and her soft warm lips pressed to his.

Oh, Eva, my darling, my love, you were so beautiful then, so delicate, so fragile and yet so fierce and so strong. And then he smiled to himself as he thought, *And I'd still rather make love to you than any other woman on earth.*

They had both grown older since then, but the mountain itself remained as it had always been. On the lower slopes the path was shaded by the groves of umbrella acacias, whose branches flared upward and outward from the trunk, like the spokes of an umbrella, before bursting into a broad, but virtually flat canopy of leaves at their top. But as he climbed higher the air cooled and grew moist, almost like mist, and the plants around him became more lush. Tree orchids bloomed in vivid hues of pink and violet in the branches of tall trees where eagles and hawks made their aeries. Leon watched the birds wheeling in the vastness of the cloudless sky scanning the bush far below them for any signs of prey.

When he reached the top he was greeted by a gaggle of small children, grinning with delight and squealing, "M'Bogo! M'Bogo!" A young woman, whom Leon knew to be one of Manyoro's new wives, looked at him with unabashed appreciation, for it was the custom among the Masai for a man to share his wives with valued guests, but only if the wife liked the look of the guest in question. She had the final and decisive say in the matter.

When Leon had first known Manyoro he had but one wife, for that was all the army would allow. She had produced three fine sons and two daughters. The Masai were, however, polygamous by tradition and it was an unspoken part of his bargain that Leon allowed them to live as they wished on his land. Having prospered mightily, Manyoro now had four wives to his name and a dozen or more new children, all of whom lived under the command and supervision of his first, senior bride. This had always been a prosperous community, whose inhabitants had been well-fed and housed in finely built huts. When Leon first arrived there, the women were bedecked in splendid ornaments of ivory and trade beads and the cattle were fat and sleek. All that was still true, but now Leon noticed a couple of paraffin lamps and, placed outside the largest and most splendid of all the huts, the incongruous sight of a set of rattan patio chairs arranged around a glass-topped table.

Manyoro was sitting in one of the chairs drinking a bottle of Bass pale ale. He must, Leon realized, be more than fifty now and had put on a good deal of weight over the years, as the visible proof of his power and prosperity. Yet there was no sense of softness about Manyoro and when he stood to greet Leon, the Masai was still the taller of the pair.

"I see you, Manyoro, my brother," Leon said, speaking in Masai.

Manyoro's face broke into a huge grin. "And I see you, M'Bogo, and my heart sings with joy."

Manyoro lifted a bottle of beer from a metal wastepaper basket filled with ice-cold spring water and offered to Leon. He was delighted to accept, for the walk had given him a powerful thirst.

"You are the only Masai I know who always has a crate of pale ale ready to hand," said Leon as he took the cold, wet bottle.

"More than one crate, I assure you," Manyoro replied. "It is a habit I learned in the army. They served this beer in the sergeants' mess." He smacked his lips with relish. "This is the best thing you British ever brought to Africa. Cheers!"

"Cheers!"

The two men raised their bottles in mutual salute, and then savored their drinks in silence for a moment. After a while they began to speak in English about their wives and children, Leon feeling almost embarrassed in this company at having just one of each, though Manyoro was keen to hear news of the son that he felt sure Eva was bearing, and of Saffron's near-victory in the show jumping.

"Ah, she has her father's spirit, that one," Manyoro said, approvingly, when he heard how Saffron had responded to being beaten. "I have never understood how your people talk of being a 'good loser.' How can losing be good? Why would a man take pride in accepting defeat? Miss Saffron is right to feel anger and shame. That way she will not make the mistake of losing a second time. Ah, but you must be proud of her, brother. She will be as beautiful as her mother, when she is grown."

"Not quite as beautiful as a Masai maiden, though, eh?" said Leon, knowing Manyoro's unshakable faith in the superiority of his tribe's females to all others.

"No, that would be impossible," Manyoro agreed. "But a great beauty among her own people, and with that fighting spirit in her heart . . . Believe me, M'Bogo, it will take a strong man to win her heart."

Next they moved on to the latest developments on the Lusima estate. Though he seldom ventured down from his mountaintop, and the estate covered the best part of two hundred square miles, Manyoro still knew everything that happened on it and there was never any need for Leon to discipline any of the herders. In the extremely rare event that one of them did anything wrong, Manyoro would already have dealt with the matter himself before Leon even heard about it.

"So, *Bwana*, what brings you here today?" Manyoro asked, calling Leon "Master" not out of servility, but respect.

"I come to you with a request, one that I hope you will find of interest," Leon said. "I dined at *Bwana* Hay's house two nights ago, and talked to a man by the name of de Lancey. He was disparaging of the Masai. He said they were lesser men, inferior to his own white tribe."

"Then this man is no more than a baboon, and a very stupid baboon at that. He should count himself lucky that I did not hear him say those words."

"Indeed he should," Leon agreed. "I, however, know the truth. So I assured him that my Masai brothers were proud warriors who have ruled this land since time began and I suggested a way in which I could prove their strength."

Manyoro grinned. "Will there be a fight? It has been too long since my assegai tasted blood. It keeps moaning to me, "Give me blood, for I am thirsty!'"

Leon fought back laughter as he adopted a pose of outrage at such rebellious sentiments. "Sergeant Manyoro! Have you forgotten the oath you swore to defend my people? Have you become a rebellious Nandi, slithering like a snake upon the dirt?"

Manyoro's broad shoulders broke into a regretful shrug. "You are right, M'Bogo, I have given my word and I will stand by it. But please, never compare me to a Nandi, not even in jest. They are the lowest people on all the earth."

"I apologize," said Leon, reflecting that it had been a Nandi arrow, stuck in Manyoro's leg, that had first brought him here to Lusima. "But let me assure you that neither you nor any of your people will be called upon to fight anyone. The *morani* will keep their blades sheathed. All I need is a man who can run."

Leon began to explain what he had in mind. But Manyoro's reaction was not what he expected. Far from being amused by the challenge, still less inspired by it, he seemed offended.

"M'Bogo, forgive me, but I am insulted to the depth of my soul. Why did you only pit three whites against one Masai? It is too easy. Ten would be more of a contest, possibly twenty."

"Now you insult my people, Manyoro. We are not all weak or lacking in endurance. I carried you on my back for thirty miles to this very mountain, when you were too badly wounded to walk."

Manyoro nodded. "That is true. But you are not like the others. You have the strength of the buffalo himself. That is why my people consider you our equal."

"I am proud to bear that honor," Leon replied. "That is why I have set this challenge, so that the Masai should receive the respect that they are due."

"For one day maybe," said Manyoro, and suddenly Leon

heard the voice of a proud man whose people were reduced to second-class status in their own land. "But that is better than no days at all. Who will de Lancey find to run against my man?"

"No one that you need fear, but some whom you should respect," Leon replied. "De Lancey is putting the word out. He'll round up some pretty tough customers, don't you worry about that. We're not all bone-idle idiots from Happy Valley, you know."

Manyoro thought for a moment then asked, "You say you will lose ten thousand pounds if De Lancey's man wins?"

"Yes."

"So if my man wins he will save you that amount. He will have done all the work. Should he not receive some reward for his efforts?"

Leon inwardly winced. Brother or no brother, Manyoro was always determined to wring the most out of any negotiation. "Good point," he conceded. "What do you suggest?"

"A man who performs a great feat should have a wife to mark his triumph."

"Sadly, I can't provide one of those."

"Then give him the cattle with which he will attract a bride and make her father think, "This is a man who deserves to have my daughter beside him.""

"Very well, I will give him a bull and three cows . . ." Leon could tell from Manyoro's face that the offer, which he had thought generous to a fault, had somehow fallen short of the mark. And then it occurred to him and he wondered how he could ever have been so stupid as he said, "And a bull and five cows to you too, though heaven knows your herds are already so mighty that you will not notice a few more."

Manyoro smiled with delight, both at the offer and the fact that Leon had understood that it should be made. "Ah, M'Bogo, a Masai always notices a new cow. You, of all men, should know that!"

"So, can I count on you to bring one of your best men to the polo fields?"

"You can count on me to bring a man. And you can count on him to win your bet. But whether he will be my best man, that I cannot say. My best might feel that this challenge is too easy. But fear not, M'Bogo, your money is safe . . . and so are my five cows and my bull besides. Now, come with me. You know there is someone else here who would rage like thunder if you should leave without seeing her."

"You know that I would never dream of doing that."

"Then come . . ."

Like an empress on her throne, Lusima Mama was sitting on a chair cut into the stump of what must once have been a towering tree. She rose as she saw Leon, her face wreathed in a loving, maternal smile, for since Leon had saved her son Manyoro's life he had become a son to her too.

Leon had no knowledge of Lusima's exact age, but she could not be less than seventy and was probably a good many years older than that. Twenty years ago she had seemed entirely impervious to the passing of time, but not even her wizardry could keep it at bay forever. Her hair was white now, her bare breasts a little saggier and less full than they had once been and her tattooed belly was just a fraction softer, the skin like crepe paper. But she held herself as tall and straight as ever, her walk still possessed a feline grace, and though there were lines around her dark eyes, their gaze could still look right through Leon, into the very depths of his soul.

A sense of great peace and security came over him, as it always did when he met Lusima. Being with her felt like stepping into a sanctuary, a place where he was always safe and cared for and he returned her smile with a warm and open heart. He held out his arms to hug her.

And then he saw something flicker in Lusima's eye and she halted in her approach toward him. Everything about her posture and expression tightened, as if she were suddenly aware of danger: as if the devil had crossed her path and something evil was prowling through the trees, waiting to attack.

"What is it?" asked Leon, alarmed by the change that had come over Lusima and conscious that it had happened while her eyes were focused on him.

"It . . . it is nothing, child." Lusima forced a wan smile. "Here, come and let me hold you."

Leon held back. "Something happened. You saw something. I know you did." He paused, summoning up his courage as if he were still a boy, rather than a grown man at the height of his powers. "You have never been false with me, Lusima Mama. Never. But I fear you are being false with me now."

Lusima dropped her hands to her side, her shoulders sagged and when she looked at him again the years seemed suddenly written upon her face. "Oh my child," she said softly, gently shaking her head. "You will be sorely tested. You will know pain such as you have never endured before. There will be times when you will not believe that you can survive it, times when you will pray for the release of death. But you must believe me . . ." She reached out, took Leon's hands and looked at him with feverish, imploring eyes, "You will find peace and happiness and joy one day."

"But I have those things already!" Leon cried. "Are you telling me that they will be taken from me? How? Tell me, for God's sake . . . what is going to happen?"

"I cannot tell you. It is not in my power. My visions come to me in riddles and half-formed images. I see a storm coming for you. I see a dagger in your heart. But you will survive, I promise you that."

"But Eva . . . and Saffron . . . and the baby. What about them?"

"Truly, I do not know. I see blood. I feel a great emptiness in you. I wish I did not. I wish I could have lied to you. But I cannot deceive you M'Bogo, and I cannot deny it. I see blood."

———

Leon spent the next few days with his stomach in knots and a permanent sense of suppressed anxiety dragging on his mind like a dog on a lead as he tried his best not to dwell on Lusima's intimations of disaster. He did not doubt that she was absolutely serious nor that there was truth in her words, for she had been right too often in the past for him to doubt her powers now. Yet experience had also taught him that there was nothing he could do to alter what fate had in store. So there was no point fretting over matters that he could not control. Even so, when Eva reported feeling dizzy he insisted on driving her to see Doc Thompson.

Before the war, Dr. Hector Thompson (to give him his proper title) and his wife had provided the expatriate community's medical care virtually single-handed. Since then, however, a European Hospital had been set up to care for the white community and the Thompsons had moved into semi-retirement, running a small general practice up-country. The Doc, a genial, reassuring Scotsman with a full head of white hair and a neatly clipped beard to match, took Eva's blood pressure and murmured, "Hmm, one-thirty-five over eighty-five, a little on the high side. Tell me, my dear, have you had any other symptoms apart from dizziness? Headaches, for example, or blurred vision?"

"No," Eva replied.

"Not felt sick or vomited?"

"Not since the morning sickness passed, but that was a couple of months ago."

The doctor thought for a moment. "You have had trouble in the past carrying a baby to term and we don't want to lose this one. On the other hand, we live at a much higher altitude than our British bodies were designed for and in a tropical climate, so there are all sorts of reasons why you might feel off-color. I advise plenty of rest and no great exertions of any kind. I'll also give you some aspirin. Take two if you feel either a headache or nausea and if symptoms persist for more than an hour or two, get in touch. Don't worry about calling me out in the middle of the night. That's what I'm here for."

The wager with de Lancey that Leon had thought so important now seemed entirely irrelevant. "I'm going to call him to say that the whole thing's off," he told Eva when they got home from their visit to Doc Thompson. "If he makes me forfeit the money, so be it. What matters is staying here with you and making sure you're all right."

"But I am all right," she insisted. "I felt a little dizzy, that's all, and you heard what Doctor Thompson said, it was probably just a spot of altitude sickness. I want you to win your wager. And I want to be there to see you win."

"Absolutely not!" Leon insisted. "You're not supposed to have any great exertions, those were the doc's own words."

She laughed, "Being a passenger on the drive down to the polo club is hardly an exertion, and nor is sitting in a comfortable chair in the shade when I get there. In any case, where do you think the Thompsons will be on the great day? Watching the race, just the same as everyone else for miles around. So if I do happen to feel a bit poorly, that will be the best place to be. Won't it?"

————

Leon could not dispute his wife's logic. And so, on the seventh morning after the dinner at Slains, he, Eva and Saffron, who was bouncing up and down with excitement at the thought of the event, set off before dawn and drove through the cool morning mist to the Wanjohi Valley Polo Club. Loikot came behind them, driving one of the estate's trucks, filled with everything the family would need to get them through the day and as many of the domestic and estate staff who could cram into the cabin and cargo area, or simply cling on to the outside of the vehicle.

The whole country seemed on the move. Farms and businesses

stood deserted by their managers and workers alike. Shops and restaurants had put "Closed" signs in their windows. Many of the chefs and shopkeepers, however, had simply shifted their operations to the polo club where an impromptu market had mushroomed, with stalls selling parasols, folding chairs and bottles of pop, alongside pits where fires were being stoked as whole sheep and great sides of beef were rotating on spits, while chops and sausages sizzled on griddles.

It was not just the colonists who had come to witness the spectacle. Once word had reached the native Kenyan population that one of their number was taking on their white masters, tribal antagonisms had been set aside, for the time being at least, and half the country seemed to be on the move—men and women of the Masai, Kikuyu, Luhya and Meru peoples— coming by foot, ox-cart, bus, or any other means they could find to join the carnival.

The settlers were all arrayed along one side of the polo field around which the race would be held, in front of the clubhouse, with native Kenyans massed opposite them on the far side. The actual field itself had been kept empty, so that the competitors could be seen at all times, to prevent any possibility of cheating. The team principals would remain in the center of the field, with those of the white runners who were still awaiting their turn to compete. Major Brett was serving as umpire while a dozen African police constables, arrayed around the course and supervised by a single white sergeant, would have the dual tasks of reporting any breaches of fair play, and also keeping the crowd in order.

"I'll be frank, Courtney, I'm not entirely happy about this whole palaver that your damned wager has sparked," Major Brett told Leon soon after he, Eva and Saffron had arrived at the club.

"I had no idea there would be quite such a turnout," Leon replied.

"Well, that's as may be. I'm a fair man, have to be in my position, so I accept that you could not reasonably have anticipated this level of public interest in a private wager between two gentlemen at dinner."

"Precisely."

"Nevertheless, I foresee the potential for considerable unrest when the native is defeated. John Masai's an excitable chap when his spirits are inflamed, particularly if he's got his hands on alcohol. I banned sales to the native population, of course, but I don't doubt they'll find a way to have a drink or two. And if they think that we have in any way conspired to make their chap lose, well, I just hope you don't have anything serious on your conscience when the day is out, that's all I can say."

For a second, Leon suddenly wondered whether the blood Lusima had been talking about might be that of the spectators. He was shocked to realize that he felt relieved at that possibility. It seemed almost like a reprieve for his family.

Major Brett interpreted Leon's silence as a refusal to accept any responsibility.

"For God's sake, man, you can't possibly believe that three Englishmen can't beat a single native, can you?"

The question dragged Leon's mind back to the here and now. "I would hardly have staked ten thousand pounds, Major, if I didn't think the Masai would win."

Brett shook his head disapprovingly. "Don't have much time for de Lancey. He strikes me as a bit of a bounder, not pukka at all. But he's got a point when he says you love the black man more than your own race. Wouldn't put it quite that strongly myself. But he's got a point."

The major took out his pipe and started stuffing it with tobacco, tamped it down, put a match to the bowl and started puffing away, encouraging the tobacco to burn. Leon was looking around, trying to spot Manyoro, but it was his competitors who appeared first.

"Speak of the devil," said Brett, looking past Leon. "De Lancey's arrived. Got his team with him too, by the look of it."

Leon turned and, sure enough, there was de Lancey, already red-faced and sweaty though the sun had barely begun to burn away the cloud that tended to hang over the valley in the early part of the day. Behind him were three men arrayed in various combinations of tennis shoes, boots, shorts, vests, shirts, scarves and cricket jumpers. A couple had actual running spikes hanging from laces tied around their necks. One wore a jumper with dark blue stripes around the V-neck and the waist and the letters "OUAC" surmounted by a laurel crown on the chest. The other had an almost identical jumper, save that the stripes were a pale sky-blue and the letters on his chest read "CUAC." Leon was familiar with the traditional rivalry between Dark Blues and Light Blues: these two were Oxford and Cambridge men, and that being the case, the letters "UAC" would surely stand for "University Athletics Club."

You never know, they might just be long jumpers or javelin throwers, he thought, cheering himself up as de Lancey stuck out a moist palm and gave Leon one of the softest handshakes he'd ever experienced. "Morning, Courtney, hope you've brought the lolly," de Lancey said. "I've recruited as good a team as you'll find south of Suez. Would you care to be introduced?"

"By all means," said Leon.

"Right-ho! Well, first I'd like you to meet Jonty Sopwith, though everyone calls him "Camel," you know, after the fighter plane."

Leon nodded. "Yes, even we Africans are aware of the Sopwith Camel. Good to meet you, Sopwith."

He exchanged handshakes, a much firmer one this time. Sopwith was pale-skinned, ginger-haired and blue-eyed. He was tall and rangy, with long legs and a barrel chest, suggesting that he had a good stride, with the heart and lungs to power it. He looked as though he was in his early to mid-twenties, just young enough to have missed the war, but in the prime years for an athlete. "You're an Oxford man, I see."

"Yes, sir. Ran in the Varsity team all three years I was there."

"What was your event?"

"I'm a pretty decent half-miler, turned out a few times at the three-A's, got to the final twice, actually."

So you're good enough to reach an Amateur Athletics Association final, competing to be British champion. No wonder de Lancey looks so cocky, Leon thought.

"And this is Dr. Hugo Birchinall," said de Lancey proudly as the man in the Light Blue jumper held out his hand. "Birchinall works at the European Hospital—his specialty was the sprint back at Cambridge."

"Good morning, doctor," Leon said, sizing Birchinall up. As befitted a specialist in the longest of the sprints, Birchinall was slightly shorter than Sopwith, but more powerfully built, heavier in the hips and the shoulders. He had short dark hair, and a swarthy complexion so that he seemed an altogether more brooding, almost menacing figure than his more boyish teammate.

A smirk crossed de Lancey's face, as if to suggest that while he had begun his introductions with two renowned athletes, he had left the very best till last. "Now for the final member of our team. I confess, he is not an Englishman, but he is white, and very proudly so, which was, I think you will agree, the essential element in our wager. So, Courtney, may I present a gentleman who has recently arrived in Kenya in search of opportunities as a farmer, Mister—or should I say *Mijnheer*—Hennie van Doorn. He's like you, old boy, a bit of a native African."

Van Doorn did not shake Leon's hand. "You any relative of that bastard Sean Courtney?" he said, in his guttural Afrikaaner accent.

"Distant cousin, why?"

"Because I lost most of my family in the war against the British, that's why."

Leon knew he meant the Boer War, rather than the more recent conflict.

"My father died fighting men like General Courtney," van Doorn went on. "My mother and my baby brother perished in the Bloemfontein concentration camp. Now I do not have any family left. Not even distant cousins."

"I'm truly sorry that your family suffered so badly," Leon said. "But I was born in Egypt. My father made his money trading up and down the Nile, and when he went to war, it was against the Mahdi at Khartoum. We had no part in what happened in South Africa."

"You have a big estate here, *jah*?"

"Yes."

"We had *'n klein plaas*, a small farm. It was on the Highveld, sixteen hundred meters up, not much lower than it is here, eh. Every day I would walk to school, six kilometers there, six kilometers back. Every day. But most of the time I did not walk, because if I walked I had to start before the sun was up and I did not like walking across the veldt in the dark, with all the wild animals out there, just waiting to have little Hennie for their breakfast. So I stayed in bed until the sun came up. But now I have a problem, for if I am late for school my teacher shall beat me and when I get home my father shall beat me even harder. So therefore I must run to school. Every day. Six kilometers there and six kilometers back. At sixteen hundred meters' altitude. So maybe this *kaffir* of yours can beat these *rooinek* Englishmen. But trust me, Courtney, he cannot beat me."

———

Leon could not deny that de Lancey had rustled up a strong trio to win him his ten thousand pounds. But where were

Manyoro and the man he was bringing to be de Lancey's opponent?

Leon looked around, scanning the crowd for the two tall,
imperious Masai he expected to see striding toward him. Then
he heard a voice shouting across the polo field, "M'Bogo!" Leon
turned and spotted Manyoro, emerging from the natives' side
of the ground. As was his custom when venturing into the
white man's world he had pinned the regimental badge of the
King's African Rifles to his red ochre *shuka*. The badge was
polished as brightly as if Company Sergeant Manyoro were
stepping out onto the parade ground and beneath it were arrayed
his many medals for bravery, campaigns against the enemy and
long service. The message was very clear: *I have served the
British Empire with honor and distinction and I deserve respect.*

Leon was about to call out his own greeting, but then he
paused, dumbstruck. For Manyoro was not accompanied by a
proud *morani* warrior who had earned his right to be considered
as a true Masai man by killing a lion with nothing but his
assegai to defend him. Instead there was a diminutive figure
who could barely be twenty, if that. He was far shorter than
any normal Masai, the shiny top of his shaven head barely
reaching Manyoro's shoulder. And while the Masai tended to
be both taller and much more slender than typical Europeans,
this profoundly unimpressive specimen was not so much slender
as scrawny, a fact made all the more apparent by the absurdly
over-sized pair of British army shorts, presumably loaned to
him by Manyoro, that were tied around his waist with string
and hung down to halfway down his twig-like calves. This
unlikely garment billowed around him as he walked so that he
looked like a small child who'd dressed up in a pair of granny's
old bloomers.

"I see you, Manyoro," Leon replied, and did not bother to
hide the irritation in his voice as he said, in English, "You
promised me a good man."

Manyoro looked back at him and flatly said, "No, I did not promise, brother. You demanded. And I told you that my best men would think this challenge beneath them. And so I have given you a runner and *Bwana* de Lancey can decide if he wants to race against him or not."

"He's hardly going to say no to that, is he?" said Leon, pointedly.

"Shall I take him away, then? You can forfeit the wager if you wish."

Leon forced himself to take his time and calmed down before he or Manyoro talked each other into a corner from which they could not extricate themselves.

"Very well, then, you had better introduce us."

Manyoro switched to Masai as he said, "M'Bogo, this is Simel. He is the son of one of my sisters. Simel, pay your respects to my brother M'Bogo. When you run for him, you run for me too, and for all our people. Do not let us down."

"I see you, Simel," Leon said.

"I see you, M'Bogo, and I promise you I will run like a wind over the grass that blows all day without ceasing."

Aye, you might at that, thought Leon. For when he looked more closely he saw the lad had a flat, well-muscled stomach hidden behind the absurdly bunched-up waistband of his shorts. And he certainly seemed healthy. He stood as straight-backed as a guardsman and his eyes were bright with life and youthful optimism. *Ah well, nothing for it now. Better introduce him to the opposition.*

Leon walked Simel over to the part of the polo field where de Lancey had set up his camp. A large tent had been erected, within which stood a couple of camp beds on which his runners could rest before their exertions, or recover after them. There were deckchairs for de Lancey and his cronies—a thoroughly rum crowd of chancers and remittance men, so far as Leon could see—and the women they had brought with them. A steady stream of porters had brought crates of champagne and Tusker,

Kenya's first brand of locally brewed beer. A campfire stood ready to provide sustenance to his opponent's entire party. A large iron kettle was coming to the boil and the smell of sausages sizzling on the grill, the whole set-up under the control of a couple of *totos*, suggested a late but hearty breakfast was being prepared.

A female face that Leon half-recognized caught his eye. It took him a second to place, but then he realized it belonged to Amelia Cory-Porter, his dinner companion a week earlier. He waved politely at her and she very pointedly did not wave back. Leon grinned to himself: *Hell hath no fury, eh? Fair enough, I showed her no interest, so now she's pitching her tent in de Lancey's camp. At least she'll be well fed.*

"Here's my man," said Leon once he had found de Lancey. He could practically see the cogs working in the other man's mind as he tried to decide whether this was some kind of set-up. Simel was grinning at de Lancey in an amiable, unthreatening fashion. He was so diminutive that his three competitors, who were now emerging from various corners of the camp to discover what they were up against, looked like champion middleweight boxers up against an untrained flyweight.

De Lancey gave Simel one last once-over, saw no threat and said, "Very well, then. You're on."

———

Jonty Sopwith had been running long enough to know that good athletes came in all shapes and sizes. This little Masai had the look of a distance runner about him. He'd said as much to Hugo Birchinall who'd agreed. "Looks like a classic Nilotic ectomorph to me. That means thin, Camel," he added, knowing that Sopwith had studied Land Economy and was unlikely to be familiar with physiological terminology. "Their light body-mass sheds heat more quickly than a more burly chap like me. Also helps them run long distances because they don't overheat, the way we do, like a car engine boiling over."

"Then we'd better get this done as quickly as possible," Sopwith said. "I'm going to take it out hard. Then he has to decide whether to match me or not. If he doesn't he'll fall way behind. If he does go with me, I reckon I can run the strength out of him, same way I did to Bobby Snelling in the '21 Varsity match, do you remember?"

"I certainly do. Dear old Snellers hung on to your coattails right up to the final bend, then you kicked again and he practically collapsed on the spot. Poor chap just didn't have another ounce of energy left in him."

"Exactly. Now, I reckon I'm good for a pretty sharp mile, at the very least. So I'm going to give it absolutely everything and hand over to you when I feel myself start to weaken."

"And then I'll come on and pick him off. Good work, Camel. That's a damned sound plan."

"So let's do the job ourselves, eh? Can't let it be said that two good Varsity men needed help from the *hoi polloi*."

"No, we certainly can't."

―――――

The tall, fair-skinned figure of Jonty Sopwith stood on the starting line beside the diminutive Simel. The two men shook hands and Sopwith said, "Good luck, old man," because it was the done thing to treat one's opponents with good manners and respect even if you then intended to grind them into the red African earth.

The starter fired his pistol and the two men set off to the sound of great roars of encouragement from the native Kenyans along one side of the polo field and the settlers on the other. As promised, Jonty Sopwith began at a punishing pace. In his introduction to Leon Courtney, he had understated his achievements, for he had a very good chance of making the British team for the Paris Olympics, two years earlier, until a badly twisted knee rendered him unable to compete. Sopwith therefore had every reason to believe that he could beat Simel, and get the job done pretty quickly too.

For a few seconds, Simel tried to keep up with the man whose hair was the color of flame-tree flowers. But then he remembered the words that Manyoro had told him, just as they were walking to the start. "Do not try to race any of them. Just run. And keep running. Think to yourself, "I am running back to Lonsonyo Mountain to see Lusima Mama and so I must run all day." But do not let the white men make you run any more quickly or slowly than you want to go. You must be a wildebeest, not a cheetah. Just run."

Now Simel understood the point of Manyoro's words. This man who had introduced himself so politely was trying to tempt him into running fast, like a cheetah. But a cheetah could not run for long at top speed. If it did not catch its prey within a few seconds it stopped, gathered its strength and then tried again, some while later. The wildebeest, on the other hand, kept moving, running all day with its brothers and sisters, from one horizon to the other.

Now I will be the wildebeest, Simel thought, and he slowed from the near-sprint in which he had started and settled into an apparently effortless, loping stride, his feet springing as lightly as an antelope's hooves from one step to the next and his hands held up high by his chest.

Within a matter of seconds a gap of five yards had opened up between the two runners. It grew wider, to ten, then twenty yards. The cheering in the white stands rose in volume. In de Lancey's camp the hangers-on were all slapping him on the back, while the women shrieked encouragement to Jonty Sopwith.

This man's even better than he said he was, Leon thought to himself. Sopwith's stride was much longer and more powerful than Simel's, like a stallion on the gallops.

Hugo Birchinall was already warming up. *They're going for the quick kill: the middle-distance man breaks him then the sprinter runs him down. Good tactics. They might just work.*

Leon looked at Manyoro. He was watching Simel intently, giving away no trace of emotion.

"You see what he's doing?" said Leon, looking toward Sopwith, who had opened up a gap of the best part of fifty yards.

"Of course."

"And will it work?"

Manyoro looked at the two runners out on the course then glanced across to Birchinall. "He certainly thinks so. He is singing his victory song before the lion has been killed."

"That's never a wise thing to do."

"No, M'Bogo, it is not."

———

Jonty Sopwith came round the final bend of the polo field and headed toward the finishing line at the end of the first lap, with the main mass of the settlers clustered in front of the clubhouse just ahead of him to his right. He glanced back over his shoulder and saw the distant figure of Simel, barely passing the corner, half the length of the polo field behind him, falling further back with every stride.

"Right, Sonny Jim, let's see how you like this," Sopwith muttered. And then he kicked again, an athlete of Olympian quality reveling in his God-given ability.

———

Simel felt a shot of alarm when he saw this opponent speed up again. He did not seem to be tiring like a cheetah. On the contrary, he was gaining in strength. He heard a deep sigh, almost a groan, coming from his people on their side of the field which was quickly swallowed up by the shouts and cheers of all the white *bwanas* and their women.

Fighting the urge to try and keep pace, Simel told himself that all was not yet lost. He still felt as fresh as he had when the race had begun, and although the gap between him and the man in front was widening, still it was not even half the full distance around the field. As he ran past the whites a few of them shouted insults at him. The words meant nothing to him, for he did not speak English. But he did not have to. The looks on their faces, the waving of their fists and the way the men shouted and the women screamed at him bore an unmistakable stamp of hostility, even hatred.

Then a thought struck Simel. *These people fear me. They are scared that I might be as good as them, or even better.*

Though he showed no expression in his face, in his heart Simel smiled. For he knew that the white men were right to be afraid. All his life he had been ashamed of being so small, but now he had a chance to prove that he could do as much for his people as any man among them.

I am a Masai. Now I must show these people what that means.

———

In the clubhouse Saffron was jumping up and down with excitement and attracting pursed-lipped looks of disapproval from the women all around her as her high, piping voice shouted out encouragement to the Masai runner. She had a problem, however. It was very hard to see the race. There were too many grown-ups in the way.

Saffy had been told to stay with her mother and was positioned beside the chair in which Eva was sitting as calmly as she could so as to expend the minimum possible energy. As determined as she was not to let Leon treat her like an invalid or be made to stay at home, Eva could hardly disobey a doctor's orders, even if her natural inclination was to leap to her feet and shout just as excitedly as her daughter for the little man who had been given the role of acting as her husband's champion.

As the runners disappeared off toward the far end of the field, Saffron turned to Eva and begged her, "Please Mummy, may I go and stand by Daddy in the middle of the field?"

"I'm not sure that's a good idea, my darling," said Eva, reaching out to take Saffron's hand. "I don't want you getting lost or trampled in the crowd. And I'm not sure Daddy really wants to have to worry about you when he's trying to concentrate on the race."

"Oh, I can get through all those people!" Saffron insisted, looking dismissively at the human barrier created by the grown-ups all around her. "And I promise I'll be as good as gold with Daddy. I won't be naughty at all." She fixed her huge blue eyes on her mother, almost daring her not to be charmed and repeated, "Please Mummy . . . please!"

Eva smiled. *I pity any poor man who tries to resist those eyes*, she thought, suddenly seeing an image of exactly how Saffron would look when she was grown into womanhood. *I certainly can't.*

"Do you absolutely promise me that you'll go carefully?" she asked.

"Yes, Mummy," Saffron nodded with a look of the utmost sincerity.

"And do you promise to be good and not to cause Daddy any trouble?"

"Yes, Mummy."

"Very well then, you can go."

"Thank you, thank you!" Saffron squealed, smothering her mother in kisses. "You are the kindest, nicest, sweetest mummy in the whole wide world!"

"Oh, and one last thing . . ."

Saffron paused in mid-stride and turned back to Eva: "Yes?"

"Tell Daddy not to worry about me. He needs to concentrate on his race. So tell him I've got a very comfortable chair and plenty of staff to look after me if I need anything. I will be quite all right. Can you remember all that?"

"Daddy's not to worry because you've got a comfy chair and everything's all right."

"Very good. Now, be gone with you!"

Eva watched as her little girl disappeared into the crowd, fearlessly darting between the adults around her. Then she gave a sharp little sigh, closed her eyes and dropped her head for a moment as a sudden sharp stab of pain struck her, like a dart thrown at her forehead, hitting right above her eyes.

It's just a little headache, she told herself as it was followed by a slight sensation of nausea. *A migraine, probably. Nothing to worry about.*

She thought for a second about sending one of the club's staff to take a message to Leon and then immediately rejected the idea. *No, I mustn't bother him. He has other, much more important things on his mind.*

———

Saffron sneaked under the rope and dashed across the track and onto the polo field before anyone could stop her. She paused for a second and looked around. It was only a week since she and Kippy had been jumping on this very same field, but it seemed like years ago. Everything looked so different now. There was a crowd of people clustered round a large tent, and she scanned them all in case she could see her father. Then she saw him a way off to one side, talking to Manyoro, and she realized she'd been looking at the enemy camp and scampered off in the right direction.

"I see you, little princess," said Manyoro as he spotted Saffron running toward him. She stopped in her tracks, two or three paces away from him and, with the utmost seriousness replied, in Masai, "I see you, Uncle Manyoro."

The tall, stately African's face broke into a broad, affectionate smile, for he considered this little white girl just as much of a niece as any of his Masai brothers' and sisters' offspring.

"Hello, Daddy," Saffron said, turning to her father.

"Saffy!" Leon exclaimed. He picked her up and swung her into the air, laughing as she squealed with excitement. He hugged her to his body, planting a kiss on the top of her head and then put her down on the ground.

"So, what brings you here, eh?" he asked.

"Mummy said I could," said Saffron, wanting to establish

that she had permission. "I couldn't see the race from the club-house because of all the people in the way. But I promised Mummy I'll be very, very good and won't cause any trouble at all."

"Hmm . . . I doubt that somehow. So, tell me, how is Mummy feeling?"

Saffron dutifully repeated Eva's message, virtually word for word.

"Good," said Leon, putting his daughter down. "I'm very pleased that Mummy is so well set. And very well done to you for remembering everything."

Saffron beamed with pleasure at her father's praise. "What's your runner called, Daddy?" she asked, once her feet were back on terra firma.

"Simel."

"He's very small."

Leon gave a rueful chuckle. "Yes, that's what I thought, too, when I first saw him. But I think he's putting up a pretty good show."

Saffron looked at the two runners who were now separated by slightly more than the length of the back straight. Sopwith had completed his second lap while she had been negotiating with her mother and making her way to where her father was standing, and was now halfway around the third. He no longer appeared to be running ahead of Simel so much as chasing him from behind.

"Is that man going to catch up with Simel?" Saffron asked.

"I hope not, my darling. But if he doesn't then Mr. Birchinall—he's the chap over there doing stretches and looking terribly keen—is going to take over."

"Oh," said Saffron, thoughtfully. "That doesn't sound very fair."

"Well, those are the rules I created."

"Well I think those rules are beastly to Simel. I'm going to go and cheer him up."

Saffron raced off to the far corner of the field and waited for Simel to run past. When he was a few paces away from her she cried out, "Come on Simel! Come on Simel!" and then dashed along beside him. Saffron could only keep up with him for a handful of strides, but the sight and sound of her encouraging their man brought heart to his supporters and they raised their voices again to urge him on.

Manyoro, however, had his eyes elsewhere. "Look at *Bwana* Sopwith, brother. His stride has shortened and his pace has slowed."

"By God you're right," Leon agreed. He had brought a pair of field glasses with him and he trained them now on Sopwith, who would shortly cross the line for the third time. "He's gasping for breath. It's the altitude, probably, he's just not used to it."

"But Simel keeps running," said Manyoro. "Soon the gap will start to open up again."

Birchinall had now taken up his position on the track at the end of the clubhouse straight, urging his teammate on. Sopwith made one final effort, summoning every last ounce of strength as he ran to where Birchinall was standing with his hand held out behind him, as if waiting for a baton. Sopwith reached out, slapped the hand and then fell to his hands and knees on the grass, his head slumped down and his chest heaving.

Now it was Birchinall's turn and he was a very different kind of athlete. He ran like a true sprinter, arms pumping, back straight, knees up high and suddenly the gap between him and Simel up ahead seemed to be narrowing again, and even more quickly this time. The spectators on the colonists" side of the field roared for their man. They flooded forward toward the rope that marked the track and the few police constables detailed to cover that side of the course—for no one had even considered the possibility that the white crowd might give way to disorder—found themselves trying to hold back a tide of shouting, fist-pumping farmers and businessmen.

Within the length of the back straight, right in front of Simel's own supporters, Birchinall had taken another fifty yards out of the gap. By the time he had run across the width of the polo field and turned the corner into the clubhouse straight, Simel was only just passing the finishing line.

The little Masai was starting to worry, darting nervous glances over his shoulder, but still he did not increase his pace.

"For God's sake, run harder, man!" Leon shouted, though he knew that Simel could not possibly hear him over the noise of the crowds.

Manyoro shook his head. "No, he must hold his nerve. That is his only hope."

"Tell that to de Lancey. He thinks he's in the money."

Sure enough, the opposition camp was already celebrating. A crate of champagne had been dragged from within the tent and the *totos* were busy opening bottles and pouring glasses. The victory toasts were just about to be poured.

———

Simel rounded the turn at the end of the clubhouse straight, his eyes wide with the fear of defeat, but sticking to the instructions Manyoro had given him, for he was even more scared of disobeying his chief than of losing the race.

Birchinall was coming up hard, still gaining, still maintaining his pace though he was far beyond the limits of his usual racing distance. His face bore an expression of savage fury, the look of a man who is fighting past the point of exhaustion, ignoring the screaming pain of his muscles, the bursting of his heart and the desperate craving of his lungs for air.

He was going to win if it killed him. He knew it. The crowd knew it. Simel knew it.

The distance between them closed. Twenty yards . . . fifteen . . . ten . . .

Simel could hear the Englishman's feet pounding toward him and the rasping of his breath, like a wild animal at his heels.

He could not help himself. He broke into a sprint.

Birchinall increased his pace still further, pushing himself far beyond his normal limits, further than he'd gone in any race he'd ever run in his life.

Still he kept coming.

Simel closed his eyes, barely even conscious that he was still running, steeling himself for the moment when Birchinall would overtake him.

And then he heard a sudden scream of pain. He opened his eyes, glanced around again, and there was Hugo Birchinall on the ground, writhing in agony, clutching the back of his right thigh, desperately rubbing at the hamstring that had given way under the intolerable stress of the race and snapped.

Simel slowed to little more than a walk. He looked back again, not knowing what to do. Another human being was injured and in pain. Surely it was right to care for him. Should he go back, or keep running?

Confused by what had happened and breathless from the additional exertion required to keep himself that fateful hair's breadth ahead of Birchinall, Simel was unaware of the shouts and gestures of both Leon and Manyoro who were now running toward the corner of the polo field where the injury had occurred, hotly pursued by Saffron and behind her both de Lancey and Jonty Sopwith. The Masai was barely moving now and de Lancey was yelling, "Umpire! Umpire! He's stopped!" But his voice was entirely lost in the pandemonium that had broken out among both sets of supporters.

Then Birchinall displayed the depths of his courage and fighting spirit. Grimacing in agony at the effort, he hauled himself to his feet and set off after Simel once again, hobbling and hopping on his one good leg. The sight of such a mighty runner reduced to this desperate parody of his former self was enough to reduce many of the women gathered under the clubhouse veranda to tears, and not a few of the men around them dabbed discreetly at their eyes or suddenly found the need to blow their noses.

Simel, however, had an entirely different reaction. He knew

that a wounded animal could be the most dangerous of all, so when he saw Birchinall coming toward him again, no matter how slowly or awkwardly, his sympathy vanished. He had a chance now to open his lead up again, and he was not going to waste it.

He did not even see Birchinall finally accepting that he was beaten and his place being taken by van Doorn. In the time it took the South African to reach the point on the track where Birchinall had finally collapsed, Simel was able to open up the gap by a couple of hundred meters.

Barely ten minutes had passed and he was two-thirds of the way to proving that even the smallest Masai was more than a match for any white man.

———

In her chair on the clubhouse veranda, Eva slipped into a light sleep that gave her a brief respite from the worsening headaches and nausea she had been experiencing. But her dreams were troubled, incoherent and suffused with a sense of threat so menacing that they woke her.

Now her head felt like it was splitting in two. *Mustn't trouble Leon*, she thought to herself, feeling slightly dizzy, as if she'd had too much to drink, though she'd not touched anything stronger than a cup of tea with lemon all day. *A couple of aspirin should make me feel better.*

Eva smiled weakly at a passing waitress. "Do you think you could possibly get me a glass of soda water, please?"

"Of course, Madam," the waitress replied.

"Thank you so much," Eva replied, and slumped, exhausted, back into her chair.

———

Hennie van Doorn possessed the bitter, unyielding toughness of a man born to pioneering Afrikaaner stock. For generations his family had struggled to take, hold and cultivate their land on the high veldt. They fought the land itself, the elements around them and the other peoples who coveted that territory for themselves, be they Zulus who considered it theirs to begin with, or British fired by an insatiable greed for more land and a greater Empire. They prayed to a God who was as hard and unforgiving as they were themselves, a God who taught them to hold grudges, seek retribution and left the turning of other cheeks to weaker, more gullible folk than them.

Simel could feel the menace emanating from this very different breed of white man, as it did from a growling lion or an angry snake. This was not a man whose limbs would betray him as Birchinall's had done. Everything about him told the world that Hennie van Doorn was going to win. No other outcome was possible. Every time Simel looked back, van Doorn was just a little bit closer to him.

The sun was rising now and the growing heat was making more and more people seek out shade wherever they could, be that within the clubhouse, in the shade of a tree or beneath an umbrella or parasol. But still the runners kept going. For Leon, the very fact that van Doorn was drawing out the kill over such a long period made it all the more horribly fascinating. It was like watching a spider taking hours to weave its web, knowing that the insects that were its prey would inevitably be caught and die when the task was complete. And Simel was finally starting to weaken.

Leon and Manyoro were now playing a much more active part in the race. Every time Simel passed their position, they marched to the side of the track, shadowed by Saffron trotting along beside them, and while the little girl cheered her hero on and Leon clapped and called out his encouragement, Manyoro provided instructions in Masai, urging Simel on and advising him how best to conserve his strength. At first, Leon understood everything that Manyoro said, for he had himself been fluent in Masai for more than twenty years. But then a time came when Manyoro's words sounded foreign to him. He had slipped into some kind of slang or dialect that even Leon could not follow.

"What were you saying to him, just then?" Leon asked.

The big man shrugged his shoulders. "It was nothing, M'Bogo."

Leon was about to pursue the matter, but suddenly he noticed that Simel's metronomic stride had started to shorten. With his hunter's instinct for a weakening prey, van Doorn was looking stronger and picking up pace. The gap between them was narrowing much more quickly.

Leon sighed and looked up to the heavens, as if seeking some kind of divine intervention. Something caught his eye. Far in the distance, beyond the furthest hills, a great mass of storm clouds had appeared over the western horizon and was now marching across the sky toward the polo fields. Leon could see lightning flashes many miles away.

Rain stops play, thought Leon. *That might be our only hope.*

————

Simel's head was rolling from side to side and his stride had lost its spring. He could feel van Doorn getting closer. His looks back down the track were becoming ever more frequent and wide-eyed. The South African was actually grinning at him now, relishing his impending triumph, picking up his pace all the time.

They were running across the field, about to turn into the back straight. Van Dorn was no more than thirty paces behind him and gaining all the time. Simel saw Manyoro, *Bwana* Courtney and his little daughter waiting by the side of the track up ahead. He had almost reached the three of them, and the gap between him and van Doorn had halved once again when he saw his chief give a fractional nod of the head. That was the signal they had agreed over the previous circuits and Simel understood precisely what it meant.

Like a man waking from a prolonged slumber, Simel came

alive again. His body lost its heavy, lifeless torpor, his head lifted and his stride lengthened. Within a dozen strides he was moving at something close to his full speed. The Kenyans massed along the back straight burst back into life as they saw that Simel's apparent exhaustion had been a ruse to draw his opponent on. They hooted with delight at the Masai's cleverness and the white man's foolishness and for every one of them shouting for Simel, there was another loudly mocking van Doorn.

The Afrikaaner paid them no attention whatever. His entire being was focused on the business of running. His smile was replaced by a grimace as he forced himself to match Simel. But matching him wasn't good enough. He had to go faster. Van Doorn had come too close to snatching an outright victory to be content with anything less now.

Simel had never known such pain. His whole body was on fire, every muscle burning, every breath a desperate, rasping inhalation, sucking air into lungs that still felt starved and a heart whose beating was like an army of drummers, pounding their sticks against his ribs.

He had been running for so, so long. And provided that he kept his pace steady, measured, moderate, he could have kept going for even longer still. But this was different. This was running like the cheetah. And the cheetah did not run for long.

Simel started to slow, and this time he was not pretending.

———

Eva's headache had become unbearable. She tried to call for a waitress to get her some more water, but when she tried to speak, she could not hear herself speak over the shouting, cheering, stamping crowd. There was a roaring sound in her ears, like surf crashing on the shore, and she was blinded by a flashing, flickering sensation as if someone was shining a light right in her eye.

She gave a cry of, "Help!" but the sound that emerged from her mouth was a feeble, incoherent moan.

A moment later a waitress passed by her chair, and the scream of horror she gave was enough to cut through the hubbub around her. A dozen or so of the people crammed onto the veranda turned and looked in horror at the sight of a woman jerking helplessly, unconsciously, like a marionette in the hands of a mad puppeteer while a dark crimson stain spread across the front of her skirt.

"Doctor!" a man's voice shouted. "For God's sake someone get a doctor!"

———

Van Doorn was at the very limits of his physical resources. But he saw the little man tying up and understood that if he could only keep going, just for a very short while, he could yet have his victory.

But could he keep going? He was suffering badly from the sun and heat and lack of water. His mouth was parched and a crust of desiccated white foam had formed at the corners of his lips. He felt light-headed, his vision was starting to blur around the edges and there was a rushing sound in his ears as if he were on the verge of fainting.

No! van Doorn told himself. *I will not give in. Only the weak let pain or discomfort affect them. I will beat this* verdoem kaffer yet!

He drove himself into one last effort and forced his shattered body to keep going, denying its pleas to slow down.

The gap was closing once again.

———

"Well, it was a good try," Leon said.

"Simel's not beaten yet, Daddy!" Saffron insisted, defiant to the last.

"I'm afraid your father is right," Manyoro said, in a voice heavy with disappointment. "Simel fought with the heart and courage of a lion. He saw off two hunters, but he could not defeat the third. There is no disgrace in that."

"I don't care what you say," Saffron insisted, folding her arms in front of her chest and glaring up at the two men, "I think he'll win."

Leon gave a rueful sigh. He was about to lose ten thousand pounds in public, and to a man like de Lancey . . . *Let that be a lesson to you. Don't make any more stupid bets at dinner tables.*

The African faces opposite him that had been so gleeful a few moments ago were now downcast. Silence had fallen as they waited for the end.

And then, from somewhere in the crowd, a single voice sang out:

We are the young lions!

A few other men joined in, somewhat tentatively:

When we roar the earth shivers!

And then more voices, more strongly:

Our spears are our fangs!

And more again:

Our spears are our claws!

An exultant smile spread across both Leon and Manyoro's faces. This was the Lion Song, passed down to all Masai boys as part of the teaching that would lead them toward manhood. Their fathers and brothers sang it, as they would one day too, when they went out to attack lesser tribes and plunder their cattle and women, or confront the mighty lion with nothing but an assegai in their hands. This song both celebrated strength and provided it. And Leon joined in with all the other Masai voices, coming together in the rich, sonorous, exultant harmonies that were one of the glories of Africa, from the velvety resonance of the basses to the highest, piping falsettos.

Fear us, O ye beasts, they sang.

Fear us, O ye strangers!

———

Across the field, Simel heard the voices of his people calling to him and now he was panting out the next lines along with them:

Turn your eyes away from our faces, you women!

You dare not look upon the beauty of our faces!

Simel was barely aware of the power surging back through him, as if carried through the air by the song itself, for his running now seemed effortless, his body almost weightless as though his spirit had left it somehow and was looking down from on high.

The Masai saw the effect of their singing on Simel, and their volume became still greater as they let him know that they and he were one:

We are the brothers of the lion pride!
We are the young lions!
We are the Masai!

Simel ran down the home straight, past the crowds of his people's white masters, barely registering their presence. The music had filled him, refreshed him and driven him on.

He was unaware of all the people rushing toward him and when the first arms caught hold of him and broke the music's enchantment he struggled and lashed out, shouting, "No! No! I must not stop."

Then Simel heard Manyoro's voice and felt the strength of his embrace as he said, "Be still, little warrior. Be still. The battle is over. The victory is won. Look . . . turn your head and look."

Simel did as he was told and stared back down the track. He saw a body lying on the turf, and men rushing toward it as they had toward him. He realized that the body belonged to van Doorn and for a terrible moment thought that he might be dead.

"Have I killed him?" Simel panted, though he was gasping for air so desperately that he barely had breath enough to talk.

"No," Manyoro reassured him. "Watch. He rises."

Simel screwed up his eyes and, sure enough, arms were reaching down, grasping the fallen runner and slowly lifting him back to his feet.

"Good," Simel gasped. "I am glad."

"You won," Manyoro said. "You ran like a true Masai, a true *morani*."

Simel smiled. And then, only then, he passed out from sheer exhaustion.

———

Saffron was still filled with the excitement of the final minutes of the race and the elation of Simel's win. But the sight of him fainting in Manyoro's arms plunged her into an abyss of fear and concern for him until he came to, blinked a few times and looked around as if unsure where he was. And then all those bad feelings vanished and she was jumping up and down and cheering at the very top of her voice as Simel was hoisted onto Manyoro's shoulders as even the white spectators joined in the riotous applause for what was so clearly such a mighty effort and a splendid triumph.

"Make that ten cows!" Leon called to Manyoro. "Simel deserves it. And, yes, ten for you too!"

The native crowd had burst past the police who had all been far too busy cheering the victory themselves to stop them and were now flooding across the polo field toward the clubhouse, dancing and jumping for joy as they went.

Amidst the pandemonium it suddenly struck Saffron that Mummy ought to be there, enjoying it all with her and Daddy.

I wonder if I should go and get her, she thought.

And then she saw Doctor Thompson pushing his way through the crowd. Of all the people all around her, whether black or white, his was the only face not alight with the sheer thrill of what they had all just witnessed. He looked somber, and she could see him becoming cross as he had to force his way through all the people blocking his way.

The doctor was looking from side to side, clearly searching for someone. Then he spotted Saffron. He'd often treated her for colds and upset tummies and general bumps and bruises so he recognized her at once and came toward her.

"Hello, Saffron," he said, not giving her his usual smile. And before she could even say hello back, he asked, "Where's your father?"

"He's over there, by Manyoro," she said, pointing toward them. "Is something the matter?"

The doctor didn't reply and suddenly Saffron had a terrible, frightening feeling that she knew what the matter was. She reached up and tugged on the doctor's sleeve. "Is Mummy all right?"

He looked down at her, his face grave, opened his mouth, but then closed it again, as if he did not know what to say. He turned his head, looked toward her father and pushed his way through the mass of people lining up to offer their congratulations.

Saffron watched the doctor talking to Daddy. She saw the happiness drain from her father's face, to be replaced by a look as sad and serious as the doctor's. Then her father turned to Manyoro, and said something. Both men looked toward her and then they started moving: her father with Doctor Thompson, heading back up to the clubhouse, Manyoro toward her.

Saffron knew what that meant. Daddy was going to see Mummy, who must be really ill, or he and the doctor wouldn't be looking so worried. Manyoro was supposed to be looking after her.

Saffron loved Manyoro. But she loved her mother more and she had to see her, no matter how ill she was. She just had to.

She thought for a second. *Black people aren't allowed in the clubhouse. Not unless they're staff. So if I can get there before Manyoro he can't come in after me.*

She looked toward Manyoro. For a second their eyes met. Then Saffron turned and dashed away, nipping between the much bigger grown-ups all around her while Manyoro had to go slowly and steadily, asking permission of all the settlers to let him through. Saffron knew that she was being cruel, forcing a man as proud and dignified as Manyoro to lower himself to men and women who weren't half as fine as him, simply because of the color of his skin. But she had no choice. She had to see her mother.

Saffron kept moving, constantly expecting to feel the weight of Manyoro's hand on her shoulder until she reached the short flight of steps leading up to the clubhouse veranda. She dashed up the steps, knowing that once she'd reached the top she was safe and only then looked around to see where Manyoro was.

The Masai wasn't hard to spot. He was a good head taller than any of the settlers around him and he was looking at her with an expression of disappointment and something else Saffron had never seen in him before. She frowned, wondering what it was and then she realized that Manyoro was in pain. He clenched his fist and bumped it against his chest, over his heart.

The pain he's feeling is for me, Saffron thought as she turned and made her way to the spot where Mummy had been sitting. Her chair was empty, but her handbag was still there, on the table beside the chair, and the book she had brought with her to read, *The Green Hat*.

Saffron remembered the first time she'd seen it, a few days earlier. "Who wants to read a book about a hat?" she'd asked.

Mummy had laughed and said, "It's not just about a hat. It's more about the woman who wears it. She's called Iris Storm and she's very daring and rather wicked."

"Is she the baddie, then?"

"No, she's more like a tragic heroine—someone beautiful and rather wonderful, but doomed."

"Oh . . ." Saffron had not been entirely sure what Mummy had meant by that, but then she'd perked up when Mummy leaned over, with a cheeky smile on her face and a wicked glint in her eye, and whispered, "Would you like to hear a secret about this book?"

"Ooh, yes please!" cried Saffron, who loved secrets and could tell from Mummy's expression that this was going to be a really good one.

"Well, Iris Storm is a pretend character, but she's based on a real person."

"Is that the secret?" asked Saffron, disappointedly.

"It's part of the secret," Eva said. "The other part is that the real woman is someone you know."

Now that was interesting. Saffron's eyes widened. "Who?" she gasped.

"I can't tell you, because it's a secret . . . but . . ." Mummy let the word hang tantalizingly in the air, "In the book, Iris Storm drives a great big yellow Hispano–Suiza car with a silver stork on the bonnet. What do you think about that?"

Saffron frowned in concentration. And then it struck her. She had seen a great big yellow car with a stork. "I know, I know!" she squealed excitedly. "It's . . ."

"Ssshhh . . ." Mummy had put a finger to her lips. "Don't say a word. It's a secret."

Moments like that, when she and Mummy were sharing things and it felt as though they lived in their own little world—although Daddy and Kippy were allowed into it too, of course—were one of the things Saffron loved about her mother. So now she smiled to herself as she picked up the book and put it into Mummy's bag, taking care not to let the bookmark fall out, so that Mummy didn't lose her place.

"Hey you . . . Missy!" someone called out. "What do you think you're doing with that bag?"

Saffron turned and saw a cross-looking man she didn't recognize.

"It's my mummy's bag," she said. "I'm going to take it to her." Then she stopped and, suddenly feeling very frightened, said, "I don't know where she is."

The man's face fell. He looked around as if looking for an escape route.

"My mummy is Eva Courtney," Saffron said. "Do you know where she's gone?"

"Ah . . . I . . . that's to say . . . must dash," the man said and disappeared into the crowd.

Saffron was surrounded by people yet utterly alone. More alone than she'd ever been in her life. She wished she'd let Manyoro look after her. She always felt completely safe when she was with him.

A waitress came up to her and got down on her haunches in front of her. "I will take you to your mother," she said, and held out her hand.

Saffron took it. The feel of the waitress's smooth warm skin calmed and comforted her a little. She walked with her into the main body of the clubhouse, still clutching her mother's handbag tight to her body with her spare hand. There was a bar inside where children weren't supposed to go, filled with men talking about the race, settling up their own side bets and loudly calling for more beer. No one paid Saffron any attention as the waitress led her across the bar and opened a door with a wooden sign on it that said "Committee Room".

"You go in there, Miss," said the waitress, softly, opening the door and gently ushering Saffron into the room.

Saffron crept in, knowing she was not supposed to be there and not wanting to disturb anyone.

She saw three people grouped around the table that stood in the middle of the room. A woman was standing at the far end with her back toward her. Saffron recognized her as Mrs. Thompson, the doctor's wife. Daddy was next to her, also with his back toward the door. Between them Saffron could just see the snowy-white top of Doctor Thompson's head on the other side of the table. He seemed to be looking down at something in front of him. There was someone next to him and as she crabbed her neck to see better Saffron realized that it was the runner, Dr. Birchinall, still in his shorts and a white cricket jumper, but with a white bandage wrapped around his injured thigh.

Only then did Saffron see her mother's legs and shoeless feet on the table, lying between her father and Birchinall.

Mummy's feet were jerking up and down, as if she were shaking or kicking them, but the way they were moving was really strange, not like anything anyone would normally do.

Saffron crept around the side of the room, until she was almost opposite the end of the table. She hadn't looked up at all, not wanting to catch anyone's eye. But finally she turned and looked down the table.

Mummy was lying on her back with her arms to her side. The Thompsons were up by her head with their arms pressing down on her shoulders. Daddy had his arms on Mummy's legs. And the reason they were all pushing down was that she was throwing herself from side to side, her body shaking and her limbs twitching.

Saffron didn't understand what was happening or why her mother was moving the way she was, or why her eyes were open but she didn't seem to be seeing anything. The beautiful face that had always looked at her with such love in its eyes was twisted into something ugly and unrecognizable. Mummy's dress had ridden up and there was a wet, dark stain between her legs and on the surface of the table. And then she groaned and it was a ghastly sound that was nothing like her mother's normal voice but more the howl of a wounded animal and Saffron could not control herself a second longer. She screamed out, "Mummy!" dropped the bag and dashed toward the table.

"Who let that girl in here?" Doctor Thompson shouted. "Get her out at once!"

Saffron saw her father let go of Mummy's thrashing legs. He stepped toward her with such an angry desperate look on his face that she burst out crying and this time when he picked her up there was no happiness, not even any affection, just his angry face and his hands holding her so tightly that it hurt.

"Mummy!" Saffron screamed again and then a third time, "Mummy! I've got to see Mummy!"

But it was no use. Her father was carrying her out of the room and across the bar and no matter how hard she punched or kicked him or how loudly she shouted, "Let me go! Let me go!" he would not loosen his grip on her.

He pushed his way through the crowd on the veranda, and walked down the steps to where Manyoro was waiting.

Then, and only then, did Leon Courtney drop his daughter to the ground, though he still held her arms so that she could not get away. He glared at Manyoro with fury in his eyes and there was not the slightest trace of brotherly affection in his voice as he snarled, "I thought I told you to look after her."

Manyoro said nothing. He just took Saffron's hand, a little more gently than her father had done, but still holding her just as tightly. Leon Courtney waited for a moment to see that his daughter was finally secured. Then he turned on his heels and ran back up the clubhouse steps.

As Saffron watched him go she felt abandoned, desolate and completely unable to understand what was happening. Her whole world that had seemed so secure and so happy just a few minutes earlier was falling apart around her. Her mother was desperately ill. Her father hated her. Nothing was as it should be and none of it made any sense.

Just then she felt the first drops of rain fall on her and spatter across the red earth all around her. There was a sudden explosive crack of thunder and only a couple of seconds later a dazzling flash of lightning. The wind whipped at her dress and within an instant her tears were washed from her face by torrential rain, and the sound of her crying was drowned by the roaring of the storm.

————

"How is she?" Leon shouted for the hundredth time, trying to make himself heard over the straining of the engine and the pounding of the rain, and received much the same answer from the back of the car as he had on every previous occasion. He was leaning back in the driver's seat, his head half-turned to the back of the Rolls-Royce.

"She's very weak, Mr. Courtney. But she's still here." Dr. Hugo Birchinall was behind him, sitting on the back seat with Eva cradled in his arms. "She's a fighter, sir, you should be very proud of her. But Mr. Courtney, may I give you a word of advice . . . as a doctor?"

"Go ahead."

"Your wife is very ill indeed. There's no guarantee she'll make it. But she certainly won't make it if we crash. So please, focus all your attention on your driving. It'll help take your mind off things."

Leon said nothing, but he turned his eyes back to the road ahead. Birchinall was right. It was an act of sheer desperation even to try to make the drive to Nairobi in this kind of weather. The distance wasn't an issue. The Rolls's six-cylinder, eighty horsepower engine would make short work of the seventy-five miles between Gilgil and the Kenyan capital if the journey ran along flat, straight roads. But the truth was very different.

Like most of western Kenya, Gilgil lay within the confines of the Great Rift Valley, the stupendous tear in the earth's surface that ran in a great arc southwards for almost four thousand miles, from the Red Sea coast of Ethiopia through the heart of East Africa to the Indian Ocean in Mozambique.

Nairobi, however, lay outside the Rift and the only way to reach it by car was a dirt road, surfaced with gravel that ran up the towering escarpment, as much as three thousand feet of virtually sheer rock at its highest points, that formed one side of the valley. The road clung to the side of this gargantuan natural wall, snaking and twisting, seeking every possible scrap of purchase as it rose and rose toward the summit.

There were no barriers of any kind at its side, nor even any markings to indicate where the road ended and the plummeting drop into the void began. Occasional trees clung to the scraps of rocky soil by the side of the road and a few enterprising, or possibly just foolhardy tradesmen had set up shacks, selling food and drinks on the very few patches of flat land, just a few yards wide, that lay between the road and the edge of the cliff.

On a clear, sunny day with a dry road beneath the wheels the view from the road, looking out across the apparently limitless expanse of the Great Rift Valley, was a sight so heart-stopping in its magnificence that it justified the nervousness that even the most cool-headed driver or passenger felt when braving the escarpment road. And the fearful could console themselves that this petrifying stretch of their journey was less than ten miles in length. But when rain fell as hard as this it might as well have been ten thousand miles, for no sensible person even attempted to negotiate what swiftly became an impossibly treacherous cross between a muddy track and a rushing stream. The water didn't just fall onto the road from the sky. It cascaded in torrents from the heights up above. So it was by no means uncommon for sections of the road's surface to be washed away in really bad storms and any hostess who invited guests for a weekend anywhere within the valley did so on the mutual understanding that, if the weather turned bad, they might be there for a week.

But Eva Courtney could not wait a week, or even a day. Her only hope was to get to a hospital and the nearest one of any size at all was in Nairobi.

"I'll try to get a message through to let them know you're coming," Doc Thompson had said. "Birchinall, you look after Mrs. Courtney along the way. Courtney, you'd better pray that fancy car of yours is as powerful as you always tell us it is. And may God be with you, for you'll need all the luck He can give."

It was barely midday by the time they had set off. Eva's first fit had passed, though others could be expected. Her face had lost its normal golden tan and was a ghostly, greyish white. Yet she seemed to be at peace, as if she were just sleeping as she was taken on a stretcher to the car and then laid on her side along the back seat. Leon had relented a little and let Saffron see her mother and whisper, "I love you," in her ear, but he had resisted his daughter's increasingly frantic pleas to be allowed to come with them to the hospital and she had been taken away, kicking and screaming, to be driven back to Lusima in the truck with Manyoro, Loikot and the staff.

The first section of the drive was relatively straightforward as the road ran southeast along the valley floor. The rain was far too much for the Rolls's windscreen wipers to cope with, but Leon knew the route so well that he only needed a few visual clues, no matter how blurred by water, to tell him where he was and there was almost no other traffic on the road to worry about. He was even able, in a desperate attempt to talk about something, anything other than Eva's plight to tell Birchinall, "This storm has come at just the right time for your Mr. de Lancey."

"How do you mean?"

"Well, I doubt he's stripped down to his birthday suit and run round the polo field in this weather. Even if he did there'd be no one still left to watch him."

"I'm glad your chap won," Birchinall said. "Pluckiest thing I ever saw, taking on the three of us like that. It would have been rotten if van Doorn had come on and beaten him at the last. Can't say I liked the cut of that Boer's jib, truth be told. Charmless bunch, aren't they?"

"True enough. But they'd probably say that charm's a luxury they can't afford. And to do the man justice, he's not like ninety-nine percent of the other white men and women who were at the race today. He's not a settler, or a colonist. He's a proper African."

"So are you, from what I hear . . . If you don't mind me saying so."

"Absolutely not, I take it as a compliment, which was how

this ridiculous bet ever happened in the first place. Christ, I wish I'd never set de Lancey that wager. We'd have spent the day at home, no excitement. Eva would have been right as rain. I'll never forgive myself if anything happens to her. Never!"

"Don't say that, Mr. Courtney. Your wife has eclampsia. It could have struck her at any time, in any surroundings. As it was, it happened at a place that was a lot closer to Nairobi than your estate is, with two doctors immediately at hand. If anything, your wager has improved her chances, not lessened them."

The road was starting to rise upward now, passing through groves of spiky-leaved sisal and candelabra euphorbia, whose succulent stems branched out and up from a central tree trunk like myriad green candles. As they went higher, more and more of the valley and the hills that rose from it were displayed before them.

"Astonishing, isn't it?" Birchinall said. "Looks like something from the dawn of time. Just the power of it all."

Leon knew just what the doctor meant, for the sun had entirely disappeared and the only illumination came from lightning bolts that could be seen flashing across the sky, striking one mountain ridge after another with their searing blasts of pure white light—the mountains just a darker shade of black against the deep purples and charcoal greys of the sky. It truly seemed as though the bolts were being hurled down from the heavens by unseen gods, as though the vast power they contained held the spark of life itself, as well as the destructive force of death.

And then the road swung upward again, curled this way and that and suddenly they were on the side of the escarpment, on a road that seemed barely wider than the car itself and, just at the point when the surface became most treacherous, so it was almost completely exposed to the full force of the wind and rain. Leon had ordered the most powerful headlights possible for his car, but the beams barely penetrated the watery, murky gloom. He could see a small patch of road surface directly in

front of the bonnet, but beyond that there was nothing but
darkness, and it was quite impossible to tell whether the blackness was simply that of the track itself, just waiting for the light
to strike it, or the empty space beyond the precipice, waiting
to hurl them to their destruction.

Leon longed to put his foot down on the accelerator, for every
extra minute spent on the journey lessened Eva's chances of
surviving it. From time to time he would hear her groan or
whimper and it struck him that these moments came not when
she emitted sound, but when the chaos outside the car had
temporarily abated enough for him to catch the audible evidence
of her suffering. But as they crawled up and up, the road became
steadily more treacherous.

The gushing water was dislodging rocks that hammered
against the wheels and the underside of the chassis, and digging
out potholes where just hours before the surface had been relatively smooth. Where the gravel had been washed away the
earth below was dissolving into a muddy slurry as slippery as
ice. More than once Leon felt the car sliding across the road,
toward the side of the track, and he had to wrestle with the
wheel to control the skid and keep them moving forward.

Is this it? he asked himself. *Is this the disaster that Lusima
Mama foretold? But how can it be? She said I would live. She
made it sound like a curse. If Eva and I could go together that
would almost be a blessing.*

And then he caught himself. *No! Whatever happens, I have
to live. There must be one of us, at the very least, to look after
poor Saffy. But, oh God, please let there be two. Please, I beg
you, let my darling Eva survive.*

———

"Do you believe in God?" Saffron asked Manyoro, as they
drove back to Lusima through the same storm, but on much
friendlier roads.

"Of course. I believe in the Father, the Son and the Holy

Ghost," replied Manyoro, whose formal education had all been provided by missionaries.

"I've already prayed to them. I prayed and prayed to make Mummy better. Do you have another God, a Masai one I can pray to as well?"

"Yes, we have a God we call Ngai. He created all the cattle in the world and gave them all to the Masai. When we drink the blood and milk of our cattle, it is as if we are drinking the blood of Ngai, too."

"Christians believe they drink Jesus's blood, don't they?"

"Yes, and that is why I believe in your God. I think he is really Ngai!"

Manyoro burst out laughing at the cunning of his theology. Then he told Saffron, "Ngai has a wife called Olapa. She is the goddess of the moon. You can pray to them if you like."

"Thank you."

"Also we believe that every person on earth has a guardian spirit who has been sent to watch over us and keep us safe. So when you pray, ask that your mother's guardian spirit is kept strong and wide-awake so that it can protect her now."

So Saffron prayed to God and Jesus and Ngai and Olapa. She prayed for Mummy and for her guardian spirit. She promised God that she would be good all the time, and never do anything naughty ever again, if only Mummy could get better.

Then she told Manyoro all about her prayers and when she had finished listing them all she asked, "Do you think that will make any difference?"

———

The nurse standing by the main entrance of the European Hospital in Nairobi screwed up her eyes against the glare of the headlights coming toward her. "Look out for a big car that has a lady with wings at the front of its bonnet," Dr. Hartson had told her. But she could not see the front of the car because the lights were so blinding. Then the car turned as it followed the drive round and now she could see it from the side and there, sure enough, was the flying lady. The nurse turned on her feet and burst through the double swing-doors into the hospital. "They are here, doctor!" she called out as she ran down the corridor. "They are here!"

Leon saw the nurse disappear into the building as he pulled up under the awning that covered the driveway in front of the entrance. He had not spoken for the final few miles of the journey, for fear of hearing words that would be unbearable. But now, as the engine spluttered and died, he could restrain himself no longer.

"Is she still breathing?" he asked.

"Just," Birchinall replied. "But her pulse is very faint."

"Thank God," Leon muttered, grateful that he had delivered Eva to the hospital alive.

"I'm afraid you're going to have to help lift her out," Birchinall said. "My leg has pretty well seized up."

"Of course."

Leon got out of the Rolls just as the hospital doors crashed open and an orderly appeared, pushing a wheeled stretcher. Behind him came the nurse and a man in a doctor's white coat whom Leon recognized as Frank Hartson, the hospital's sole consultant surgeon. They had met once or twice at social occasions, and so far as Leon could tell, Hartson seemed like a perfectly decent, intelligent fellow, if not the liveliest mind one was ever likely to encounter. Now this man would have Eva's life in his hands.

Leon ran round to the rear door of the car and opened it wide as the stretcher came to a halt just a few feet away. Then he put one foot into the well in front of the passenger seat, leaned in and placed his arms under Eva's shoulders, between her body and Birchinall's.

"I have the legs, *Bwana*," the orderly said.

"Lift on three," Leon told him. "One . . . two . . . three!"

The two men lifted Eva's limp, unresponsive body up off the seat and Leon watched in horror as her head rolled helplessly against his arm. Her eyes were closed. There was crusted spittle at the corners of her mouth. When he looked down at her skirt it was wet and pungent with blood and urine.

"Oh my poor darling," Leon murmured.

He placed her on the stretcher and watched as the orderly strapped her down. Then he took her hand and looked down at the face that had captivated him so utterly for so long. "Good luck. God speed. I love you so very, very much," Leon said and for a second he thought he saw, or perhaps it was just his longing that made him imagine a flicker of her eyelids and the tiniest fraction of a smile.

"I'm sorry, Mr. Courtney, but we really have to get your wife ready for surgery," Hartson said.

"I understand." Leon forced himself to let go of Eva's fingers.

"Dr. Birchinall is in the car," Hartson told the nurse. "He needs crutches. Please get some for him and then come straight to the operating theater." He turned to the orderly. "Tell Matron I need to operate as soon as possible. So please prepare Mrs. Courtney for surgery immediately. Got that?"

"Yes, doctor."

"Off you go then."

As the orderly pushed the stretcher away toward the heart of the building, Hartson turned to Courtney. "I'm sorry we have to meet in such grim circumstances. Look, I don't know how much Thompson has said to you about your wife's condition . . ."

"Nothing beyond what he said when she first went to see him. We didn't really stop and chat today, what with the convulsions."

"Quite so. Well, here's the situation. As Birchinall may have told you, we're pretty certain your wife is suffering from eclampsia, which is what we call a hypertensive disorder. In layman's terms, she's got very high blood pressure and excess protein in her blood and urine. The seizures she's suffered are characteristic of the condition. But I have to warn you that eclampsia can also lead to kidney failure, cardiac arrest, pneumonia and brain hemorrhage. I'm afraid to say that these can, on occasion, prove fatal."

"Why in God's name didn't Thompson do something about it days ago, if she was so ill?" Leon asked, failing to keep the anger out of his voice.

"With the resources available to him he couldn't have predicted what would happen. The initial symptoms of dizziness, headaches, mild nausea could apply to all manner of conditions, many of them relatively trivial. And your wife is a pregnant woman living at altitude. She could feel sick or have a sore head and there'd be nothing whatever to worry about. The advice he gave was entirely appropriate. It's just rotten luck that there was in fact something serious going on."

"So what can you do now?"

"Ideally I would give your wife something to lower her blood pressure, but I fear we may be past that now. With your permission I will try an emergency delivery by caesarean section. I have to tell you that there is a high chance that we will lose the baby and a somewhat smaller but still significant chance that your wife will not survive the operation, also. It rather depends on the degree of organ damage she has already suffered."

Leon tried to cut through the emotions that were crowding out his rational mind and make some sense of what Hartson had just said: that calm, unflappable English voice delivering such devastating, heartbreaking news. Leon wanted something he could fight, an enemy he could defeat, for what in God's name was the point of his existence as a man if not to protect his woman and his child? But there was nothing to be done, for the war was all within her, out of his reach.

"Do I have your consent?" Dr. Hartson repeated.

Leon nodded. "Do whatever you think is best, doctor. And if it comes to a choice . . ." Leon stopped, choking on his words as he fought back desperate tears, "for God's sake, please . . . save Eva."

"I'll do my very best, I promise you," Hartson said. He half-turned, about to walk away, then stopped and looked back at Leon. "There's a waiting room just down the corridor. Take a seat in there, why don't you? I'll have someone bring you some tea, good and sweet to keep your blood sugar up, eh?"

Hartson had taken half a dozen steps down the corridor, when Leon said, "Doctor?"

Hartson stopped: "Yes?"

"Good luck."

Hartson said nothing, just looked for a couple more seconds at Leon, then went away toward the operating theater.

Leon watched him go, gave a heavy sigh, then went in search of the waiting room.

An hour passed in the waiting room. There were four battered old armchairs and Leon sat in each one of them as he tried to find somewhere he could be still without needing to get up and pace around the room, just to work off the tension that had his guts as tight as drumskins. A low wooden table sat in the middle of the room, surrounded by the chairs. A few dog-eared old issues of *Punch* were scattered across its surface, next to a dirty Bakelite ashtray. Leon picked up the magazines in turn, flicked through their pages, gazed blankly at the cartoons, hardly even seeing the drawings, still less appreciating their jokes. The tea arrived after the best part of half an hour's wait and he gulped it down in a couple of minutes. The sugar perked him up, as Doctor Hartson had predicted, but the additional energy only made his restlessness worse.

As Leon was leaving the clubhouse, back at the polo club,

Doc Thompson had pressed a packet of Player's Navy Cut cigarettes into his hand, saying, "These may come in handy."

"I don't smoke," Leon had replied but in the chaos Thompson hadn't heard, so Leon had shoved the cigarettes into his trouser pocket and forgotten all about them. Now he took out the crushed and crumpled pack. Thompson had stuck a book of matches into the pack. The words "Henderson's General Store, Gilgil, Kenya" were printed on the flap of card that covered the matches.

As a boy, Leon had grown up with the smell of the cheroots that his father Ryder Courtney kept clamped between his teeth as he navigated his river boats up and down the Nile or haggled with the men from whom he bought and sold. When the clash of wills between father and son became too intense for them to remain in the same house, Leon had left the family home in Cairo to seek his fortune in the new colony of British East Africa, as Kenya had then been known. The smell of cigar smoke had always been associated in his mind with his father, and everything he was trying to escape, and the only time he had ever smoked had been during the war when, like virtually every other soldier in the British army, he did it to pass the time and ease the tension in the long hours of tedium and apprehension that preceded the start of any battle. The day he left the army, he threw away his smokes, but now he realized that Doc Thompson had not so much given him the packet of Player's as prescribed it for precisely this helpless period of waiting for news that might very well be bad.

Leon lit up his first cigarette, felt the familiar sensation of the smoke filling his lungs and then the long, slow, relaxing exhalation as it poured back out again. There were eight more in the packet and Leon smoked them all over the next two hours. By that point the air in the waiting room was thick with smoke, his clothes stank and his mouth tasted as filthy as the ashtray that was now half-filled with his cigarette butts.

Leon suddenly felt a desperate need for fresh, clean air. He walked out of the waiting room, along the corridor and through the two swinging doors into the world beyond. The area in front of the European Hospital and the road on which it stood was laid out in a pleasant garden, bounded on three sides by the drive, and on the fourth by the wall that ran along the road on which the hospital was located. Benches had been placed for patients and their visitors to sit on. The storm had passed, night had fallen and the air was as cool and refreshing as water from a mountain stream. Leon wiped the rainwater off one of the benches with his hand then sat down on it, stretched his legs out in front of him and leaned back, gazing up at the majestic, infinite beauty of the stars in the southern sky. There was no traffic on the road outside and the only sound to be heard was the noise of the insects chattering away in the bushes and trees. Leon closed his eyes and for a moment a sensation of deep peace and relaxation spread through him, easing the tension from his muscles.

Then he heard the clatter of the doors.

Leon opened his eyes, sat up straight on the bench and looked toward the hospital entrance. In the harsh white glare of the light that illuminated the spaces beneath the awning, Leon saw Dr. Hartson walking toward him. His shoulders were slumped, his tread was heavy and there was an air about him that Leon had seen in soldiers who had just taken a beating and lost comrades in the process.

And then he knew the message that Dr. Hartson was bearing with him on that slow, exhausted trudge across the lawn and it was as if all the constellations had suddenly vanished from the sky and blackness fell upon Leon Courtney. For he had lost the sun and moon and stars that had illuminated his existence.

Hartson had reached him now. He must have known that he had no need to tell Leon what had happened. So he just said, "I am so very sorry, old man. We did everything we could, but . . ."

Hartson may have finished his sentence, but if he did Leon Courtney never heard him. For now the dam inside him broke and all he could hear was the sound of his own sobbing.

———

In her room at Lusima, Saffron lay awake for what seemed like hours before she dropped into a fitful sleep, plagued by dreams that were filled with anger, danger and a terrible sense that something was missing, no matter how hard she tried to find it. Then she woke suddenly. There was someone in her room, she knew there was. She sat up straight, eyes wide, staring from side to side, straining her ears for any sound, but although that sense of another presence very close to her remained, there was no sign at all of anyone she could see or hear.

She turned on her bedside light.

The room was empty. The door was closed.

And then, as suddenly as it had appeared, the presence vanished and, in a moment of absolute clarity, Saffron understood.

"Mummy!" she cried out. "Mummy! Come back!"

But Mummy was gone and she wasn't ever coming back. Saffron knew that now, and with that knowledge all the comfort and security her mother had brought with her disappeared from Saffron's life and an entirely new chapter of her existence began.

———

At the age of thirteen, Leon had sent Saffron to Rodean, a girls' boarding school in Parktown. "It's time you got a proper education," he'd told her. "When I'm gone, you'll be in charge of the estate, and all my Courtney business interests. You need to know about more than cookery, needlework and flower arranging."

"But why do I have to go all the way to South Africa?" Saffron protested. "I'm sure there are good schools in Kenya too."

"Indeed there are. But I've asked around and it seems that none of them offers the kind of education for girls that you will get at Roedean. It's the sister establishment of a very famous girls' school in England. Literally so, apparently: three sisters started the place in England and then a fourth one came out to South Africa and started the place in Jo'burg with a chum. That was thirty years ago and apparently it's gone from strength to strength since, a really top-notch place. And Saffy . . ." Leon's voice had softened as he started to speak from the heart, rather than the head, "it's no life for you here, rattling around the estate with just me and the staff for company."

"But I like rattling around the estate! It's my home. And all the people on it are my family," Saffron pleaded.

"I know, my darling, and there's not one of them that doesn't love you as their own. But you need to be around girls your age, and you need women you can look up to and learn from. There are things I just can't teach you. Things only women know. And . . . well . . . you know . . ."

Yes, of course Saffron knew. In the end, so many conversations with her father came back to the great hole in their lives where her mother should have been. He had never found another woman to replace her. There had been plenty of women who liked the idea of being Mrs. Leon Courtney and mistress of one of the largest, best run and most breathtakingly beautiful estates in East Africa. Several of them had found their way to Lusima and done their best to impress Saffron's father by sucking up to her.

"If one more silly woman tells me that she's sure we shall be the most terrific chums, I am going to scream," Saffy had told Kippy, during one of their daily heart-to-hearts (though in truth the pony was only really interested in the apple that she knew her mistress was hiding behind her back). But each of the women disappeared within a matter of days, weeks, or in one case a full three months, and Saffron had long since given up paying any attention to any of them.

That did not, however, mean she loved her father any less, or was bored with her home. Lusima was a magical kingdom in which she was the Crown Princess and there was nowhere else in the world she wanted to be. So she had fought with every logical argument she could muster and every emotional trick she could play, but it had done her no good. Her father had made up his mind, and when Leon Courtney did that, no force on God's earth could budge him from his decision.

———

Going to Roedean meant that Saffron would have to leave home for the first time. Leon knew that the experience was bound to be hard for her, so he was keen to make it as exciting as possible, to distract her from any thought of homesickness for as long as possible. To that end, he did not take her on a steamship to Durban, the nearest port to Johannesburg, but instead booked tickets on the final legs of the brand new Imperial Airways service from England to South Africa. And he did not take her to Johannesburg. Instead, shortly after Christmas 1932, he and Saffron flew all the way to Cape Town.

"I thought it was time you met the South African branch of the family," Leon told her, "starting with your cousin Centaine."

"That's an odd name," Saffron replied.

"It's French, and it means a hundred. So 'Une centaine d'années' means 'a century.'"

"Well that's even odder. Who calls a girl 'Century'?"

"Someone whose daughter is born in the first hour of the first day of the first month of the first year of a century might, if they were French. Centaine's maiden name was de Thiry and she met my cousin Michael in France when he was stationed there with the Royal Flying Corps during the war. Michael was a fighter pilot."

"Did they fall in love?"

"Yes."

"How romantic!" Saffron's imagination instantly conjured up an image of a dashing pilot and a beautiful French girl swooning at one another, though she still knew too little about love to have much of an idea what would happen after that.

"I've decided that Centaine is a lovely name," she said, with characteristic decisiveness. But then something struck her. "You said Michael was a fighter pilot, and you haven't said we're meeting him in South Africa. So . . ."

"He died, yes. The damn Germans shot him down."

"So how did she end up in South Africa?"

"Well, Michael and Centaine got married," Leon began. In truth, he had always had his doubts as to whether the knot had ever been tied, but the family had accepted Centaine as one of their own and any doubts had been discreetly swept under the carpet. "When he died Centaine was pregnant with his baby, and she had no family left in France so it was decided to send her down to South Africa because she and the child, when it came, would be safer there."

"Wasn't there any war in South Africa, then?"

"Nothing to write home about. South West Africa had been a German colony, so plenty of people there were on the Kaiser's side. So were some of the Boers, because they hated the British. The Germans actually planned to help the Boers rise up and conquer South Africa but . . . well, that never happened."

Mostly because your mother and I stopped it happening, Leon thought, but did not say. Instead he went on, "Anyway, there was far, far less fighting of any kind in South Africa than there was in France, so it should have been much safer for Centaine to be here, except for one thing . . ."

"Ooh, what?" asked Saffron, who was becoming more curious about Centaine by the minute.

"The ship Cousin Centaine was on was torpedoed by a German submarine. Somehow she survived and was washed ashore on the coast of South West Africa."

"What a lucky escape!"

"Yes, but her troubles weren't over, because, as you should know if you've been paying attention in geography lessons, the coast there is part of the Namib Desert, which is one of the oldest and driest deserts on earth. That's why they call it the Skeleton Coast. There's no water there, no food, nothing. Not for a white man, anyway."

"So why didn't she die?"

"She was rescued by a San tribesman and his wife. The San have an extraordinary ability to survive in the desert and they kept Centaine alive until her baby son was born. Anyway, while she was travelling with them, she found a diamond, just lying on the ground."

"A diamond!" Saffron exclaimed. "Who'd left it there in the middle of a desert?"

"No one left it there," Leon laughed. "It was an uncut diamond. It was there naturally. So Centaine claimed the land and all its mineral rights and it turned out that there were a lot more diamonds where that first one had come from. So she became the owner of a diamond mine."

Saffron's eyes were as wide as huge sapphire saucers. "Goodness! Cousin Centaine must be the richest woman in the world!" she exclaimed.

"Well, she has been very rich, that's true. But these are hard times for everyone and there's not much of a market for diamonds these days, or anything else, come to that. I think she's been lucky to keep hold of the mine at all, to be honest, but now I gather she's putting her home outside Cape Town on the market. All its contents too, apparently: pictures, furniture, family silver, the lot. That's one of the reasons I wanted to see her. Thought I might be able to help."

Saffron thought that this was a rather sad subject, so she decided to change it. "Can you tell me about Centaine's son? What's his name? How old is he?"

"He's called Shasa and I suppose he must be fifteen by now. I think you were born about eighteen months apart."

"What's he like?" she asked, really meaning to say, "Is he handsome?" but not daring to be that obvious.

"I honestly don't know," her father replied. "I've met Centaine a couple of times, but not her lad. But I'm sure you two will have plenty to talk about."

———

When they landed at Winfield Aerodrome, just to the east of Cape Town, the first thing Leon and Saffron saw was an enormous yellow Daimler parked on the field, barely twenty yards from where the Atalanta had come to a halt.

"Look at that car!" Saffron said to her father, pointing in the Daimler's direction. "It's even bigger and yellower than Lady Idina's Hispano–Suiza!"

Before Leon could reply the driver's door swung open. A car like this was usually driven by a uniformed chauffeur, but what emerged instead was a woman so striking that Saffron stopped dead in her tracks and simply gazed at her in wonder.

"Is . . . is that Cousin Centaine?" she gasped.

"It is indeed," Leon replied.

With just one look, Saffron was lost in admiration for Centaine. She was as beautiful as a queen in one of Saffron's old books of illustrated fairy tales, as slender as a wand, with impeccably bobbed black hair and eyes so mesmerizingly dark that they seemed almost black too. But it wasn't just her beauty that made Centaine regal. It was the way she carried herself and the fierce determination in the line of her jaw.

Saffron had spent almost half her life without a female role model, but now, looking at Centaine, she was gripped by an emotion that she did not quite recognize at first, though she knew somehow that she had felt it before. And then she realized that this was just like seeing her equally beautiful, stylish mother when she was a very little girl: that same sense of awe in the presence of feminine beauty and grace and the same longing that maybe, just maybe, she might look a little like that herself one day.

Leon strode over to say hello and as he approached, Centaine smiled and suddenly revealed the other side to her personality: charming, flirtatious, deliciously female in the presence of a man.

What a couple they'd make, Saffron thought, looking at her tall, strong, handsome father beside this ravishing woman.

Taken aback by this entirely unexpected idea she chided herself. *Don't be so silly!*

Then another figure emerged from the car. And suddenly Saffron had something much more important to think about.

————

Shasa Courtney had not been keen on being dragged out to the aerodrome to meet his cousin from Kenya. She was being sent to Roedean, for a start, and everyone knew that Roedean girls were plain, spotty swots who all wore glasses and did nothing but read books. They weren't interested in boys. They just wanted to go off to university and get jobs that were meant for men. Plus, this Saffron girl was only thirteen, whereas he was only a few months from his sixteenth birthday and was just about to go back to his school, Bishops, as Head Boy. Clearly she could not possibly be of any interest to him.

Then he saw a girl get off the plane. And that had to be Saffron because there was only one other female emerging from the Atalanta and she was a silver-haired granny on the arm of an equally elderly man. But on the other hand, that girl—the one with the shiny, dark-chocolate-colored hair blowing against the breeze, wearing a skirt that the wind was pushing against her long legs so that he could see the shape of her slender thighs and her flat tummy and the wicked, tantalizing, infinitely mysterious bit in the middle—that girl, who had now spotted him, he could tell, and was looking at him, staring at him in fact, so that he felt as though she could see right through him . . . *that* girl couldn't be Saffron Courtney. Could it?

————

"Centaine! How splendid to see you again," Leon said.

"And you Leon," she replied, kissing his cheeks with the elegant affection of a born-and-bred Frenchwoman.

He stepped back and gave her an appraising up-and-down. "You look . . ." he was about to give her appearance a conventionally flattering compliment when the warmth of her smile and the way it lit up her eyes made him change his mind. "D'you know, you look extraordinarily happy. Good news?"

"Yes!" she said.

"May I ask what it involves?"

"Later." She took his arm and turned back toward her car. "Your daughter is quite ravishing, Leon. It will not be long before she is driving men wild. Perhaps you should forget school and send her off to a convent!"

"Steady on, old girl," Leon replied. Like any doting father, he had always taken it for granted that his daughter was the prettiest little girl in the world. But the thought of her as a sexual creature, even as a hypothetical, far-distant possibility, had never occurred to him. But now he followed Centaine's eyes and watched as Saffron and Shasa approached one another.

"By God, you really can see the family resemblance," he said.

"Mmm . . ." Centaine murmured in agreement, for it was true that the two youngsters were so similar as to look more like siblings than cousins. Shasa's eyes were an even darker blue than Saffron's, perhaps, but they both shared the same dark hair and slim, limber build. He was only just growing out of an almost girlish beauty, but was not yet a man. She still possessed the last vestiges of her tomboy days, though faint traces of approaching womanhood were beginning to appear in the slight broadening and rounding of her hips and the first traces of her breasts.

"Look at them, sizing one another up," Centaine said.

"Like young lions."

"I wonder how long it will take them to realize that they share a sadness: Shasa without a father, Centaine without a mother. Both of them so rich in one way, and so deprived in another." She snapped herself out of her reverie. "Come! You must be exhausted after your journey. I must drive you back to Weltevreden."

"Have you had to let the chauffeur go? So many people one

knows have done that," Leon asked, hoping that his tone was sufficiently sympathetic that the remark did not seem tactless.

Centaine laughed. "Heavens no! I don't believe in having chauffeurs. I refuse to be controlled by any man. Even if he's just driving my car!"

———

Saffron and Shasa spent the journey from the aerodrome to his mother's estate talking about his school and speculating about hers. Each was forced to conclude that their prejudices were, perhaps, unfounded. As Centaine had anticipated, they soon established that they had each lost a parent. Neither of them wanted to talk about the experience, but a mutual understanding had been established: they had both been through a similar ordeal and it gave them a bond that did not need to be expressed.

Saffron was charmed by Weltevreden. Like Lusima it was set among hills, but this country was not so newly claimed from Mother Nature. Europeans had lived in the countryside around Cape Town for centuries and they had somehow softened the edges of the landscape; the earth seemed richer, the Kikuyu grass greener. Weltevreden even had its own vineyard, and pretty whitewashed cottages were dotted about the place.

"Oh look, Daddy, a polo field!" Saffron exclaimed.

"Yah," said Shasa, coolly, "we run a team here, the Weltevreden Invitation. We won the junior league here a couple of weeks ago, actually. I scored the winning goal."

"I love polo!" sighed Saffron.

"A lot of girls do," Shasa said. "I think it's a bit like the olden days. You know, medieval maidens watching all the knights jousting and stuff."

"No, I don't mean *watching* polo. I suppose that's all right. But it's not half as much fun as *playing* polo."

"But you can't play polo!" Shasa protested. "You're . . . well, you're a girl!"

Neither of the two youngsters saw Leon roll his eyes as he

contemplated the terrible mistake the lad had just made, or noticed Centaine's smile as she found her unswerving loyalty to her son being trumped by her support for a fellow female.

"I do so!" Saffron protested. "And I'll prove it, too!"

Before the argument could go any further, Centaine was calling out, "We're there."

White-jacketed male staff and housemaids in smart black uniforms were waiting to greet them as they stepped out of the Daimler.

"Welcome to Weltevreden," Centaine said.

Saffron looked around in wonder at a full-sized reproduction of a French château that made her home at Lusima look like a tumbledown farmhouse. She was led into a cool, quiet hallway lined with paintings.

"I love your pictures, Cousin Centaine," she said.

"Thank you, my dear. If you like, I can show you around some of the other ones in the house, as well. I think you would like them."

"Thank you, I would."

"Mater's got a landscape by a chap called Alfred Sisley that was painted on the estate where she was born, and a Van Gogh picture of a wheat field," Shasa boasted.

Centaine flashed him a frown of disapproval and then turned to her guests, "Now I'm sure you'd like to freshen up and change before . . ."

"Actually," Saffron interrupted her, earning a cross look from her father in turn, "I would like to play polo with Shasa. If he doesn't mind playing with a girl."

"Oh, all right," he grouched.

"Well you can't play in that dress," Centaine pointed out. "You can borrow some of my riding breeches and a pair of my boots. I can't promise that they'll fit but it's better than nothing." She signaled to one of the maids. "Could you please show Miss Courtney where my riding gear is kept?"

"Yes, Ma'am. Come this way please, Miss."

"I'll get changed too and meet you back here in a few minutes, then," said Shasa, and dashed up the stairs to his room.

"Saffy's mad keen to be up and doing. But I must say I would appreciate the chance of a bath, a shave, a fresh change of clothes and, if you have it, a nice glass of whisky," Leon said, when he and Centaine were alone.

"Of course," Centaine said. She glanced at an antique grandfather clock whose gentle ticking could be heard now that their children had disappeared. "It's quarter to six now, so by the time you've freshened up the sun will be—what is it you English say?—over the yardarm."

"That's the one."

"Then it will certainly be time for a drink."

———

Leon Courtney sank into the welcome embrace of a leather armchair that could have come straight from a gentleman's club in Pall Mall, gratefully took the heavy crystal glass of single malt Scotch that the footman had presented to him on a silver tray and looked at Centaine. She had changed into a crystal-beaded evening dress and was cradling a freshly shaken martini.

"So," he said, "tell me about that smile. It's hardly left your face since we arrived here, and I don't believe it's entirely due to the pleasure of our company."

"Not entirely, no," Centaine agreed, "though it is very nice indeed to see you here."

"I'll be honest: I was expecting to find you on your uppers. The word on the family grapevine was you'd called in the chaps from Sotheby's and everything was up for grabs. But I never in my life saw anyone less on their uppers than you have looked today."

"The stories were true," Centaine said. She took a sip from her cocktail glass and placed it on a table beside her. "I was in real trouble. Who isn't these days?"

"Who indeed . . ."

"But I had a stroke of good fortune on the stock market. I happened to be holding a great many shares in mining companies when the government took South Africa off the gold standard."

"Ah, I see," said Leon thoughtfully. "Clever you."

For years, many of the world's major currencies had been pegged to the gold standard, meaning that their worth had in theory been backed by gold. This had kept the price of currencies artificially high, so they were hugely overvalued when the Crash of 1929 was followed by economic depression across the western world. As countries came off the gold standard, their currencies were able to drop in value, making their exports much cheaper to foreign buyers and thus boosting their economies. South Africa had been one of the very last countries to remain tied to gold, sending the exchange rate of the South African pound far above that of British sterling and thus making South African gold, diamonds and wool so expensive that no one bought them any more. The decision to come off the gold standard and let the South African pound find its true value had been made only a matter of days earlier. The immediate effect had been to transform the country's trading position. Shares in mining companies suddenly rocketed. Anyone who had bought at the bottom of the market stood to make an enormous profit.

"I won't ask how you pulled off your coup," Leon went on, though every commercial instinct he had told him she must have had inside information about the government's decision. "I shall simply congratulate you on becoming a true Courtney. We've always found ways to make a killing. The first Courtneys got rich by looting Spanish treasure ships in the service of our King."

"Looting other people's treasure—that's the basis for the whole British Empire," Centaine said, with a wry smile.

"That . . . and defeating the French."

"Touché!" she laughed.

Just then the doors to the drawing room in which they were sitting were flung open and two hot, flushed adolescents, with dust-covered clothes and hair matted by sweat, burst into the room.

"So, how did it go?"

"I showed him!" Saffron cried triumphantly. "I made him back off."

"Only because I let you," Shasa retorted.

"Calm down, Shasa, and tell me what happened," Centaine commanded.

"Well, Mater, we went down to the stables and I told her that I had two ponies, and one of them was Plum Pudding, who's really steady and experienced, and the other one was Tiger Shark, who's quicker and stronger, but wild and really hard to control. And I said she could choose which one she wanted to ride, and I thought she was bound to pick Plum Pudding . . ."

"But I chose Tiger Shark!" said Saffron.

"Of course you did," said Leon, who had seen that one coming the moment he heard Shasa's descriptions of the two beasts.

"And we played for a bit, just knocking up and it was fun and Shasa was quite good . . ."

"I'm better than "quite good!" Shasa protested, indignantly but also accurately.

"And then the ball was in the middle of the field and we both went for it," Saffron said.

"We went "down the throat," Shasa said. "Just like I did with Max Theunissen in the final, do you remember, Mater?"

Centaine's face suddenly whitened. "Going down the throat" was the polo expression for a full frontal charge between two players, riding directly at one another, head-on, and Shasa had pulled off the very same trick to win his polo tournament. It had been one of the most terrifying moments of Centaine's life, seeing a berserker madness seize her son as he'd hurled Tiger

Shark at the Theunissen boy and his pony. If the two horses had collided at full gallop they would certainly have had to be put down and both their riders could have been seriously injured or even killed. At the very last instant, Theunissen's nerve had cracked, he had pulled away and Shasa had smashed the ball past him and into the goal.

The idea that he had even considered pulling off the same trick on a guest, and, what's more, a guest who was a relative, a girl and younger than him, appalled her.

"You did what?" Centaine gasped. The question was rhetorical. Before her son could answer she got to her feet, looked Shasa in the eye and rasped, "How dare you? How *dare* you? That is unforgivably bad-mannered, stupid, irresponsible, and dangerous behavior. You're lucky both of you aren't on your way to the hospital. Go to your room right now. Right now!"

Shasa looked mortified. He bit his bottom lip, trying to hold back his tears. Then Saffron piped up, "Excuse me, Cousin Centaine, but it wasn't Shasa's fault. I was the one who charged at him. And he got out of the way . . . And I know you weren't being a scaredy-cat, Shasa, even though I said you were. You just didn't want to hurt me."

Silence fell upon the room. Leon hesitated for a moment, not wanting to take charge in someone else's house, and with their child, but he realized he was the only person in the room not yet involved in the argument.

"Right," he said, "let's sort this out, shall we? Saffron, you did very well to own up. But you shouldn't have charged Shasa. You put both of you in danger and you and I both know that you only did it because you were being pig-headed about doing anything a boy could do and wanted to show Shasa up. Now you've got him into trouble and I think it's a pretty poor show. You owe him an apology."

Saffron screwed up her face, realized that she was in the wrong and said, "I'm sorry, Shasa. I didn't mean to get you in trouble."

"That's all right."

"As for you, Shasa," Leon went on, "let this be a lesson. It's both rude and extremely unwise to be ungentlemanly to a lady, particularly a Courtney lady, because believe me, my boy, they fight back. Honestly, if there is any young man on earth who ought to know what women are capable of it's you. Just think of your mother, for heaven's sake, and all she's achieved. Do you doubt her abilities, just because she's a woman?"

"No, sir."

"And are you sorry for doubting Saffron?"

"Yes, sir."

"Good. That's settled then, and no harm done. Now, Saffron, you've had a very long day. I think you should go and have that bath and perhaps, if you ask Cousin Centaine nicely, she'll have some supper brought to your room. A bit of food and an early night is what you need, my girl."

"An excellent idea," said Centaine. "And I think you should do the same thing, Shasa. Bath, supper and bed . . . and then we can all have a fresh start in the morning."

———

Shasa and Saffron walked upstairs together. When they got to the landing they paused before they went off to their rooms.

"I wouldn't have backed down, you know, when I went down the throat," Saffron said. "Even if you hadn't got out of the way."

"I know," said Shasa. "And I wouldn't have got out of the way, either, if it had been anyone else coming toward me."

"I know," she said.

With that they each satisfied their pride and went off to their baths with their honor and dignity intact, knowing that now they would be friends for life.

———

Saffron was sad to leave the haven of Weltevreden. As a motherless only child, she had loved having a relative her age to play with, and an older female role model to look up to. But after the blissful bucolic luxury of Centaine's Cape Town estate, the size and noise and bustle of Johannesburg were an overwhelming assault to her. The city was five times as big as Nairobi, with more than a quarter of a million inhabitants, and they all seemed to move with a speed and urgency she had never experienced before, as if every single one of them had something urgent they simply had to achieve, right this very second.

"That's the Johannesburg Stock Exchange," Leon told her as they passed an ornate building, fronted by great marble columns, that covered an entire city block on Hollard Street. "The companies that control half the world's gold and diamonds are traded there."

"It looks like a palace," Saffron said.

"Well it is, in a way. It's the palace of Mammon, the demon of money."

Over lunch, Leon gave Saffron a quick explanation of how company shares and stock exchanges worked and was surprised by the speed with which she picked up the ideas he was presenting to her. So far, he felt, the day had gone well. He'd been perfectly happy purchasing Saffron's tuck box, on which her name was even now being painted in elegant black capital letters. And having led countless groups of travelers and hunters across the wilds of British East Africa during his pre-War days as a safari guide he was completely at home debating the best possible trunks to buy to carry all Saffron's increasingly vast amounts of baggage.

After leaving the restaurant where they had lunched, they arrived at the school outfitters. Suddenly talk turned to dresses, blouses, pinafores and other items of youthful female attire and Leon's expertise gave way to bafflement. When the shop's manageress, who'd had no need even to glance at the list to know what it contained, got on to the subject of gym knickers a look passed across her father's face that Saffron had never in all her life seen before.

Oh my goodness, he's blushing! she thought to herself, desperately trying to keep a straight face. *He's so embarrassed he doesn't even know where to look.*

"Perhaps it would be best if Father took a seat and let Miss Courtney and I proceed by ourselves," the manageress said. "I take it, sir, that I have your permission to select the items that Miss will need for her time at Roedean?"

"Yes, yes, absolutely, whatever she needs, excellent plan," Leon had blustered. Saffron couldn't swear to it, but she was almost certain the manageress, who had seemed rather fearsome when they had first been introduced, actually winked at her as they walked away to deal with those mysterious aspects of female existence that were best kept hidden from the uncomprehending eyes of men.

Saffron had felt as though she was being initiated into some mysterious but exciting new world as the manageress, whose name was now revealed to be Miss Halfpenny, took an appraising look at her chest, said, "Someone should have bought you a brassiere by now, young lady." She sighed, "But that's a mother's job . . ."

"I don't have a mother," Saffron said. "She died when I was seven."

"I'm very sorry, but I'm afraid I feared as much. When a girl walks in with her father . . ." She left the sentence unfinished, but then gave a brisk sigh and said, "Never mind, best just get on with it, hadn't we? Lots of children don't have a mother, or a father, or even both, what with the war and the Spanish Flu and who knows what. But they find a way to manage and I'm sure you will too. Just let me help you and I'm sure we'll sort you out with everything you need."

Saffron had been hearing this kind of stiff-upper-lip encouragement for years, but she sensed a genuine kindness in Miss Halfpenny's voice. As she rummaged in glass-fronted drawers for bras and knickers and stockings, occasionally holding up an item in front of Saffron's coltish, long-limbed frame, checking it for size and either discarding it on one pile or placing it on another, much larger heap of things to be tried on, Miss Halfpenny chatted away about what Saffron could expect at Roedean, and what the teachers and girls were like.

"Your father couldn't have picked a better place. Roedean girls, in my experience, are bright, independent, thoroughly modern young ladies. Plenty of them go on to university, too. And they are all trained to be able to earn their own living."

"Daddy said I needed to know about more than cookery and needlework and flower arranging."

Miss Halfpenny gave an approving nod. "Well said, that man. And I'm sure he's thinking about your mother and what she would have wanted for you and he's trying his very best to make her happy."

"I hadn't thought of that," said Saffron. But from the moment Miss Halfpenny said those words, her attitude to her new school changed. She resolved that she would do everything to make her mother happy, too, with the result that having turned up at Roedean in mid-January for the first day of the new academic year she plunged into school life with all the energy she possessed. Her naturally athletic physique and fiercely competitive nature made her a demon on the hockey pitch and netball court and her rapidly growing height saw her cast for many a male role in the school's dramatic productions. It took her a term or two to learn how to adapt to boarding school life, which requires pupils to be able to get along with people with whom they share not only classrooms but also dormitories, bathrooms and every meal of the day. Saffron soon made friends, however, for her classmates knew that while her temper could be stormy she was neither malicious, nor deceitful: she said precisely what she thought, for better or for worse, and once decided on a course of action stuck to it, come hell or high water. If her ancestors were looking down from on high they must have smiled, for no Courtney had ever done anything else.

————

Soon after his return from South Africa, Leon had to go into Nairobi to carry out various administrative chores related to the Lusima estate. He took a room at the Muthaiga Country Club, a private, membership-only institution that was the social hub of the expatriate community in Kenya. For all its social cachet, the Muthaiga was not a particularly impressive piece of architecture, being little more than a greatly expanded bungalow, with pink pebbledash walls, painted metal window frames (for wooden frames soon rotted away in the subtropical climate) and a few classical columns by the entrance to provide a sense of colonial prestige. Inside, one walked over floors of highly polished wooden parquet, past walls painted in shades of cream and green. It looked, as Hugh Delamere had once remarked to Leon, "Like a cross between my old prep school and a suburban nursing home."

Arriving back at the club one evening, after a long day of meetings with lawyers and accountants, Leon sank into one of the chintz-covered armchairs that dotted the members' lounge. A uniformed waiter immediately appeared and took his order for a gin and tonic. The drink appeared beside him only moments later and Leon signed for it on a colored paper chit: nothing as grubby as money was ever seen to change hands within the club's portals. Leon took a sip of the ice-cold drink, put the glass back on the side table and leaned back in his chair, eyes closed as he let the cares of the day slip away.

Then he heard a familiar voice: "Evening, Courtney, mind if I join you?"

"By all means, Joss," Leon replied.

Over the past few years a lot had changed in Josslyn Hay's life. For one thing, he was now the twenty-second Earl of Erroll, having inherited the title on his father's death, along with the honorary post of Lord High Constable of Scotland. He had not, however, inherited any money, for his father had not been a wealthy man, and the lack of cash had led to the breakdown of his marriage to Lady Idina. His second wife, Molly, was, like

Idina, a wealthy divorcée and, once again, Joss saw no reason whatsoever why his marriage vows should apply to him. He still looked as he always had done: his hair swept back and blond, his head slightly turned, so that his half-closed blue eyes looked slightly sideways at anyone he was talking to. And one look was still enough to land the great majority of women who happened to catch his fancy.

So far as Leon was concerned, Joss Erroll, as he now liked to be known, was an unprincipled rogue, no matter how elevated his title might be, and if he ever so much as glanced at Saffron he'd horsewhip him all the way to the Mombasa docks and throw him onto the first outbound steamer he could find. But until that time, Leon was perfectly happy to enjoy Joss's company. It was certainly more agreeable than that of a great many other expats he could think of.

"Have you heard about this business at the Oxford Union?" Joss asked, once he had been served a drink of his own.

"What business is that?" Leon replied.

"A bloody rum one, I can tell you." Joss took a cigarette from a slim silver case, tapped it against the table, lit it and sat back, savoring the first inhalation. "They had a debate with the motion, "This House will under no circumstances fight for its King and Country.""

"Bloody Hellfire! I trust the motion was soundly defeated."

"Fraid not, old boy, it was carried by almost three hundred votes to one hundred and fifty. A two-to-one majority."

Leon looked aghast. "Are you seriously telling me that the flower of young English manhood, the fellows who are supposed to be the brightest and best of their generation, have declared that they will never fight for their country?"

"Apparently so," Joss replied. "The Huns, or the commies, or even the damn French can pitch up on our shores, march across the country, rape our womenfolk and pitchfork our babies, and the brightest brains in the kingdom will simply say, "By all means, feel free.""

"I don't believe it," said Leon. "Of course the last war was bloody. And I know people say it was the war to end all wars. But this lily-livered pacifism is nothing but cowardice and treachery. There are times when the nation simply has to be defended and a man has to answer the call."

"Couldn't agree with you more, Courtney. But then again, you and I are simple, straightforward chaps. We're not like these intellectual Oxbridge types."

"Well, I grant you," said Leon, "there is no one on earth as dangerous as a really clever fool. But even so, how in God's name were the audience at the Union persuaded to support the motion?"

Joss took a long lazy drag on his cigarette as a sly smile played across his lips. "Oh, you'll love this . . . the chap proposing the motion, Digby I believe was his name, said that we should all follow the example of Soviet Russia, which was the only country fighting for the cause of peace . . . a rather interesting paradox, that, I thought: fighting for peace."

"Perhaps that's what the Reds were doing when they seized power in a bloody revolution and murdered the Tsar and his family," Leon observed.

"Ah, yes, that must have been it. How foolish we were not to spot their peaceful intentions. Anyway, when Master Digby had said his piece he was supported by a philosopher called Joad—can't say I've ever heard of him but apparently he's considered quite the coming man in philosophical circles—and he suggested that if Britain should ever be invaded there was no point fighting our enemies with weapons. We had to engage in a campaign of non-violent protest, like Mister Gandhi goes in for, in India."

"Good grief," gasped Leon. "Can you imagine it if these people get their way? Enemy planes will start bombing London and their tanks will roll down Whitehall, and all we'll have to defend us will be Joad and a bunch of conscientious objectors from Oxford University sitting in the middle of the road, chanting for peace?"

"Well, look on the bright side, Courtney. Most people don't go to Oxford University."

"Well, I suppose that's a reassuring thought. Care for another drink?"

The following evening, Leon wrote one of his regular letters to Saffron. He gave her a vivid account of the debate, as discussed by him and Erroll, and let her know in no uncertain terms of his extreme disapproval of its outcome and of the Oxford students who had voted for it. "I warn you now, my girl, if you should ever be courted by an Oxford man I will refuse to allow him into my house. I'm sure you will read these words and think, "Oh, the old boy's just having his little joke," and you may be right. But I am shocked to think that a supposedly great university should have become a nest of Reds, traitors and pacifists and I would disapprove most strongly of you having anything whatever to do with it."

Saffron received the letter a week later in South Africa. She had never given much thought to any universities, let alone Oxford, but the idea of students being so provocative and so tremendously annoying to their elders pricked her curiosity. So she asked her form teacher, "Please Miss, can girls go to Oxford University?"

"Indeed they can, Saffron," her teacher replied. "None of our pupils has ever gone to Oxford, or not yet, at any rate. But our sister school in England regularly puts girls up for both the Oxford and Cambridge entrance examinations, with considerable success."

"So if I went to the other Roedean, I might be able to get into Oxford?"

The teacher laughed. "Well, I suppose so, Saffron. But you would have to work rather harder than you do presently. There are very few places for young women at England's great universities, so competition to get in is very fierce indeed."

To some teenage girls, those words might have been enough

to put them off the very idea of university education. But Saffron was different. The thought of going halfway across the world to engage in a winner-takes-all contest filled her with excitement and enthusiasm.

"Have I been any help to you, my dear?" the teacher asked.

"Oh yes, Miss," beamed Saffron. "You have been a very great help indeed!"

Of all the discoveries Saffron had made since arriving at her new school, the most surprising was that she enjoyed her lessons much more than she'd expected. She was hardly an intellectual, for whom thought was preferable to action, but she had a quick mind, grasped ideas easily and, because she enjoyed the feeling of getting things right, worked to make that happen as often as possible. Sadly, however, there were so many other things going on in her life that work was not always possible, or not in Saffron's view at any rate, with the result that her school reports were filled with teachers' pleas that if only Saffron could possibly give her studies her full concentration and effort, great things would surely follow. Now, however, she had a purpose, a goal at which to aim. And once she had her mind set on something, she pursued it with a determination a terrier would have envied.

In mid-January 1934, Saffron flew back down to Johannesburg with her father for the start of the new school year. She assured him that she was perfectly capable of handling the journey alone, for she had already flown unaccompanied from South Africa to Kenya and back again for her mid-year holidays, but he insisted. "What kind of a father would I be if I didn't take my daughter all the way to school, at least once a year," he said. "Besides, who's going to pay for all your shopping if I'm not there to do it?"

That was a point to which Saffron had no counter, for another expedition to the emporia of Johannesburg was required to replace everything that she had either broken, worn out or grown out of during her first year. When they went to the outfitters, Leon doffed his hat to Miss Halfpenny, gave her a winning smile as he said how charmed he was to see her again and obediently did as he was told when Miss Halfpenny said, "Father may leave us now. We ladies will manage quite nicely by ourselves."

Leon felt an unexpected pang of disappointment at his dismissal. But there was something else, too, a bittersweet realization provoked by two little words: "We ladies." That was what Miss Halfpenny had said, and she was right. Saffron was becoming a young lady. She wasn't just his little girl any more. And as much as Leon was proud at the woman he could see his daughter becoming, it saddened him, too, to say goodbye to his little girl.

––––––––––

Five thousand miles from Johannesburg, at the Meerbach Motor Works, a sprawling citadel of industry that covered several square kilometers in the southeast corner of Bavaria, Oswald Paust, the Head of Personnel, was coming toward the end of his annual report to the company's trustees. "After many months of hard work, the task of ridding the company of all Jewish employees, as well as other undesirable races, workers with any form of mental or physical deformity, no matter how minor, and sexual or political deviants is very nearly complete," he proudly asserted. "I can now confirm that Jews, who used to form some 4.2 percent of the workforce, have entirely disappeared from all our factories, workshops, design studios, maintenance depots and offices . . ."

His next words were drowned out as the trustees banged the palms of their hands against the boardroom table around which they were gathered as a sign of approval.

"As I was saying . . ." Paust went on. "There are six remaining cases of so called "*Mischlinge*", which is to say mongrels who have one Jewish parent, or one or more grandparents. I am presently in discussions with representatives from the SS Race and Settlement Main Office to determine whether the fact that none of them shows any signs of Jewish appearance, or practices any Jewish religious or domestic customs, entitles them to any special consideration. I am deeply indebted to *Herr Sturmbannführer* von Meerbach for his assistance in this regard."

More palms were slapped against the great oak tabletop and the massive, brooding figure at the end of the table nodded his head in acknowledgement of the tribute.

"The work has not, of course, been without difficulties," Paust said, in the tone of a man who has taken on a great burden, but borne it willingly. "It was relatively easy to weed out the communists, since we already knew who the troublemakers and strike leaders were. These people have never kept their affiliations quiet. Establishing the deviancy of suspected homosexuals, however, required considerable investigation, which proved expensive. Nevertheless, a little over one percent of our workers were found to be practicing homosexuals and lost their jobs as a consequence. It must be noted, unfortunately, that the loss to our workforce from these two groups was disproportionately skewed toward higher skill occupations, so that our legal, accounting, marketing, design and research departments have been quite severely affected and may take some months to recover from the loss of experienced and, if I may say so, talented personnel. Of course it is no surprise that the Jew, with his greedy, disputatious nature, should gravitate toward legal and financial work, while the effeminacy of homosexuals may give them a certain aesthetic flair in the design of advertising posters, for example, or even aircraft fuselages. But I feel sure that the trustees will accept that any short-term loss of company income will be more than outweighed by the benefits of knowing that our workers are all decent, healthy Aryan folk."

This time the banging was markedly less hearty. As keen as the trustees were to ensure that they maintained the highest standards of racial, sexual and political purity, they were even more interested in maintaining the highest possible profit. *SS-Sturmbannführer* Konrad von Meerbach had dropped his aristocratic title in favor of his Nazi rank, but he remained chairman of the company that bore his name. Clearly irritated by the want of enthusiasm for Paust's conclusions, he made a point of slamming his great lion's paw of a hand, its back covered with a furry mat of ginger hair, so hard that all the pens and coffee cups sitting in front of the company trustees rattled with the impact.

"Thank you, Paust," said von Meerbach, rising to his feet. He was still young, in his very early thirties, but his physical stature—for he had the massively muscled shoulders, thick chest, tree-trunk neck and glowering brow of a heavyweight boxer—and inborn air of dominance gave him the authority of a much older man. "I am deeply appreciative of your efforts and I am sure that all my fellow trustees would wish to join me in applauding your achievements." He gave half-a-dozen hearty claps, prompting six of the eight other attendees at this meeting of the Meerbach Family Trust to take the hint and join in with equal heartiness.

The only two whose applause seemed perfunctory at best were a thin, nervous-looking woman in her mid-sixties, whose fingers were otherwise occupied holding a long, black cigarette holder, and a young man sitting next to her. He was not clad in a formal business suit and stiff collar, as the other men present all were, but preferred a jacket cut from heathery gray-green tweed, a flannel shirt and a knitted tie over a pair of gray worsted trousers. He looked like an academic or some form of intellectual—neither of which was a remotely complimentary description in Germany any more—and the impression of nonconformity was reinforced by the sweep of dark blond hair that insisted on flopping down over his right eyebrow no matter how often he swept it back up to the side of his head. He could, however, afford to treat Konrad von Meerbach more casually than the others did for he was his younger brother, Gerhard, and the woman sitting next to him was their mother, the dowager Countess Athala.

"You may go now," said Konrad, and Paust scuttled from the room. Konrad remained standing. He looked from one side of the long, rectangular table to the other, scanning the faces pointing back at him.

"I am shocked, gentlemen, truly shocked," he said, "at the idea that anyone here . . . any . . . single . . . one," he repeated, jabbing a finger onto the table with each word, "could possibly consider it more important to grab a few more Reichsmarks than to carry out the work to which the Führer has sacrificed his entire life, namely the purification of the Aryan race. Anyone would think that you were Jews, the way you place money first, above all else, when we all know that our first duty is to our Führer. I would give away these factories here, all the estates around them, even the *schloss* that bears my family name, all the great works of art and furniture within it, everything I own, in fact, before I parted with this . . ."

Konrad pointed to the Nazi badge on his jacket lapel: the black swastika on a white background surrounded by a red ring and outside that a gold wreath, running right around the badge. "The Führer himself pinned this golden badge, awarded for special services to the Party, on my chest, because he remembered me from the early days, this rich kid, not even twenty, who joined the march through Munich, November the ninth, 1923 . . ."

"Oh God, here we go again . . ." Gerhard sighed to himself

" . . . who stood shoulder to shoulder with the others who were proud to call themselves National Socialists, who did not break ranks when the police fired on us. Oh yes, the Führer remembers those who stood by him then and who remain true to him now. That is why I combine my role as the head of this great company with the even greater honor of serving as personal assistant to *SS-Gruppenführer* Heydrich, and why I am privileged to enjoy the confidence of the most senior members of our Party and government. And this is where I come full circle, gentlemen—and Mother—for it is precisely because I put the Party first, and everyone knows it, that I am now able to tell you that the Meerbach Motor Works is about to enjoy the greatest prosperity we have ever known."

He put his hands on his hips and looked around triumphantly as the room once more echoed to the sound of flesh and bone upon wood.

"Over the next four to five years the Reich will embark upon a period of military expansion that will make its enemies quake in fear. German factories will build aircraft by the thousands and tanks by the tens of thousands. The days when our nation was forced to bow its head by the Allied Powers will be gone for good, just as the Jews whose betrayal undermined our country and led to its defeat will be gone. And all these fighter airplanes and bombers and transports—warplanes unlike any the world has ever seen before—will need engines. All these new tanks, with designs far, far superior to any other tanks on the face of this planet—for who can match Germany for engineering genius?—will require engines to power them, too. And who will supply these engines? Who else but a company cleansed of Jews and commies and perverts, a company whose loyalty to the Party is unquestioned, a company, in short, like the Meerbach Motor Works!"

Konrad bowed his head in modest appreciation of the applause his words had provoked, sat back down again and then, when order had been restored, said, "And so, let us proceed with the private element of the meeting. Herr Lange, perhaps you would give us your report on the state of the Meerbach Family Trust's funds at the present time."

A short, bespectacled man consulted the papers in front of him and proceeded to give a long and extremely detailed account of capital, income and expenditure, delivered in a flat, nasal monotone. His droning intonation, however, could not disguise one salient, inescapable fact. The Meerbach family was extraordinarily wealthy: not merely rich, but blessed with a fortune on a par with the Rothschilds, the Rockefellers and the Fords.

The Meerbach estate stretched for more than thirty kilometers from one end to the other along the shores of the Bodensee. The bank deposits in Frankfurt, Zürich, London and New York matched the reserves of many a nation.

When the recital of facts and figures was complete, various other items on the meeting's agenda were dealt with before Konrad said, "Very well, I think we can now break for a very well-earned lunch. Unless there is any other business anyone wishes to raise?"

His tone very strongly suggested that there ought not to be and there was much shaking of heads from the men in suits. But then Gerhard von Meerbach raised his hand. "Actually," he said, "I do have a request to make."

"Oh really, what is that?" Konrad snapped back, with no suggestion whatever of brotherly love.

"I'd like some more money."

When Oliver Twist asked for a second helping of gruel he did not provoke a more horrified response than the collective gasp that went up around the table.

"More money?" Konrad sneered. "You have a perfectly good allowance. You must be far better off than all your layabout student friends. Besides, I thought you commies weren't interested in money or material possessions."

"For the thousandth time, Konnie, I am not, nor have I ever been a communist. Besides, I can't see why you hate them so much. You belong to the National Socialist Party. The communists worship Russia, or as they insist on calling it, the Union of Soviet Socialist Republics. You're a socialist, they're socialists. Excuse me if I can't spot the difference."

The words were intended to provoke and the only reason Konrad didn't charge round to where his brother was sitting, haul him bodily from his chair and give him the thrashing he deserved was that he knew he was being baited. Breathing hard as he fought to control his temper he said, "How much do you want? And why do you want it?"

"I'd like five thousand Reichsmarks, please. I want to buy a Mercedes."

"So you want to spend our money on a competitor's car?"

"Think of it as a form of industrial espionage. I want to see what the competition is up to."

"But you can buy a perfectly good car for far less than five thousand."

"I don't want a perfectly good car. I want the best. And I want it because I'm a von Meerbach and, unlike you, Konnie, I actually know and care about technology. You may be a good Party man, but can you strip down a car's engine, clean and service its parts and then put it back together again? I can. And the car I want, the Type 29 Mercedes 500K, may look like a runabout for playboys and their girlfriends, but it has a five-liter, supercharged engine that can produce one hundred and twenty kilowatts of power and reach top speeds of more than one hundred and sixty kilometers per hour. It also has a suspension system that is undoubtedly the most advanced in the world. Finally, it is unquestionably, indisputably German. The Führer himself is driven around in various models of Mercedes-Benz. How can you object if I want the same car as him?"

Konrad von Meerbach looked at his younger brother with steely blue eyes. *You may be able to take engines apart, baby brother,* he thought. *But you have never been in the basement of the Gestapo headquarters at number eight, Prinz-Albrecht-Strasse, just down the road from Heydrich's office, where I work when I am in Berlin, and seen a man being taken apart, seen his mind and soul . . . what was it you said? Ah yes, stripped down and cleaned and put back together again. But I have. I've heard them scream in pain and beg for mercy. I've seen them betray themselves, their friends, their families, anything and everything just to make the pain go away. And don't think that you, with all your arrogance, your privileges and your smartass student attitudes, would be any different.*

"Fine," he said. "Have your money. But don't blame me when you crash your stupid car."

The meeting broke up. Konrad was first to leave the boardroom, with the others trailing in his wake. As they were about to follow everyone else through the door to the hall outside, Athala von Meerbach put a bony hand on her younger son's arm. Once upon a time she had been a great beauty, with ash-blonde hair, high cheekbones and delicate features that made other women feel that their own appearance, no matter how attractive, was somehow clumsy and unrefined in comparison. But an unhappy marriage and half a lifetime of loneliness and disillusion had ravaged Athala, leaving her cheeks gaunt and her skin lined and blue veins clearly visible through her wrinkled, semi-translucent skin. Now she looked up at Gerhard and said, "Wait a second."

He stopped in his tracks. "Yes, Mother?"

She looked at him with the eyes of a woman who has heard too many male lies, excuses and bogus arguments not to be able to spot another. "Tell me, darling boy," she said, "why do you really want that money?"

––––––––

Once he had delivered Saffron to school, Leon did not fly back to Nairobi, but headed down to Durban and boarded the first passenger vessel he could find that was bound north. While he was in Johannesburg he had received a telegram from his brother David, who was now the managing director of Courtney Trading, the firm their father had founded. The message simply read.

CT situation desperate. Family's future in jeopardy. Please come to Cairo soonest.

"Your part of the family's future may be in jeopardy, Davey-boy, but not mine," Leon muttered when he first received the telegram. "I've only got ten percent of the company, and one hundred percent of my own loot, thank you very much."

He had been about to draft a reply in that ungenerous vein,

but stopped himself just in time: *Don't be such a bloody idiot. No need to make the same mistake twice.*

More than twenty-five years had passed since the day Leon had left home and he hadn't returned to Cairo since. His stubborn refusal to go back and make peace with his father had been one of the few subjects on which he and Eva had disagreed. Having lost her father when she was still a girl, she could not bear to see the man she loved deliberately cut himself off from his.

"You're just being stubborn," she used to say. "All you have to do is go to Cairo, shake his hand and make your peace."

"Why should I go there?" Leon would reply. "He's as rich as Croesus. He could come down to Kenya any time he wanted."

"Because you were the one who left. And because he's just as stubborn as you are and one of you has to be man enough to end this stupid feud."

"I'll do it when this damn war is over," Leon would say. But then the war had ended and he changed his excuse for not doing anything to, "How can I leave you when you're pregnant with our child?" Then Saffron had arrived and no matter how many times Eva had said, "I'll come with you. I'm perfectly well and a baby is very portable," or, "Very well, then, I will stay here with Saffron and we shall be perfectly able to take care of ourselves until you return," it still was not enough to make Leon take the first step north to Cairo.

Then his father had died and was buried by the time the news of his passing reached Leon. The opportunity to make his peace with his old man had gone forever and Leon bitterly regretted his failure to do anything while he still had the chance. Eva had been right. It had simply been a matter of stubbornness and foolish pride and now that he was a father too he realized how much Ryder must have missed him and how deeply his mother must have been hurt by their falling out.

The ship that was taking Leon back up to Mombasa was en route to Suez so he simply extended his ticket and cabled his brother in Cairo:

ON MY WAY. INFORM OF DEVELOPMENTS C/O P&O SHIP BRABANTIA.

The journey north, around the Horn of Africa and then up the Red Sea to the Suez Canal, took three weeks, and virtually every day saw Leon in the ship's radio room, either dictating a cable to Cairo or receiving one in reply. The situation was very clear, and all too typical of the times they were in. In the ten years after the end of the war, Courtney Trading had built on the legacy left by its founder. With Leon, the oldest of Ryder Courtney's sons, absent from the family and Francis, the second son, so badly wounded in action that he was unable to work full time, responsibility for managing the company had fallen upon David, the third son, named after his maternal grandfather David Benbrook, who had died defending his family at the siege of Khartoum. With the global economy booming and mass production making cars affordable to millions of new customers, and the aircraft industry expanding at breakneck pace, David had concluded that, of all the family's interests, their investments in Persian oilfields had the best long-term prospects. Accordingly he had borrowed heavily to finance expansion of both their drilling and prospecting operations, and the tanker fleet that carried the oil to refineries in Great Britain and Europe. The strategy would have paid off handsomely had not the Wall Street Crash of 1929 sent the global economy plummeting into a terrible depression. With the supply of oil increasing, for all the world's petroleum companies had been expanding, and the demand suddenly falling, the bottom dropped out of the market and the price of oil fell through the floor.

Backed by Francis and also Dorian, the youngest of the four Courtney brothers, David had held his nerve. He had not canceled his contracts with shipbuilders. Instead he had renegotiated new, lower prices, knowing that yards were willing to cut their profit margins to the bone rather than lose work completely.

He even bought out some of his partners in the Persian fields whose pockets were not as deep as his for a fraction of the true value of their holdings. Eventually, he reasoned, the world would go back to work again, demand for oil would pick up and the price would rebound.

But the world wasn't returning to work. The depression continued to get worse and worse. Now Ryder Trading was not the hunter but the prey. The debts accumulated by the expansion program could no longer be financed and the company was facing the very fate it had imposed on others: selling everything at a rock-bottom price, and giving every penny from the sale to its bankers. The only hope was for someone to come to the rescue. And in the eyes of his younger brothers, that someone had to be Leon.

———

Gerhard von Meerbach walked along the street that led toward the marshalling yards, his jacket collar raised to ward off the chilly winter wind and his cap rammed over his eyes. The noise of the people and the occasional cars and trucks all around him was drowned by the sound of the locomotives and rolling stock being shunted into place to serve the tens of thousands of people who would be leaving Munich Central Station, three kilometers down the tracks, within the next few hours. This was Laim, a tough, uncompromising, working-class neighborhood, where the pristine streets in the smarter parts of the city gave way to cracked pavements strewn with discarded newspapers, rotting vegetables and dog mess. It was crammed with men and women: some quietly going about their business; others leaning on doorways and lampposts, cigarettes in their mouths, watching the world go by; others again pointing fingers, shouting and swearing in coarse accents that made Gerhard feel nervous about opening his own mouth and revealing his educated, aristocratic intonation.

He had dressed for the occasion in his oldest, scruffiest suit, one he'd been wearing to lectures, building sites, parties and countless late nights in smoky bars and cabarets throughout his student years. Its black fabric had been rubbed to a greenish sheen with age and over-use, there were patches on the elbows and close examination would reveal crude darning where a former girlfriend had mended one of the trouser pockets that had almost been ripped off in a particularly wild bout of student horseplay. He was wearing his oldest shirt without the stiff collar that would normally be attached to it and had borrowed one of the oily flat-caps, worn by the mechanic when he was servicing the family's fleet of cars, that hung from a peg in the converted stable building at the Schloss Meerbach that now served as a garage.

He passed a tailor's shop on whose window someone had painted a crude Star of David in whitewash, with the word "*Jude*" scrawled next to it. Underneath it was a poster that screamed, "Don't buy from Jews!" The shop was closed and the door padlocked. The dummies in the window were covered in dust and one had fallen over. The Jews, it seemed, had been driven out.

From a *bierkeller* came the smell of stale drink and the sound of raucous voices joining in the old drinking song "Lang Lang Ist's Her" to the accompaniment of an accordion. A man outside the *bierkeller* looked furtively to one side and then another and then shoved a crudely printed pamphlet into Gerhard's hand. "You look like a friend," he said, then scuttled back into the shadows.

Gerhard glanced at the pamphlet, which was entitled, "ISK— Journal of the International Socialist Combat League" and carried the headline, "International Socialism on the Autobahn!" Below that was a picture showing men working on a brand new stretch of high-speed motorway between Frankfurt and Darmstadt, the first of its kind in the world and Adolf Hitler's pride and joy. The story beneath it described the workers" discontent with their poor pay and intolerable living conditions.

But they were striking back, the writer said. They were staging protests, slowing the pace of construction, even daubing slogans on the new bridges across the road.

Gerhard stopped dead in his tracks. Could any of this possibly be true? The cinema newsreels had been full of stories about the new autobahn and none of them had mentioned discontent among the workforce, who were always pictured with broad smiles on their faces as they toiled for the good of the Fatherland. Nor had anyone said a word in public about any painted slogans. *Well, they wouldn't, would they?* Gerhard thought, crumpling up the pamphlet and shoving it into the nearest rubbish bin. Then he, too, looked around, just as the ISK activist had done, just as everyone did in Munich, the city that had spawned the Gestapo, where the eyes and ears of the secret police were assumed to be ever vigilant, everywhere. Gerhard had taken a tram to Laimer Platz, watching all the other passengers as they got on and off and then checking to see that no one had followed him when he alighted. On the walk down Fürstenrieder Strasse he'd paused every so often to look in shop windows and see what was happening behind him, just as he had seen actors do in films. But there had been no sign of anyone on his tail, so he'd pressed on toward his destination.

And now here he was, walking up the short flight of cracked stone steps to the entrance of an apartment building. The brickwork around the door was stained where water had flooded down the wall from overflowing guttering above and the mortar between the bricks was crumbling away and in desperate need of repointing. The front door was not locked. Gerhard pushed it open and walked into a hallway lined with bicycles propped up against both walls. A small board showed the numbers of the flats that opened off the staircase rising up in front of Meerbach. He saw a name scrawled by the final number, 12(b): Solomons.

Oh, Izzy, has it come to this? Gerhard thought, remembering the days when his mother used to take him to visit the Solomons at their splendid house on Königinstrasse—Queen Street—just opposite the English Garden. The Solomons had been family lawyers to the von Meerbachs for generations and were so perfectly assimilated into upper-class German life that, as Gerhard's mother used to say, "One would hardly know that they were Jews at all."

A display cabinet in the dining room proudly bore the decorations Isidore Solomons, the family's golden boy, had won in the war. He had fought as proudly and valiantly for Germany as any man in the Kaiser's army and, as he miraculously survived while so many others died around him, he had risen from a humble *Leutnant* to *Oberst*, or colonel, in the process. Solomons had served in the 15th Bavarian Infantry Division, part of the Fifth Army under Crown Prince Wilhelm of Germany, the Kaiser's heir. The Prince's handwritten letter of commendation, praising Solomons for his gallantry, had taken pride of place in the cabinet, next to his *Pour le Mérite* medal, the legendary Blue Max. It was the highest honor that any German military man could receive and had been awarded to him in recognition of his extraordinary courage under fire at Verdun, and his selfless willingness to risk his own life to protect those of the men who served under him.

Solomons did not like to talk about his wartime experiences. But Gerhard could remember sitting on the great marble staircase at Schloss Meerbach one New Year's Eve, watching the guests arrive for the night's celebrations. Gentlemen had been invited to wear their decorations. Isidore Solomons had walked in, looking tall, saturnine and impeccably dressed with the blue cross on his chest, hanging from a black and white ribbon, surrounded by a cluster of golden oak leaves, with the words "*Pour le Mérite*" inscribed upon its face. Men had taken one look at it and greeted him with the kind of deference they might have shown to royalty, while women seemed like moths drawn to his flame as other richer, more powerful, even more famous men—for the guest list included a number of celebrated actors, writers, painters and musicians—walked by entirely unnoticed.

And now the Solomons were reduced to this, walking up and down the stairs that Gerhard was now climbing, where the paint was peeling off damp-ridden walls and the pervasive odor of stewed cabbage and stale sweat mingled with the stench of human filth from the toilets—one to every two floors, Gerhard noticed as he recalled the gleaming marble bathrooms of the old Solomons house.

Finally he reached the top floor. He walked along a cramped corridor, barely wider than his shoulders, then knocked on the door marked "12(b)."

"Come in, my dear fellow," said Isidore nonchalantly, as if nothing had changed, ushering Gerhard into a cramped sitting room, filled with incongruously grand furniture that Gerhard recognized from the house on Königinstrasse. Solomons was as impeccably dressed, shaved and groomed as if he were still one of the smartest lawyers in Munich. He waved a hand at a room that looked immaculately maintained, save for the bed-linen neatly folded up at the end of a sofa on which one member of the family must have slept.

"You look well," Gerhard said. "As if you're just about to go to the office."

Solomons shrugged. "One tries to maintain one's standards. And actually I do keep my hand in—unofficially. In this neighborhood there are always people in need of legal advice. Most of them can't afford to pay, but it keeps me occupied and . . . well, let's just say that some of my clients are in a position to make sure that no one bothers us here. That is worth a lot these days."

"Is Claudia around?" Gerhard asked. "I suppose the children must be at school."

"Actually the children are being educated at home these days. It was made clear to us that their presence was no longer welcome at their school. Ah well, I would have found it hard to pay the fees anyway . . . So, to answer your question, Claudia is not in at the moment. I sent her off to the park with the children and my mother. I thought it best that we spoke alone. I hope you agree?"

"Absolutely . . . of course," Gerhard replied, trying to maintain the pretence that they were chatting casually, just as in days gone by. But it was impossible. "Izzy . . . Mr. Solomons . . . I'm so, so sorry. It shames me to see you like this."

"Nonsense, dear boy, think nothing of it. We have a bedroom, a kitchen, a shared bathroom and toilet on the next floor down. Hardly the same as Königinstrasse, of course, but it's positively palatial compared to my quarters at Verdun. And there are far fewer rats."

Gerhard laughed. Solomons was more than twenty years his senior, old enough to be his father. He had inherited the position of family lawyer from his late father at the end of the war. Having grown up without a father of his own, for he had only been three when his was killed in action at the very start of the war, Gerhard had needed an older man to turn to for advice, or just a pair of ears willing to listen to his troubles, and Isidore Solomons—quick-witted, urbane, steeped in legal knowledge, utterly loyal to the von Meerbach family and blessed with an innate wisdom worthy of his name—was the natural choice.

"Konrad should never have dismissed you. He should have fought harder to persuade his friends in the Party to grant you an exemption from the anti-Jew laws. You were awarded the Max, for heaven's sake."

Solomons gave a shrug and a wry, sad smile. "It turns out the *Pour le Mérite* isn't what it used to be. I don't blame Konrad. The fact is, I couldn't do my job properly any more and it wasn't going to get any better, either. Mark my words, Gerhard. What has happened so far is only the beginning."

"Then he should have given you a proper settlement. After

all these years, these generations, it's the very least my family could do for yours."

"Well, that's true. But Konrad has his own career to think about. I hear he is working directly for Heydrich now, as some kind of adjutant, no?"

"That's right. He's Heydrich's personal secretary. They're working in Berlin now that Heydrich's got the whole Gestapo and Security Police under him. Konrad travels with him everywhere. He's even been up to the Führer's chalet at Berchtesgarten."

"Tea on the terrace with Adolf and Eva, how *gemütlich*!"

"Not so charming really, I suspect. Anyway, you can rest assured there's at least one of us who understands the concept of a debt of honor. I managed to get five thousand Reichsmarks from my trust fund. The trustees think I'm buying a Mercedes. Let's just hope they don't ever expect to see it."

"Thank you, Herr von Meerbach," said Solomons, suddenly sounding much more formal as Gerhard removed an envelope from his inside jacket pocket and handed it over. "You are too generous. Most people could not earn that in a year. It will help us more than you can know."

"Most people aren't von Meerbachs or Solomons." Gerhard paused. "I won't ask what you're going to do with it. I don't want to know. But whatever you do, and wherever you may go, I will always wish you well. And . . ." Gerhard sighed. "This isn't just about all that family stuff, though I did mean what I said. It's personal, too. As long as I live, I will never forget your kindness to me, or all the times you took the trouble to listen to me and help me. Never."

Solomons put a fatherly hand on Gerhard's shoulder. "You are a good man, but these are not times for good men. So remember, you must be as hard, and determined and, if necessary, as ruthless as the bad men who are on the rise, all across Europe. You have to fight their fire with fire, or they will triumph and all will be lost. Tell me, are you familiar with the work of William Butler Yeats?"

Gerhard shook his head.

"He is an Irish poet, very good I think. He has a poem called "The Second Coming." He writes in English of course, but I have his works in a German translation." Solomons walked across to a rickety wooden bookcase and took out a small volume that proudly bore the marks and creases of a much read and much loved book.

"Yeats wrote this in 1919, when the blood had not yet dried from the last war, but he was already, like a prophet, seeing the next one approaching," Solomons said, leafing through until he had found the right page. "*Ach so*, I have it! Listen to these few lines, Gerhard, for they tell us much:
Things fall apart; the Center cannot hold;
Mere anarchy is loosed upon the world,
The blood-dimmed tide is loosed, and everywhere
The ceremony of innocence is drowned;
The best lack all conviction, while the worst
Are full of passionate intensity.
"You are one of the best, Gerhard. One of the very best. And so you must have as much conviction and as much passionate intensity in the good things that you do as the worst in all the evil acts that they commit. And stay alive. For God's sake, Gerhard, do as I did at Verdun and above all, whatever else may happen . . . stay alive."

———

The four Courtney brothers met for lunch on the terrace of Shepheard's Hotel in Cairo, where Leon was staying, having taken the train there from the port of Suez. The weather was pleasantly warm, which meant blissfully cool by Cairo standards. Leon had booked the table and arrived early, sipping a pre-prandial gin and tonic as he watched the world go by: Europeans in suits and hats; Arabs in their flowing robes; street traders calling out for customers as they walked down the street bearing large baskets laden with almonds and apricots;

street urchins begging for strangers' spare *piastres*; horse-drawn carriages fighting for the right of way against donkeys and carts and drivers furiously tooting their horns. The women's clothes had changed while Leon had been away, there were many more cars and bicycles, and the smell of exhaust fumes now mingled with the eternal aroma of dust, dung, wood smoke and spice that had hung in the air here since time immemorial, but the essential nature of the city remained the same.

But what of his brothers? Would he even recognize them after all this time?

A white-jacketed waiter appeared at his table and said, "Your guests have arrived, *effendi*."

Leon looked past him to see the three men walking toward him. He spotted David at once. He had been a tall, skinny stick of a lad when Leon had last seen him and he looked exactly the same even though he was now approaching forty. Even his sandy hair, the fairest in the family, was as tousled and apparently unbrushed now that he was a serious businessman as it had been when he was a schoolboy. Dorian, too, was immediately recognizable. Dark and elfin in the slightness of his body and the quickness of his movement, he had inherited their mother's artistic talents. By the time he was ten or eleven he could draw brilliantly wicked cartoons of his big brothers, or turn his hand to watercolor landscapes that could have been mistaken for the work of adults. Judging by his crumpled, sand-colored linen suit, with the trousers held up by a tie rather than a belt and a dark blue shirt open at the neck to reveal a cotton neckerchief, he was still the artist of the family.

That left Francis, the closest of the three brothers to Leon in age: too close, perhaps, because Leon had always felt that Francis looked on him with rivalry rather than love. But the best part of thirty years had passed since those days, and those years had included a war in which Francis had suffered more than any of them, and been changed more than any of them, too.

But had he changed for the better, or the worse? That, thought Leon as he watched Francis walk toward him, limping slightly and carrying a stick to help support him, was the key to the plan he had in mind: the key, indeed, to the survival of Courtney Trading itself.

Davy's a reasonable chap. If he sees that I'm being fair, he'll accept it. Dorian will tag along with him. But what about you, Frankie-boy? Which way are you going to jump?

———

Captain Francis Courtney had been serving in the Mediterranean Expeditionary Force that had landed at Cape Helles in western Turkey in April 1915. On the northern side of the Cape lay the waters of the Aegean. To the south were the Dardanelles, the straits through which all sea traffic between the Mediterranean and the Black Sea had to pass. The Dardanelles lay in the hands of the Ottoman Empire, which had sided with Germany in the war. If they could be secured by the Allies, however, that would enable direct communications between British forces in North Africa and the Middle East and their Russian allies on the far shores of the Black Sea. The original aim of the Dardanelles Campaign, as it was initially termed, was to use French and Royal Navy battleships to force a passage through the straits by sea. In the eyes of Winston Churchill (or "that damn fool Winston' as Leon Courtney termed him from that moment on), the operation should have been straightforward. The Ottoman Empire was decadent, inefficient and weakened by internal revolt. The Royal Navy was the greatest maritime force the world had ever seen.

Unfortunately, however, a combination of minefields in the water and Turkish gun batteries on the shore devastated the British and French fleets and forced a humiliating retreat. It was then decided that the Turkish guns had to be attacked from the land and so the second phase of the campaign began. It was a campaign involving British, French, Indian, Australian and New Zealand troops and it was the Australasian forces and the casualties they suffered that epitomized the combination of heroic fighting by the troops and total strategic failure by their commanders. For this was Gallipoli, and even by the standards of the Great War, a conflict not short of blood-soaked catastrophe, this was a disaster of spectacular dimensions. Contrary to public perception, the British troops, who formed the great majority of the Allied army, comprised around two-thirds of all the killed and wounded. And one of them was Francis Courtney.

———

To his father's disappointment, when Francis had first been called up his poor performance in basic training led to him being adjudged as "not officer material" and sent to the ranks. By the time of the Gallipoli campaign he was a lance corporal working for the regimental quartermaster, for whom he was a clerk, checking supplies in and out. While Ryder Courtney may have regarded this as a sorry state of affairs, Francis was delighted. The honor of starting one's military service as a second lieutenant was far outweighed in his eyes by the appalling casualty rates among young subalterns. Let them lead charges against trenches defended by machine guns: he was much happier in the quartermaster's stores, filling out chits and keeping orderly accounts. But then, toward the very end of the Gallipoli fiasco a man called Garden, a captain in the Special Brigade of the Royal Engineers, arrived at the front, hot foot from Egypt. He brought with him three thousand cylinders of chlorine gas, for some desperate desk-wallah, two thousand miles away at the War Office in London, had suggested that gas might be the way of dislodging the Turks from their positions and turning disaster into triumph. This, however, was not only an immoral idea but an impractical one. The sea breezes that swirled around Cape Helles were far too changeable and just as likely to blow a cloud of gas straight back onto the British lines as to send it across to the Turks. To make matters worse, the Turkish positions were on higher ground than the

Allied ones and chlorine, being much heavier than air, tends to sink downhill, rather than floating up.

So the plan was abandoned and the gas canisters put into storage until such time as they and Captain Garden could be sent back to Alexandria. By complete chance a stray Turkish shell exploded near the dump where the gas canisters had been piled and a piece of shrapnel from the shell pierced one of the cylinders. Francis Courtney had been inspecting the dump at the time, to check that the records showed the correct quantities of munitions in storage. He had in fact been walking past the chlorine cylinders when the shell landed. The explosion threw him, shocked but unhurt, to the ground just as a heavy stream of chlorine was emitted from the ruptured canister.

A burning pain ripped through his eyes and throat, a giant fist seemed to clamp itself around his chest and his lungs seized up, so he felt as if he were suffocating. He somehow managed to stagger to his feet and stumble away from the gas, an action that saved his life. Even so he was seized by spasms of coughing and retching. His eyes were blinded by the tears produced by his desperate body as it sought to remove the irritation. His mouth, meanwhile, went to the opposite extreme: he was parched with thirst and his tongue felt thick and furry. Francis collapsed to the ground where he was found by a stretcher party, lying on his side with his head aching and his mouth open in a desperate attempt to let the fluid in his lungs flow back out of his body. His face was a pale greenish yellow, and over the next few hours other parts of his body put on a macabre display of vivid color as the gas and the oxygen deprivation that it caused took their toll: the jaundiced pallor of his face slowly gave way to a vivid, violet red complexion, while his fingernails went from a healthy pink to a deathly blue. He was exhausted and yet restless, struggling for breath, seized by the anxiety, bordering on panic, that comes with an inability to breathe. Everything hurt, his whole body was erupting in protest:

coughs, vomit and diarrhea, one after another in an endless, random succession.

Finally Francis slept. He awoke feeling much better. But a few hours later a second wave of physical torment broke over him as his shattered body, its defenses broken, gave way to an acute bronchial fever. The coughing returned and the white handkerchiefs he held to his face were soon coated with green, blood-streaked mucus. As his temperature rose beyond one hundred and four degrees Fahrenheit, his pulse became faint yet rapid. For a few hours he became delirious and the doctors at the military hospital felt certain that he would be another addition to the ever-growing list of fatal casualties. But then, when all seemed lost, the fever broke. Francis had survived.

"It was being a Courtney that saved him," Leon's mother had written in her letter telling him what had happened. "Frank was just too stubborn to die and your pa refused to take no for an answer. He went all the way to the War Office to get permission to ship Frank back to Alexandria and then made d___ sure that he had the best doctors and nurses in the Levant to look after him. With God's will, we hope he will pull through."

It was a slow business, even so. Francis spent almost four years recuperating: first in hospital, then at a sanatorium and finally at home. In the end, he had emerged much weaker and with an acute sensitivity to bright light: hence the stick and dark glasses. But compared to many of the blind, the crippled and the mutilated veterans who had become such a horribly familiar sight on postwar streets, Francis Courtney had got off lightly.

"I'm so glad to see you looking so well, Frank," Leon said, in a tone that left no doubt that he meant what he said.

Francis reacted as if insulted. He gave a dismissive little grunt and his mouth was twisted into a bitter grimace as he said, "So, you wouldn't come back when your brother was lying wounded for months on end. And you still wouldn't come when your father was dying. But the moment your money's at risk you come running. Excuse me if I'm not impressed." His voice had a wheezy edge to it and when he'd said his piece he gave a rasping, hacking cough that seemed to Leon to be as much a sign of his brother's anger as any purely physical gesture.

"Steady on, Frank," said David. "No need to rake over old ground, eh?"

Leon ignored the provocation. "Well, it's good to see you, anyway," he said and held out a hand.

Francis pointedly ignored it.

"Thank you so much for coming all this way, Leon," said David, playing the peacemaker. "I very much hope we can sort something out for all our benefit."

His handshake was firm and confident, the grip of a man who was used to taking responsibility and standing by his word.

Dorian stood back for a second, eyeing Leon as if he were sizing him up for a portrait. Then he said, "Hmm . . . somewhat battered by old age, but still essentially the same big brother." Then he grinned and, to Leon's surprise, gave him an affectionate hug. "Good to see you, old man."

"You too," said Leon. Then he waved a hand toward his table and said: "Why don't you sit down and order some drinks? They make a damn good G'n'T, as this empty glass can testify."

"That sounds like a splendid idea," said David.

Dorian thought for a second. "I think I'll have a vodka martini, if that's all right, big brother."

"By all means. How about you, Frank?"

"Johnnie Walker, neat, no ice, and make it a double."

The drinks were obtained, food was ordered, served and consumed. All the while, the four men's conversation was just the normal talk of brothers who have long been parted from one of their number. Leon asked after their mother and sister and caught up on the details of their various families. David was married with two children: a boy of ten and a girl of seven.

Francis had been married but his wife Marjorie had long since left him and he had not found anyone new. Dorian, meanwhile, was entirely unencumbered by any marital ties, clearly preferring to play the field with a constant stream of women.

"I don't believe he's ever painted a woman's portrait without taking her to bed," David remarked.

"Oh, that's not fair," Dorian insisted. "A chap asked me to paint his mother a few years ago. He told me that he wanted something to remember her by when she was gone. She was a splendid old bird, seventy-five if she was a day, but still in remarkably good physical fettle, and bright as a button with it."

"Tell me you didn't . . ." said Leon, laughing.

"Of course not!" Dorian exclaimed, as if outraged by the very suggestion. "That's precisely the point I was trying to make. I do have my limits." He paused for a moment and then added, "Though I have to admit the thought did cross my mind . . ."

"I really don't think that Dorian's total absence of sexual continence is either an interesting or fruitful topic of conversation," said Francis irritably. "Can we just get on with our business? That's why we're here, isn't it? And, let's be honest, Leon, you wouldn't have come all this way to discuss it unless you thought you could profit from our misfortunes. So why don't you tell us exactly how, precisely, you intend to do it?"

———

Leon looked at his brother. He understood now that Francis carried his deepest scars on his soul, rather than his body. That was where the real damage lay and it was all the more dangerous as a result.

He took his time, refusing to let Francis goad him into haste or ill temper. Instead, he summoned the waiter and ordered coffee for them all, then said, "Very well, why don't I start by summarizing the situation as I see it. And then we can discuss what to do about it. I have my ideas, but I'm sure you will all have ones of your own, too."

"That sounds fair enough," said David. "Fire away."

"Right then . . . The first thing I want to say is that I think you acted entirely reasonably, Davy. It's absolutely clear to me that the demand for oil-based fuels is only going to grow—even ships are as likely to be powered by diesel as coal these days—and there was no reason why you should have predicted this endless damn depression when absolutely nobody else did. So, I see no need for recriminations.

"On the other hand, there's no getting away from the fact that Courtney Trading is in dire straits. It's not just the oil. All Dad's investments in the South African mining industry are suffering. Gold and diamonds are the last things anyone's buying these days. Even Egyptian cotton's going through a slump. And of course shipping has come to a virtual standstill because no one can afford to trade. So there's nothing taking up the slack. And the company's total debts stand at a little over six million pounds by my rough calculation . . ."

"Six million, two hundred and thirty-nine thousand, four hundred and seventy-two pounds, seventeen shillings and ten-pence was the precise figure when our chief accountant last worked it out," said David.

"Well, the seventeen and ten shouldn't be any problem," said Dorian, blithely.

"And it's borrowed at an average of around eight percent per annum interest," said Leon.

"About that, yes," David agreed.

"Which means that in round figures Courtney Trading needs to find half a million pounds a year to meet the interest, let alone repay any of the principal, and that's impossible when none of its businesses are making any money."

"Thank you so much, Leon, for telling us what we already know," said Francis.

"Indulge me, Frank, there's a good chap. You see, I think that the very scale of the company's debts is what will give us leverage with the bankers. Any creditor with half a brain will know that if we have to sell up, we'll get a pittance and they'll be lucky to get a tenth of their money back. It's far better for them if we stay in business."

"Frank does have a point, Leon," said David. "We have managed to work this out for ourselves and I've been hammering the message home to the banks for months. In fact, that's the only reason they haven't foreclosed on us already. But they're getting to the point where they're ready to write off the loss."

"Quite so . . . But if they knew that the interest would be covered for a period of, say, four years—absolutely guaranteed—they would be much calmer, wouldn't they? And if they knew that their capital investment was safer, then they might be amenable to renegotiating the terms of the loan. After all, interest rates now are far lower than they were when you made these deals. The Americans are down to about two percent. I don't see why we couldn't get our creditors to accept a four percent return, if they knew they were going to get paid."

"But they're not going to get paid, are they?" Francis protested. His voice rose in volume as he raged, "It doesn't matter if the interest is eight percent, four percent or the square root of bugger-all, we can't bloody well pay it."

"I really don't think it's a good idea to let the whole of Cairo know that," said Leon. "And in any case it's not true. You may not be able to pay it. But I can."

"How?" asked Francis, bitterly. "Magic beans?"

"No, gold sovereigns. One million pounds' worth of them."

"And you have that, do you, one million pounds in gold? Are we really expected to believe that? What did you do, dig up a treasure trove of pirate gold?"

Leon shrugged, "This is not the time to go into details, but that's as good a way of describing it as any other."

David frowned. "This gold of yours, Leon, assuming that you

have it . . . It is legal, isn't it? I mean you didn't come by it criminally, or anything?"

"I didn't rob a bank if that's what you're worried about. It was the spoils of war, if you really want to know, taken from our nation's enemies. Which, as our dear, departed father would surely have said, if he were here now, was how we Courtneys made our family fortune in the first place."

"The fine Courtney tradition of barely legalized piracy" . . . wasn't that his phrase?" asked Dorian with a grin. "You must admit, Davy, the old man was—in the nicest, most charming possible way, of course—an absolute rogue and a scoundrel. He'd be thrilled to hear that his oldest son had taken after him so splendidly. A million pounds in gold, eh? Dad would have been proud of you, Leon . . . and a little jealous too, I dare say."

"Suppose you give us this money," said Francis. "What do you want in return?"

"Good question, Frank," said Leon. "I've been trying to work that out for myself. The first place, I've been wondering whether to do anything at all. I don't mean to sound callous, but the plain truth is that if Courtney Trading goes bust it really won't trouble me—financially, at least. On the other hand, it will cause you chaps very considerable inconvenience. What's more it will destroy Dad's legacy, which means more to me than I dare say you imagine. But what troubles me most of all is that our mother and sisters will be left without a means of support, and I'm not prepared to accept that under any circumstances. So the company has to be saved.

"Now, Dad left you three twenty-five percent of the company each because you'd stayed in Cairo and could be expected to run the show. My share was cut to ten percent because I'd walked out . . . and before you say anything, Frank, I have never had any complaint about that. And Mater, Penny and Becca each got five, which should have been ample to keep them decently supported for life.

"I could, of course, simply give them each enough to make up for the loss of their Courtney Trading shares. That would be much cheaper for me in the short term, but there's no possibility of profit in the long term and I am absolutely convinced that the company has a very fine future if it can survive the present crisis. So here is what I will propose. I will give Courtney Trading one million pounds. And in return I will receive an additional forty-one percent of the company, taking my share up to fifty-one percent. I have to be the majority shareholder, after all, to make sure my investment is protected."

"But that's daylight robbery!" Francis exploded. He looked around at the others. "What did I say? He's just a bloody thief." Then he turned his acid gaze on Leon. "You bastard! You know perfectly well that it's worth far, far more than that."

"Not at the moment it isn't," David wryly observed.

"Precisely," said Leon, doing his best to remain calm. "And this way you will still retain a stake, and keep it for long enough to see it grow in value so that you will actually be much better off in the meantime. Look, Frank, I'm staking virtually all of my liquid assets on this company. If this goes wrong, I could end up on Queer Street too. So I want a damn good premium or I'm walking away and keeping my money safe and sound in the bank vault where it now resides."

"How do you propose we give you this forty-one percent?" Dorian asked.

"Essentially, you transfer a proportion of your shares to me. It's up to you to decide who gives me what. But I think Davy should have the second biggest holding after me, because he's the poor sod who'll have to make the whole project work. I don't want the womenfolk to lose out too badly, and by the way, I'll cover their living expenses for the next four years because one of my conditions is that no one, myself included, gets a dividend from the company in that time. Of course, you three can claim wages for the work you do. Again, Davy gets the lion's share."

Leon looked around the table. David had taken a notebook from his jacket and was writing calculations as he worked through the financial implications of Leon's proposal. Dorian was leaning back in his chair, casually smoking a cigar and making eyes at a very pretty woman at the next table, whose husband had his back to him and was therefore none the wiser. Francis angrily stubbed out a cigarette and beckoned a waiter over to him. "Get me a whisky," he said. "And make it a damn strong one."

"I agree with Leon that the ladies should only have to hand over a minimal amount," said David, looking at the numbers jotted on the notepaper in front of him. "I suggest a contribution of two percent, shared evenly between them. That leaves us chaps to find thirty-nine percent, which divides very neatly by three into thirteen each. Jolly kind of you to offer me more, Leon, but we should do this equally or not at all. I take it, incidentally, that we aren't seeing any of the actual money."

"No, it all goes into the company's accounts," Leon said. "If we can halve the rate of interest, a million pounds should tide the company over for four years, and if things still haven't got any better by then, well, it really won't make any difference if Courtney Trading goes under because the whole world will be bust."

"Excuse me for my limited appreciation of financial matters," said Dorian, "but if I understand you correctly, your basic proposal to us is that half a sixpence is better than none."

"Correct."

"But if things do get better, then you will have an awful lot more sixpences than the rest of us. I take the point that you're the one who's risking his money. But we are giving up our birthright, handing over our mess of pottage, or whatever that chap in the Bible did. It seems to me that if things go well, and your money is completely safe, and suddenly worth an awful lot more than one million pounds, we should have some of our pottage back. If you see what I mean."

Leon smiled, "Ma always used to say that you weren't as

green as you're cabbage-looking, Dorian, and I can see that she was right. Very well, here's what I suggest. If, at some later date, Courtney Trading is back on its feet and, as you say, its value is greatly increased, then you can buy back half of the shares you gave me, for their face value, plus four percent interest for every year I've held them."

"By God, is there no end to your greed?" Francis sneered. "Charging your own brothers interest? Are you sure you're not a Jew, Leon? Shylock himself would be proud of you."

"Is there no end to your bitterness, Frank?" replied Leon, in a tone less of anger than regret. "In the situation Dorian is envisaging, the shares will be worth far, far more than they were—twice, perhaps even ten times as much. So if I am charging four percent interest, you can happily pay it and still be hugely in profit. All I am doing is making sure that I am not actually losing money, bearing in mind that it could just sit in a bank earning interest anyway."

"What do you think, Davy?" asked Dorian.

"I think it's a very fair offer. Leon still stands to make a very considerable profit if things go well, which is fair enough in the circumstances. But he's giving us a chance to share in that profit. And since we have no chance of profit whatsoever at the moment, that strikes me as a very fair deal."

"So do you accept my terms, David?" Leon asked.

"Yes. We'll have to get lawyers to draw up the papers, but in principle you can count me in."

"Dorian?"

"Oh, I'm just the layabout artist of the family. If it's good enough for Davy it's good enough for me."

"How about you, Frank? I want unanimous agreement on this. I can't have us split from the very beginning. There's no chance of the plan working if we aren't all committed to it."

"I don't trust you," said Francis. "You'll find a way to trick us, I'm sure of it."

"That's what the lawyers are for," said David. "To make sure no one tricks anyone and all the contracts are completely above board."

"But why would I want to trick anyone?" Leon asked. "I have no reason to do that. I'm doing this for all the reasons I've already stated: to preserve Dad's legacy, to help Mother and the girls and, yes, because I think there's a genuine business opportunity here—for all of us. Look, if you don't trust me, I will get up from the table right now, walk away and you won't ever have to hear another word about any of my wicked schemes."

"Leon's right, Frank," said David. "He doesn't need Courtney Trading, but we do need a million pounds."

"So we should accept his terms because he's got us over a barrel, is that what you're saying?"

"No, we should accept his terms because we won't get better ones anywhere else and because we owe it to our parents and our sisters not to let our personal feelings get in the way of doing the right thing."

There was still a little whisky left in the bottom of Francis Courtney's glass. He downed it, slammed the glass back down on the table and glared at Leon. "Very well then, I can see I have no alternative but to accept your terms. I'll sign whatever papers the lawyers put in front of me. I'll put on a brave face in public. I'm used to that. But don't think I like it, dear brother of mine. Because I don't. Not one little bit."

———————

A short while later, as the four Courtney brothers all went their separate ways, Dorian stayed behind for a moment to have one last word with Leon.

"Are you going to see Mother while you're here?" he asked.

"Absolutely. I was planning to have dinner with her tonight, as a matter of fact. Just thought it was best to get this business out of the way first."

"Yes, that makes sense. Look, I'm sorry about Frank. He can be awfully unreasonable these days."

Leon shrugged. "Well, he's had to endure a hell of a lot, what with his wounds, losing his family. It's enough to make anyone testy."

"Hmm . . . You're right, of course, but it's not quite that simple. It wasn't actually getting wounded that made Frank this way. It was when he got better."

"How do you mean?"

"In a sort of way, I think he quite enjoyed being the family invalid. He was the center of attention. I mean, Dad was absolutely obsessed by doing everything possible to make Frank better . . . as he would have been for any of us, of course, including you, Leon. So Frank was endlessly being fussed over and made to feel special. The whole business of going to see him was tremendously dramatic. The windows would be shaded and Frank would be lying in bed, coughing feebly. Only Marjorie was allowed to approach him."

"It must have been terribly hard for her. I don't suppose one can blame her for not coping."

"Quite so," Dorian agreed. "But oddly enough, that wasn't the part she couldn't cope with. I mean, Marjorie's a smashing girl and she was an absolute brick when Frank was in hospital. The problems started when he came back home."

"Why so?"

"Well, there was no reason for Frank not to lead a perfectly normal life, and I don't think he liked it. Suddenly, people weren't paying him nearly as much attention. Everyone said, "Jolly good to see you, old man," and then just got on with things as usual. Frank couldn't seem to cope. I think the gas affected him in the head more than the body. He changed, psychologically. I mean, he wasn't such a bad chap, really, in the old days. But now there was this air of gloom and self-pity all around him. And then, of course, Dad became ill . . ." Dorian stopped, looked at Leon and sorrowfully said, "You really should have come home."

"I know . . . Believe me, I know. I don't think there's anything I regret more."

"Ah well, no point fretting about it now. Anyway . . . as I was saying . . . Dad became ill and of course everyone's attention turned to him and his needs."

"And Frank felt let down by that? Surely not."

"I'm rather afraid he did. He certainly became more and more bitter, that's for sure. And that's what drove Marjorie away. She just couldn't stand the person he became. And if you ask me, that's what has stopped him finding a new wife, too."

Leon gave a rueful sigh. "It's so sad, and so counterproductive. It sounds like Frank has got himself trapped in a really vicious circle. The more bitter he is, the less people warm to him, and that only makes him more bitter."

"And more dangerous," said Dorian. "I know he's gone along with your plan for the time being. He knows he doesn't have a choice. But I don't think he wants it to succeed. I think he wants you to be proved wrong, even if it means him losing everything."

"Oh, come on. He surely wouldn't go that far. Once the money starts rolling in, he'll come around."

"No, he won't. That's the whole point. If the money comes in, that means you were right, and it also means that you're getting more than the rest of us. No, I couldn't care less, because all I need is paint, canvas and a place to lay my head. And Davy won't mind because he's a pretty decent sort, really, and he understands that this is the only way that the company can survive. But Frank is different. He would rather we all failed than that you succeeded."

"I see."

"I hope you do, big bro. So take my advice, even if I am the baby of the family. Keep your eyes wide open. And watch your back."

———

Leon dined with his mother, and it was good to begin the process of rebuilding a relationship that for more than a quarter of a century had consisted of nothing more than occasional letters from her and even less frequent replies from him. She had cried.

He had felt a whole host of emotions that he couldn't quite make sense of. This was the kind of time when he missed Eva more than ever: she would have helped him untangle the knots in his head and his heart. But for now the unresolved feelings made him restless. There was no point going to bed, he knew he wouldn't sleep. So when she returned to Shepheard's Hotel Leon headed for the bar, grabbed a stool and ordered a brandy.

"Kind of a pity to drink alone, don't you think?"

The voice was female, American. It took Leon a second to realize she was speaking to him. He turned on his stool and saw the woman the voice belonged to. She'd gone for the Jean Harlow look—platinum hair, Cupid's bow lips, big come-hither eyes and a black cocktail dress that left her creamy shoulders completely bare and her splendid breasts only marginally less so. The Blonde Bombshell look wasn't exactly subtle. But no man with red blood in his veins could deny that it was effective.

"Are you gonna say something, maybe invite me to sit down, or do I gotta stand here all night while you look at me like a starving man in a butcher's shop?"

Leon smiled. "I apologize. You took me by surprise. My mind was, ah . . . elsewhere."

"Well bring it back here then and ask me what I want to drink. Hell, I'll save you the trouble. Hey, Joe!" She waved the barman over. "You know what I want, right?"

"Certainly, Mrs. Kravitz. An Old Fashioned, made with Bourbon and not Scotch, easy on the water with an extra cherry on top."

"Attaboy."

"Good evening, Mrs. Kravitz," Leon said. "My name is Courtney . . . Leon Courtney."

"Good evening to you, Mr. Courtney. My name is Mildred, but I'd rather you called me Millie."

"How about Mr. Kravitz, what does he call you?"

"Oh, I don't know. "Sweetheart" if he's feeling friendly. "You dumb bitch" if he ain't."

"Will he be joining us for drinks?"

"God, I should hope not! Far as I know he's off in the desert somewhere, looking at pyramids and ancient mummies. Though he could be in a whorehouse right here in Cairo, for all I know."

"Is he an archaeologist?"

"Hymie Kravitz, an archaeologist? Ha! That's a good one. He's no kind of -ologist, trust me. Not unless you can get an -ology in ass-licking. No, my Hymie's a studio executive at Metro-Goldwyn-Mayer. His boss, Mr. Thalberg, he's Head of Production, has an idea to make a motion picture set in Ancient Egypt. You know, King Tut, Cleopatra, all that jazz. Maybe get Cecil B. DeMille to direct it. And he's thinking, maybe they should make it right here in Egypt. Y'know, so it feels real. Anyways, he sent Hymie over here to take a look. And, I mean, it was obvious within ten minutes you could never make a Hollywood picture in this dump. But Hymie can't just say that. He's got to give it his best shot, so he's off scouting locations and talking to folks that know about dead Egyptians."

"And he left you here in the hotel? Foolish man. Must be very boring for you."

"Tell me about it, Leon. I thought it would be romantic. Y'know, me and Hymie cruising down the Nile, riding camels, posing by the pyramids and whatnot. Instead, all I do is sit around this damn hotel. Hell, I can sit on my ass at home in Bel Air. What's the future in that? But, say, what about you . . . and Mrs. Courtney?"

"Well, I'm here on business. And I'm widowed. My wife died a few years ago."

"Oh gee, I'm sorry. Damn, I can be dumb sometimes."

"Don't worry about it. You meant no harm."

"Maybe I should have that on my tombstone: *Here lies Millie Kravitz. She meant no harm.*"

"Either that or: *She was a good girl, really.*"

Millie looked at Leon over the top of her Old Fashioned. "Well aren't you the sly dog, Leon Courtney?"

He knew for certain then that they were going to end up in bed. They each had another drink and then went up to his room. "I guess your business pays well," Millie said when she saw its size and luxury.

She stepped out of her teetering heels and barely came up to his shoulder, but he wasn't complaining. As petite as she was, every inch of Millie Kravitz was built to please. Her figure was a true hourglass, with a full, round, peachy backside that just begged to be caressed, grabbed or spanked, depending on the mood of the occasion, and a waist so slender she looked like she could be snapped in two if a man tried hard enough. When she slipped out of her dress, letting it slide down her body and land in folds at her feet, Leon saw that her breasts owed nothing to corsetry or the cut of her dress: they really were just as full and soft and inviting as advertised.

As he looked at her, Leon grinned, even as he felt himself swelling. "I see you're blonde all over."

She looked down at her platinum pudenda. "Yeah, the peroxide stung like a bitch, but the rug gotta match the drapes, right?"

Leon didn't say anything. He just grabbed her, pulled her to him and laid her down on the bed; she looked up at him as he mounted her. There were times when he could take it nice and slow, teasing and petting and gradually bringing a woman to that point of arousal and hunger at which the act of penetration had become an overwhelming need for them both. But this was not one of those nights. He just took her because that's what he wanted and he knew that she did too. This was not romance. It was sheer animal instinct and it was hard and fast and he knew from her screams and the clawing of her scarlet nails down his back and the desperation with which she arched her spine to let him further and further into her that she wanted it that way too. As her moaning and writhing and desperation reached its climax he felt the muscles far inside her fluttering around him and knew that she had come. He let himself go then, thinking of nothing but his own pleasure as he drove even faster, even harder, even deeper, the tension growing more unbearable until that final, explosive release came and he collapsed onto the bed beside her.

They both lay there, sweaty and exhausted, staring up at the ceiling.

"God, I sure needed that," Millie gasped.

"Me too."

She snuggled up to him with her head on his shoulder, her legs wrapped around his thigh and her fingers playing idly with the hair on his chest. Then her fingers fell still and her breathing changed and a moment later Leon realized that she was crying.

"What's the matter?" he asked.

"Oh I don't know," she sniffed. "It's just, that was great and I'm not kidding, I really needed it so bad. But I guess I need something else, you know? Something more."

"Yah, I know."

"And I ain't gonna get it from you, am I? Which is a real pity, cause you're a handsome bastard, and you're a lot more loaded than Hymie . . . in more ways than one."

"Thank you for the compliment."

"Believe me, honey, I'm thanking you. Anyway, I should stop going on. Who needs a broad getting weepy on them in the sack? But . . . you know what I mean, right?"

"Yes, Millie, I know exactly what you mean," Leon said.

They fell asleep in each other's arms. When Leon awoke, the sun was streaming into his room through a gap in the curtains and he was alone in the bed. There was a piece of hotel notepaper on the pillow. Leon rubbed the sleep from his eyes and picked it up. The note read,

———

Nice knowing you, Mr. C. Love M xxx

He looked for her in the hotel dining room when he went down for breakfast and in the bar before lunch, but there was no sign for her. As he got into the taxi that would take him to the station and the train to Suez, Leon knew that he would never see Millie Kravitz again. But he also knew that she was right. He needed something more.

In the late 1850s, having made his fortune from manufacturing steam engines, Gerhard von Meerbach's great-grandfather was invited to join a royal hunting party at Hohenschwangau Castle, the recently built country home of King Maximilian II of Bavaria. The castle stood atop a rocky crag on the site of a medieval fortress and was built in keeping with that style. It was ringed by high, crenelated walls, around whose battlements guests could stroll and look down upon the frigid, crystalline waters of the Alpsee, the lake that washed against the foot of the crag, or gaze up at soaring peaks, marching away in serried ranks as far as the eye could see. Within the walls stood a mighty, foursquare keep, that looked ready to withstand any invading army. The medieval theme continued within the keep, where chambers were decorated with murals showing kings and queens going about their fairy tale lives and the heavy wooden furniture was carved in a Gothic style. Yet the sense of antiquity was deceptive, for the castle had been built with every modern comfort and luxury that the mid-nineteenth century had to offer.

Old Man von Meerbach was so taken with the king's castle that he immediately decided to build one just like it, except that his was bigger and named after himself. Thus Schloss Meerbach had risen from an equally picturesque site on the shores of the Bodensee near Friedrichshafen, east of Munich. The *schloss* had been the most magnificent residence in the kingdom of Bavaria until Maximilian's successor, "Mad" King Ludwig II, embarked upon a program of castle building so

wildly extravagant and excessive that not even his richest subjects could possibly compete.

Gerhard von Meerbach was born at Schloss Meerbach. He
knew every single square centimeter of the huge building, from
the subterranean depths of the lowest cellars, which had been
designed to look like medieval dungeons and in which four
generations of von Meerbach fathers had threatened to lock
their misbehaving sons, right up to the servants' quarters
crammed in under the roofs. And the older he had grown, the
more Gerhard concluded that he really hated the place.

There was something oppressive about the monumental, over-
bearing scale of Schloss Meerbach. The main reception rooms
were paneled in wood stained almost black by years of smoke
from candles, gaslights and cigars, from which hung larger than
life-sized portraits of von Meerbachs, past and present. The men
had a very particular look about them. Much like the castle
that bore their name they were undeniably powerful and imposing, but their strength seemed deigned to intimidate and
bully those weaker than themselves, rather than protect them.

Gerhard's father, Count Otto, had chosen to be painted in his
flying gear, standing in front of a biplane powered by one of
the rotary engines that had propelled the Meerbach Motor Works
and the family's fortunes to even greater heights than before.
He was standing with his legs apart, his hands on hips and his
eyes boring into anyone who looked at the picture, as if daring
them to defy him. Gerhard had only been three when his father
died and had few memories of their time together, but he felt
that he must have been very frightened of him, for he could
not look at that hard, obdurate face beneath the bristle of short-
cropped ginger hair without feeling a tremor of anxiety. That,
not the pain of losing a father's love, was what he had been
left with.

Gerhard himself was of a very different physical type, inherited
from his mother's side of the family. Though by no means
weak-looking, he was much slimmer in build: lithe rather than

thickset and with more conventionally handsome, regular facial features. His eyes were a soft marble gray but had the unusual property (which Gerhard had discovered from the way that the women he seduced gazed at them) of appearing to change color depending on the light around them, so that they carried a hint of blue, or even hazel, depending on the circumstances. His tastes, too, were far removed from the Gothic grandeur of Schloss Meerbach. He was a child of his times, training to be an architect in the Modernist style, in which walls were white if they existed at all, light flooded in through the biggest possible windows, and form was reduced to pure, clean, geometric simplicity.

Still, even Gerhard had to admit that there were times when the sheer grandeur of the castle could make it a splendid backdrop for the family to entertain their guests. Tonight for example was the moment at which Konrad von Meerbach had shown himself to be a man whose influence straddled the old Germany and the new. He was entitled, as the eldest son of an aristocratic family, to call himself *Graf* or Count von Meerbach, yet chose not to, declaring such a badge of inherited privilege unbefitting to his National Socialist principles. Tonight he had hosted a grand dinner at which the guests were taken from the finest old aristocratic families of Bavaria, the wealthiest industrialists of the region and their new Nazi masters, who were now busily constructing the foundations of the Thousand Year Reich. The guest of honor was *SS-Gruppenführer* Reinhard Heydrich himself, the newly appointed commander of both the Gestapo, the national secret police and the SD, or *Sicherheitsdienst,* the Nazi Party's own intelligence agency.

Heydrich's arrival at the party reminded Gerhard of the effect Izzy Solomons's Blue Max had created a dozen years earlier. In this case the magnetism was provided not by a decoration for valor, but by the black dress-uniform Heydrich was wearing, or more specifically, its jacket. This was short, cut like a tailcoat from which the tails had been removed so that it stopped at the waist. The only color came from the slash of lipstick red on Heydrich's left arm, where he wore a swastika armband. There were silver braid epaulettes on his shoulders, denoting his rank, which was also indicated by a collar patch on which were embroidered the three silver oak leaves of a *Gruppenführer*. On the right side of his chest a silver death's head grinned at the world around it in horribly macabre good humor.

Gerhard was very far from being a Nazi supporter, but with his trained eye he could not deny the evil genius with which everything about the Party's visual image, from the vast scale of the Nuremberg Rallies, with the Cathedral of Light formed by the searchlight beams rising like giant columns into the night sky above the Zeppelin Field, to the piercing gaze of that little silver death's head, was designed to underline the idea of absolute, inevitable dominion over the world. And Heydrich, the prodigy of the Nazi Party, could carry it off with an élan that was entirely missing from most of the Nazi leaders.

Gerhard had always thought of Hitler, Himmler, Goebbels and their ilk as laughably far removed from the master race of which they spoke so avidly. Heydrich, however, was different. He was a tall, slim, elegant man, as glamorous as a film star, with blond hair brushed back from his temples, narrowed, quizzical eyes, a long, fine-boned but slightly hooked nose and surprisingly full, sensuous lips. He came from an artistic family—his father was a modestly successful opera singer and composer—and he possessed almost film-star-like charisma. To his discomfort, it struck Gerhard that had he met Heydrich in other circumstances he might have found him very likeable. In conversation, he did not rant, or pound the table, or berate any of the other men and women around it. He laughed, he gave way graciously to let others have their say, and he was courteous to a fault to the women on either side of him. It was only when one listened closely to what this handsome devil with his honeyed voice was saying that one began to get a glimpse of the cold, calculating malice that lurked, like a viper in a flowerbed, behind that delightful façade.

When dinner was over, Gerhard had planned to slip away to his room. Though he had been brought up to be able to make polite conversation to anyone at any time, he had very little in common with anyone else in attendance that evening and wanted to write a letter to a girlfriend in Berlin, describing his impressions of the night while they were still fresh in his mind. But as he was discreetly making his way to the door of the large drawing room to which the guests had all retired, he felt a tap on his shoulder.

It was his older brother Konrad, proudly wearing his *SS-Sturmbannführer*'s uniform: a rank equivalent to an army major. "Come with me, please," he said, with chilly politeness, as if talking to a suspect apprehended on the street, rather than a member of his own family.

"Thanks, but I'm just going up to bed," Gerhard replied, affecting not to hear the menace in Konrad's voice.

"You misunderstand me. That was not an invitation. That was an order. Come with me. Now."

Members of the von Meerbach family did not make scenes in front of their guests. So Gerhard went with Konrad, smiling at a couple of other guests who caught his eye as they walked out of the drawing room and across the marble-flagged great hall of the castle to an oak door, studded with black nails on the far side. This was the door to Konrad's study, but to Gerhard's surprise he knocked and waited for a call of "Enter!" from within.

Gerhard followed his brother into the study. Directly opposite the door, sitting behind the desk that had for more than a hundred years belonged to the head of the Meerbach family, was a now familiar, golden-haired figure. He stood and held out a hand.

"Ah, Herr von Meerbach, thank you for joining us. I don't believe that we have been properly introduced. My name is Reinhard Heydrich. Won't you please sit down?"

Gerhard shook the proffered hand and took one of two wooden chairs arranged opposite the desk. His brother sat in the other.

Doing his best to maintain his composure in the face of a summons to the most powerful secret policeman in Germany, Gerhard asked, "May I ask to what I owe the pleasure of meeting you, *Herr Gruppenführer?*"

Heydrich smiled as if this were just a casual social encounter. "Oh, we can come to that in a moment," he said. "But first, tell me a little about yourself. You are twenty-three years old, is that correct?"

"Yes." Gerhard noticed that a pale gray cardboard file, containing a number of sheets of typed paper, was open on the desk in front of Heydrich. *My God, is that my file?* he thought. *Is that what Germany is coming to?*

"And you are studying architecture in Berlin, no?"

"That's right. I am a student in the College of Architecture at the Berlin University for the Arts."

"And before that you spent three years at the Bauhaus School, formerly known as the Great Ducal Saxon Art School, in Dessau."

"Yes."

"May I ask what attracted you to the Bauhaus?"

"Certainly. I was a great admirer of its first director, Walter Gropius, and of the Modernist principles that he advanced. By the time I arrived, however, his place had been taken by Ludwig Mies van der Rohe. He was in my view an even greater architect. Aside from that, some of the greatest artistic minds of our time have been teachers at the Bauhaus. For anyone of my generation who is interested in the arts it was a natural choice to make."

"By "greatest minds" I take it you refer to men such as Paul Klee, Wassily Kandinsky and László Moholy-Nagy?"

"That's right."

"I take it you are aware that we now consider their work to be degenerate trash?"

"I am aware of that. Of course, that particular critical analysis had not been made at the time I applied for admission to the Bauhaus."

Heydrich's eyes bored into Gerhard, as if deciding whether the latter's words had been unacceptably mocking, then he wrote a brief note on the file.

"This Modernist trash has strong Semitic influences, I am sure you would agree," Heydrich remarked, putting down his pen.

Gerhard stood his ground. "With respect, *Herr Gruppenführer*, it is correct to say that Moholy-Nagy is of Jewish descent, but the other men you have mentioned were not. Indeed, there were men on the faculty who held opinions on the Jews that you might find sympathetic. Certainly there were very few, if any Jewish students at the Bauhaus during my time there."

Heydrich frowned, looking uncertain for once. Gerhard did his best not to smile. *You didn't know that, did you? Now what are you going to say?*

Heydrich cleared his throat, glanced at the file. "You were still enrolled at the Bauhaus when it moved to Berlin . . ."

"That is correct."

"Where it was closed on political grounds."

"Strictly speaking, Mies closed the school voluntarily, having received permission to continue."

"Don't try to be clever with me, Herr von Meerbach. The Gestapo closed the school. Maria Ludwig Michael Mies, alias Mies van der Rohe, known to close associates as Mies: born 27 March 1886 in Aachen, Prussia . . ." Heydrich paused for a beat to let Gerhard appreciate the depth of his knowledge and what that implied, " . . . appealed to my predecessor in Berlin and was given a reprieve. He then understood that it was not in fact wise for him to continue. He is currently unable to find work in this country. People do not want this "Modernist" architecture you value so highly, Herr von Meerbach. You should bear that in mind. But, to return to our discussion: Gestapo agents in Berlin were rightly concerned that the Bauhaus was a nest of communist subversion that actively promoted anti-German ideas and therefore could not be tolerated by the Reich. Tell me, are you a communist?"

Gerhard could not help himself. He burst out laughing. "Not you too! As I told your colleague, my brother, I am not a communist. Look at me, *Herr Gruppenführer*. Here I am, in my family's castle dressed for dinner in my white tie and tails. Do I seem like a communist to you?"

"This is not a laughing matter, and I strongly advise you not to treat it as such. Answer my question. Are you a communist?"

"No, I am not, nor have I ever been a communist, nor voted for the Communist Party. Yes, there were plenty of students at the Bauhaus who had communist sympathies, as there were at every other university in the land. But I was not one of them, nor were they allowed to form an organization within the Bauhaus. And if you must know, I will tell you what I actually believe, which is that a modern form of architecture, based on the latest principles of engineering, science and manufacturing, is in keeping both with my own family's industrial heritage and with the thoroughly German principles of craft and quality as represented by the German Association of Craftsmen, of which I am a member. I want to tear down the slums of our industrial cities and produce clean, airy, healthy homes for ordinary, hard-working German families to live in. What the hell is communist about that?"

As the impassioned question hung in the air, Heydrich leaned back in his chair and his cold, skeptical eyes examined Gerhard like a butterfly collector looking at a specimen pinned to a board. "Do you have any idea how privileged and how arrogant you sound?" he asked in a calm, untroubled voice that was far more unnerving than any furious shouting would have been. "The very fact that you, a mere student, feel free to address me of all people in this way, in front of your brother, without considering the very grave risk you are running, or the embarrassment and shame you are bringing upon your family . . .

Trust me, Herr von Meerbach, no ordinary German would be so foolish as to speak as you have done."

"I apologize if I have caused offence, *Herr Gruppenführer*," Gerhard said, respectfully, but still looking Heydrich in the eye. "That was not my intention. I was merely seeking to establish the truth, which is that I am not a communist."

"You are, however, a Jew-lover."

The words hit Gerhard like a blow from a Brownshirt's truncheon. "I'm . . . I'm sorry . . . ?" he stammered. "What do you mean?"

"Exactly what I say. Some five weeks ago, on the morning of 7 March—my birthday, as it happens—you drove to the outskirts of Munich from where you caught a tram to Laimer Platz. From there you walked down Fürstenrieder Strasse, making a series of hopelessly amateur attempts to check whether you were being followed. You were, of course, even if you clearly did not know it. You paused to accept an item of forbidden communist literature . . ."

"I did not accept it!" Gerhard protested. "The man shoved it into my hand."

"And you looked at it with considerable interest for one who says that he does not have communist sympathies before throwing it away. You then proceeded to your destination, the apartment where your family's former lawyer—the Jew Solomons —now lives. Do you deny that this is the case?"

"You know that I can't deny it. That is what happened. And excuse me if I am being arrogant again, but may I ask, is it a crime to speak to someone who gave loyal service both to my family, and to our country, just because he is a Jew?"

"No," Heydrich admitted. He pondered a moment and then added, "Thank you. You have made me realize that we must tighten the laws regarding all forms of association between Aryans and Jews. But even now, a case could be made against you for providing the financial means to allow a Jew to leave Germany without permission."

"What do you mean?"

"Oh, come now. You gave Solomons five thousand marks. It was your preposterous attempt to persuade your trustees that you needed money to buy a smart car—as if a student, even one from your family, would drive around in a Mercedes grand tourer—that alerted your brother to what you were up to. He very properly informed me and a watch was placed on you."

Gerhard turned, aghast, to look at Konrad. "You betrayed me? Your own brother? How could you?"

"Because he is a patriot and a good Nazi," Heydrich said before Konrad could answer. "And perhaps because he is a good brother and hopes to save you before it is too late."

"Save me from what? How can it possibly be a crime to talk to a man who was awarded the Blue Max for his courage at Verdun? Isidore Solomons was a colonel, personally commended by Crown Prince Wilhelm himself. To me, he is the very best kind of German."

"He's a filthy Yid, a greedy, treacherous, conspiring rat, like all the rest of his race," sneered Konrad.

"How can you say that?" Gerhard asked, his voice rising in appalled incomprehension. "He was our friend. We went to his family's house. We stood there, you and I, while he told us about the history of the *Pour le Mérite*, our eyes popping out of our heads when he took it out of the case and showed it to us. You thought he was a hero. You did! How can you deny it?"

"I was a child. Now that I am an adult, I have learned the truth about the Jews. They are nothing but sub-human scum. All of them."

Heydrich held up a hand in admonition. "No, *Sturmbannführer*, your brother has a point. We must be aware of the existence of what one might call "the good Jew." People may know such a person—their doctor, for example, or a kindly woman who mends their clothes, or even, as in this case, a war hero. They will think to themselves, "Well, Herr Levy or Frau Goldschmidt isn't such a bad sort. They can't be as bad as these Nazis say." It is for us to educate them so that they understand that these good apples are the exceptions and that all the rest are rotten. And since it is not possible to sort out the minuscule number of good from the vast numbers of bad, then they must all be dealt with in the same way. But to get back to this particular Jew, Isidore Solomons and his family. Do you happen to know where they are now, Herr von Meerbach?"

"I assume that they are still living at the same apartment on Fürstenrieder Strasse."

Heydrich sighed. "Really? You think Solomons and his spawn are still sitting there in that disgusting slum block—the very kind that you wish to tear down and replace with shiny Modernist houses—when he has five thousand Reichsmarks sitting in his wallet, along with all the gold and diamonds you can bet he has hidden away? No. Try again."

"He did not look to me like a man who had diamonds hidden away anywhere. As you say, why would he be living like that if he had?"

"Because, Herr von Meerbach, Solomons is a Jew. And Jews have learned that their greed and usury and vile treachery inevitably bring down the justifiable anger of the decent people amongst whom they live. So they always—but always—have the means to run away, like the rats they are. And diamonds— so small, so light, but so very valuable—are the perfect form of portable wealth. So, tell me, please: where is Solomons now?"

"I don't know. I promise you, *Herr Gruppenführer*, on my life I do not know."

Gerhard's heart was beating hard now, his body flooding with adrenaline as it responded to the threat Heydrich posed and the fear he induced. He felt the sweat starting to prickle under his arms. "I'm telling the truth. I swear it!" he added, unable to keep the note of desperation from his voice.

"What do you think, *Sturmbannführer*? Is the suspect telling the truth?"

"I think he's a filthy liar," said Konrad as the word "suspect" echoed around Gerhard's brain.

Gerhard looked at his older brother and saw the hate etched into his twisted features. The two of them had never got on particularly well. They were very different characters. But he had never had the faintest idea that such bitter hostility had been burning away inside Konrad's heart.

"I am not lying," he repeated, trying not to scream the words in frustration. "I do not know where the Solomons family has gone, or even if they have gone anywhere at all. I gave him some money because I believed he deserved some kind of settlement from our family after all he had done for us. I gave him as much as I could manage, though it was far less than he deserved. I did not ask him what he planned to do with it and he did not tell me."

Heydrich said nothing. He let Gerhard sit there and watched as he wiped a hand across his brow to rid himself of the beads of sweat collecting there. Finally he said, "Actually I believe you. Solomons is too good a lawyer to tell you anything that might incriminate you or, more importantly from his perspective, himself. I am satisfied that you do not know where the Jew has gone. Luckily, however, I do. He and his family crossed the border into Switzerland—without proper papers, naturally— some three weeks ago and are now resident in Zürich, where he has found employment in a the legal firm of Grünspan and Aaronsohn—fellow Jews, of course. I assume he had already arranged the position there before he left, indeed before he took your money. Hmm . . . I wonder if he will pay it back?"

"I would not ask him to."

"Just as well, since that would be against his religion."

Konrad snickered sycophantically at his boss's wit as Heydrich went on, "The Swiss authorities have asked us whether we wish them to deport the Solomons and we have decided, on balance, that this will not be necessary. Your protestations about Solomons's military record might well be echoed in the press, particularly the foreign correspondents. A man who fights nobly for his country is a hero in any language, even if he was once an enemy. If anything were to happen to Solomons, it would be a distraction for us to have to explain that away. So he is better off in Switzerland where he will keep a low profile, I am sure, for he knows that we could reach out and deal with him at any time, should he even think of causing trouble.

"You, however, have caused trouble, and you are right here. Let me be frank, Herr von Meerbach, the Reich rewards loyal citizens, but punishes dissenters and deviants mercilessly. Two years ago, my commander *Reichsführer-SS* Heinrich Himmler opened a camp near the town of Dachau, just outside Munich. Do you know the place?"

"I know the town of Dachau. I was not aware of any camp there."

"No? Well, let me tell you about it. This camp is intended for political and social undesirables: communists, criminals, sexual deviants, intellectuals . . . Jew-lovers. People, in short, who have no place in a healthy Aryan society. The regime there is hard. Inmates are completely isolated from the outside world: no visits, no letters in or out, no newspapers or radio broadcasts, nothing that in any way connects inmates to the society they have themselves rejected. There is forced labor, every day. There are no weekends or holidays in Dachau. The rations provide the absolute bare minimum required for survival, so there are no fat inmates at Dachau, either. Discipline is absolute and punishments brutal. A man who commits the most minor infraction has his wrists bound behind his back and then attached to a hook, three meters above the ground. He then hangs there, in agony, as his arms are slowly torn from their sockets. For more serious offences, execution is carried out instantly, without either trial or any form of appeal."

Heydrich paused. "You look pale, Herr von Meerbach. Could you be so good as to get your brother a glass of water, please, *Herr Sturmbannführer*? I believe he needs it."

It took Konrad a little under three minutes to leave the study, go to the drawing room, find one of the crystal jugs filled with iced water, pour a glass and return to Heydrich and Gerhard. In that time Heydrich did not speak. He sat quite motionless and simply looked at Gerhard with reptilian coldness, letting the description of Dachau sink into his mind and fire his imagination with vivid images of unspeakable suffering.

Konrad placed the glass in front of his brother and Gerhard downed it in one.

"Better?" Heydrich asked. "Now, listen very carefully to me Gerhard von Meerbach, for your life and your family's reputation depend upon it. I could have you arrested this instant and sent directly to Dachau. You will be sleeping there tonight and you will never set foot outside its fence, if I say so. Do you understand?"

"Yes." It was just a single syllable, but Gerhard found he could barely force it out of his mouth, so tightly was his throat constricted.

"However, you share one quality, apart from treachery with Isidore Solomons, which is to say, you are a potential embarrassment. The Meerbach Motor Works is a vital part of our industrial armory. Furthermore, your brother's commitment to Nazi ideals is a very clear sign to other members of the social and commercial elite that their class is as much a part of the new order in Germany as anyone else, and that as much loyalty is expected from them as it is from those whom they regard as their inferiors. It is very tempting indeed to punish you, and do so publicly, in such a way as to make it clear to all classes of the population that no one is above the law of the Reich and no one can escape its justice and its retribution. As you can imagine, that would be a message greatly welcomed by the lower orders in society. But it is an unfortunate fact of life that the Reich needs the great industrial families as much as they need us, and while it may be necessary to secure their cooperation by fear, it is preferable to have them as allies, and even—as in your brother's case—enthusiastic supporters. Again, there is part of me that relishes the idea of making an example of the two of you as a sort of Cain and Abel of the Reich: the good, noble brother versus the wicked betrayer of his family's honor. Even now . . ."

Heydrich sighed, "*Ach*, what a story Goebbels would make of that! But you are lucky. Your fate hung in the balance as I arrived here. But then I met your mother. Such a charming lady, so proud of both her sons, but widowed so young. "This woman has already lost a husband," I said to myself. "Can I now deprive her of a son?" So, in the end, I decided upon a different solution to the problem. Would you like to know what that is?"

"Yes . . . yes please," Gerhard was shocked to realize that he was almost begging.

"Very well, then, this is it. You, Gerhard von Meerbach, will become a model citizen of the Reich. You may continue your architectural studies, but not at the Berlin University of the Arts. Instead I will apprentice you to Albert Speer, First Architect of the Reich. You will learn about the true, Nazi principles of architecture, as laid down by the Führer himself, as you work on buildings designed to glorify the Reich. In your spare time, you will busy yourself with an activity that is perfectly suited to your family's proud history of providing engines for our nation's warplanes."

"You want me to work in our factory?" Gerhard asked.

Heydrich laughed. "Well, if you insist . . . But no, I had something else in mind. As you doubtless know, Article 198 of the Treaty of Versailles prohibits Germany from having an air force. This is an absurd limitation on our right to self-defense and one of many good reasons why the Führer has totally repudiated the Treaty in its entirety. As a result we are now training pilots as reservists for the Luftwaffe, so that when the time comes to show the world the true strength of the Third Reich there will be enough men to provide us with absolute command of the air.

"You will therefore become one of these reservists. You will spend weekends, and a prolonged period every summer training to be a pilot. You will wear your Luftwaffe uniform with pride. At no time, whether at work, or in training, or when you are with your family and friends, will you deviate by so much as a millimeter from the approved Party line. You will give the Nazi salute, declaim, "Heil Hitler!" and mean it. Should the topic of the Jews arise in conversation, you will let no man outdo you in your condemnation of their race and its evil, scheming ways. Should the discussion turn to the arts, you will denounce the decadence of abstract daubs that look like nothing more than something a monkey could produce by flinging paint at a canvas."

"You want my soul," Gerhard said.

"Yes," Heydrich replied. "I want your soul, and should you be filled by some misguided spirit of principle or nobility and decide that you would rather sacrifice yourself than give in to me, let me add this. If you are denounced as a political dissenter and Jew-lover, I will not stop there. All your friends, your fellow students, the women you have loved—everyone who has ever had anything to do with you will find their lives examined in every detail by the Gestapo. They will be arrested and questioned. Their property will be searched. And if my men find anything, no matter how trivial, that suggests that they are undesirable, they will join you at Dachau. So you will not just be condemning yourself. You will condemn them too. So, do you accept my conditions?"

"What choice do I have?"

"None. I want your solemn agreement to commit yourself wholeheartedly to the Nazi cause, given to me and witnessed by your brother. Now."

Gerhard swallowed hard. He longed to spit in Heydrich's face, to tell him where he could shove his demands and to hell with the consequences. He didn't care what Dachau was like. Better to suffer there and be true to oneself, than to live a lie in comfort. But he could not betray his friends. He could not condemn them to the camps.

"I will," Gerhard said, and it felt like handing his soul to the devil himself.

"Thank you," said Heydrich. "That wasn't so hard, now, was it?"

He stood up straight, as did Konrad, then looked hard at Gerhard.

Gerhard stood too.

Heydrich flung out his right arm in front of him and shouted, "Heil Hitler!"

"Heil Hitler!" echoed Konrad.

Silence fell for a second. Then a third arm rose into the air and was held out in the Nazi salute.

"Heil Hitler!" cried Gerhard von Meerbach.

In May 1934, Francis Courtney set off for England, taking a ship from Alexandria to Piraeus, the port of Athens, and then travelling across the Continent by train to London. His older brother, he knew, increasingly chose to travel by air, but he made it very plain to the other members of the family that he disapproved of such extravagance. "It's all very well for Leon to throw money around. He stole our shares from us, he can afford it. But I am quite content to travel in a more modest style, as befits an English gentleman."

"I wasn't aware that any of us were either English or gentlemanly," Dorian had replied. "But if that's how you want to get to Blighty, Frank, who am I to tell you otherwise?"

Frank's principal reason for making the journey was to see his surgeon, Dr. Harold Gillies. He had been suffering minor problems with his skin graft: a small patch appeared to have died off, leaving a sore, small suppurating area that had to be covered at all times by a dressing. But that was not the only reason Frank wanted to be in London. There was another man he wanted to see: Oswald Mosley, leader of the British Union of Fascists, or the Blackshirts as they liked to call themselves.

His was a name that was increasingly heard among the men

who discussed politics at the Cairo Sporting Club, where Frank liked to play the occasional round of golf, demanding a special handicap as he did so, to allow for his war wounds. "Of course the man's an absolute bounder," one of Frank's cronies, a liquor importer called Desmond "Piggy' Peters, declared one morning as they were walking to the first tee. "I'm reliably assured that he married the Curzon girl, Cynthia I believe she's called, for her money and is now having it off on the side with her sister and her stepmother."

"Bloody hell," said the third member of the game, a cotton trader by the name of Hatton. "You have to admire the nerve of the man."

"And the stamina," said Frank.

When the men's laughter had abated, Piggy Peters continued, "But Mosley's no fool. Been a Member of Parliament for the Tories and the Socialists and would have made a better Prime Minister than any man in either party, so I'm told. But he couldn't be doing with the old way, d'you see? Times are too serious, more radical measures required, that's his assessment of the situation, and who's to argue with that, eh?"

"No one with any brains," Frank agreed. "It's patently obvious the whole bloody world's going to the dogs. Capitalism's on its uppers. The Reds just want to control the whole world. And the bloody Jews don't care who wins because they control the banks and the commies, both."

"The Hebrew only thinks about two things, himself and his money, not necessarily in that order," Hatton observed, to harrumphs of approval.

"It's not just that. Look around the colonies, the darkies are as bad as the Jews. That Gandhi fellow in India wanting independence, ungrateful little man, after all we've done for that country."

"Well, that's Mosley's point, as I understand it," Piggy said. "He thinks it's time we put ourselves first, looked after number one, as it were. He says there's a third way that's not capitalism and not communism, but fascism. And when you look at what that Hitler chappie's doing in Germany, you can't argue, I don't think."

"God knows he's a ridiculous-looking man and what was he in the war, just a corporal, wasn't it?"

"So was Napoleon and he didn't do so badly," Hatton pointed out.

"But he's putting Germany back on its feet," Frank went on. "Damned impressive, I call it. He's given the people back their self-respect."

"Exactly! And that's what Oswald Mosley is going to do for the British, you mark my words," said Piggy Peters.

"I'm going home in a few weeks' time, have this damn skin graft attended to. I think I might just make it my business to find out a bit about this Mosley fellow."

"I think I may be able to help you there, Frank. Couple of chaps I do business with in London are quite prominent supporters of the Blackshirt movement, absolutely hugger-mugger with Mosley himself. Let me know when you're going and I'll wangle you an introduction to the great man."

* * *

Gillies repaired the skin graft and Frank spent two weeks in a sanatorium by the sea at Eastbourne while the operation healed. On the morning of 7 June, feeling better than he had done in months, he took the train to London, checked into a respectable but modest hotel, and then set off for the Olympia exhibition hall on the Hammersmith Road in West London, where Mosley was holding a rally of his supporters.

Twelve thousand fascist sympathizers were due to attend the event. But ranged against them were thousands of protesters who had come to attend a demonstration organized by the London District Committee of the Communist Party. A press release had been sent out to all London's newspapers, the newsreel-makers and the British Broadcasting Corporation declaring that "the workers in the capital city will resist with all means the fascist menace."

That very morning the *Daily Worker*, a Communist mouth-piece, had warned the Blackshirts that "the workers' counter-action will cause them to tremble."

For their part the Blackshirts made it perfectly clear that they had no intention of canceling the event or backing down in any way. Left and right were going to war, and neither much minded who got in the way.

———

Frank emerged from Olympia station, just yards from the hall, to find that the short journey to the main entrance had become a gauntlet as anyone who wanted to watch Mosley speak had to run as fast they could past an angry mob of protesters waving anti-Mosley placards and red banners bear-ing the yellow hammer and sickle of the Soviet Union. They were faced by hard-faced fascists, dressed in black from head to toe, and only too ready to trade a punch to the head or a kick to the guts for every word of abuse shouted at them by a protester. Between the two forces a thin blue line of policemen, a few of them mounted on horseback, tried to maintain a safe passage for civilians caught in the furor.

The deafening noise, the press of bodies and the overwhelm-ing impression of chaos that could at any moment tip into outright anarchy only served to fire Frank with more enthusi-asm for Mosley's cause. Any man who could provoke such hatred from people Frank despised must be doing something right. And the way the mob was behaving merely underlined the desperate need for order and discipline to be imposed upon the people by a strong man for their own good, and damn democracy and the people's rights. Those were old ideas, failed ideas. The times required something new.

As he walked at a steady pace, refusing to be driven into a run by the mob, his temper rising with every pace he took, Frank suddenly felt something wet strike the left side of his face. He put a hand up to his cheek, examined what it found, saw a warm, bubbly blob of saliva and realized he'd been spat on.

Outraged at the insult, Frank turned to his left and saw a young woman just a few feet away. She was scruffily dressed, standing with a group of men, all with their shirts undone at the neck, not a hat between them. And they were all laughing at him. The girl looked right at him and mimicked the act of spitting in his direction. Then she laughed again.

It was more than he could stand. He took a couple of swift paces toward the group, propelling himself forward with his walking stick, its steel tip striking sparks as it hit the paving stones. "Don't fall over, Dad!" one of the men shouted at him. Frank's face was contorted in a furious snarl as he raised his stick and lashed out at his tormentors. He hit the girl flush in the face. She screamed and bent double, blood seeping between her fingers as she pressed her hands to her head. Her companions dashed toward Frank. He flailed at them with his stick but they kept coming and one landed a punch on Frank's shoulder that knocked him back. Still they kept coming, as possessed with blind anger as he had been, bent on exacting revenge. Suddenly, Frank felt desperately afraid. He had provoked these hooligans and now they wanted their revenge. He lashed out again, but someone caught his stick in mid-swing and ripped it from his grasp. Desperately he cowered like a boxer caught on the ropes, hunching his shoulders, holding his hands up by his head to try and protect himself. He was waiting for the first punch to land when he felt a rough hand grabbing his shoulder and pulling him back out of the way. Frank fell backward onto the pavement. He propped himself up on his elbows to see a knot of Blackshirts piling into the demonstrators, laying into them with practised, brutal efficiency. Frank scrabbled for his hat, which was lying on the ground beside him and put it back on. Then he rose rather shakily to his feet. The Blackshirts had put the opponents to flight. One of them emerged from the mêlée holding Frank's stick.

"Does this belong to you, sir?" he asked. His accent was lower-class, but efficient and respectful, Frank thought, like a sergeant speaking to an officer.

"Yes, yes it is, thank you."

"Rotten, isn't it, the way them commie scum assault decent gentlemen like yourself? Don't you worry, sir, we don't stand for it."

"Well said, young man," said Frank and he touched the brim of his hat in salute as he went on his way. Inside the hall there was more fighting, for some demonstrators had managed to get hold of tickets and infiltrate the event itself. The start time was delayed for thirty minutes, then forty-five and almost an hour had passed by the time the house light suddenly dimmed. A great roar went up as mighty spotlights cut through air made heavy by the countless cigarettes smoked by the audience as they had waited for this moment. The bright white beams picked out the blazing red banners of the British Union of Fascists, each bearing the party symbol of a white lightning bolt inside a blue circle. The banners were being carried two abreast by twenty Blackshirts marching down the aisle that ran down the center of the auditorium, past thousands of supporters all holding out their arms in the fascist salute. At the head of the party marched another Blackshirt, the commander of their unit.

A chant went up, thousands of voices shouting, "M-O-S-L-E-Y! Mosley, Mosley, Mosley!" And then the beams swept past the banners and found the man marching behind them, the man who had filled the hall and the streets outside: Oswald Mosley himself.

Everything about his appearance was designed to create an impression of strength and virility. Mosley was thirty-seven, the absolute prime of a man's life, tall and straight-backed. He wore black trousers held by a broad black leather belt. A close-fitting black polo-neck jumper covered his strapping chest and he held his head high, more like a gladiator entering the arena than a politician about to make a speech. His hair and mustache were as black as his clothes. This was Britain's Hitler.

Frank found himself caught up in the hysteria, saluting, applauding, chanting as Mosley reached the front of the crowd and mounted the steps to the platform from which he would speak. Only now did Frank notice that Mosley had a slight limp, but somehow that discovery did nothing to detract from his conviction that this was the strongman the country and the Empire so desperately needed.

The standard bearers took up their positions on either side of the platform, all standing to attention.

"Color-party, present arms!" shouted the Blackshirt commander, as if they were Guards at the Trooping of the Color.

At once, the men lowered their flagpoles to the diagonal, pointing out at the crowd. A few voices of dissent could be heard, scattered around the huge arena. Mosley and his Blackshirts ignored them.

"Color-party, stand easy!" the commander cried, and as one the men stood legs slightly apart. Mosley remained silent, motionless, waiting for his people to calm themselves.

The hubbub ebbed away and the thousands who had been on their feet took their places in their seats. Then Mosley began. "Thousands of our fellow countrymen and women have come to hear our case and thousands have joined the fascist ranks," he said, in a voice that was unmistakably upper-class, without being absurdly highfalutin". He had the rich, sonorous tone and perfect diction of a great Shakespearian actor, so that the words he said were imbued with significance and gravitas. And the very sound of his voice gave him an air of authority, one that immediately impressed itself upon a crowd raised since birth to respect their betters and obey their leaders.

"This movement is something new in the political life of this country, something that goes further and deeper than any other movement this land has ever known," Mosley went on and

Frank Courtney, sitting halfway back on the floor of the Olympia hall, felt special because he was part of that movement, a cog in the machine that was going to transform the Empire.

Then the spell was broken as a couple of protesters leaped to their feet and shook their fists at the stage as they shouted at Mosley.

He gave an easy, confident, reassuring smile as black-shirted stewards found the hecklers and dragged them from their seats. "Take no notice of these small interruptions," Mosley said. "They don't worry me and they needn't worry you."

The crowd roared in approval, feeling that they had been as defiant as their leader. Nothing would stop him stating his case, or prevent them hearing it.

"This meeting is symbolic of the advance of the Blackshirt cause in the first twenty months of its existence," Mosley continued. "In that time, fascism in Great Britain has advanced more rapidly than in any other country in the world. Not because our people had to adopt fascism. Not under the lash of economic necessity, as in other lands, but because they desire a new creed and a new order in our land."

The speech continued for an hour as Mosley spoke, entirely without notes, yet without stumbling or repeating himself or at any moment losing the power and flow of his argument. Frank was overwhelmed. He felt as though he had been waiting his whole life to hear the words that had just been laid before him. They made sense of so much. They addressed his bitter sense of grievance and injustice and promised a world in which he could be one of the winners, one of the new masters. Piggy Peters had been as good as his word and spoken to his friends in the Mosley camp, who had ensured that Frank's name was added to the list of guests at a small reception, held backstage after the event was over. His sense of privilege was raised even higher as he saw the envious glances being cast in his direction as the Blackshirts guarding the way to the reception parted to let him through.

Frank found Piggy's contact and introduced himself. "Mr. Courtney, how splendid of you to come all the way from Egypt, just for us, what? Look, Oswald will be dashed keen to meet you. He's very keen on spreading the word out to the colonies and anyone who can lend a hand is greatly appreciated."

A few minutes later, Frank found himself in the presence of the great man himself. Mosley was as impressive close up as he had been when performing to his thousands of followers. His grand oratory gave way to overwhelming charm. He focused all his attention on Frank, noticed his stick, inquired how he had come by his injury and said, "Good man. You served our country with honor, and I salute you. I have a bit of a bad leg myself, as you may have notice. I picked it up in '16 when I was with the Royal Flying Corps. I wish I could say I came by my wounds in honorable combat, but the truth is I crashed my plane while I was trying to impress my mother and sister with my prowess as a pilot. Damn foolish, don't you agree?"

Before Frank could answer Mosley went on, "Now, I hear you're quite the coming man in Cairo. Let me assure you that I would appreciate any help you could give the cause out there. We have to bring the Empire with us if we are to succeed. Excuse me one moment . . ."

Mosley turned away for a second and waved toward the most beautiful woman Frank had ever seen in his life. She was as slender and graceful as Botticelli's Venus, brought to life in modern dress. Her hair was a dark honey blonde and her clear, pale blue eyes were framed by eyebrows shaped like perfectly drawn arches. Her nose was straight, fine and very slightly tilted upward, her scarlet lips were disdainfully sensual and her chin, fractionally too strong to be conventionally pretty, merely added to the sense that she was in every possible way a thoroughly superior being.

"Darling, do come and meet Mr. Courtney," Mosley said. "He's going to do wonderful things for us in Egypt. Mr. Courtney, may I introduce Mrs. Diana Guinness."

"I'm so pleased to meet you," said this vision of female love-liness. "Anyone who fights for our cause will always be a friend of mine."

"I do assure you, Mrs. Guinness, that you can absolutely count on me," said Frank.

She clasped his hand, looked deep into his eyes and said, "Thank you so much, Mr. Courtney."

A moment later, Mosley and his mistress had disappeared without a backward glance. Their work was done. Frank Courtney was utterly won over to the cause of British fascism.

———

On a fine afternoon in high summer Gerhard von Meerbach clambered into the tiny open cockpit of the Grunau Baby glider that sat on the runway of the private airfield that formed part of the Meerbach Motor Works complex. He bent his head, making sure not to hit it on the raised wing that swept in a single pure and uninterrupted sweep of fabric and plywood over the top of the feather-light craft. This was the Ford Model T of gliders, a design barely more complicated than the sort of kit a schoolboy might build with balsa wood and paper, but it had opened up the skies to tens of thousands of Germans. And, in so doing, it had enabled a nation banned from possessing an air force by the Treaty of Versailles to train its next generation of pilots.

Gerhard strapped himself in, pulled his leather helmet over his head and did up the chinstrap. He checked his controls to make sure that the glider's flaps were all working. Then he waved his arm to indicate his readiness.

A member of the ground crew raised a white flag, and more than one thousand meters up the runway another flag was lifted to indicate that the signal had been received. The second flagman was standing by a hefty Mercedes L6500 truck on which a massive motorized winch—powered, naturally, by a Meerbach engine—had been mounted. The engine had been thrumming for the past couple of minutes as it was brought to full power. Now a lever was thrown, gears engaged and the drum of the winch started rotating, slowly at first and then gathering speed.

A cable of light, high-tensile steel wire ran from the winch to the nose of the glider. For a few seconds the winch did nothing but take up the slack. Then Gerhard felt the tug as the line tightened and then the forward motion and the breeze in his face as the Grunau Baby began rolling down the runway. The breeze turned to a gale as the glider reached its take-off speed of eighty kilometers per hour and then, just as a sail fills at the touch of the breeze, so the wing responded to the rush of air across its surface and Gerhard felt the first glorious moment of release as the glider left the grasp of the earth below and, defying gravity, rose up into the sky.

When the altimeter showed a height of five hundred meters, Gerhard released the clip that held the cable, which plummeted back down to earth. Now, at last he was truly free.

The glorious armies of alpine peaks, the lush green meadows and the dazzling sparkle of the waters of the Bodensee were magnificent enough when seen from the windows of the Schloss Meerbach. They provided endlessly changing backdrops of color, light and form to walks, cross-country ski trips or hunting expeditions on the estate. But nothing compared to their loveliness or majesty when seen from the air. And gliding, Gerhard had discovered, was the purest of all forms of flight. An engine gave off deafening noise, constant vibration and choking exhaust fumes. But a glider was as silent as a soaring eagle, as it rode the invisible currents of hot air that picked it up and carried across the sky.

Gerhard's face was wreathed in an exultant smile. *Thank you, Konrad! Thank you,* Gruppenführer *Heydrich! You have no idea of the gift you made to me when you ordered me to fly!*

Here, in this most joyous solitude, he was liberated from the cares of the world down below. Over the past three months his life had been transformed. He had been forced to drop many of his old acquaintances; for fear that he might lead the Gestapo toward them. Other friends, including his very closest, had dropped him of their own accord, appalled by his apparent capitulation to the bigotry and wickedness of Nazi ideology. To them, the sudden appearance of a Party badge on Gerhard's shoulder and his appointment to the staff of Albert Speer's design office was evidence that he had chosen to betray his conscience, political ideals and architectural creativity. "Once a spoiled rich kid, always a spoiled rich kid," one of Gerhard's oldest, closest companions had sneered. "In the end, you couldn't resist it, could you? They put it all on a plate for you: privilege, advancement, a seat at the top table. And you couldn't say no."

It tore Gerhard apart that he could not tell anyone the truth. He hated himself every time he nodded approvingly or even spoke up in support when a guest at the family dinner table made an anti-Semitic remark. He barely said a word at work without first running his comments through in his mind to check that they were in accordance with approved Nazi thinking. Konrad had asked him one day, "Berlin is a city of four million people. How many Gestapo men do you think it requires to keep every one of them in order?"

"I don't know," Gerhard had replied. "Ten thousand? Twenty thousand?"

"No, you are completely wrong. There are barely five hundred Gestapo officers in all Berlin. But then again, there are also four million. That is the genius of the system. Everyone watches everyone else. Everyone is a policeman. You have no idea how much information is brought to our attention every day. So many people reporting so many neighbours, workmates, friends, even family members. It is all we can do just to file all the accusations."

Konrad had looked at Gerhard then and the smug, bullying look in his eyes was as clear as any spoken threat: we are watching you, we have eyes and ears everywhere, you are never safe. It could be that pretty girl who works as the office secretary, or that friendly fellow who invites you out for a drink, or the landlady of your flat. It could be absolutely anyone. You are never safe from us. Never!

But up here, high in the Bavarian sky, there was no one to spy on Gerhard, no one to report him for independent thoughts or rash bursts of improper speech. Up here he could recover some sense of his true self. And as his eyes ranged over the wondrous scenery and toward the Swiss shoreline on the far side of the Bodensee—how tempting it was, sometimes, just to turn the nose of the glider toward that safe haven and leave his cares behind!—so his mind returned as it often did to the postcard he had received just ten days after his encounter with Heydrich. It was a typical tourist card that showed a view of the steam engine that carried passengers up what was said to be the steepest railway line in the world to the top of a mountain called the Rothorn. And the message was equally innocent:

Hey Gerd, you should come to Switzerland. The girls here look even better than the mountains! Looking forward to seeing you again. If you need anything from here—cheese? chocolate? fancy watches?—just let me know. Your pal, Maxi.

Gerhard had known at once that Maxi was Isidore Solomons, the proud holder of the Blue Max. *Thank God the card arrived after I met that SS bastard*, he thought now. *I could never have lied to Heydrich that I didn't know where Izzy was. He would have seen through me at once.*

"If you need anything . . ." that was the key line, Izzy's sign that he had a debt of honor to Gerhard. One day, it might be called upon. Until that day, however, Gerhard would not mention anything to anyone. And when the glider came back down to earth and real life began again, he would not allow himself even to think about Isidore Solomons.

———

By the time her third year at Roedean began, Saffron had that wonderful feeling of being completely at home in her school and wholly at ease with everything involved in getting there and back. Leon, too, was far more relaxed, not least because his daughter's evident enjoyment of her education brought him tremendous pleasure, even if it was even harder for him that he could not share it all with Eva. "Off to see the splendid Miss Halfpenny," he said, straightening his tie before they left for the outfitters. "Pity she'll kick me out within ten seconds of our arrival. Damned handsome woman, that one."

"Daddy, really!" Saffron exclaimed in mock outrage. "You can't talk about Miss Halfpenny like that. She's not one of your lady friends. I mean, she's much too old, for a start."

Leon laughed as he opened the car door for Saffron to get in. "My dear girl, I would estimate that Miss Halfpenny is only around thirty. And in case you haven't noticed, I will celebrate—or possibly mourn—my forty-seventh birthday this year. A woman of thirty may seem ancient to you, but to me she's a mere slip of a girl."

As they drove into central Johannesburg, Saffron turned her father's words over in her head. She had never really stopped to think about Miss Halfpenny's looks, not least because the way the manageress dressed was intended to make her seem eminently respectable rather than attractive. But now that she considered the question, Saffy decided that she could see what her father meant. Miss Halfpenny had lovely auburn hair, even if she did wear it in a prim little bun. And though her features were not pretty-pretty—her nose was too long, her cheekbones too pronounced—they were elegant, symmetrical and fine-boned. She had nice hazel eyes, too, and, though her job did not encourage levity, Saffron had seen Miss Halfpenny smile enough times to see how it lit up her face.

Having considered all these questions in the abstract, Saffron was keen to see the object of her deliberations again to observe her more closely in the flesh. But when she and Leon arrived at the shop they discovered that Miss Halfpenny was no longer employed there. "Her mother took poorly and she had to go back to England to look after her," the new manageress said. "But I would be pleased to cater to your requirements. Come this way . . ."

"Well, I'll leave you to it," said Leon, looking much less cheerful than he had as they arrived at the shop. Saffron had hardly been any more cheerful as she followed the unfamiliar face off toward the clothes racks and drawers.

It had not been an auspicious start to the new school year, but things had improved since then and now here Saffron was, just three weeks away from Christmas, coming in to land at Nairobi. She had taken her School Certificate exams in English language and literature, mathematics, science, history, geography, art, French, Latin and (to Saffron's tremendous indignation at the very idea of being examined in the skills that her father had so strongly dismissed) domestic science. She was reasonably sure that she had passed them all, with Credit or even Distinction grades in most of them. Between gritted teeth, if sufficiently tortured, she might even have admitted that she quite enjoyed her cookery lessons and was actually rather proud of the pineapple upside-down cake she had produced in her exam.

But those days were behind her now. She was sixteen years old, legally entitled to leave school and, so far as she was concerned, practically a grown woman. Her father would be waiting for her on the aerodrome's flat grass field. Kippy, who was by now far too old to ride, but still tended with loving care by the stable-boys, was waiting for her at Lusima. And there was a surprise waiting for her. A happy smile spread across Saffron's face.

Home! she exulted. *I'm almost home!*

————

"Would you care to give me your coffee cup, please, Miss Courtney?" the Imperial Airways steward asked the poised young lady of sixteen whom he was serving, almost shouting to make himself heard over the roar of the four rotary engines that powered the Armstrong Whitworth Atalanta airliner. "We'll be landing in Nairobi soon."

Saffron smiled up at the steward in his smart white uniform. His peaked cap made him look like a naval officer who had, quite by chance, found himself acting the role of a cabin boy on this Imperial Airways flight.

"Of course, Symons, here you are," she called back, handing him the bone china cup and saucer. "I thought it was particularly good today."

Symons smiled. "I made it nice and strong for you, just the way you like it, Miss. Almost home, eh?"

"Yes." After three years of air travel, Saffron was well used to the volume required to converse in the air. "My father cabled me just before we left Jo'burg. He said he had a surprise for me when I got home. I'm a little worried because he didn't say if it was a nice surprise or a nasty one. I do hope it's nice."

"I'm sure it will be. I'll bet he's bought you something extra special for Christmas. The way your father talks about you when he flies with us, I know he'd only ever want nice things for you. Proud as punch he is, though better not tell him I said so!"

"I won't, but thank you very much for saying so, anyway, Symons. That was very sweet."

The steward beamed affectionately and walked back between the cabin's seven pairs of passenger seats toward his galley in the rear of the plane. He and his colleagues, who were permanently stationed in Africa by Imperial Airways, along with the company's own pilots, navigators, mechanics and ground staff, had all come to know Saffron very well over the past three years as she flew back and forth between Nairobi and Roedean, on the northern edge of Johannesburg.

———

The Imperial Airways Atalanta came to a halt on the landing strip at Nairobi Aerodrome. When she'd emerged from the plane and had her passport stamped, Saffron looked around the tiny terminal that served both departing and arriving passengers before spotting her father and dashing toward him with a jubilant cry of, "Daddy!" But as she disentangled herself from their hug—that wonderful moment, so long anticipated, when she could relish the feeling of absolute safety that came from having his arms around her and the man-smell of him as she put her head to his chest—she saw a woman, waiting patiently for father and daughter to finish their greeting, clearly waiting to say hello.

She was wearing a loose linen robe that hung to her knees. It was white, but decorated with delicate, brightly colored embroidered flowers around the neckline and on the hems of the three-quarter-length sleeves. Beneath it she wore pajama-like trousers, also white, which gathered at the ankle. Her shoes were simple, open sandals. Her short, gray hair was held in place by a silk scarf around her head, she was wearing dark glasses, and she carried an open straw bag, which hung from her shoulder on a leather strap. The gray hair suggested that she must be quite old, but her figure was slim and lithe and there was something about both the way she dressed—which was quite unlike anything Saffron had ever seen before—and the way she carried herself that seemed irrepressibly youthful.

Who is she? Saffron wondered. And then an appalling possibility struck her: *Is this Daddy's surprise? Does he want me to meet his new wife?*

The woman caught her eye, smiled and said, "Hello, my dear. My name is Saffron Courtney."

Saffron's head spun: *What did she just say?*

"Saffron . . . meet Saffron," Leon said, seeing her confusion. "This is your grandmother, darling. My mother. We named you after her."

Oh, thank goodness for that! Saffron was hugely relieved, but also dumbfounded. She had never in her life met a grandparent before, and the woman in front of her now wasn't at all the sort of cuddly old creature she'd always imagined as a granny.

"I am so, so pleased to meet you at last," her grandmother said. "Come here and give me a hug."

Saffron did as she was told and found herself enveloped in a scent that seemed impossibly spicy and mysterious, as if it had been stolen from the innermost chambers of a sultan's harem. With every second that passed, Saffron found herself becoming more captivated by her newfound relative.

"I think your clothes are just wonderful," she said. "It's midsummer, but you look as cool as a cucumber."

Her grandmother smiled. "Thank you, my dear, how sweet of you to say so. The truth is, I've lived in North Africa all my life and I long ago realized that it was absolutely crazy to go around dressed in clothes designed for cold, wet days in England when one was right next door to the Sahara Desert. I know people are always saying that white women can't survive the sun . . . Do people still have that lunatic habit of putting their daughters into hats lined with heavy red felt?"

"Oh yes, lots of girls have to wear those," Saffron said. "But I never have."

"Well, that's because you come from a family that actually knows how to live out here. Personally, I took my cue from what I observed on my travels through Mesopotamia, Ethiopia, Egypt, Morocco . . . all over the place, actually . . . and adapted the local clothes to my tastes and needs. I'm a painter, you see. So I have to have clothes that are comfortable to work in. No corsets. No stockings. Can't be doing with that nonsense, unless I'm forced to dress up."

"I agree," said Saffron. "It's so lovely to get out of school uniforms and starched dresses and spend my holidays in my riding breeches or just some shorts."

"That's my girl! Now, before we go any further, we need to

decide upon names. I know that some grandmothers are happy with "Granny" and "Nanny" or even "Nan"—though not in polite society, I might add. I, however, like to be known as Grandma. So can we agree on that?"

"Absolutely, Grandma," Saffron said, loving this unexpected chance to say the word.

"Good. And you, my boy, may call me Mother, or if we are feeling particularly friendly, Ma."

"Yes, Mother," said Leon, wearily, not noticing the wink his mother had aimed in Saffron's direction.

"Very well then," Grandma declared. "You may now take us all to lunch."

———

"I thought we'd eat at the Stanley," Leon said as he drove them away from the airport, toward Delamere Road, where the New Stanley Hotel stood. "The Muthaiga's really not a suitable place for mothers and daughters. It's become even rowdier than usual lately. Chaps swinging from the lights, pretending to be monkeys, getting drunk in public and taking all their clothes off."

"Oh but I love all that!" Saffron exclaimed. The night she always spent at the Muthaiga before catching the plane to Johannesburg was one of the highlights of the whole journey to school.

"Well, I'm sure your grandmamma would not."

"Oh Leon, really!" Grandma objected. "I'm hardly a doddering old maid. I was a married woman by the time I was fifteen, and I'd already lived through the Siege of Khartoum by then, practically seen my poor dear father killed before my eyes and had a few adventures with your own father that really aren't suitable for young ears."

"Grandma!" Saffron gasped, instantly forgetting about the Muthaiga. "How could you be married at fifteen? That's not even legal!"

"It is in Abyssinia, which is where your grandfather and I

had our wedding. And I may say, it was quite an occasion. The
Emperor and Empress themselves attended the service."

Saffron's eyes opened wide in astonished admiration. "An
Emperor . . . and an Empress?" she gasped.

"Oh yes, my dear, Empress Miriam and I were the best of
friends. Like you, she was kind enough to take an interest in
the way I dressed. She used to come to me for advice, actually,
although in her eyes I was rather an old maid. She'd been married at thirteen, you see."

"Goodness."

"How old are you, Saffron?"

"Sixteen, Grandma."

"A fine age. I was sixteen when your father was born."

"Oh," said Saffron, who now understood why her grandmother looked so unusually youthful.

"Well, anyway," Leon continued, struggling to lead the conversation back to safer ground, "Mayence and Fred Tate, who've
run the hotel for as long as anyone can remember—good chap,
Fred, bumped into him a lot in the war—have just done the
place up and I must say they've done an excellent job, and . . ."

"Were you shocked when Grandpa asked you to marry him?"
Saffron asked, ignoring her father.

"Well, it wasn't really a case of him asking me," Grandma
replied. "You see, what happened was . . ."

"I really don't think Saffron wants to hear this story," Leon
interrupted.

"Oh yes I do!"

Saffron snuggled deeper into the leather passenger seat,
making herself comfortable, feeling very much as she had done
as a little girl, safe beneath her blankets as her mother read her
a bedtime story as Grandma continued, "My sister Amber and
I were supposed to go to live with your great-uncle Penrod's
family, the Ballantynes, at their estate in Scotland, to be brought
up as good British girls with a governess. We were due to sail

from Djibouti on a ship called the *Singapore*. But I was desperately in love with Ryder Courtney . . ."

"How old was he, Grandma?"

"A little more than twice my age, but I didn't care. I knew he was the love of my life, knew it in the depths of my heart, and I wasn't going to let him go. So I ran away, and the ship had to leave without me. Ryder found me eventually—after I'd sent him off on a false trail down the road to Abyssinia, rather cleverly I thought . . ."

Grandma flashed a cheeky little smile at Saffron, who suddenly saw a glimpse of the impish, rebellious, but adorable girl she must have been. "The poor man tried to be cross with me but I could see that his heart wasn't in it because I knew that he loved me just as much as I loved him, he just hadn't realized it himself. So I told him that we were to be married and that it was quite all right because I had already spoken to the Empress. She thoroughly approved of the plan and had agreed to sponsor our union, so really there was absolutely no good reason not to get married and he, bless him . . ." Now the smile on Grandma's face was wistful and Saffron thought she could see the beginning of a tear in her eye as Grandma said, "That darling man said that it was not the worst notion he had ever heard of, and then he kissed me, and I was the happiest girl in the world."

"Oh, Grandma . . ." Saffron sighed. "That is such a beautiful story."

"Don't you worry, my dear, that is only one tiny part of a much, much longer tale and I dare say I will tell you a bit more before I leave."

"Please, please do, that would be marvelous!"

"Well, here we are," Leon said with relief, pulling up outside the hotel.

It was a white-painted three-storey building. The entrance was flanked by two towers topped by little cupolas that made them look like a matching pair of pepper grinders. The façade was pierced by high arches that rose up to the first floor to reveal bedrooms set back behind balconies decorated with baskets of brightly coloured flowers. They were to lunch outside, but just before the maître d' escorted them to their table, Leon said, "Excuse us one moment," and then told his mother and daughter, "Come with me."

He led them across to an old acacia tree, and when they came closer they saw that the trunk was ringed by a series of cork noticeboards, all of them covered with letters, telegrams, or just pieces of folded paper with names scrawled upon them. "This is the New Stanley Hotel thorn tree, Nairobi's unofficial post office. If you want to get in touch with someone in Kenya, and you don't know exactly where they are, just stick a message here and sooner or later it will be found."

"I'd like to stick a message that says, "I'm hungry. Where's lunch?" Granny said.

"I'm starving too," Saffron agreed.

They ate well, as one always did in Kenya, for the land was so fertile and the climate so balmy that virtually all fruits and vegetables grew year-round and the huge tracts of grazing produced delicious pork, lamb and beef. Grandma quizzed Saffron about her sporting triumphs, discovering that in the past year she had been the captain of the school hockey and netball teams as well as winning the individual tennis trophy.

"She also rides as well as any horseman I've ever seen. She can hit a gamebird on the wing like Dead-Eye Dick's little sister. And not only can she drive a car, she also knows how to change a tire, top up the oil or water . . ."

"And I know how to turn one of my stockings into a fan belt!" Saffron added.

"I wouldn't let her set off around the estate unless she could manage a few basic running repairs," Leon explained. "Can't have her being helpless if she has a breakdown while she's miles from home."

"I see . . ." said Grandma thoughtfully. "Tell me, Saffron, have your lessons been going well, too?"

"I think so, Grandma. I'm just waiting for my exam results. I think they shouldn't be too bad."

"What she means is she's hoping for Distinctions all round," beamed Leon.

"Good . . . good . . ." Grandma said, though she sounded surprisingly unimpressed, for a woman who had just been informed that her granddaughter was both a sporting and academic paragon. "Tell me dear girl, since you are so formidably well educated, what do the following three people have in common: Elsa Schiaparelli, Main Rousseau Bocher and Madeleine Vionnet?"

Saffron was flummoxed. She glanced toward her father but he simply shrugged as if to say, "I haven't got a clue."

"Umm . . ." she desperately wracked her brain, remembered that Grandma was a painter and took a guess. "Are they all artists?"

"In a manner of speaking, I suppose you could say they are. But what sort of artists?"

"Uh . . . Uh . . ." Saffron's voice rose in something close to panic. "Sculptors? Painters?" Desperately she tried to think: *What other kinds of artists are there?*

"They are all couturiers," Grandma said, and then, realizing from the continued look of bafflement on Saffron's face that she did not know what a couturier was, added, "They create very beautiful, expensive, perfectly made-to-measure dresses and evening gowns for rich and fashionable women."

"Oh," said Saffron, feeling utterly crestfallen.

"And you, my darling child, would look utterly ravishing in any of their creations, which is why they would fight to have you as their customer. Do you have any idea at all how perfectly lovely-looking you are, Saffron? . . . No, one look at your face tells me that you don't." She turned toward her son. "Leon, your daughter is a marvel. You have provided for her as well as any father could. You have given her a splendid education. Your love for her is as delightfully obvious as hers for you. The one thing you have not done, because you could not possibly do it, is to show her how to be a woman."

"If Eva hadn't died . . ." Leon began, and then fell silent.

Grandma reached out her hand and placed it on her son's arm. "I know, darling, I know . . . You suffered a terrible loss and you have been nothing short of heroic, raising a daughter and, by the way, keeping your mother and sisters very well provided for too. Courtney Trading seems to be flourishing."

Leon grinned with relief. "Yes, things have been picking up lately. The world's still a long way from being properly back on its feet. But I think we're actually ahead of the pack. All the bankers have been paid off ahead of schedule, so we're debt-free. It's Davy you should be thanking, though, Ma. He did all the hard work. I just signed the checks."

"Well, he couldn't have done it if you hadn't come to our rescue. That was a very fine thing you did, Leon, even if not everyone recognizes the fact. Now, I'm going to take Saffy off to do some shopping."

"What for?" asked Saffron, wondering whether her grandmother was suddenly going to make expensive hand-made dresses appear by magic in the modest little shops of Nairobi.

"Christmas presents!" announced Grandma decisively. "Have you bought your father one yet?"

"Actually . . . no."

"I suspected as much. Now, Leon, you stay here and have a nice cup of coffee, chat to your chums in the Long Bar—I'm quite sure you know half the men there—and generally pass the time until we ladies return. Saffron?"

"Yes, Grandma?"

"Follow me!"

————

Saffron was thrilled by the sudden arrival in her life of this extraordinary woman. First she had met Cousin Centaine, now

Grandma Saffron. Bit by bit a proper family, with all sorts of relations, was starting to assemble itself around her. Together they went off and browsed the shops in the new Stanley Arcade, set into one outside wall of the hotel. In one of the shops, which sold menswear, Saffron went off in one direction, to look at a rack of ties that might provide a possible candidate for a present, while Grandma busied herself elsewhere. Saffron was just running a couple of rather beautiful, brightly patterned silk ties through her hands, wondering whether she could ever persuade her father to wear one, when she heard a harsh, female voice say, "You must be the Courtney girl. My, haven't you grown up?"

Saffron turned around to see a woman whose type was all too familiar in Kenya. She had obviously once been quite pretty and from her haughty attitude, extravagantly coiffed, bright blond hair and thick makeup she believed that her looks were still intact. But that fatal combination of too much sun and far too many drinks over rather more years than she would care to admit had left her skin as leathery as her crocodile-skin handbag. There were deep wrinkles around her eyes and her top lip was grooved with the lines that come from being so often pursed around a cigarette.

"I'm sorry," said Saffron. "I don't think we've been introduced."

"I dare say you're right," the woman said. "My name is Amelia Cory-Porter. I used to know your father, briefly. He made quite a pass at me, as a matter of fact."

I don't believe that, Saffron thought, and then something in the bitterness of the older woman's voice told her, *but I bet you made a pass at him, didn't you? And I bet he blanked you, too.*

"Really?" she replied. "How interesting."

Amelia Cory-Porter looked at Saffron with something she had rarely if ever before encountered in her life: undiluted malice. "By God, you're as arrogant and full of yourself as he was, too. Look at you, pretty as a picture, rolling in money. Who'd ever guess that your mother was a tart?"

The words hit Saffron like a punch to the gut. It was as if all the air had been knocked from her body. She could hardly breathe. Somehow she managed to gasp, "No she wasn't."

"Oh, I'm afraid she very much was, my dear. She made her living spreading her legs for some fat German until she decided she fancied a bit of younger meat and set her sights on your father. Poor chap didn't know what hit him, from what I heard."

"No, no she wasn't like that," Saffron sobbed. "She wasn't like that!"

Through her tears, Saffron saw her grandma coming toward her and heard her asking, "What on earth is going on here?"

"She . . . she . . . she said Mummy was a tart," Saffron sobbed.

"I think I'll be going now," said Amelia Cory-Porter.

"Stay right there!" Grandma commanded in a voice that would have made presidents and generals halt their stride. "What on earth do you think you are doing, reducing a sweet young girl to tears with such vile filth?"

"You call it filth, I say it's nothing but the truth. Her mother was a German's whore. She was a tart . . . and a traitor too."

Grandma took another step closer to Amelia. "I dare say you'd know a thing or two about sleeping with men for money, yourself, though by the look of you you're probably finding it rather harder to work up any interest these days."

"I'm not going to stay here and listen to rubbish like that."

"You are going to stay here until I tell you to go. Now, listen here, you common little minx, if you spread another word of this vile slander to anyone, anyone at all, our family will come after you with every legal means at our disposal, and we will ruin you, utterly and completely. Do I make myself clear?"

"I really don't think there's any need to make threats . . ."

"I will ask you again: have I clearly conveyed the conse-quences of any further vile slanders?"

Amelia Cory-Porter seemed to be deflating before her eyes,

like a balloon filled with poison gas that had just been pricked by a sharp pin. "Yes," she muttered.

"Good. Now, consider this . . . my son, Leon Courtney, is at this moment less than two hundred yards away. He is an exceptionally decent, honorable gentleman, but when he hears what you have said to his daughter he may not be able to stop himself giving you the thrashing you so soundly deserve."

"Well, I think I should be going then," Amelia said, though she did not actually move.

"Yes, I think you should. And I'd go a long way away, too, if I were you. Now, be gone with you. And pray to God I never set eyes on you again."

"Thank you, Grandma," Saffron said, watching Amelia Cory-Porter scuttle out of the shop. "But all those horrible things she said . . . I have to know if they're true."

Leon waited until they had all returned safely to Lusima and had a light supper before he took his mother and daughter into his study, the most private and intimate corner of the house. His mahogany desk stood by the bay window, facing inwards into the room. One wall was entirely covered in bookcases, an open fireplace dominated another. Above the mantelpiece hung a portrait of Eva, painted a year after Saffron's birth. The artist was a White Russian called Vassileyev who had fled the Revolution, washed up on the shores of Kenya and made a modest living from the commissions he obtained from the expatriate community and tourists. Vassileyev did not pretend to be anything more than a jobbing painter, yet in this one work he had excelled himself, for he had perfectly caught Eva's beauty, and also the joy in her heart. Here was a young woman, blissfully married, with a baby she adored, living in paradise and preserved in all her perfection forever.

Leon made sure that Saffron and his mother were comfortably settled and provided with drinks: a good, stiff whisky for

Grandma and a small gin with a lot of tonic and lemon for Saffron. He poured himself a brandy and placed himself by the fire. For some reason he didn't feel that this was a tale he could recount sitting down. He wanted to be able to move and work off a little of the tension that telling it would generate. He sipped his brandy slowly as he looked up at Eva's portrait. Even now, almost a decade after her passing, his love for her had not dimmed. "Please forgive me, my darling," he whispered to the picture. Then he turned to face his audience.

"I had always hoped, perhaps naively, that I would never have to tell you what you now want to know," Leon began. He spoke slowly, choosing his words carefully and bestowing upon them a certain formality. "This was in part because some of what I have to say concerns matters that are officially classified. I am about to break the law by speaking about them to you, and you both will break the law if you discuss them with anyone else. And I really do mean anyone else at all, ever. So first, I must ask you both to promise, on your words of honor, never to repeat a word of what you hear tonight. Do you promise me that, Saffron?"

"Yes, Father," she replied, with equal seriousness.

"And you, Mother?"

"Yes, of course dear, I quite understand."

"Very well, then . . . There was a second reason why I hoped that this moment would never come, Saffron, and that is because I know how much it would upset your mother. She was the love of my life. She was as brave as she was beautiful. She brought me more happiness than I ever dreamed possible. She gave me you, my darling, the finest daughter any man could wish for, and she loved you with all her heart, as she loved me too."

"I know, Daddy," said Saffron, and her eyes filled with welling tears.

"She was also a true patriot. You already know that she served the British Empire during the war and was decorated for her valor . . ."

"Yes."

"But what you don't know is that she served the Empire before the war too."

"May one ask how?" Grandma inquired.

Leon nodded, "Yes, on this one night you may." He took another drink from his brandy and then said, "Eva was a spy, an agent for the Secret Service Bureau, in its foreign espionage department, or the Secret Intelligence Service as they call it nowadays. So now I hope you understand why this is all top secret."

"Good heavens," Grandma said as Saffron asked, "What kind of a spy?"

"I'm coming to that, but first you need to know a little about Eva's background. She was born in Northumberland. Her father, Peter, was English but her mother was German—you must remember, Saffron, that in those days the links between England and Germany were very strong, and our two countries were not enemies. Her parents were not rich, but they loved each other and they loved her, so she grew up in a happy home. But then, when she was twelve, her parents both contracted a disease called polio myelitis. Eva's mother died . . ." Leon looked at Saffron. "Yes, I know, to think that Mummy would herself die young is almost unbearable. Her father survived the disease but it left him crippled. His legs withered away and he was confined to a wheelchair."

Leon paused to finish off his brandy. He placed the empty glass on the mantelpiece above the fireplace, looked up at Eva's portrait for moral support and went on. "Your mother, like you, Saffy, was a bright girl and had the chance to go to Edinburgh University, but she turned the offer down because she wanted to stay at home and care for her father."

Leon paused and gave a wistful smile.

"What is it, Daddy?" Saffron asked.

"Oh, nothing, I just remembered Mummy saying that she called her father "Curly" because he didn't have a hair on his head. Anyway, Curly was a brilliant engineer and inventor, and he came up with brilliant ideas for high-powered internal combustion engines. He patented his designs, but he didn't have the money to develop them and bring them into production. But a German industrialist did have the money. He offered Curly a partnership and waved a contract under his nose. Curly, being a boffin, didn't know the first thing about contracts and he couldn't afford a lawyer, so he put his name to the contract and, to cut a long story short, signed away all his rights to his life's work and his patents. The German went away and made his already massive fortune even larger, while poor Curly died in poverty."

No need to tell her how he died, Leon thought to himself. *Blowing his brains out with a shotgun, Eva having to clean the bloodstains off the wall.*

"Your mother was sixteen—your age—at the time, and she was left all alone in the world, penniless, with no one to look after her," he said.

"Oh, but that's awful!" cried Saffron. "Why didn't the German take care of her? He'd made so much money out of Curly's inventions. He could afford it."

"He could indeed, but he had the hardest, meanest, cruelest heart of any man I ever met."

"You met him? How?"

"Wait, my darling. All in good time . . . Now, young Eva had to find some way to support herself, so she went to work as a factory girl in a nearby mill. But then, one day, a woman called Mrs. Ryan arrived at her doorstep, saying that she had known Eva's mother, had heard of the tragic events of the past few years and wanted to help. Eva went to live in Mrs. Ryan's house in London. Mrs. Ryan was a firm believer in the greatness of the British Empire. She used to talk endlessly about what a blessing the Empire was to the world and what a privilege it was to serve it, if one was ever called upon to do so. And Eva agreed, because she was suddenly enjoying all the benefits of living in the Empire's capital city. She had her own room, all nicely furnished; smart clothes; a tutor to teach her etiquette; a riding master and her own horse—a filly called Hyperion. All in all she soon became a very proper young gentlewoman. She also had German lessons. That was the one thing Mrs. Ryan absolutely insisted upon—daily German lessons.

"What your mother did not know, however, was that she was being trained. You see, there are many ways in which a spy network can obtain secret information. It can infiltrate enemy organizations with its own agents, operating undercover. It can bribe, persuade or blackmail enemy personnel to betray their own cause. It can beat or torture enemy captives. Or it can take advantage of the male sex's irrepressible desire to impress, seduce and conquer the female of the species, particularly if she is very, very beautiful.

"Eva, of course, was incomparably lovely. She was also very bright—she could have gone to university, remember. And finally, she was burning with the desire to avenge her father and right the wrong that had been done to him. All this made her extremely useful to the Secret Intelligence Service. For by now, the political winds had shifted. The Germans were making no secret of their desire to challenge the British and take over the mantle of the world's greatest power. Germany's armed forces were expanding at a tremendous rate, as was its armaments industry, part of which was owned by the very man who had stolen Curly Barry's designs. So Eva Barry was given a new identity. She became a haughty German aristocrat called Eva von Wellberg. She was introduced to the man who had ruined her father and . . ." Leon paused, steeled himself, took a deep breath and said, "and she became his mistress."

Saffron could not help herself. "So she *was* a tart!" she sobbed. "That horrible woman was right."

Grandma took her in her arms. "No, darling, she wasn't . . . that's not what your father is saying at all. Sometimes, we women have to make very hard choices. We do what we must to survive, as my own sisters did when they were prisoners of the Mahdi, after the fall of Khartoum. Or we do what our country requires of us. We can't fight with our fists or guns in the way men do, so . . ."

"So we become prostitutes?"

"That's quite enough!" Leon snapped. "I will not have you talking about your mother like that. She did something she knew was rotten because it had to be done. Look at me . . . look at me, girl!"

Saffron raised her head from her grandmother's embrace and turned her eyes back to her father.

"I have killed more men in the service of my country than I care to think about," Leon said. "Killed them with these hands. I've left them crying for their mothers, bleeding their lives away into the dirt. So if your mother is a prostitute, then I am a murderer, and a mass murderer at that. But I know that I did what I did in a just cause, serving my King, standing up for freedom and decency, just as my darling Eva did too. And how some cheap little tramp like Amelia Cory-Porter has the brass nerve to throw vicious accusations at your mother, who had more goodness and decency in her little finger than that woman has in her whole raddled body, is completely beyond me."

For a moment no one said anything. Saffron looked at her father, trying to make sense of everything she'd heard. There had been so much to take in. And she'd never heard anything like the way he had spoken just then, with so much raw passion. Her breathing calmed and her tears stopped flowing. "Here . . ." Leon said, taking the silk handkerchief out of his lapel pocket and handing it to her. She used it to wipe her eyes and nose and handed it back. She sniffed, gave him a brave smile and said, "At least now I know what to buy you for Christmas."

"A man can never have too many handkerchiefs," Leon agreed.

"Might I ask how the story of Eva and the mysterious German ended?" Grandma asked.

"The two of them came on safari to East Africa, just a few months before the war. I was their guide. Eva and I fell in love. When the safari ended, she had to go back to Germany and we both feared that was the end for us. But then the war broke out, and the Germans conceived a plan to join up with the old Boer rebels in South Africa and rise up against British rule. The rebels needed arms and money to pay troops. Eva's German industrialist had just the means of getting the cargo to them much more quickly than any conventional means of transport—a mighty airship, even bigger than a Zeppelin, called the *Assegai*. He insisted on commanding the expedition and on taking his mistress with him, unaware that she was spying for the enemy and had alerted us of the plan. I intercepted the *Assegai*. I didn't have the means to shoot her down so I dropped fishing nets down onto her engines, tangled up the propellers and crippled her that way."

"But Mummy was on board!" Saffron exclaimed.

"She wasn't supposed to be. I saw her just as I was making my attack."

"And you went ahead, anyway?"

"Yes, of course. I had no choice. It was my duty. We both understood that."

"But Mummy survived . . . how?"

"Thanks to the one decent thing that damn German ever did. He stuck a parachute harness on her and threw her off the airship."

"Did he die on his airship?"

Leon thought for a moment. *Should I tell her? Why make things even worse? But how can I let Eva be the only one who bears any blame?*

"No," he said. "He had a parachute too. It got caught in some trees, just before he landed. Mummy found him hanging there, wriggling as helplessly as a fish on a line, but she didn't have the heart to kill him in cold blood. Some of his men came up and captured her. He was about to give her a very nasty, painful death when I came upon the scene."

"Did you . . ." Saffron could not finish the sentence.

"Yes, girl, I did. I shot that bastard through the chest and have never suffered a single second of remorse since. He deserved it. And as he roasts away in Hades he should count himself lucky that I got to him before Manyoro did, or his death would have been a lot longer, drawn-out and infinitely more painful."

"Ah, Leon, how like your father you are . . ." Grandma sighed. "He would have loved that story, and understood it perfectly, too: both your role and Eva's. But tell me, how much money was this airship carrying?"

"Approximately five million German marks, in gold coins."

"How much would that be in pounds sterling?"

"A little less than two million."

"And was it ever recovered?"

"Yes."

"Who by?"

Leon said nothing.

"Ahh . . ." said his mother, putting one and one together and coming up with two million.

"Oh . . ." said Saffron, suddenly understanding why she lived on such a magnificent estate. Then her brows furrowed as a thought struck her and she said, "Daddy?"

"Yes?"

"You never told us what the German man was called."

Leon paused, thought for a moment and then said, "I don't suppose there's any reason now not to tell you, not after you've heard everything else . . . Very well, then, his name was von Meerbach. Count Otto von Meerbach, to be precise."

———

Three days before Christmas, as they were all sitting around the breakfast table, one of the house staff came in bearing a telegram for Leon, sent to him by the headmistress of Roedean. It read:

PLEASED REPORT SAFFRON EXAM RESULTS. FOUR CREDITS, SIX DISTINCTIONS (INC DOMSCI FUNNIEST). SPLENDID.

"Well done, you brilliant girl, well done!" he exulted, reaching out his hand to squeeze hers. "I couldn't be more proud of you." He leaned back in his chair and took another, puzzled look at the piece of paper in his hand. "There's only one thing I don't quite understand. What on earth is "domsci"? And what's so funny about it?"

Now it was Saffron's turn to be baffled. "I don't have any idea, Daddy. May I have a look?"

Leon handed the telegram over to his daughter and watched her face go from frowning concentration to wide-eyed horror as she gasped, "Oh no!" followed in immediate succession by helpless fits of the giggles.

"I'm sorry," he said, "but would someone please tell me what on earth is going on?"

"Oh, Daddy, don't look so worried!" Saffron laughed. "D-O-M-S-C-I is short for "domestic science." Miss Lawrence knows I hated it. So it's funny that I ended up doing quite well."

"You did a lot better than "quite well." I'd have given my eye teeth to get a Distinction in anything at all."

"You could have got any result you wanted in any subject you chose, dear boy, if only you had also chosen to do some work," Grandma pointed out. "There was never anything wrong with your brain, merely your desire to actually use it."

"I was an idle young beggar, wasn't I?" Leon admitted. "So, now that you've got these wonderful exam results, what are you going to do with them? Back to Roedean for Sixth Form, I suppose?"

"Hmm . . . yes . . . in a way . . ." Saffron said, mysteriously.

"What do you mean, "in a way"?" Leon asked.

"Well, I do want to go to Roedean for Sixth Form . . . but I want to go to Roedean in England." Saffron saw her father was about to say something, but kept talking, determined not to let him get a word in until she'd made her case, particularly since her opening gambit had been carefully calculated to make it almost impossible for her father to deny her. "The thing is," she said, "I've been thinking a lot about what I want to do, and I was so sad when you told me about Mummy, who never went to university, even though she was clever enough. It was awful that she never had the chance to show what she could do as a student. So I think it's really important that I should make the best of my ability and my opportunities."

"I agree," said Leon, though there was a hesitation in his voice that betrayed his strong sense that his clever little girl was laying a very large trap, into which she expected him to fall.

"So I've been talking to some of the mistresses at Roedean and they've been telling me about their sister school in England. Apparently it's tremendously strong academically, even more than the one in Jo'burg, and it sends tons of girls off to university, including Oxford and Cambridge."

"You are not going to Oxford!" Leon snapped, suddenly seeing precisely why she'd been leading him on. "It's a nest of cowards, traitors and Reds. I absolutely forbid it!"

Saffron groaned inwardly. She hadn't forgotten her father's letter on the subject, but she had hoped that for once in his life he might have moderated his opinion just a little. "For goodness sakes, Daddy, all the people who voted in that silly debate must have left Oxford by now. All I care about is that it's one of the greatest universities in the world."

"Well go to one of the other greatest universities then."

"I can't. Oxford is the only one that has the course I want to do."

"What's that, then: waving the white flag?"

"Oh for heaven's sake, Leon, don't be so ridiculous," said Grandma. "What on earth has put these silly ideas into your head?"

"There's nothing silly about them at all, Mother. You must know perfectly well that the Oxford Union voted that its members would never, under any circumstance, fight for their King and country. I'm sorry, but that's simply unacceptable. Too many fine young men died fighting to keep us free, including some damn good friends of mine. It's just an insult to their sacrifice for the next generation to turn into a bunch of bloody conshies."

"Is it?" Grandma asked. "I should have thought that a conscientious objection to war was the only decent, moral response to its horror. You forget, my dear, I grew up with war. I saw it destroy my childhood home. It took my father and, indirectly, my oldest sister. When I became a mother it turned my second son from a kind, loving, delightful boy into a bitter and twisted man. I'm sure that if, God forbid, there should ever come a time when the British Empire needs defending from another barbarian horde, the young men of England will do their part, just as they always have done. But for now, let them stand up for peace. There's not a woman on earth who wouldn't applaud them for it."

Saffron's head had been turning from her father to her grandmother and now back to her father again, like a spectator at a tennis match watching the ball hit from one end to the other. Leon took a deep breath, composed himself and then said, "Look, Ma, I know how utterly vile war is. It was bad enough charging round East Africa after von Lettow. God only knows how much worse it was for the poor chaps in the trenches. And yes, it's terrible to see what's become of Frank. But it's just not right for young men now to turn their backs and say, "That's not for me." It makes us veterans wonder what any of it was for."

"It was for the freedom to have debates and speak out on both sides and vote on the result, my darling," said Grandma, with a much gentler, more comforting tone to her voice. "You fought so that those young men could say their piece. And you also fought so that your daughter could make her own way in the world. So, Saffron, tell us why you want to go to Oxford, and why your father should doubtless have to pay a handsome sum for you to be able to do so."

Greatly relieved that peace seemed to have broken out again, Saffron said, "Well, Daddy has his estate and all his business interests and eventually he'll need someone else to run them, and he doesn't have a son, so . . . well, I just thought I should to be prepared, in case I ever have to do it. And Oxford has a course called P.P.E., which stands for Philosophy, Politics and Economics, which I think would be terribly interesting, and also really useful."

"Given the fact that your father's business interests now stretch all the way from the gold and diamond mines of South Africa to the oilfields of Mesopotamia, an understanding of economics will indeed be essential," Grandma said. "And since his assets in Abyssinia, obtained by his father from the Emperor himself when we were very first married, are now threatened by that ghastly little man Signor Mussolini, I should say that you may well be in need of a grasp of politics too. A study of philosophy should make you a more logical and even more moral thinker. Well done, Saffron. That's a first-rate idea."

"Thank you, Grandma. But Daddy . . . do you really own all those things?"

"I have shares in a family firm that has those interests, yes."

"I had no idea that there was, well . . . so much. I just thought it was the estate and . . . actually I'm not sure what else I thought there was."

"That was exactly what I'd hoped you would think, Saffy. I didn't want you growing up a spoiled little rich girl, who only thinks about money and how to spend it. That's not what life should be about."

"I don't think money matters at all, Daddy, really I don't."

"Well, it matters when you don't have any, believe me. But I know what you mean, my darling, and I'm very pleased you feel that way. Now, Ma, you evidently approve of Saffron's plan to go to Oxford—although I imagine it's extremely hard to get in, so we can't take it for granted. What do you think about her going to school in England first?"

Grandma smiled, "Well, I'm a fine one to talk, since I spurned the chance to go there myself. Mind you, I was desperately in love, and my man was in Africa, so that was rather different. You aren't secretly planning to marry a much older lover, are you, Saffy?"

"No Grandma, I am absolutely not!" Saffron laughed.

"Just as well. It was a miracle my marriage worked as well as it did. But to answer your question, Leon, I think it's a splendid idea. Whether or not money is a good thing, Saffron is going to inherit an awful lot of it, and the social position that comes with that. She needs to learn how to act like a British gentlewoman, rather than an African tomboy."

"I say, Ma, that's rather harsh!" Leon objected. "She's a perfectly lovely girl."

"Of course she is. But at this precise moment, she would be as out of place and ill-equipped in a smart Mayfair cocktail party as a London debutante would be if you picked her up and dropped her in the middle of the African bush."

"I would much rather be in the bush . . ." Saffron sighed.

"I'm sure you would and I have no doubt you could cope without the slightest trouble. But you need to learn about the supposedly civilized world, too, because it's every bit as much of a jungle. The predators—male and female alike—have just as sharp claws as any lion or cheetah, and just as hungry appetites."

"That sounds awful. I'm not sure I want to go now."

"Yes, you do. Life in a city like London, or Paris, or even Cairo can be wonderfully stimulating, exciting, thrilling . . . Oh, my dear, what I would give to be as young and as pretty as you. You will have the whole world at your feet and it will be the most marvelous feeling in the world. You just have to know the rules of the game. And you'll never learn them living out here in the back of beyond."

"I just want to get away from horrible old women like Amelia Cory-Porter. I hate the way it is here, everyone knowing everyone else, sticking their noses into each other's business, spreading beastly lies about other people."

"I'm afraid you'll find women like her wherever you go," Grandma said. "And men who are utter rotters and scoundrels too. But it's different in a great city. You have more room to be yourself. No one can watch you as closely as they can in a smaller community."

"Then I do want to go . . . Please, Daddy, do you think you might say I can?"

"Well," said Leon, thoughtfully, and Saffron beamed in delight because she knew from that moment that he wasn't going to say, "No."

"If I recall correctly, the British school year begins in September," Leon continued. "So that means you wouldn't be able to start for nine months. The question is, what should you do until then?"

"Why do I have to wait until September to go back to school?" Saffron asked. "I'll be seventeen by then and nineteen by the time I leave. That's too old to be at school. I'd rather start right away."

"But you will have missed a term, so you'll be behind the other girls," Leon pointed out.

"Then I'll just have to work harder and catch up. I'd rather that than be the old maid of the class."

"You are no one's idea of an old maid, my dear," Grandma pointed out. "But I do take your point." She thought for a moment. "You must go with her, Leon. And when you get to England, stay there for a few months. Speaking as one of your shareholders, albeit a very minor one, I believe it's time Courtney Trading had a London office. Perhaps you could set it up while Saffron spends her first two terms at school, and then you could both go traveling around Europe in the summer."

"That would be wonderful!" Saffron enthused.

"Very well, then, that's settled."

"Hold on a minute," Leon interjected. "We don't know whether Saffron can go to school in England. They may not have a place for her. Even if they do, everything has to be organized in a couple of weeks. She can't just turn up and say, "Let me in!""

"My darling boy," said Grandma, "this is the modern age. There are telegrams and telephones with which to communicate and airplanes to take you halfway around the world in a matter of days. Use your initiative, Leon. Get in touch with the head-mistress in Jo'burg, ask her to pull strings, make a discreet donation as a parting gift to the school if that helps oil the wheels. You have always been able to achieve whatever you wanted, when you put your mind to it. So . . ."

"I'll put my mind to it," Leon said.

———

Leon made calls, sent telegrams, pulled strings and booked tickets. By the second of January 1936, with school due to start on the sixth, he and Saffron were both in London. But after a couple of days in London, Saffron was wondering whether she'd made the right decision to come to England. The weather was cold and damp and gray. The pavements were covered with a slurry of semi-molten slush and grime. They could see Green Park from their hotel window, but as she looked at the monochrome tones of the dead grass, the bare trees and the footpaths Saffron moaned, "It looks more like Gray Park to me."

The sun never seemed to shine in the daytime and thick, choking fogs, heavy with the smell of car fumes and coal fires, descended at night, making it impossible to see more than a few feet into the murk. The filthy air seemed to have seeped into the buildings, so that all the great monuments to which her father dutifully took her, from Buckingham Palace to Westminster Abbey and St. Paul's Cathedral, all the great department stores, all the government offices on Whitehall were stained in shades from pigeon gray to a blackness so deep and dirty that they seemed to be hewn from coal, rather than constructed in brick or stone. The greyness was reflected in the dullness of the clothes people wore, the pallor of their complexions and the tasteless food they ate. Even the last few Christmas decorations still hanging in shop windows or draped across the streets seemed to have been leached of all their festive colours. And however much Saffron had been overwhelmed at first by the size of Johannesburg, London was on a different scale altogether.

Coming into the center of the city from Croydon Aerodrome they drove for mile after mile past identical streets of terraced houses and one town center after another: each clustered around an Underground station; each with its own municipal hall, library, baths, shops, pubs and restaurants; each with streets more crowded than any Saffron had ever seen, and each just one of a myriad separate suburbs of the great, sprawling city.

Leon did his best to show his daughter the very finest that the center of the Empire had to offer. He booked a suite of rooms at the Ritz, which was gloriously indulgent, with a bedroom for each of them, huge beds with mattresses thick and comfortable enough for the fussiest princess and a bathroom that shone with the reflections from the polished marble walls and floor and the gleaming chrome of the baths and taps. He took her to the London Palladium, to see the Crazy Gang, and

even though she did not have the first idea who all the per-
formers were, nor why the audience lapped up their catchphrases
with such delight and obvious familiarity, still she found herself
caught up in the atmosphere and was soon laughing and clapping along with everyone else. Leon also discovered the joys of
the Lyon's Corner House tearooms that seemed to be present on
half the streets of central London. "They know how to make a
proper cup of tea here," he said approvingly. "Good and strong,
in a simple cup, reminds me of the army." But even so, though
both Saffron and Leon did their best to keep their spirits up,
they both had the same thought repeating itself in their minds:
I wish I were back in Kenya.

But they had both come too far to change their minds now,
even if that were something that ever came easily to either of
them. So they had to make the best of it. Once again Leon found
himself heading off with Saffron on another expedition to buy
yet more school uniforms and equipment and, having asked the
Ritz concierge where one went for such things in London, was
directed to Daniel Neal, the leading light in school outfitting,
whose flagship store was in Portman Square, just north of Oxford
Street.

"Goodness, it's huge!" Saffron said as they emerged from the
taxi and found themselves confronted by three plate-glass windows, each as wide as a typical London townhouse and all
decorated with mannequins of impeccably dressed schoolchil-
dren. The shop filled the ground and first floor along half the
length of a massive modern mansion block that took up most
of one side of the square.

"Well, I think we can assume it will have everything you
need," said Leon, who was keen to buy the maximum number
of necessary items in the minimum number of shops and the
smallest possible time. "Come on, let's find out."

They walked in and then stopped dead as they looked around
and tried to work out where on earth they could find everything
they required. Across the floor they could see a woman in a

smart black dress. Her back was turned to them, but she was clearly giving instructions to one of the shop assistants.

"That's the ticket, someone in authority," said Leon and started making his way toward her. By now the woman had sent her underling on her way but, clearly being the kind of perfectionist who noticed the smallest fault and felt bound to correct it, was bending over a table, making fractional adjustments to a display of jumpers.

"Excuse me, Miss," said Leon. "My daughter and I need assistance."

The woman straightened and turned to face them. A puzzled expression crossed her face, the look of someone who has just seen something or someone in an entirely unfamiliar context yet knows that they are familiar, but can't quite work out how.

A similar bafflement, now turning to mutual embarrassment as both grown-ups found themselves in the same predicament, had seized Leon and for a moment he and the woman both just stared at one another, neither knowing quite what to say.

And then Saffron realized exactly who the woman was.

———

"Miss Halfpenny! It's me, Saffron Courtney . . . from Jo'burg. I went to Roedean."

The manageress's face was at once lit up by a warm, engaging smile. "Of course! I knew I remembered you . . . and your father, too."

"Leon Courtney," he said, holding out a hand. "I don't believe we've ever been properly introduced."

"Harriet Halfpenny . . ." She frowned. "Hmm . . . I'm not sure whether I should be quite so familiar with customers, but it really is an unexpected delight to see you both again. May I ask what brings you here?"

"The same as brought us to the last shop we saw you in: school uniforms for Saffron."

"May I ask which school in particular?"

"The same one, Roedean," said Saffron. "Except this one's in England."

"Very well then, you will need a blue blazer, blue skirts, white shirts and a tie striped according to your house colors."

"I don't know what house I'm going to be in. It's all been awfully sudden," said Saffron.

"Never mind, I'm sure you can get the right one at the school itself. You'll also be requiring shoes, stockings, gym kits, of course, as well as nighties. We only have a limited range of those, I'm afraid, I suggest Selfridges or John Lewis if you want a wider selection, and likewise for dressing gowns and undies."

"Oh Lord . . ." groaned Leon.

Miss Halfpenny looked at Leon, then turned her eyes toward Saffron, who gave a little shrug that said, "No, it's still just the two of us."

"Would you like me to take care of everything, Mr. Courtney?" Miss Halfpenny asked. "As I recall, Saffron and I used to manage pretty well by ourselves."

Leon was about to agree, but then changed his mind. "Actually, I think I'll come with you. When I think of all the dangers I've faced like a man, it seems a bit feeble to run away from a bit of shopping."

"Well said, sir!" Miss Halfpenny said, with a little clap of her hands. Leon looked delighted by the compliment and Saffron, observing the way the pair of them were grinning at one another, suddenly realized that her school uniform was suddenly a very long way from being the most important thing about their shopping expedition.

She thought about the care her father had taken to dress smartly and look well groomed on the days when they had visited the school shop in Johannesburg, and of his disappointment when he was told that Miss Halfpenny had been forced to return to England. She thought of all the women who had told her that they would be her friend: *But Miss Halfpenny already is my friend. I really like her because I know how nice she is.*

As they went round the shop Saffron did everything she could to include her father in her conversations with Miss Halfpenny and was delighted when he said things that made her laugh or say, "Quite right, Mr. Courtney." It struck Saffron that she was seeing a completely new side to her father. He was relaxed with Miss Halfpenny, more ready to laugh at himself and even flirtatious in a way that was really quite sweet because he was so obviously unaware he was doing it. *She makes him happy,* Saffron thought. And then, *But what would people say if Leon Courtney married a shopgirl?* And then, *Who cares what anyone else thinks? She's the right person for him, that's all that matters. In any case she's not a shopgirl, she's a manageress. And Daddy hates snobs, anyway, so that's that.*

By the time Miss Halfpenny was ringing up all Saffron's new clothes at the till, while assorted underlings packed them away in shopping bags, Saffron had decided that it was her job to keep the two grown-ups as close to one another as possible for as long as it took for them both to realize what was best for them. She was just pondering how to do this when Miss Halfpenny said, "There are an awful lot of bags. If you don't want to be troubled with them I can have them sent round to wherever you're staying."

"Thank you," said Leon. "We're at the . . ."

"Oh, don't you worry, Daddy, I'm sure we can manage," Saffron interrupted, feeling absolutely certain that if Miss Halfpenny knew they were staying at the Ritz, she would immediately feel that they were far above her station and abandon any thought of romance.

"Oh, well, if you don't mind lugging a couple of bags yourself, darling."

"Not at all," said Saffron and then, feeling that strong and purposeful action was required, said, "Would you like to have tea with us, when you finish work, Miss Halfpenny? It would be so nice for us to talk to someone else who knows Africa. And Daddy has developed an absolute passion for Lyon's Corner Houses."

"I quite agree, they're admirable institutions," said Miss Halfpenny. "But I don't get off until five, and I'm sure you have better things to do this afternoon than take tea with me."

Leon didn't say anything. Saffron, who was standing next to him, with the counter between them and Miss Halfpenny, gave him a hefty kick on the ankles, just as if she were booting a horse into action.

"Nonsense!" he said, nobly resisting the temptation to kick his daughter right back. "I can't think of anything more pleasant."

Miss Halfpenny pondered the invitation. "Is Piccadilly Circus at all convenient for you?" she asked.

"Absolutely. It's just down the road from our hotel."

"Very well, then," said Miss Halfpenny, becoming her usual, businesslike self again. "Do you know the Trocadero on Piccadilly Circus? It has a magnificent entrance, with great big columns and a pediment above it, just like a Greek temple. It's quite the tourist attraction. And it's even run by Lyon's, just like the Corner Houses, so the tea should be to your taste."

"In that case, Saffron and I will meet you at five thirty, just inside the magnificent entrance. How does that sound?"

"Like the most tremendous fun," said Harriet Halfpenny.

———

"Welcome to the Troc," said Miss Halfpenny when she met Leon and Saffron.

"You look nice," Leon said.

"Thank you."

"I love your hair, Miss Halfpenny," Saffron said. "It looks so nice down."

She had noticed at once that Miss Halfpenny had unpinned her hair, which now fell in auburn waves around her oval face.

She had put mascara and liner around her hazel eyes, too, and rouged her lips and cheeks. Saffron was delighted. *You want to look nice for him. And you really do!*

"Ah, so that's what it is. I knew something was different," Leon said. "Well, it's jolly nice, anyway. Now, there seem to be a stack of different rooms to go to in here. What do you suggest?"

"That depends," said Miss Halfpenny, "do you like music and dancing, Saffron?"

"Oh yes, but I'm useless at dancing. I've never really learned how to do it at all."

"Then it's time you learned. Follow me."

The interior of the Trocadero resembled a grand opera house, rather than a tearoom. A grand, red-carpeted staircase decorated with murals depicting the legend of King Arthur and his knights of the round table rose through the heart of the building, wrapping around a bronze statue of a classical goddess, who held up a light designed to look like a flaming torch. Palm fronds sprouted from pots and urns at the foot of the stairs and along the first-floor landing. There was a splendid bar with a sign by the entrance that said "Gentlemen Only."

"That really makes me want to go in it," Saffron whispered to Miss Halfpenny as they walked by.

"I shouldn't think we're missing very much," she replied.

Saffron heard a jazz band, playing somewhere in the building. The music grew louder as they drew near and then they entered a great salon. Small round dining tables, crowded with people, were packed close together on the floor, with the only open space reserved for the shiny wooden dance floor. Saffron looked up and saw the band, seated on the balcony that ran right around the room, with more tables, from which diners could look down on the scene below.

"Let's go up there!" she said, pointing to the balcony.

"Excuse me," said Leon and went in search of the maître d'.

"So . . . this is the Empire Hall," said Miss Halfpenny to Saffron. "What do you think?"

"It's amazing! I'm so glad you suggested it."

"Ah! I think we may be in business. Your father is calling us."

Sure enough, Leon was waving at them from across the floor. He was standing next to a plump, mustachioed man in a black uniform.

"*Ah, cosi belle signorine!*" the maître d' exclaimed. "Signor, you did not tell me that your wife and daughter were so beautiful."

"Well . . ." Leon began, and then stopped himself and instead said, "They are rather lovely, aren't they?"

Well done, Daddy! Saffron thought as she followed the maître d' up the stairs.

"One little moment," he said as they reached the balcony. He flicked his fingers, summoning two waiters as if by magic. Then he issued instructions in a flurry of words and gesticulations and, by another act of conjuring, space appeared where there had been none and was instantly filled by a table, right by the balustrade, covered in a crisp white cloth, polished cutlery and gleaming glasses.

"Would the *signore* care for anything to drink?" the maître d' asked when they had all been seated.

Leon consulted his watch. "Hmm . . . very nearly six o'clock. It's really too late for tea, don't you think? A bottle of champagne will do very nicely."

An ice-bucket appeared on a stand beside the table, followed soon after by a wine waiter who deftly popped the cork, poured champagne for all three of them—Saffron was thrilled that her father did not stop the waiter as he filled her glass—and then placed the bottle into the bucket.

"Cheers!" said Leon, raising his glass. "Here's to Africa . . . and London . . . and to you, Miss Halfpenny. Where would we be without you?"

"Somewhere not nearly as nice," said Saffron, raising her glass.

The conversation did not flag for a second as they enjoyed their drinks. Then Miss Halfpenny said, "I think it's time I taught you a few dance steps, Saffron."

"What? In front of all these people?"

"Go on," said Leon. "I dare you."

"Promise you won't laugh if I'm hopeless?"

"I promise. I shall stay up here, watching you both from afar."

The two women went down to the dance floor, where half a dozen couples were dancing to the waltz that the band was playing.

"I'll be the man," said Miss Halfpenny. "So, start by putting your right hand in my left hand . . . good. Next, put your left hand on my right shoulder . . . excellent. Now just watch my feet and try to follow them with yours, as if you were looking in a mirror. Off we go!"

They set off across the floor and within a few steps Saffron's feet were hopelessly tangled up and Miss Halfpenny's toes were smarting from having been trodden on.

"I'll never get the hang of this!" Saffron protested.

"Yes, you will. Now try again."

By the sixth try, Saffron had mastered the basic step. By the end of the second song she was moving almost gracefully. When the song ended, she looked up at the balcony and saw her father clapping. He gave her a little nod, to signal his approval. Then, as the music started again, she saw him get up from the table and make his way along the balcony toward the stairs. Miss Halfpenny had seen him too. They stepped to the side of the dance floor and waited for Leon to join them.

He arrived a few moments later. "Well done, Saffron, you picked that up very quickly. I'm impressed. Now it's time your clumsy old father had a go. May I have the pleasure of the next dance, Miss Halfpenny?"

"Yes," she said. "You may."

He took her in his arms and Saffron saw that her father was not in the slightest bit clumsy, nor did he resemble an old man. As they stepped onto the dance floor and joined the other couples, Leon held Miss Halfpenny with an air of confident command and she, Saffron noticed, responded by relaxing her shoulders and molding her body to his, just fractionally, but enough. She tilted her head so that she was looking up at him and their eyes met and Saffron caught it, at once, the spark between them, the instant connection.

Saffron skipped upstairs, her feet hardly touching the steps beneath them, so happy that it was almost as if she were the one falling in love. After all these years, her father had finally found someone. Saffron raised her eyes, as if to the sky. She wondered if her mother was looking down on them. Saffron knew that if she were, she would be happy too.

———

The school had reserved two coaches on the Brighton train and the platform at Victoria station was filled with schoolgirls, and their parents saying goodbye. Like the others, Saffron was already dressed in her uniform, for school rules applied from the moment the girls stepped on board the train. Leon tipped the station porter, who had taken Saffron's luggage on board, then turned to her and said, "Good luck, old girl. I hope you have a splendid first term. Just keep your nose down, work hard, be your usual charming self and I'm sure you'll find that you'll have fitted right in before even you know it."

"Don't worry, I will," Saffron replied. "And Daddy . . ."

"Yes?"

"I really, really like Miss Halfpenny."

"We seem to be in agreement, then, because I rather like her, too."

"I know. And I don't mind at all."

"Oh don't you now?" Leon grinned. "How very gracious of you! Now, come here and give your father a hug."

Saffron snuggled into her father's embrace, got up on tiptoe to give him a kiss on the cheek and then said her final goodbye. A moment later, she was on the train and instantly turned her mind to school and the term ahead, with barely a thought for the father she was leaving behind.

Her first problem was where to sit. Every compartment she looked into seemed to be filled with girls, all abuzz with conversation, picking up their friendships after the weeks apart over Christmas. Finally she came to one in which there was just a single girl. She was blonde and Saffron noticed that while all the other girls seemed to have found ways of making their well-worn uniforms just a little bit more relaxed, some even verging on the scruffy, this girl's was as smart as a new pin. Saffron had been feeling a little self-conscious in her own immaculate uniform and had been well aware of the inquisitive eyes being turned in her direction and the huddled whispers as girls speculated on who the new girl might be. But perhaps she was not alone, after all. She opened the compartment door and stepped inside.

"Do you mind if I sit here?" she said, indicating the seat opposite the one on which the blonde girl was perched.

"Not at all, please go ahead," the girl replied. She sounded a little nervous and her accent was foreign, though Saffron could not place it.

"Hello," she said. "I'm Saffron Courtney."

"Good afternoon, Saffron. My name is Francesca von Schöndorf."

"Oh, are you German?"

Francesca's face fell. "Yes," she sighed, as if she knew that this would not be welcome information.

"Are you a new girl too?" Saffron asked.

"No, already for one term I have been at Roedean."

"I'm only just starting. I used to be at the other Roedean, in South Africa."

"There is a Roedean in Africa?" Francesca sounded amazed at the very idea. "I did not know that. So you are South African, ja?"

"No, I come from Kenya. So what's school like?"

"Difficult, I must say," Francesca admitted. "The teachers are very good, yes, and the situation is remarkable, right by the sea on high, how you say . . . *klippen*?"

"Cliffs?"

"Yes, of course, cliffs. So the sea is very beautiful, although often it looks gray because the sky also is gray . . ."

Saffron laughed. "I know! Everything in England is gray!"

For the first time Francesca relaxed enough to smile. "I think so, too!"

"How about the other girls?"

Francesca's smile turned to a grimace. "Not so good . . . I mean, many of the girls are very nice. But there are some who do not like me."

"Really? Why not?"

"Because I am German. Maybe they have fathers who died in the war, or they think all Germans are monsters, but in any case they let me know that I am not welcome."

"I think that's beastly! It sounds to me as if they're just bullies. They're looking for any excuse they can find to be horrible to other girls, so they pick on you for being German."

"Yes, this is maybe true. Of course, I cannot tell my parents what happens. They would not believe it because they have lots of friends and family in England. My father used to know the Kaiser and of course the grandmother of the Kaiser was Queen Victoria of England. My grandmother was English, too, actually."

"What a coincidence! My grandmother was German."

"Really? You are not teasing me?"

"Not at all. She was my mother's mother. I never met her because she died when my mother was just a girl."

"Oh that is so sad. But your mother can tell you about her, no?"

Saffron shrugged. "No, my mother died when I was seven."

"Oh, I am so sorry."

"That's all right. You weren't to know. But tell me all about your family. Fancy your father knowing the Kaiser. Is he terribly grand?"

As it turned out, he was. The von Schöndorfs were an old Bavarian family, although for all her talk of palaces and castles, Francesca gave the impression that her people were not as rich or as mighty as they once were and were increasingly forced to sell family portraits, heirlooms or properties just to make ends meet. For her part, Francesca was thrilled by Saffron's descriptions of Lusima and amazed when Saffron described encounters with rhinos, elephants and even lions as everyday occurrences.

The two girls talked all the way to Brighton, and then on the coach that took them to the school. They stood together in line as the girls all snaked past the teaching staff who were, as school custom dictated, lined up to shake the hand of every girl in the school, and then Francesca, who told Saffron that her family all called her Chessi, showed her around. Both girls now knew that they had at least one person they could always sit next to and at the start of any school term that made all the difference.

———

Leon walked back across Green Park to the Ritz, glad of the chance to stretch his legs. He felt as though he had a lot of nervous energy to work off. *By God, I feel like a bloody schoolboy*, he thought to himself. *Get a grip of yourself, man!*

Earlier in the day, while Saffron was busy packing, he had sent a messenger round to the Daniel Neal store, with a note addressed to Miss Halfpenny, inviting her to meet him for dinner at the Ritz. The messenger had been instructed to wait for her reply, and duly brought it back to the hotel.

"Thank you for a delightful, but rather sudden invitation," Miss Halfpenny had written in a neat, feminine hand. "I need to think about it. But I will send you a proper answer as soon as I can."

None had arrived before Leon had taken Saffron to her train.

The business of getting his daughter off to school had occupied his mind until she was actually on the train, but the moment their farewells were complete, Leon's attention, like Saffron's, had shifted elsewhere: in his case, right back to Miss Halfpenny. He stepped through the gate from the park onto Piccadilly, turned right and had to restrain himself from running the final few yards along the street, underneath the hotel arches, through the front entrance in and up to the reception desk.

"Is there a message for Mr. Courtney?" he asked, when he reached his destination, doing his very best to seem offhand.

The young man behind the desk had to concentrate hard, as if dragging the very deepest recesses of his memory before he could finally answer, "I believe that does ring a bell, sir, yes. Excuse me one moment."

He went away to consult a rather older, more imposing functionary, further up the desk. The younger man returned, bearing a note, which he then looked at before saying, "Miss Halfpenny called for you, sir. She says she would be delighted to accept your invitation and will meet you for dinner at eight."

"Excellent news!" said Leon, and pressed a ten-shilling note into the young man's hand.

"That's very generous of you, sir, much obliged. And may I wish you a most enjoyable evening."

Leon visited the hotel barber to have his hair neatly trimmed and his chin shaved as close as an expertly wielded razor could manage. He had already taken the precaution of having his dress shirt and dinner suit cleaned and pressed and was looking the picture of manly elegance as he went downstairs at half-past seven. The same staff member was still behind the desk and was only too happy to oblige when asked if he could direct Miss Halfpenny to the Palm Court when she arrived. Leon went on ahead and procured a table nestled in the most discreet corner he could find, which was no easy task in a white, pink and gold-painted salon, with a glass ceiling and

mirrored walls whose entire purpose was for guests to see and
be seen. Then he ordered a whisky on the rocks and waited
for his guest to arrive.

———————

Harriet Halfpenny stepped out of the cab, gave a shilling to
the footman who had opened the door and stood for a moment
on the pavement as she composed herself. She forced herself
to hold her head up and walk into the Ritz as if she owned
the place. Her first destination was the cloakroom, where she
deposited her overcoat, which suddenly seemed embarrassingly
cheap and tatty, though it was a perfectly warm, serviceable
garment. Next she went to the ladies' room and inspected her
reflection. Her delay in replying to Leon Courtney's invitation
had owed nothing to any reluctance to see him. She had simply
been unable to contemplate walking into the Ritz in the dress
she wore to work. In her lunch hour she had dashed out to
Selfridges and spent a sum of money that was way beyond her
means, one that would have her living on bread and water for
the next month, in fact, on a long evening dress in green silk.
Harriet did not think of herself as having the body of a great
seductress, but she was reasonably tall and long-limbed and
had, thanks to her many years of membership of her local
netball club, kept her figure reasonably trim. Her breasts were
neat, and actually rather fuller than might have been expected
from her naturally slender, narrow-hipped build. And now she
came to look at herself, the dress did seem to fit very well,
and whatever assets she had were being displayed to her best
advantage. *Right you are, girl*, she told her reflection in the
mirror. *Over the top you go*.

   She went to the reception desk, could not help smiling when
the young man behind it said, "Mr. Courtney is going to be
very pleased to see you, Miss," and made for the Palm Court.
She had to make an effort to keep her jaw from dropping as
she walked in, for the room was sumptuous. The palms after
which it was named were dotted around the edge of the room,

but her eye was struck by a huge floral centerpiece at its heart, which was festooned with huge, pink roses whose blooms seemed to defy the winter outside.

Harriet searched for Leon Courtney. And then, there he was, in the far corner, rising to his feet to greet her. *By God, you're a good-looking man*, she thought. With his height, his broad shoulders and his immaculately tailored dinner jacket, Leon cut an imposing figure. But it was his face that she loved. That deeply tanned skin made all the Englishmen around him look pallid and whey-faced. It set off the white of his strong, square teeth, just as the lines around his eyes framed his clear, dark eyes. Oh, those eyes! There was strength, and intelligence, and warmth, and the hint of possible anger in them, but also there was sadness.

This was a man whose wife had died and never been replaced, though goodness knows enough women must have tried. So why did she, a spinster who worked in a shop, think that she stood a chance when all those others had failed? It was an absurd proposition, or at least it should have been. But Harriet had seen the way he looked at her when he thought her attention was elsewhere. She knew how pleased Saffron had been to see her and how much her approval would mean to her father. It had been Saffron who had made the running on her father's behalf, acting the matchmaker. But none of that really counted for any-thing now. All that mattered was the feeling that had filled her when Leon had first held her on the dance floor at the Troc, the look in his eyes when he gazed at her, and the unmistakable evidence of his arousal when she pressed her body against his.

He had seen her now and a broad grin was crossing his face, in an expression of undiluted, boyish glee. *He's thrilled to see me!* she thought and then they were saying hello and not quite sure whether to shake hands, or kiss, or what to do at all.

"Remind me, what did I say you looked like, the other evening at the Troc?" Leon asked.

"You said I looked nice."

"Did I now?" He looked at her again and now his eyes conveyed an entirely new message that Harriet had never seen in them before. Now they were hungry, predatory, penetrating so deep into her she had to grasp the top of the chair by her side for fear that her knees would give way completely if she did not.

"Well, you don't look "nice" now, my darling. You look absolutely ravishing."

Harriet's pulse was racing as his eyes continued to bore into her. She felt the molten heat between her legs as a little devil inside her head was saying, *Just throw me over the table and take me now!* But then Leon smiled, the spell was broken and he said, "I ordered champagne cocktails for us both. Just like last time . . . only a little more exciting."

Harriet sat down, composed herself again as she sipped her drink and then, doing her very best to sound like a sophisticated woman making polite conversation, asked, "Are you staying here, while you're in London?"

"Saffron and I took a suite. It's a bit fancy for me, to be honest. I'm just a scruffy old African at heart."

"You don't look very scruffy."

He shrugged. "That's the army for you, teaches you to scrub up smart when required. Honestly, I'd be just as happy sleeping under the stars, next to a nice campfire. But this isn't really the weather for it, or the place, so here I am. It was nice for Saffron, anyway."

"She's a wonderful girl."

"Yes, she is . . ." Leon paused and looked at Harriet again, not quite as hungrily, perhaps, but still his eyes were dark and serious as he said, "She thinks the world of you, too, you know. It's, ah . . . it's the first time she's felt that about anyone. Since her mother died, I mean."

Harriet knew full well that Leon was speaking about himself, as well as Saffron. "Look, Mr. Courtney . . ."

"Please, for heaven's sake, call me Leon."

"Very well, Leon . . ."

"Should I still call you Miss Halfpenny?" he asked, with a teasing look in his eye, before she could go any further.

"No," she giggled. "Call me Harriet."

"All right, then, Harriet it is. Now, what were you about to say before I so rudely interrupted you?"

"Just this: you are obviously a very successful man. You fly from Africa to England at a moment's notice and book a suite at the Ritz. Your suit is beautifully tailored . . ."

"By a splendid Indian gentleman in Nairobi who charges me almost nothing . . ."

"Well, wherever you get it, the point is that you are you, and I am just a thirty-five-year-old spinster who works in a shop. And I can't quite see how I can hope to be worthy of you."

"Well, if you are a thirty-five-year-old spinster then I am a forty-eight-year-old widower, so that makes us even," he replied. "And as for working in a shop, let me tell you the way I see it. I respect anyone who gets up in the morning, stands on their own two feet and puts in a hard day's work for a fair day's pay. I admire you for doing your job, and doing it damn well, I might add, far more than some la-di-da society woman who lives off her daddy, or her husband, or her trust fund and never does a hand's turn in her life.

"Look, Harriet, let me put my cards on the table. I know . . . Hell, I've probably known from that first day in Johannesburg . . . that you are not only the most attractive woman I've met in God knows how long, but you're also the best woman, too. You're strong, and independent, but also kind and funny and warm. I saw the way you took Saffron off, that very first time, and looked after her and made her feel at ease. I thought of all the other women I've known, because I've not been a monk, believe me. Not one of them ever got on as well with Saffy, no matter how hard they tried, as you did from the moment you met her. That told me a helluva lot about the kind of woman you were."

"Thank you," murmured Harriet, who suddenly found that she wanted to cry.

"You don't have to thank me. I should thank *you*. The third time Saffy and I went back to Jo'burg, I told myself I'd buck up and ask you out for a drink, or dinner or something. Then the woman there told me you'd gone back to England and I was kicking myself. I couldn't believe I'd been so stupid and let you get away. But now you're here, and you're giving me another chance. And believe me, Harriet, I intend to take it."

He paused. "That's all I have to say," he added and gave her a sweet, self-deprecating smile.

"Don't worry. That's all you need to say."

"Good. Now, shall we order some food? I don't know about you, but I am absolutely famished."

Harriet did not sleep with Leon Courtney that night, though she was sorely tempted. Denying herself as much as him, she restricted their intimacy to a brief kiss as they were saying goodbye, while the hotel footman summoned a taxi. After their second dinner she let him see her home and had the very great pleasure of kissing him at length, and feeling his hands exploring almost—but not quite—every inch of her body in the back of the cab as it drove to her very modest little terraced house in the deeply unfashionable backstreets of Fulham. She had inherited the place from her mother, who had died a year after her return to England. It shamed Harriet to find herself feeling grateful for her mother's passing: it meant she was free to do as she pleased.

On their next date they went to the pictures, just like a pair of courting youngsters. The film they chose was *The 39 Steps*. All Harriet's friends said it was tremendously good, but she emerged from the cinema none the wiser for most of the film had been spent smooching with Leon in the next seat, rather than watching Robert Donat's adventures on the screen.

They continued in this fashion for another fortnight, both deliriously happy but increasingly frustrated. Leon was generous, kind, amusing and never once made her feel that she owed him anything in return for the dinners he bought her, and then the dresses to wear to the dinners, and then a pair of earrings and a pearl necklace to go with the dresses. "Without you, I would be alone, and bored and completely lacking in any idea of where to go," he said. "And with you, I'm the happiest man in London."

Harriet found herself wanting to tell Leon if something funny happened to her, or she saw a newspaper story that she knew would interest him, or even if she had been forced to endure an exceptionally rude customer and just needed to get it off her chest. She was fascinated by the life Leon had led in Africa, and when he talked about his estate at Lusima, she longed to see it, not just because she knew it would be quite unlike anything she had ever experienced in her life—wilder, more beautiful, filled with extraordinary animals and people—but because it was his place, and he loved it so, and she wanted to be part of that love.

Then one day, he said, "Do you fancy a weekend in the country? I've been invited to meet all my English cousins. They have a place down in Devon. It's called High Weald, been in the family since the seventeenth century. I've never been there myself, but I'm told it's very lovely." He paused and stroked his chin in mock contemplation. "Hmm . . . hope they've improved the plumbing and heating since they moved in. Maybe installed the odd lavatory or two, that sort of thing."

Harriet giggled. "I thought you were the hardy outdoorsman who liked to sleep out under the stars. Why would you care about plumbing and heating?"

"I must be getting soft since I met you."

"Soft in the head, certainly."

"Anyway, would you like to come along?"

"Are you sure? I don't want to feel like I'm spoiling a family occasion."

"Nonsense, you won't spoil anything. I've told them all about you and they can't wait to meet you. We can leave after you finish work on Friday afternoon and I promise I'll have you back in London, safe and sound in time for Monday morning. Please . . . I really would like it very much. And before you ask, yes, of course you will have your own room. We aren't married and the English members of the Courtney clan are sticklers for etiquette. Though I dare say our rooms won't be too far apart . . ."

Harriet had never been to a country house party, but she'd read enough novels to know that while the social rules might be scrupulously observed on the surface, blind eyes were turned to anything that happened once the lights were out. Leon's invitation was a declaration of intent.

"Yes," she said, "that sounds wonderful. I'd love to come."

———

High Weald was nestled between rolling hills that looked out toward the sea. Its lawns ran down to a low cliff, where a path descended to a sandy cove. On a cold, still day in late January, with the sky as cloudless as midsummer, mirrored in the flat-calm sea, it was a perfect place for two lovers to walk to hand-in-hand, for the man to lead his woman safely down the steep, stony path and for the two of them to stand, arm in arm, and look out across the waters.

They held each other differently now, in the way that two lovers do after their bodies have joined as one, with that perfect, effortless match of one form to another that told them both that they were made to be together. Harriet pulled Leon still closer to her and sighed contentedly. Then her sigh became a yawn.

"Bored of me already?"

"Just tired," she said, her voice muffled by the way her head was half-buried in his overcoat. "You've completely exhausted me, you wicked man."

"Well the fresh sea air should wake you up. Come on . . ." He pulled her off him. "Take a few deep breaths, that's the spirit!" Harriet did her best to oblige but then he said, "Right, now for some bracing exercise. Ten jumping jacks . . . One! Two!"

"No, shan't!" she said, defiantly yawning again.

"Oh all right, you win . . . lazy-bones," Leon said. He wrapped his arms around her again. "You must admit though, it was a very nice way to get exhausted."

"Mmm . . ." she nodded and he bent down to kiss the top of her head.

"I love you so much, Hattie, my darling."

She looked up at him. "I love you, too. With all my heart. And I love the way you kiss me, and I love the way you touch me, and stroke me and . . ." She reached out and stroked his crotch, gently rubbing her hand up and down the front of his trousers until she could feel him and then she said, "And I love that most of all. I love when you're inside me. I love the way you taste and I love your smell."

Leon grunted like a lazy, contented lion.

"Do you want to know a secret?" she asked him. He nodded and she said, "Remember that first dinner we had together, just the two of us, at the Ritz?"

"How could I forget?"

"When we first said hello, the way you looked at me, the things it did to me . . . you could have had me there and then."

"I'm going to have you now," Leon said. He led her back up the beach to where the sand was dry. Then he took off his coat, placed on the ground and she lay down upon it.

"Christ!" he muttered, placing himself on top of her. "It's bloody cold. I might get frostbite on my cock."

She gave a low purring laugh. "Silly man. Why don't you put it somewhere hot?"

He reached down and she opened her legs and lifted her bottom off the ground so that he could tug her skirt up around her hips and pull her knickers down her legs. She kicked them off and his hand felt for the soft, hot, wet, yielding core of her. Then it was her turn to feel for his fly buttons and the slit in his underpants and then she had him in his hands and he sprang free from the clothes that had confined him and she guided him into her, groaning with pleasure as she took him again.

Now he didn't give a damn about the cold. He couldn't care less that they were right out in the open and if any other members of the house party walked down to the cliff's edge they would certainly be spotted. All Leon cared about was his love and desire for his woman. He wanted her to feel it and know it in ways that went far beyond words. He wanted her to take pleasure in him and from him and his whole being was focused on her, all his senses alert to every sound, every movement she made. He kissed her and she responded and the boundaries between them blurred, like two watercolors on a piece of paper, joining as one to create something entirely new. She was his woman now and they would never be divided.

"Marry me," he said. "Please, I beg you. Marry me."

"Oh God," she moaned. "Yes," and then, her voice rising with every repetition, "Yes, yes, yes, yes, yes!"

———

The other members of the house party were delighted that the weekend had been graced by such a happy event. Champagne was brought up from the cellar, corks popped and toasts drunk to the happy couple. When Leon and Harriet had arrived at High Weald on Friday evening, they did so as strangers to his English cousins. But they were such an obviously delightful and well-matched couple and their happiness was so infectious that by the time they came to say their farewells on Sunday afternoon, both sides felt like family.

"Thank you so much for having us," Leon said to his host, Sir William Courtney, while the staff loaded his and Harriet's luggage into the car that would take them to catch the London train.

"My dear chap, it's been an absolute pleasure. It's not every day an engagement is announced beneath one's roof. It'll be the talk of Devon before the week is out, you mark my words. And well done, old man, Harriet's a splendid girl. You've found yourself an absolute cracker there."

Harriet meanwhile was kissing goodbye to Lady Courtney. "You must both promise to come to stay again before you go back to Kenya," her hostess said, with a squeeze of Harriet's hand to emphasize that this was a genuine invitation, not a mere pleasantry.

"We'd love that," Harriet replied, thinking how strange and also how wonderful it was to have become one half of a "we" after so many years of just being "I".

"And do bring Saffron down with you. I'm greatly looking forward to meeting her."

They were all smiles as they waved goodbye and the happy glow lasted all the way to Exeter station. But once they were settled in their first-class compartment and the train began the journey as dusk fell on the Devonshire countryside, Harriet became quieter, more melancholy.

At first Leon assumed that she was simply exhausted. Neither of them had slept more than a few hours over the entire weekend and their nights had been anything but restful. But as the time went by he realized that something was clearly bothering Harriet. This was the first time he had ever seen her unhappy and it troubled him deeply.

"What is it, my darling?"

She sighed, "I don't know . . ."

Leon knew enough about women not to believe that for a moment. But he also knew that there was no point forcing the issue. "Well, if there is something on your mind, you can tell me. I love you very much, Harriet Halfpenny, and nothing you say could ever change that."

"I fear that this might," she said, looking up at him with such sadness in her eyes that he had to reach out and take her in his arms.

"Darling Harriet," he said, kissing her hair and gently stroking her, trying with every means at his disposal to make her feel safe, and loved, and protected. She was crying now and, once again, Leon was grateful for the handkerchief he always wore in his breast pocket.

He waited until the crying had passed, then pulled back a little so he could look her in the eyes and very quietly said, "Please tell me. I just want to help."

"I'm just so worried that you'll be disappointed in me."

"Never!"

"It's just I would have told you before you asked me to marry you but you . . ." Harriet managed a faint smile, "You took me by surprise."

"I took myself by surprise, come to that! But it was a jolly nice surprise, don't you think?"

"Oh yes . . . the nicest. But there's something I have to tell you, and if it makes you want to change your mind, then I won't blame you or hold it against you."

A note of anxiety entered Leon's voice. "What could possibly make me do that? For goodness sakes, darling, please tell me. You've really got me worried."

"Well, it's very simple," Harriet said, gathering herself. "When I was very young, during the war, I had a sweetheart. We were going to get married, but he was killed in the Hundred Days Offensive, just a month before the Armistice. But he'd come home on leave in the spring and, well, I was pregnant . . . and I lost the baby . . . and, and . . . oh Leon, I can't have any more. I won't be able to give you a child!"

The resolve that had enabled her to tell her story cracked and Harriet fell back onto Leon's chest, sobbing.

"Oh, Harriet, you silly, wonderful, beautiful girl, I don't mind about that. I don't mind at all."

She looked up, hardly believing that could be true. "Really?"

"Really . . . In fact, I had been wondering how I was going to tell you that I didn't want us to have children. I thought you would be terribly disappointed. It's partly because I'm getting on a bit and I don't want to be a doddery old man who's old enough to be his children's grandpa. But the real truth is, I have already lost someone I loved very, very much because she was carrying my child, and I simply could not bear to lose you the same way. Even now, after all these years, there's a little voice in my head that tells me I killed Eva."

"But you didn't. You mustn't think that," said Harriet, reaching out to Leon, their roles reversed as she offered comfort to him.

"I know it's foolish, but I can't help it. And if you were pregnant . . . well, I'm not sure how I would cope, to be honest. So you don't have to worry in the very slightest. I am blessed with a wonderful daughter and that's good enough for me. All I want from you, my darling, is you. You are perfect in my eyes, and I want you till the day I die."

"I think you're just as silly as me," Harriet said, snuggling up against her man.

"Then we're the perfect couple, aren't we?" he replied.

————

Saffron was granted a weekend leave from school to attend her father's wedding. Leon married Harriet at Chelsea Town Hall and Saffron was both the bridesmaid and the only guest, for this was a very private occasion. Afterwards they lunched at the Troc, where Mr. and Mrs. Courtney had their first dance as a married couple. The same maître d' who had looked after them before was on duty. He recognized the gentleman with his two *"belle signorine"* at once and his smile only broadened when Harriet held up her left hand, with its gold wedding band and the diamond and sapphire engagement ring Leon had bought her at Garrard & Co., the Mayfair jewelry house that had catered to British royal families for the past two hundred years. She was beaming with delight as she said, "And this time, I really am his wife!"

They were all going on from the Troc to Victoria: Saffron to take the train back to school, while Leon and Harriet boarded the Simplon Orient Express service to Venice, but first Saffron and Harriet retired to the ladies' room for a private, woman-to-woman chat.

"I just wanted to say, thank you," Harriet said as they were both standing by the mirror, attending to their faces. "I'm sure that lots of girls in your position would hate the idea of their father finding someone new, and they'd be absolutely poisonous. I can't tell you how much it means to me that you have been so nice and so welcoming."

"Oh, I would have been poisonous . . . really poisonous if I'd wanted to be," Saffron said, making them both laugh. "But not to you, because I knew that you weren't like all the others. You didn't want anything from him. You didn't try to suck up to me." Saffron took Harriet's hand in hers. "I think you're lovely, Harriet . . . Oh, is it all right if I call you Harriet?"

"Of course! It is my name and you certainly can't call me Miss Halfpenny any longer."

"Well, I might sometimes, just to tease."

"Don't you dare!"

"Anyway, I love how happy Daddy has been since he met you, and I love it that of all the people in the world who could have been my stepmother, you're the one who is. And I really, really hope you have an absolutely super-smashing time on your honeymoon. There's only one thing I'm sad about . . ."

A look of alarm crossed Harriet's face. "Really? What's the matter?" she asked.

"I don't know, I just wish I could be there when you see Lusima for the first time. It's so magical."

"I wish you could be there too. But we won't be going out until Easter. I have to finish working my notice . . ."

"Do you really have to do that? Can't you just leave?"

"I could, yes. But then I would be letting my employer down and making more work for my colleagues and I would hate to think that I was the kind of woman who would do such a thing. Besides, the girl who's replacing me needs to be taught how everything's done."

"You know, you're a bit of a bossy-boots . . . in the nicest possible way," Saffron laughed.

"I dare say I am," Harriet admitted. "But in any case, your father needs to get the new office up and running and we think we might get a little house so that we all have somewhere to stay when we're in town. Perhaps you can help me decorate it. We can choose curtains and carpets and whatnot."

"I'd love that!"

"Good, then that's settled. We'll do all that before we leave, and it then won't be long before you come out for the summer holidays. I will still be terribly new to Kenya, so you can show me all around Lusima, and take me to all your favorite places."

"I will, I promise," Saffron said. "Now. We'd better get back to our table. Daddy will be wondering where you are. Come on, Mrs. Courtney, your husband awaits you."

"Mrs. Courtney . . ." murmured Harriet, still trying to get used to her new name. "Fancy that."

As an architect, Albert Speer stood for everything that the Modernists who had taught Gerhard von Meerbach at the Bauhaus most despised. His work did not look forward, but back. His desire was not to build modern homes and workplaces, but to create monstrous copies of ancient Greek and Roman buildings, on a monumental scale that dwarfed even the mightiest Classical temple or amphitheater. And he did this not to improve the lives of ordinary people, but to glorify his master Adolf Hitler.

Yet however much Gerhard hated to admit it, even to himself, there was something profoundly exciting in finding oneself so close to the center of power in Germany. The Führer saw himself as a frustrated artist and architect, so took a close personal interest in all the plans that Speer drew up, for they envisaged nothing less than a total rebuilding, even a re-imagining of Berlin. It did not matter what existing streets or buildings stood in the way, Speer and his team, among whom Gerhard now found himself, were free to design on the basis that anything that stood in their way would simply be obliterated, if Hitler liked what they proposed to put up instead.

The scale on which Speer was planning gave Gerhard entry into the magnitude of Hitler's ambitions, for what they were creating was not the capital of a country, or even an expanded Reich, but of a global empire. Elsewhere in Berlin another architect, Werner March, was supervising the construction of a Olympic Stadium seating one hundred thousand spectators. It frustrated Speer that March was working in concrete, steel, bricks and mortar, while he was still restricted to pencil, ink and paper, but he got his own back by proposing structures that would make March's apparently splendid stadium look like an insignificant pimple.

There would be a grand, triumphal boulevard called the Avenue of Splendors slicing through the heart of the city. Its commencement would be marked by a triumphal arch, many times larger than the Arc de Triomphe or the Brandenburg Gate, and it would lead to a Great Square covering three hundred and fifty thousand square meters of open space. Along one side would rise the Führer's own palace, built on a scale that would dwarf Versailles. Directly opposite the Arch, on the far side of the Great Square, would stand the People's Hall, whose domed design was inspired by Hitler's own sketches. The dome of the hall was intended to be two hundred meters high and two hundred and fifty meters wide: so huge, in fact, that one of the tasks assigned to Gerhard was to conceive of ways to prevent clouds forming inside the dome and raining on the people within it.

Craftsmen had been working for months to create a room-sized model of the entire scheme showing a huge section of the new city with all its streets and major buildings.

One day in late February 1936, Speer told his staff that the Führer himself would be paying a personal visit to their studios to examine the model and go over the plans.

"The Führer is under great strain at the moment," Speer explained. "There are matters which I am not at liberty to discuss that may very soon transform the position of the Reich, and make the German people a power within Europe once again. The Führer bears the entire weight of responsibility for our glorious future upon his shoulders. He needs, and deserves the chance to relax, to take his mind off his responsibilities, if only for a few brief moments. It is our great privilege to be able to provide him with that opportunity. I therefore call on all of you to do everything in your power to make our glorious leader's visit an enjoyable one."

The announcement threw the entire office into something close to a frenzy. The female staff dashed to the ladies' rooms to make themselves look beautiful for their master. The men put on jackets, straightened ties, combed their hair and tried to adopt the proper attitude. "But what should that be?" they asked one another. Did Hitler want to see confident, purposeful men who could be entrusted with the creation of his capital? Or should they be deferential, modest and silent until spoken to?

And then, suddenly, he was there, that instantly recognizable face, already known to all the world, but dressed in a tweed suit, rather than the usual brown uniform jacket: the great architect now, rather than the great leader.

Gerhard was as transfixed as everyone else. *If Jesus Christ himself had appeared here we could not be more in awe of him*, he thought, suddenly realizing that he was no different to anyone else, no more capable of remaining independent or skeptical in the presence of the Führer.

They had been told to keep working while the visit was in progress: "The Führer wants to see activity and progress," Speer had said. So Gerhard dragged his eyes away from Hitler and back to his drawing board. He was drawing a ventilation duct for the dome of the People's Hall when he heard a coughing noise, clearly designed to attract his attention, just over his left shoulder.

Gerhard looked round and there, less than two meters away, was Adolf Hitler, with Albert Speer beside him. Gerhard jumped from the high stool on which he had been perched and, as an immediate reflex action, saluted the Führer with a cry of "Heil Hitler!"

Hitler responded with a salute that was little more than a flick of the wrist and then Speer said, "This is one of our most promising young staff, Gerhard von Meerbach."

"Of the engine-making family?" Hitler inquired, looking at Gerhard.

"Yes, my Führer. My brother Konrad is the present Count von Meerbach."

"Von Meerbach is not only a promising architect, he is also a volunteer pilot in the Luftwaffe."

Hitler nodded approvingly. "You see, Speer, this is National Socialism at its best. Here we have a young man from an aristocratic family, yet he does not waste his time in a world of privilege. He helps to build the Reich and also to defend the Reich." Then he stepped forward and gave Gerhard an avuncular pat on the arm. "Well done, young man," he said, and his blue eyes looked right at Gerhard, who found himself transfixed. Hitler possessed a form of charm that was something close to mesmerism. To be in the Führer's presence, eye to eye, was to be utterly persuaded of his greatness so that one wanted nothing more in life but to do whatever one could to serve his cause.

"*Ach so*, I see you are working on the Great Hall. So, tell me von Meerbach, what do you think of my scheme for the building?"

And Gerhard found himself saying, as if no other words were possible, "I think it is magnificent, my Führer."

———

Saffron and her new friend Chessi von Schöndorf had made a deal in the very first days of their friendship. Chessi would help Saffron to learn to speak German and in return would be taught enough Swahili so that, as she put it, "I can to my parents the most great shock give! They send me to England to speak English better, but now I shall pretend that I am at Roedean only speaking African. They will not know what has happened."

This was, Saffron agreed, an excellent scheme. In the event, however, she only learned two words. *"Hujambo"*, which meant "Hello" or "How are you?" and *"Sijambo"*, which was the conventional reply, meaning, "Fine." When Saffy and Chessi were overheard using *"Hujambo?"* *"Sijambo!"* as their greeting to one another, their in-joke became an instant craze throughout the entire school as four hundred and fifty English schoolgirls and a very few foreign students put on their idea of African voices and pretended to be Zulu or Masai princesses.

The craze was over in a matter of weeks, but by that time its two originators had entered the ranks of the most popular girls in their year, a position that only became stronger for Saffy when her skill on the sports field, allied to her good looks, made her the target of a hundred adoring "pashes"—as the younger girls' crushes on the older ones were known—from the junior end of the school. Popularity had always found Saffy without her having to look for it. For Chessi, on the other hand, this sudden acceptance by girls who had previously been cold to her was a thrilling new experience. She immediately set her Swahili studies aside and plunged into her exciting new social life. Saffron, meanwhile, stuck to her guns, gradually improving her German until she and Chessi could chat to one another, even if she regularly had to reach for English words and phrases when the German ones were still unknown to her.

After weeks when it seemed as though the Easter term would go on for ever, it suddenly seemed to be over in no time at all. She spent the first half of the four-week holiday in London with

Leon and Harriet. They had bought a flat in Chesham Court, an apartment block newly converted from a Victorian mansion on Chesham Place in the heart of Belgravia, just a few minutes' walk from Sloane Square in one direction and Knightsbridge in the other: right in the heart of one of the smartest and most attractive parts of town.

"You can stay here when you need to spend a night or two in town," Leon told Saffron. "We've hired a part-time house-keeper, Mrs. Perkins. Give her a couple of days' notice before you arrive and she'll have the whole place freshened up. I dare say she'll even cook you a meal or two if you ask her nicely."

As promised, Harriet let Saffron help her with the decoration of the flat and the two of them spent a week scouring department stores like Peter Jones and Harrods, and a mass of antiques shops, upholsterers, carpet-sellers, fabric merchants, furniture shops and purveyors of sheets, carpets, curtains and knick-knacks of all sort. They also shopped for clothes, for Harriet needed outfits suitable for her new life in the tropics, from safari clothing to wear on the estate to the evening dresses required for the annual horse-racing week in Nairobi for which female guests at the Muthaiga Club (and no one stayed anywhere else for race week) were expected to appear in a new gown every night. Saffron, meanwhile, had already received her first invitations to her new friends' birthday parties and country-house weekends and so required everything from party frocks to hunting tweeds.

Leon made a show of immense distress at the bills the two women in his life were running up, but they all knew it was just a sham. He was by nature a generous man and it pleased him that he had the means to indulge a wife and daughter who gave him so much happiness in return. Since Saffron would have to look after herself for long stretches of the year, when she was in England and Leon was in Africa, he opened an account for her at Coutts bank, complete with checkbook, to be funded by an allowance of thirty pounds a month—a sum which left Saffron wide-eyed with amazement and gratitude. He also said that she might take advantage of the account he had set up at Harrods, on two conditions: first that she should only buy things because she truly needed them, rather than wanted them, and second that she informed him, in writing, of any purchase over five pounds, so that he could make sure than the first condition was being met. "I am treating you like an adult, rather than a child, and giving you access to grown-up sums of money. Now it's up to you to be grown-up in how you use them."

This seemed entirely reasonable to Saffron, who appreciated the trust and responsibility Leon was bestowing on her and, as a result, was determined not to betray his faith in her.

"Bear this in mind," he said. "I wouldn't want any daughter of mine to seem like a poor relation. But I wouldn't want her looking like a spoiled brat either. So find the middle way, and stick to it."

* * *

Saffron, Harriet and Leon spent the second weekend of the Easter holiday at High Weald, where Sir William and Lady Violet assured Saffy that she was always welcome to come and stay for half-terms, or holidays, for it simply wasn't possible or practical to go all the way to Kenya more than once or twice a year. The Courtneys' own children, Philippa and Michael, were six and four years older respectively than Saffron. Mike was halfway through his officer training course at the Royal Military College, Sandhurst, and Philly was already married to a City stockbroker, with her first baby on the way and a half-timbered mock-Tudor house in the Surrey suburbs to look after. "I'm afraid we're just a pair of old sticks," Lady Violet, who was only in her mid-forties and still retained much of the delicate, English-rose prettiness of her youth, told Saffy. "But a lot of the other families round about us have children your age and there's always masses going on—riding, sailing, tennis parties and all that sort of thing—so we'll make sure you don't have to sit around being bored by us for too much of the time."

The Courtneys kept a stable with half-a-dozen horses in it. Saffron was very taken by one, a powerful stallion, whose rich brown coat was as glossy as a well-polished mahogany dining table.

"Ah, that's Tanqueray, Mike's hunter," Lady Courtney told her. "Mike calls him Tank because he's such a great big brute of a beast. He's over seventeen hands, you know."

"Would Mike mind awfully if I took Tanqueray out?" Saffron asked. Before they'd all gone out to the stables she had put on her jodhpurs and was carrying her riding cap, just to be ready in case she had the chance for a ride.

"Are you sure that's a good idea, my dear? He really is a man's horse. Mike is six foot tall and played rugby for the county when he was at school and even he says it takes all his strength to keep Tank under control sometimes."

"I'm five feet nine and a quarter," Saffron said. "Everyone at school calls me Saffy Stringbean because I'm so tall. So I can ride a big horse."

There was a paddock just beyond the stable yard, where half-a-dozen elderly fences, their paint now flaking and wood slowly rotting, had been arranged many years earlier, when the Courtney children were in their gymkhana-going years. Saffron pointed in that direction. "Perhaps I could take him out there just for a little trot, to see if it was too much for me," she suggested. "He wouldn't able to run away with me because it's all fenced in."

"Hmm . . ." Violet pondered. "What do you think, Leon? Is Saffy up to it?"

"There's only one way to find out," he replied. "But listen to me, Saffron: take it nice and easy, do you hear?"

"Yes, Daddy."

"Just a gentle trot, and if that goes well enough a nice easy canter. But no more than that!"

"No, Daddy."

"Well, if you're sure, Leon," Violet conceded, making it quite plain that she regarded this as a highly unwise exercise. She told the stable boy to saddle Tanqueray and soon the sound of horse's hooves on cobblestones echoed around the yard. Saffy went up to Tanqueray, who looked at her with something close to disdain. Evidently he was as skeptical as Lady Violet that this long, slender slip of a female human could stand a chance of controlling him. Saffron stood by Tanqueray's massive, sculpted head, stroked his hard, muscular cheeks, talking to him all the while, getting him used to the sound of her voice. When the trip to the stables had been brought up over lunch, she had taken the precaution of discreetly sneaking a half-eaten apple out of the dining room. She now removed this from her pocket, still hidden within her hand, checked to see that Leon and Violet were engaged in their own conversation and not, at this precise moment, paying any attention to her and slipped it under Tanqueray's nose. He took the hint at once and snaffled the apple in the blink of an eye. Saffy gave Tanqueray's cheek a final pat and asked the stable boy for a leg-up.

"You sure, Miss? Hell of a beast, this'un, pardon me saying so."

"Quite sure, thank you."

She placed one foot in the lad's cupped hands and sprang up into the saddle. A second later, before Tanqueray had any opportunity to object, she was walking him across the yard toward the five-bar gate that led into the paddock. The stable boy ran ahead and opened it to let the horse and rider through. Leon and Violet followed them and stood by the rails that surrounded the paddock to see what would happen next.

"I do hope she will be all right," said Violet, apprehensively.

Leon put a foot on the lower rail and leaned forward onto the fence. "I'm more concerned for the horse. He has no idea what's about to hit him."

Saffron trotted, just as she had promised . . . but only for a matter of seconds. She managed a nice, relaxed canter, for as short a span of time again. Then she leaned forward and said, "Right, my lad, let's see what you're made of," and kicked Tanqueray into a gallop, riding full pelt across the paddock toward the first fence.

Saffron whooped with delight. Now, for the first time since she had landed in England, three months earlier, she felt absolutely in control. For the next five minutes she drove Tanqueray back and forth across the paddock, approaching the fences from every conceivable angle, in every possible sequence, getting a feel for the horse beneath her, learning his individual mannerisms and quirks, feeling for the perfect, natural rhythm between her and him, like a yachtsman finding the perfect balance between his boat and the wind.

For animals, as for people, authority is best exercised as something so inevitable, so assured that neither side ever questions it. Men and women will happily follow a leader who gives them a sense of absolute confidence and control over his destiny and theirs. And horses will obey the hand of a rider who conveys that same air of command. Saffron had never considered how or why she could make a horse do what she wanted. She just knew that she could, knew it without the faintest shadow of a doubt and, like the perfect self-fulfilling prophecy, the horses she rode knew it too.

"My goodness," said Lady Violent Courtney as Tanqueray thundered past her with Saffron crouched over him in her characteristic jockey style. "That girl rides like the wind."

"I know," grinned Leon. "Just wait till you see her shoot."

———

A fortnight after Hitler's visit to Speer's studio, German troops marched into the Rhineland. Since the end of the war this great swathe of German territory on either side of the Rhine had by order of the Treaty of Versailles been a neutral, demilitarized zone into which no German forces were allowed.

Until the start of the 1930s it had been occupied by French and British troops. Now Hitler had defied the Allied powers and demonstrated that he could get away with it, for there had been no response to his unilateral action. The Rhineland was truly German once again and there was nothing anyone could do about it.

Irrespective of his politics, Gerhard was a patriot and he too was caught up in the jubilation that had filled the overwhelming mass of the German people in the wake of Hitler's triumph. Three-quarters of his life had been led in the shadow of defeat and the shame that came with it. Foreigners had drawn up treaties that denied Germany the means to defend itself and imposed reparations that beggared a once-prosperous people. Gerhard had never suffered materially, as so many of his fellow countrymen and women had done, but he felt the humiliation of his country's debasement just as acutely. So he felt the renewal of national pride as well, and shared the pleasure of it too.

With the march into the Rhineland still fresh in the nation's mind, Hitler called a national referendum. It took the place of a conventional election and asked for a single yes or no response to what were in fact two questions: do you approve of the re-occupation of the Rhineland and of the election of the following candidates (all of whom were members of the Nazi Party, bar a few token and entirely spurious "independents") to the Reich parliament? Of forty-five million voters, more than forty-four million voters responded, "Yes."

Gerhard was one of them. Then, on the morning after the result of the referendum came in, he had the chance to take a brand new fighter plane up for a training flight. It had been developed by the brilliant engineer Willy Messerschmitt at his company Bayerische Flugzeugwerke—another Bavarian company with which the Meerbach Motor Works had long had close links, which was the reason Gerhard received an invitation to try the new aircraft. It had been given the designation Bf 109 and it represented, he instantly realized, little short of a revolution in fighter design.

It looked sleek, yet also tough and purposeful, with wide, up-tilted wings that were squared off at the tips and a glass canopy that kept the pilot protected from the elements but provided perfect all-round vision. There were a few drawbacks with the 109. The cockpit was cramped for a man of Gerhard's height and, once landed, the aircraft sat with its tail on the ground and its nose tilted upward, making it hard for the pilot to see where he was going when taxiing on the runway. It also took a bit of getting used to a single-winged craft that was bigger and heavier than the flimsy, but nimble biplanes with open cockpits that the veteran Luftwaffe pilots were accustomed to.

"They're like a bunch of old women, complaining that everything's going to hell and nothing is as good as the old days," Messerschmitt had told Gerhard. "But you are young. You never knew the old days. I think you will like it."

Messerschmitt was right. From the moment the 109 was airborne it was a revelation to Gerhard: so fast, agile and strong that no matter how roughly Gerhard threw it about the sky it responded without complaint.

His only disappointment was that this prototype model was fitted with a British engine, a Rolls-Royce Kestrel; "God in heaven, Willy, why didn't you ask us?" Gerhard asked. "We could have made an engine worthy of such a magnificent design."

Toward the end of his flight, as he was heading back to the airfield, with the adrenaline-driven excitement of the aerobatics he had been performing giving way to the deep contentment that he always felt in the air, Gerhard found himself looking back on everything that had happened to him and to his country over the past month.

The Rhineland was only the very first step on a much longer path, so far as Hitler was concerned. That much was obvious from the plans for the rebuilt Berlin. It was also very clear to Gerhard, from his own responses to Hitler's personal presence and to the whole nation's joy at his success, that the Führer had the power to make Germany do whatever he wanted. And if Willy Messerschmitt's Bf 109 was anything to go by, and there were tank designers and naval architects producing similar weapons for use on land and sea, the German armed forces would have the tools with which to carry out any tasks the Führer set them. On the surface that seemed like a glorious prospect but then there was that other vision of Nazism: the one Gerhard had received on that night in his father's study, when Heydrich had sat behind the old man's desk and painted a picture of a very different Germany, one in which the government had absolute power, individuals were helpless and Jews, or communists, or homosexuals—anyone, in fact, who did not fit the Nazi vision of an acceptable German—could be persecuted, punished and killed without the slightest right to any defense. That would be the empire that Hitler would rule from his palace in the new Berlin.

Leon had now set up the London branch of Courtney Trading and got it running to his satisfaction. Now it was time to take his bride to Kenya. As always, Leon was going by air.

"I've never been up in an airplane in my life, I've always traveled by boat," Harriet admitted to Saffron as they stood in the main bedroom of the Chesham Court flat, surrounded by open trunks, suitcases and strewn clothes. "Now I'm going all the way to Africa."

"Don't you worry. It can be noisy, and smelly, and bumpy sometimes and some people get airsick though I never do," Saffron said, and then, seeing the look of alarm on Harriet's face, quickly added, "But I'm sure you won't be bothered by any of that at all. And just wait till you fly over the Alps, and past the pyramids, and along the Great Rift Valley. Even if you are feeling a little poorly, you'll soon forget about it when you look out of the window and watch the world going by."

Saffron, too, was on her travels a few days later, making her way by rail to Nuremberg, where Chessi von Schöndorf and her parents would meet her. At about the time that Gerhard von Meerbach had been taking the Messerschmitt through its paces, Saffy had been changing trains at Cologne and walked across a concourse packed with German soldiers in uniform. A week earlier, the Führer himself had paraded through the streets of the city at the head of a massive column of gray-uniformed troops and the station was still bedecked with the scarlet Nazi banners that had been hung to celebrate the great day and there were posters everywhere declaring the achievements of National Socialism.

Nuremberg was even more Nazified for this was the site of the great annual rallies that Saffron had read about and seen in newsreels even when she was in Africa. But there was Chessi on the platform, waiting to greet her with a great shriek of delight, a flurry of hugs and giggles and high-pitched, over-excited cries of *"Hujambo?" "Sijambo!"* The von Schöndorfs could not have been more welcoming and charming and it was all Saffron could do to persuade them, as politely as possible, that they really did not have to speak English to her and that she was actually very keen to practice her German. They drove to Regensburg, which was the nearest town to their family's ancestral home, and took her down narrow streets past high medieval houses with steepled roofs, and an old cathedral with two ornate spires, and through an arch in a building like a castle gatehouse onto a centuries-old bridge across the River Danube. "It's just like a fairy tale!" Saffron sighed. "I've never seen a more beautiful town in my life!"

For the next ten days she lived as a member of the von Schöndorf family and what struck Saffron was how similar their life was in so many ways to that of the Courtneys in Devon.

The food was a bit different, of course. She came down to breakfast on the first day to find slices of cheese and cooked meats, black bread and coffee, when the Courtneys never began the day without a good bowl of porridge, followed by any combination they fancied of kippers, deviled kidneys, eggs, bacon, sausages, tomatoes, mushrooms and, of course, a proper cup of tea, with plenty of toast and marmalade to follow, if required. But those gastronomic details aside, the country life of long walks, cross-country rides, long conversations on rainy afternoons and songs around the piano in the evening was really no different. And though Chessi's father was, perhaps, a little more formal and regimented than Saffron's, there was no difference at all in the obvious love he felt for his daughter and her three younger brothers.

One night, Baron von Schöndorf announced that there was a film being shown at the local village hall that night. After supper the entire household, staff and family alike piled into an assortment of cars and drove down to the village. It was clear when they walked into the hall that absolutely every man, woman and child present knew the von Schöndorfs, who were greeted like something close to royalty and shown to a row of seats that had been specially reserved for them. The film turned out to be Charlie Chaplin's *City Lights*. It was a silent film and, there being no language barrier, could be enjoyed by anyone, anywhere, equally. Here was an English comedian, who lived in America, reducing two hundred German country folk to helpless laughter at Chaplin's foolery and tears at the plight of the blind flower-girl that the little tramp with his bowler hat and cane befriended.

As Saffron and her new German friends drove back up to the Schöndorfs' house, Saffron thought about the common humanity that was so evident in the fact that her responses to the film had been no different to any of the Germans in that hall. They wanted nothing more than to live in peace and

get on with their lives, which was all anyone in England, or
Kenya for that matter, wanted too. Surely their leaders would
realize that. Surely they wouldn't lead the world into war
again.

————

For thousands of years people had lived in the place that
Egyptians called al-Qahira. The pharaohs, Macedonians and
Romans had come and gone. Coptic Christians, Jews and con-
quering Arabs had all created their own communities. But for
Francis Courtney, Cairo was, and had always been a British
city. He grew up in a large house close to his relatives the
Ballantynes in the Garden City, where quiet, winding streets,
planted with shady trees, were lined with the villas and man-
sions of the colonial elite. Life in those houses was essentially
British and when the Courtney brothers had been taken to the
Gezira Sporting Club, which stood on an island in the middle
of the Nile, surrounded by another European suburb, Zamalek,
they played tennis, cricket, golf and polo, as English gentlemen
did wherever they went in the world.

Now, though, Francis was getting to know another Cairo.
This was a much more crowded, dirty, but also more vibrant
world, heady with spices, the aroma of thick, dark Turkish
coffee and the smoke from countless shisha pipes. This was
where, in great secrecy and taking endless precautions to ensure
that he was not followed, Francis Courtney, director of Courtney
Trading, stalwart of the British community in Cairo, had on
three separate occasions come to a small room behind a modest
restaurant on a shadowy sidestreet to meet Hassan al-Banna,
founder of the Muslim Brotherhood.

Al-Banna was a decade younger than Francis, but, like Oswald
Mosley, he was fired by a vision. And that vision touched
something in Francis, just as Mosley's had done. For in the two
years since that moment of revelation at the British Union of
Fascists meeting at Earls Court, Francis had come to the reali-

zation that he not only wanted to see the creation of a new, better, purer Britain, he wanted the destruction of what had gone before. His motivation did not arise out of idealism, but from hatred and resentment. These emotions had their roots in his feelings about his brothers, Leon in particular. But they had grown from there to encompass everything he had always taken for granted but now found himself despising: all the cocktail parties filled with women who would not sleep with him; the sports he could no longer play; the friends whose numbers seemed to shrink with every passing year; the family business that was now thriving again and—despite his smaller share-holding—making him richer than he had ever been in his life. Yet that very growth in Courtney Trading's profits and the expansion of its businesses only made Francis even more em-bittered for it was making Leon richer still.

Francis wanted to tear the whole stinking edifice of British rule in Egypt to the ground. And, while he was at it, he wanted to bury the country's Jews in the ruins. Hassan al-Banna shared both these ambitions. He was, like so many revolutionaries, the child of a relatively prosperous, privileged family, and had been working as a schoolteacher in Ismalia, close to the Suez Canal, when he founded the Muslim Brotherhood. Ever since, he had denounced the rule of Islamic lands by colonial, infidel overlords and called upon his co-religionists to prepare themselves for a great *jihad* that would see them take back control of their own destinies.

It had been his old chum Piggy Peters who first alerted Francis to al-Banna's dreams of a great uprising. "Mark my words, Courtney," he said over his third pink gin, one long, hot after-noon, "the wogs are getting restless. Chum of mine who works on the Canal tells me that there's some new gang called the Muslim Brotherhood, campaigning among the workers, getting them all het up about the evil infidels, telling Johnny Arab he should be leading a life of purity and devotion, reading the

Koran all day long, God knows what other nonsense. Anyway, the upshot of it all is, rebellion is brewing in the ranks. Still a way off anything actually happening. But it's on the way."

"Bloody hell, Piggy, that's a damned unhappy prospect," Francis had said, but privately he was intrigued. He made further inquiries, discovered that al-Banna had relocated to Cairo and wrote to him, signing himself "An Admirer' and offering financial assistance to the Brotherhood.

Hassan al-Banna had been wary in the extreme, fearful that he was being led into a trap. But when one five-hundred-pound donation was followed by another and no police came smashing through his door, he sent an intermediary to a rendezvous with his mysterious donor and that meeting was followed by face-to-face encounters with Courtney himself.

"Your assistance has helped me greatly," al-Banna told him. "The Brotherhood's message of liberation and religious observance is spreading. We have friends throughout the *ummah*, both here in Egypt and elsewhere. We are talking to them, planning with them, preparing for *jihad* together. Look to the north, my friend. Observe the gestures of the Black Hand. You will see what your money is buying."

Francis had already learned that the "*ummah*" was the greater Islamic community around the world, irrespective of national boundaries. At Easter 1936, when the Arabs in Palestine, stirred up by a militant Islamic group that called itself the Black Hand, took the first steps toward outright rebellion against British rule and thereby launched a general strike, he understood what al-Banna had been talking about.

But that had not been the only message the leader of the Muslim Brotherhood had brought him. "You are not the only inhabitant of *Dar-al-Harab*, the infidel empire that we call the House of War, who shares a common cause with us," al-Banna had said. "Others agree with us that our greatest of all enemies, even above the British, can be found in Zion. They have come to me offering assistance, just as you did, and I have taken the liberty of directing them to you, believing that you may be their friend as you are mine. They will make contact soon."

Not long afterward, Francis Courtney was invited in his role as a director of Courtney Trading to attend a form reception at the German Embassy, held to mark the visit of a German trade delegation to Egypt. It comprised officials from the Reich Ministry of Trade and Commerce, accompanied by a number of prominent businessmen, almost all of whom, Francis noticed, had a Nazi Party badge pinned to the left lapel of their dinner jackets.

One of the ministry men, who introduced himself as Manfred Erhardt, made it his business to introduce Francis to a number of the most influential businesspeople and to make it plain to them that Courtney Trading was a highly successful, influential and potentially useful company of which Francis was a very senior director and shareholder. "Herr Courtney can supply us with oil for our factories, cotton for our mills and diamonds for our mistresses," the official had said to his fellow delegates and the laughter that followed had set the mood for some very positive and potentially profitable conversations.

"Thank you," Francis said afterwards. "That was damn kind of you. We could have spent years trying to break into the German market and not achieved as much as this one evening has done."

"My dear fellow, think nothing of it," Erhardt replied. "I gather that we have mutual friends and mutual interests that—how shall I put it—extend beyond the world of commerce, no?"

"Ah, yes, I believe we do. I assume you have been following recent events in Palestine?"

"Of course, with great interest. Now, I must not detain you any longer. But I feel sure that tonight is the start of a partnership between Courtney Trading and the Third Reich that will prove beneficial to both parties. And I hope, also, that you and I will be able to have further discussions, about subjects of mutual interest in the weeks and months to come."

"You're staying here in Cairo, then?"

"For a while, I think, yes." He smiled affably. "How would an Englishman say it? Ah yes . . . You haven't seen the last of me, old boy."

————

Mr. Brown was very clearly a man of considerable eminence, for he spoke very casually and without any sense of showing off about his encounters with Prime Ministers, from Gladstone—Mr. Brown had been a very young man at the time of the great man's fourth and final administration—through to the present occupant of No. 10 Downing Street, Stanley Baldwin. His opinions were judicious, measured, but not without a certain cutting edge. "Mr. Baldwin has already served two Kings of England in his first year in office, and it would not at all surprise me if, within a very short while, he is serving a third," he remarked over dinner at one of the finest ducal dining tables in England, one June evening in 1936. He had saved his remark until the ladies had left the table for, as he liked to say, "It is foolish, and even unfair to expect confidentiality as well as beauty from the fairer sex." (In truth, Mr. Brown's career had relied very considerably on the ability of women to extract secrets from hopelessly indiscreet men. But then, little about him was entirely as it seemed.)

"Dash it all, man, you can't say a thing like that," the duke had exclaimed, calling over a footman to refresh his glass of port. "His Majesty's a young man, still in the prime of his life. No reason at all to suppose he won't live for a good long while yet. Outlast us all, I dare say."

"With respect, your grace, I was not suggesting that the King would die, merely that he would no longer be our monarch."

Six months later, Edward VIII had indeed abdicated, giving up his throne for the love of a serial adulterer whose lovers, if Mr. Brown's information was correct, included the German Ambassador in London, Joachim von Ribbentrop. At another dinner, just before Christmas, the duke who had been Brown's host told his guests, "I'll tell you the queerest thing. A chap called Brown, sitting right here, at this table, as good as said that Edward was going to give up the throne, months before the balloon went up. I pooh-poohed him, said he was talking rot. Well, it just goes to show how wrong one can be, eh? Funny old cove, Brown. I'm damned if anyone knows exactly what he does, but he seems to have all the inside gen."

"D'you know," one of the other guests remarked, "I'm not even sure that I've ever heard anyone address him by his Christian name. Don't have an earthly what it is, as a matter of fact. Isn't that strange?"

"Mr. Brown's very charming," the attractive marchioness whom the duke had insisted should be sat next to him said. "Of course, he must be seventy if he's a day, but he still has a rather naughty little twinkle in his eye, which is quite sweet."

"Well, I'm almost seventy. I hope I can still twinkle sweetly!" said the duke.

"I wouldn't say you twinkle sweetly. I think you do it rather naughtily."

The duke was delighted with that. Once the laughter died down, the conversation turned back to the crisis in the House of Windsor. "How can one have a King who can't string two words together without gobbling like a Christmas turkey, that's what I want to know?" the duke had asked. It was only later, when the women were in the drawing room, waiting for the men to finish their conversation, that one of them mentioned Mr. Brown again and said, "The thing I like about him is that he listens to what one has to say. One spends so much time having to pretend to be fascinated by the most frightful bores droning on about themselves, but he is actually interested in one's life and one's opinions. And so one finds oneself saying all sorts of things that would never normally pop out of one's mouth. I have a feeling that he was quite a ladies' man in his day."

Mr. Brown was indeed a great listener. He knew that he was

expected to sing for his supper and so made sure to have a few carefully selected titbits of Westminster or Whitehall gossip to pass on to his hosts, be they the owners of grand houses on Park Lane, or the Masters of Oxford and Cambridge colleges who regularly invited him to dine at their high tables. But he had long since learned that he didn't have to talk very much at all, provided that what he said was sufficiently interesting to make an impression. For the rest of the time he paid attention to what everyone else was saying. And as he went about his business in the eighteen months after the abdication, Mr. Brown kept hearing snatches of conversation about a remarkable girl who had arrived in England from darkest Africa and caused quite a stir in the closed little world of upper-class England in which everyone knew one another, had gone to the same schools, served in the same regiments or come out at the same debutante balls. All the most important families were inter-related and women in particular could explain in great detail the ties of blood and marriage that linked them to this great landowner, or that political titan. So when someone new arrived on the scene, blessed with gifts that marked them out from the herd, they very soon made a name for themselves.

So it was with Saffron Courtney. "I was down in Devon the other day, spent a weekend with Gilbert and Gladys Acland, down at Huntsham," a retired general told Mr. Brown over sherry at the Army and Navy Club, or "the Rag" as its members called it in Pall Mall.

"How is Acland?" Mr. Brown had asked.

"Same as always. Splendid fellow, decent as the day is long. His proudest boast is that in all the years he has been the Member for Tiverton he has never seen fit to open his mouth in the Chamber. "You won't find a single trace of me in Hansard," that's what he says. Typical Acland!"

"He is known as a good Committee man, though. He does a great deal of work behind the scenes."

"He was a damn good soldier, too. Served in South Africa

and in the war, colonel of his regiment, won an MC. Of course he's also Master of the Tiverton Foxhounds and the weekend I was there, he was hosting a meet at Huntsham. The Aclands had some other chums over for the weekend, the Courtneys, do you know them? Sir William and Lady Violet, live at a place called High Weald, charming couple."

"I believe we've met," said Mr. Brown, whose ears had pricked at the mention of the name "Courtney."

"Well they'd brought a young cousin of theirs over, name of Saffron Courtney. Roedean girl, parents live in Kenya, staying with them for half-term, or some such. Well, I'm getting on a bit, same as you Brown, but I don't mind saying, if I were a young subaltern again, full of the joys of spring, I'd have made a play for young Miss Courtney. By God, she was a pretty young filly. Tall, mark you, looked me in the eye, but deep blue eyes, rosebud lips. What I'd give to be young again, eh?"

"Did you happen to catch who her people were?" Brown asked, thinking, *Can this possibly be Eva's little girl?*

"Funnily enough, Violet did mention something, let me think . . . Yes, that's right. Her father's a chap called Leon Courtney. Used to be a white hunter, I think. You know the sort, made a living taking rich tourists out on safari. He's as rich as Croesus himself now, apparently. No one's entirely sure how. He lost his first wife, the girl's mother, but remarried recently. Young Saffron's rather in favor of her new stepmother, as I recall."

Yes, it is! After all these years, Mr. Brown thought as he casually asked, "Did you join the hunt?"

"I certainly thought about it. Won't deny it was damned tempting, but I'm afraid my days of riding to hounds are over. Wish I had gone, though, because once everyone got back, all that anyone could talk about was the Courtney girl's performance."

"How so?"

"Well, the general gist of it was that they'd never seen anything like her. Her mount was a bloody great hunter that the

Courtneys keep for their son, seventeen hands if it was an inch, absolutely not a lady's horse. Plenty of chaps, experienced horsemen, old cavalry types—some of 'em were speculating about how long it would be before the girl came a cropper, and serve her right, getting on a horse like that. Well, the hunt trotted off to some copse where the local peasantry claimed to have seen foxes. They all waited around, the way one does. Hunting is like war in that respect: endless waiting interspersed with sudden bouts of extreme activity. But anyway, the hounds eventually took the scent, gave tongue and it was tally-ho and off they all went, what?"

"Absolutely."

"Now, I don't know if you're familiar with hunting in that part of the West Country . . ."

"Not especially."

"Quite unlike anywhere else. You see, the fields tend not to be separated by walls or hedges, but by banks. About head high, I suppose, very steep, with just enough width on the top for a horse to gather its feet before it jumps down the other side. Of course, riders who aren't used to this sort of thing tend to need a bit of time to master the technique, get used to it all."

"I can well imagine."

"But not our Miss Courtney. She had that brute of a stallion up and over the tallest, steepest banks without even blinking. Acland said it was like watching Fulke Walwyn take Reynoldstown over the jumps at Aintree. The girl was a complete natural, apparently. Wonderful seat, brave as a lion, but unfortunately had not the first idea about proper behavior. Not surprising, I suppose, if she's grown up in the wilds of Africa. At one point, I'm told, she dashed past the whippers-in and was riding alongside the Huntsman, which is as far from the done thing as one can possibly get. Acland had to have a word with Bill Courtney afterwards, ask him to read his young cousin the rules, as it were. But he couldn't bring himself to be angry with her. No one could. She was just such a splendid horsewoman, d'you see?"

"I knew her mother," Mr. Brown said, unable to keep an uncharacteristic note of sentiment from his voice and immediately regretting his indiscretion.

"Was she a beauty too?" the general asked.

Mr. Brown decided he might as well continue to play the game. "She was, without a doubt, the single most beautiful woman on whom I have ever clapped eyes."

"I see . . . know her well, did you?"

Mr. Brown gave an enigmatic, but suggestive shrug.

"You sly old dog!" said the general and then repeated, "Ah what I'd give to be young."

———

Saffron arrived back in Kenya for the summer holidays to find Lusima in a state of frenzied activity. A team of Indian builders and decorators—for in Kenya, the settlers always hired Indians to build and maintain their homes, just as they chose Somalis to serve in them—had set up an office and dormitory in one of the outbuildings, while Harriet supervised the total transformation of the interior of the house. Saffron's initial reaction was shock: Harriet had written to her to say that she was doing "a little bit of redecoration", but Saffy had no idea that this was what she had in mind.

"Nor did I," confessed Harriet when Saffron asked. "But as soon as I started making one room look nice, well . . . come with me. I'll show you what I mean."

She led Saffron into the drawing room, whose most striking feature were two sets of French windows that opened onto a terrace beyond which one could see the garden and a spectacular view of the Aberdare mountain range, rising up in the distance. Saffron's first impression was how much brighter the room seemed and then she began to spot all the changes that had made it that way: the fresh white paint around the windows, the cornicing around the top of the room and the ceiling itself: a new, pale rose colored carpet; fresh wallpaper and large vases filled with lovely roses from the garden. She also noticed something else:

Harriet hadn't changed the pictures on the wall or the framed photographs on the piano, some of which showed the family when Eva was still alive. She had put her stamp on the room, but acknowledged everything that had gone before her.

"It looks really nice," Saffron told her.

Harriet heaved a sigh of relief. "I'm so glad you like it. I've been so worried in case you didn't. Now, let's go into the dining room."

Saffron walked into the room where she had eaten so many meals, always sitting in her chair, always looking across the table to the antique mahogany sideboard in which the china and silver were kept. The furniture had all been removed, for the Indians were due to start work on the room within the next few days. But that only served to highlight how dowdy and faded the floor-to-ceiling curtains over the windows were, how worn the carpet, how cracked and dirty the paint on the skirting boards.

Saffron saw at once why the process of redecorating, once started, was bound to consume the whole house. But she had to bite her lip, for the sight of a room she had loved for so long looking quite so dowdy and sad made her want to cry. "Oh . . ." she said, for once in her life quite lost for words.

"I know," said Leon, walking into the room behind her. "Makes you realize how I just let the place go to seed."

"No you didn't, Daddy. You just didn't . . ." Saffron cast around for the right word.

"I didn't pay attention," Leon interrupted her. "I suppose I was just being a typical man, concentrating on business and the estate and all the things that interested me and not actually paying any attention to the house, or anything in it."

"I've had to change all the bed-linen," Harriet said. "The sheets were so worn I could practically see right through them and the towels . . . well, the least said about them the better."

"Not really my sort of thing, buying linens," Leon admitted. "And I'll tell you something else, Saffy, the grub's a lot better round here these days, too."

"Dinner last night was delicious, now you come to mention it."

"Well, I had a chat with *Mpishi* and his *totos*," Harriet said, as Saffron and Leon exchanged amused glances at how fast she had picked up the Swahili words for a cook and kitchen-boys. "In my experience staff actually like to be kept on their toes. It shows them someone cares. If they cook well, I make a point of complimenting them and if they don't they soon hear about that too. I think we all understand one another."

"I think they're all completely petrified of you, my darling," Leon said. "But devoted to you, too, which is as it should be. Now, the reason I was looking for you two was that I suddenly realized that the rest of the estate might have been quietly wasting away for the past ten years, just like the house has done. And since my study is about to get the Harriet Courtney treatment, it seemed like a good time to go on a proper tour of inspection. So I'll be heading off at crack of dawn tomorrow, Manyoro's coming with me, just the two of us, on foot, sleeping under the stars. It will be like old times."

"I wish he was that enthusiastic about spending time with me," Harriet remarked, with mock disappointment, though the smile on her face suggested that she knew very well how much Leon loved her company.

"Did you say that you're redecorating the study?" Saffron asked, with a note of anxiety in her voice. "What are you doing about . . ." she paused and glanced apologetically at Harriet before concluding, "about Mummy's picture?"

"That's a very good question," Leon replied. "Harriet and I talked about it at length. I don't think it would be right for any man to start a new life with his second wife if the first one is still hanging around the house like Marley's ghost."

"But Mummy's not . . ."

"Wait! Hold your horses, Saffy, and let me finish . . . I love that picture as much as you do. Which is why, at Harriet's suggestion, I have asked Vassileyev to copy Mummy's head as a much smaller portrait, which we will hang somewhere, though I haven't decided exactly where just yet. Meanwhile the original portrait will be properly packed for storage so that you can have it when you are old enough to have a place of your own."

"And we're going to get a new picture done . . . of us," Harriet said, stepping across to Leon and taking his arm. The two of them looked at Saffron and she realized from the way they were looking at her that they were hoping for her approval.

This role reversal was something she had never experienced before, but their happiness and their hope that she would be included in it was so obviously sincere that she was completely won over.

"I think that's a lovely idea," she said. "But when it's done, you shouldn't hide it away in the study. You should put it in the dining room where everyone can see it."

"Well, that's a thought," said Leon. "Now, if you ladies will excuse me, I have to sort out my kit for the great trek around the estate."

"It makes such a difference, you being here," Saffron said to Harriet when they were alone again. "It's like the secret garden coming to life again."

"Oh, I loved *The Secret Garden* when I was a girl!" said Harriet.

"Me too, though I always cried and cried when Colin's father came back to the house, no matter how many times I read it. I think I was really imagining Mummy coming back to me."

"I never knew my father. He left my mother before I was even born. I still wonder if he's out there somewhere, just waiting to see me again . . ."

Saffron rushed across and gave Harriet a hug. Harriet squeezed her back, but then, after a few seconds, stepped back and said, "So, shall we go and have a look at your room? I didn't dare touch a single thing without your permission, and you have my promise that if anything is done, it will be exactly as you like it."

———

The following morning, Saffron was awake before dawn. She pulled on a pair of shorts and a jumper and went downstairs to the kitchen where she made herself a cup of tea and then took it outside. The air was still chilly as the very first faint light of the new day drew a pale golden line along the eastern horizon as Saffy sat down on the steps that led from the kitchen into the back yard, with her knees drawn up to her chest and her mug clutched in both hands to keep them warm.

Slowly that side of the house began to stir into life as the first *totos* emerged from their sleeping quarters to start work baking the fresh rolls for breakfast.

They grinned to see Saffron, who greeted each man by name, for she had known them all her life. Speaking in Swahili, scattered with the occasional Arabic phrase, she asked after their families, some of whom were thousands of miles away in Somalia, taking the trouble to listen to their answers and respond with as much interest as she would to one of her friends.

Finally the reason for her early rising appeared.

"Uncle Manyoro!" she cried and dashed toward him just as if she were still a little girl.

They exchanged greetings and then he looked at her with a serious, almost frowning expression on his face and said, "You have changed, my little princess. You have become a woman." Then his face was illuminated by a huge smile as he said, "Now I shall call you my queen."

A *toto* appeared, without needing to be called, and respectfully handed Manyoro a cup of the strong, black, heavily sweetened coffee without which he could not properly begin his day.

"So, Saffron, what has made you wait for me here, outside on this step, in the cold morning air, when you could be warm in your bed inside?"

"I needed to know something."

"And what would that be?"

"What do you think of Harriet? Do you like her? Do you think that everyone on the estate will like her?"

"Hmm . . ." he replied, sipping his coffee. "I can hear from your voice that you like her very much and that you want me to say yes."

"Don't you want to say yes?" Saffron asked, suddenly alarmed.

Manyoro took some more coffee then said, "You know that I loved your mother very much. She was my brother's woman and so she was like a sister to me."

"Yes, I know."

"When she was gone, the light went out of my brother's life. He walked and talked and appeared to be a man, but he was really just an empty shell. The loss of your mother had taken away his heart."

"I know . . ."

"So for all those years, I felt his sadness and it made me sad too. I had my wives and my children and they made me happy. I wanted my brother to be happy too. Now he has a new Mrs. Courtney . . ." he paused and Saffron could scarcely bear the tension until Manyoro said, "And now the light has returned to my brother's eyes. Now his heart beats again. Everyone can feel it. Their chief has a woman. She has made him a man again. And that makes them happy. That makes me, very, very happy."

"Oh, Manyoro, I'm so glad!" said Saffron wrapping her arms around one of his strong biceps. "I feel just the same way. It's like the house. I didn't realize how shabby it had become until I saw how Harriet was making it all new. And I didn't really know how sad Daddy had been until I saw how happy he was with her."

"She is a strong woman, too . . . I like that. A man like M'Bogo needs a mate who can match his strength with hers." He chuckled. "*Mpishi* told me a story about his new mistress. He said she is very strict. Everything has to be done in exactly the right way, just as she commands it."

"I know," giggled Saffron. "I've seen her giving orders."

"So he asked himself, "What will happen if I do not do exactly as the mistress says? Will she notice it?"

"Oh dear . . ."

"So one day, when he cooked dinner, he made the meal perfectly, everything as it should have been . . . except for the potatoes. He had been told to make boiled potatoes, but instead he fried them. He fried them as well as he could. But still they were not boiled."

"So what happened?"

"The meal was served. Every scrap of food was eaten. Afterwards, Mrs. Courtney came into the kitchen. She praised *Mpishi* and the *totos* for the meal. She said the food was delicious and that the boys had served it very well. She turned to leave and then, just as she got to the door, she turned around and said to *Mpishi*, "But if you ever cook the potatoes the wrong way again, I will have to have words with *Bwana* Courtney and ask him to have you dismissed.""

"Oh no!" Not even Saffron had thought Harriet would be so severe. "How terrible for *Mpishi*!"

"Not at all, he was extremely delighted. He said to me, "I have been invisible since the first *memsahib* died. Now they see me again and all is well." And he is right, all is well."

Manyoro got to his feet and said, "Now I must leave you. Your father will be wondering where I am. And I must not keep him waiting. It would make Mrs. Courtney very angry, and she might have me dismissed!"

And with that, guffawing mightily at his own joke, Manyoro went into the house, leaving Saffron glowing with happiness on the step behind him.

———

Gerhard and Konrad von Meerbach did not make a habit of spending time together, not if they could avoid it. But on a perfect summer's evening, with the air warm and still, Konrad happened to find himself at a reception held on a terrace by the bank of the River Spree to celebrate the successful completion of all the preparations necessary to ensure the complete success of the Olympic Games that would be held in the city

in barely two weeks' time. Konrad was delighted to have received an invitation, since this was very much an occasion for
the rulers of the Reich, who had issued all the orders, than the
bureaucrats, artisans and laborers who had done all the work.
He was wearing his SS dress uniform, which was all the more
impressive since a recent promotion had put a silver oak leaf
on his collar tab, and feeling all the more smug for all the
admiring glances he was receiving from the women that he
passed by.

There was, Konrad well knew, an infallible correlation between the wealth and power of the men at any given occasion
and the beauty of the women. On this occasion, the men were
the most powerful in all the Reich and the female guests were
correspondingly lovely. The balmy weather had inspired many
of them to wear light silk dresses that exposed their arms, their
shoulders, their décolletages and, in some cases, draped so low
around their naked backs, barely covering the tops of their
buttocks, that they could not possibly be wearing any under-
garments. It was on nights like this that Konrad was grateful
for his wife Trudi's acceptance of his decision that she should
remain in Bavaria to raise their two-year-old son and newly
arrived baby daughter. Trudi was a pretty, docile, but insipid
blonde whose most appealing feature was that she was a great-
niece of Gustav von Bohlen und Halbach, or Gustav Krupp as
he now liked to be known, having married the heiress to the
great Krupps steelmaking and armaments company. It was good
for Konrad's personal status and the Meerbach Motor Works
business to be in with the most powerful industrial dynasty in
Germany. And it was good for his sex-life if his wife was several hundred kilometers away in a delightful house in the
grounds of Schloss Meerbach while he was chasing women in
Berlin.

He was just deciding which of the women to target first when
his eye was caught by the sight of a familiar figure in an elegant,

but rather too casually cut suit, smiling charmingly at three little beauties who seemed enthralled by his company.

No, it can't be . . . God in heaven, it is. Damn him!

Konrad forced himself to grit his teeth and paste a sickly smile across his face: it was a worthwhile sacrifice if it got him any closer to the women. "Gerd, what a pleasant surprise to see you here. Come now, brother, introduce me to your delightful friends."

"Of course," smiled Gerhard, while the young women simpered at the big, tough-looking SS officer who had just arrived on the scene. "Konnie, let me introduce you to Gerda, Sabi and Jana. Ladies, this is my big brother, *SS-Standartenführer* Konrad Graf von Meerbach."

Konrad clicked his heels and nodded his head to the ladies. "I am honored to meet you."

Gerhard smiled, for all the world like an affectionate younger brother who was delighted to be able to show off his impressive older sibling. "You picked a perfect time to pop by, Konnie. I was just about to tell the girls about my recent meeting with the Führer himself."

"Your what?" Konrad replied, completely unable to keep the shock or incredulity out of his voice. The smart-assed little pup had to be up to some kind of tomfoolery. It was inconceivable that he was telling the truth. "Is this some kind of a joke? I have to tell you Gerhard, it is in very bad taste if it is."

"Fear not, old man, this is nothing other than the absolute honest truth. It was my genuine honor and privilege to meet the Führer when he paid a visit to the Speer architectural practice, where I work. He even patted me on the arm and said I was an example of National Socialism at its best."

Konrad felt the sense of self-satisfaction that had been buoying him up so pleasurably just a few moments before evaporate into the Berlin night, leaving him bitterly deflated. For years he had boasted of his closeness to the most powerful figures in the Nazi hierarchy, and he was telling nothing but the truth. He worked every day with Heydrich, spoke frequently to Himmler and had been introduced to Bormann and Goebbels. He had often even been in the same room as Hitler. But never, not once had he actually exchanged words with the Führer.

"How did this encounter take place?" Konrad said, doing his very best not to let too much of the poison in his heart seep into his words. It would not do him any good with the women if he were seen to envy his younger brother.

"Well, I have the honor of working on the plans for the future transformation of Berlin into a capital worthy of the Reich. This is a project very dear to the Führer's heart, and so . . ."

Gerhard told the story of his meeting with Hitler. It was painfully obvious to Konrad that he was telling the truth, not least because of the relish with which he described the Führer congratulating him for both building the Reich and defending it.

"How can you be an architect and a Luftwaffe pilot?" one of the girls—Konrad thought she might have been the one called Jana—asked.

Because I damn well ordered him to be! thought Konrad.

"Oh, I'm just a reservist, a part-time fighter pilot," Gerhard said, with a self-deprecating smile that had the three girls practically melting into a puddle in front of him.

"Do you like flying?" Sabi piped up, casting big brown doe eyes in Gerhard's direction.

"I absolutely love it," he said. "There is absolutely nowhere in the world where I feel more at peace, more absolutely in control of my destiny, and more surrounded by the glory of this wonderful planet than when I am up in the sky, as free as a bird. It's the most wonderful feeling you can imagine."

As the girls sighed adoringly, Konrad contemplated the bitter irony of the situation. He had sent Gerhard off to do a job he should have hated, and join a branch of the armed forces to which his free-spirited character should have been entirely unsuited. And the little bastard had ended up becoming the Führer's personal pet—Gerhard had returned to the story of his meeting and was recounting every word of his conversation about the Great Hall.

"It's really just boring stuff, lots of talk about vents and air-circulation," Gerhard said.

"How can it be boring, telling us what the Führer said?" asked Sabi.

"Is it true that when you meet him, it's not like meeting anyone else on earth?" Trudi wondered.

"Yes," said Gerhard, "that is absolutely true. It is a quite extraordinary experience."

Konrad didn't think that anything could top the surprises that had already been flung at him, but Gerhard's awestruck praise of Hitler beat them all.

"So you, my skeptical, rebellious brother now accept that the Führer is the greatest man of our times?"

"I accept that he has a power that is truly unique," Gerhard replied. "When he looked right at me, standing as close to me as I am to you all now, it was like nothing I have ever known before, and for that moment there was nothing he could have said that I would not have believed and no order he could have given that I would not have obeyed. And I am absolutely certain that any one of you would have felt exactly the same thing if you had been in my place."

Silence fell over the little group. No one knew quite how to follow that. Konrad cleared his throat. "Well, I must be going. People to meet, things to do—this is a working event for me, I'm afraid. Good to see you, Gerd. My congratulations on your remarkable encounter with the Führer. That is a rare privilege. Ladies . . ."

He bowed again and walked away. There had been no point at all in staying. He simply couldn't compete with Gerhard.

Konrad paused by the balustrade at the edge of the terrace

and looked out across the river, taking in the scene. He lit a cigarette and smoked it thoughtfully, and as he did so his spirits, so recently deflated, began to rise again. This evening might have appeared to be a triumph for Gerhard. But surely, on reflection, he, Konrad, was the true victor. For he had taken a rebel who had to be forced, virtually on pain of death, to toe the Nazi line and set him on the path to becoming a true believer. Gerhard's conversion to Hitler's cause, that afternoon in Speer's office, had been a modern-day equivalent to St. Paul's conversion to Christianity, when he saw God on the road to Damascus.

You belong to us now, little brother, Konrad thought as he threw the end of his cigarette into the murky waters of the Spree. *You belong to Adolf Hitler!*

———

Gerhard asked Sabi if she wanted to leave with him, then Jana asked if she could come too. So he slipped a ten Reichsmark note into one of the wine waiter's hand and was given a bottle of the excellent French champagne that the waiters had been serving in return. They went back to Gerhard's apartment where they quickly polished off the champagne and then a bottle of schnapps that Gerhard had in his drinks cabinet. Then he discovered that there was most of a bottle of an excellent Riesling in his refrigerator, so he took that into his bedroom and the girls followed him in one on each arm, giggling as they kicked off their high heels and slipped out of their dresses. Then Gerhard had both of the girls and then lay against the quilted headboard of his king-sized bed, watching while they played at kissing and petting one another until he was fully restored and able to join in again, too.

When every permutation had been worked through and they were all exhausted Jana and Sabi fell asleep, one on either side of him. Gerhard, however, was still wide-awake, still restless despite his physical fatigue. He slipped out of the bed and watched as they rearranged themselves in their sleep until they were curled up in a tangle of soft curves, gold and chestnut hair, and warm, sweet skin like two pretty, pampered little kittens in a basket. He went out onto the balcony of his apartment and, in an unconscious echo of his brother's actions, smoked a cigarette as he looked out at the sleeping city.

Gerhard had been corrupted, he knew that. Not completely perhaps, but even if he had not sold his soul—not beyond redemption—he had at least allowed it to be used for causes in which he did not believe. In return he had received a new form of status to go with that which he had inherited, for the Führer's personal approval had marked him out as a coming man and, like a singer becoming a star overnight after a single brilliant performance, he was now regarded everywhere as a coming man in the Party and the Reich. He was not exactly famous, but, as the women in his bed demonstrated, he received the perks of one who was.

He consoled himself with two thoughts. The first was that his flying still remained pure and unsullied as an expression of his true self. And the other was that he had been more careful than anyone realized when he described Hitler's effect upon him. He had seen how furious Konrad had been when he discovered that his despised brother had been blessed by the Führer in a way he had never been. But he had also seen the first signs of the smugness returning to Konrad's features when he heard what must have sounded, to his ears, like the praise of a besotted, adoring devotee. For it would never have occurred to Konrad that Gerhard did not glory in Hitler's powers of mesmerism, just as he would have done, that in fact Gerhard was terrified by the way that he had been seduced and what that told him about the way that the whole country had fallen under Hitler's spell.

But can I escape that spell? Gerhard asked himself. *Do I have the willpower and the courage to resist it?*

And the reason he was still so wide-awake and quite unable to sleep was his fear that the answer was: *No.*

———

Saffron went back to Roedean in September and settled down to the final year-and-a-bit of school. When the autumn term ended, two weeks before Christmas, she found that she was almost sorry to be flying out to Kenya for the holiday: not because she did not want to see her father and Harriet, but because it meant missing so many of the balls and house parties to which her school friends and family members had invited her. She arrived back at Lusima, where all the renovation work had finally been completed, to discover that Harriet had created a miniature gallery of family pictures that ran up the stairs from the front hall to the bedrooms. She had contacted Grandma Courtney in Cairo who had sent her a small pencil portrait of Leon as a boy, and some ancient photographs of him with his parents and brothers. Centaine had contributed a photograph that she had taken of Saffron and Shasa during the visit to Cape Town four years earlier, and another shot of Shasa in his polo gear, about to compete for South Africa in the Berlin Olympics. Harriet's own childhood was represented too, along with a photograph of all the shopgirls, herself included, at the school outfitters where she had first met Leon and Saffron. And there, discreetly placed among them, was the head of Eva that Vassileyev had copied from his own portrait of her. He had somehow added a slightly wistful air to her expression that gave a sense of her absence, as if she were gently regretting that she could not be there among them all in person. By including Eva as part of a wider family, Harriet had found a way to honor her importance to Leon and Saffron without in any way being overshadowed by the past.

Saffron was touched by the thoughtfulness of the gesture and the trouble Harriet must have taken to assemble all the various pictures. But there was no hiding who was mistress of the Lusima estate now. Harriet presided over a great Christmas tea party for all the estate workers and their families, with little presents for all the children. There was a dinner to celebrate Saffron's arrival from England, attended by local families she had known all her life. When the ladies retired from the table, Saffron was struck by the degree to which the other women in the local expatriate community, even those who came from much smarter backgrounds, had not only accepted Harriet as her own, but even deferred to her a little. Of course, Harriet happened to be the wife of one of the richest men in the entire country, but that would not, of itself, have prevented catty remarks designed to put her in her place: gentle, and even not-so-gentle reminders that she had been a shop manageress not so very long ago. There was an assurance, however, about the way she carried herself, and a strong suggestion of barely hidden steel that silenced any doubters, even before they had opened their mouths. If anything, by transforming the appearance of Lusima, and raising the standards of the household so dramatically, from the delicious food, to the impeccable service, to the basket of perfectly ironed hand-towels in the spotless downstairs lavatory (where amusing cartoons hung on the walls and a small vase of scented flowers was placed on the deep-set windowsill), she had made people see Leon in a different light. He had been looked on as a former white hunter: handsome, even charming when he wanted to be, but still a little rough around the edges, who happened to have come into a large amount of money in mysterious circumstances. Now he was fast acquiring a new identity as a gentleman landowner and pillar of the community.

It struck Saffron, as she lay in bed after the dinner party running over the evening's events in her head, that she was changing too, just as her father was. Thanks to the flat in Chesham Place she had been able to spend weekend exeats, a half-term and a few days waiting for her flight up in London. She was getting to know the city a little better now and leading a life that was very different to her tomboy existence in Kenya. She saw girlfriends for lunch or tea in fashionable restaurants and cafés. They furthered her education in the pleasures of shopping, even when one didn't really buy very much but just scouted all the nicest shops, looking at the other customers

Penny had inherited Grandma Courtney's artistic gifts. She had recently moved from Cairo to London and was renting a studio-cum-flat in Tite Street, off the King's Road in Chelsea.

It was a colorful, Bohemian quarter and Penny's friends were all painters, poets, musicians and actors, none with two pennies to rub together and all of them filled with a variety of passions, be they creative, political or sexual. Here was another new world for Saffron to explore and she soon learned that she had to dress down for evening at Aunt Penny's just as she had to dress up for cocktails at the homes of her debutante friends. But she loved the free and easy world of late-night dinners in cheap Greek restaurants and endless conversations on the meaning of life and love over bottles of rough red wine just as much as the smartest ball in Eaton Place or Park Lane, where knots of passers-by would gather on the pavements to watch the girls arrive in their gowns and family jewels, before dancing the night away to Ambrose and his orchestra. And every Friday afternoon, without fail, found Saffron at one of London's main-line rail termini, en route to that weekend's house party, where some combination of hunting, shooting, dancing and dining awaited. For no one, not even the most radical of Aunt Penny's friends, spent a single weekend in London if they could possibly avoid it.

As winter turned to spring and the first cricket matches of May heralded the onset of another English summer, Leon and Harriet arrived back in England. Leon attended to business at the office on Ludgate Hill while Harriet helped prepare Saffron for the Season. This was the summer-long round of events, both private and public—for the Wimbledon tennis, Henley regatta and the cricket match between the schoolboys for Eton and Harrow (all of them future husband material for the debutantes) were all a part of it—that formed the "coming out" of upper-class girls as they left the shelter of their family homes and were thrown on the marriage market.

Saffron had not the slightest intention of finding a husband: she had Oxford to attend and, though she had not yet mentioned this to her father, a business career of her own to start first. Still she played along with the game, going to the annual Queen Charlotte's Ball where the girls all curtseyed before a giant cake and then curtsying again, this time for the King himself when she was introduced at Court by her Cousin Violet. In order for a girl to be allowed this honor, she had to be accompanied by a sponsor who had herself been introduced in the past and Violet was only too happy to do it.

In July, Saffron, Penny and Harriet persuaded Leon to accompany them to the London exhibition of German Expressionists, internationally renowned artists including Kokoschka and Kandinsky who had all, to a man, been banished by the Nazis. Just that month, Hitler had raged against them as "lamentable unfortunates who plainly suffer from defective sight. They can live and work where they choose, but not in Germany."

"I'm hardly an admirer of Mr. Hitler, but I think he may have a point," muttered Leon, as he looked at the paintings, most of which, in his view, came under the category of "a six-year-old could have done better" or, in some extreme cases, "a monkey." But then he stopped in front of a painting by an artist called Magnus Zeller, which the card beside it revealed was called "Der Hitlerstaat (The Hitler State)." It showed a ruined landscape across which an army of slaves, whipped by men in black SS uniforms, were dragging a giant cart on which was mounted the monumental statue of a seated ruler who looked like an Ancient Egyptian pharaoh. The entire picture was painted in a bleak palette of gray and browns, and the only splashes of bright color came from the Nazi banners that fluttered around the great king's feet.

Leon stopped dead in front of the picture and stared at it intently, not saying a word. Finally, he turned to Saffron and asked, "You've been there, tell me: is this how it will all end?"

Saffron thought of all the banners she had seen on her visits to Germany. She cast her mind's eye over all the propaganda posters. There were more of them every year and their tone was becoming progressively more hostile: not celebrating the Nazi government's achievements but berating its enemies, particularly the Jews. There were more anti-Jewish slogans painted on walls and shop windows—or perhaps there just seemed to be more because she could understand them so much better now. But then she thought of the von Schöndorfs and their friendship and generosity toward her, feelings that had been echoed by the overwhelming number of people she had met in Germany. And yet, she had seen those black uniforms, too.

"I don't know," she said, finally. "But I fear that it might."

Two days later Saffron was at home in Chesham Place when her father came back from the office. "I've been talking to Hartley Grainger. I told him not to renew any of our German contracts when they come to the end of their terms. No need to do anything dramatic just yet, so we won't cancel any that are still active. Just won't look for new deals, that's all. Your uncle Frank won't be happy. The German trade is his baby. But I think you're right, Saffy. I think we're in for rough weather and it's time to start battening down the hatches."

For the past two years Mr. Brown had found himself encountering mentions of Saffron Courtney wherever he went. In Oxford she was regarded as Zuleika Dobson, Max Beerbohm's fictional *femme fatale*, whose beauty drives university men mad with passion, brought to life. In Scotland, staying with her Ballantyne cousins over the New Year, she had caused as much astonishment with her marksmanship on a pheasant shoot as her skill and daring on a horse had done in Devon. A fellow guest at the house party told him, "The ghillie turned to Ballantyne and said, 'Yon wee lassie's putting every gun in Scotland tae shame.'"

"Of course, the Courtney girl's absolutely ravishing." Lady Diana Cooper, one of the great beauties of a slightly earlier age, and still ravishing in her early forties, had mentioned Saffron to him one evening at a cocktail party in Berkeley Square. "What I rather admire is the way she handles her money. It's perfectly obvious that she has an awful lot of it. I can assure you that any woman looking at her would know at once that all her dresses are hand-made, and not by some little old lady-who-does, either. I was talking to Hardy Amies just the other day and he was in raptures, talking about what a delight it was to dress her. Eddie Molyneux adores her too, he'd use her as a mannequin if he could. Of course she has that slightly boyish figure, which all the queers love, and dresses hang so much more elegantly if one's not too curvy. But the admirable aspect is her understatement."

"How do you mean?"

"Well, she's very young and, not to put too fine a point on it, colonial. She hasn't grown up in smart homes, surrounded by well-dressed women, who know how to be *comme il faut*. In a way, that's part of her charm. She has a slight air of wild-ness. One gets the impression she could go off hunting lions without turning a hair. So one might expect her to be a little vulgar, overdone."

"Just a little too flashy?"

"Exactly. Dear Mr. Brown, you are so nice to talk to. You always understand just what one means."

"I do my best, Lady Cooper. But how does this absence of vulgarity manifest itself?"

"Well, by its absence!" she laughed. "I mean, whenever one sees Saffron Courtney one always thinks, that's a very well-dressed girl. Her shoes are always just right for her dress and for the occasion. Her handbags are delightful. Her jewelry is very nice but discreet. Actually, that's the word for it: discreet. Either someone has told her, or she's worked out for herself, that with looks like hers and that dazzling personality, she doesn't need her clothes to be anything but a very chic, elegant backdrop."

"I hesitate to make an observation about women, particularly with regard to their relations with other women . . ."

"Very wise. It's not a subject upon which men are likely to have anything remotely useful to say."

"But let me suggest something, just as a hypothesis . . ."

Lady Diana smiled. "Very well then, Mr. Brown, just this once, since you are really quite perceptive, for a man."

"I think Miss Courtney's intelligence is evident in the freedom with which you, and other ladies to whom I have spoken, compliment her. I can imagine a girl like her, arriving in England, blessed with wealth, looks, a remarkable sportswoman . . . Well, such a creature might cause considerable ill feeling among some members of her sex. Not you, of course, Lady Cooper, you have no need whatever to fear competition . . ."

"You said that just in time."

"But other women, particularly of Miss Courtney's own generation, and perhaps a few years older than her, might resent the competition she presented to them and feel inspired to spread malicious gossip, or criticize her behavior. You know the sort of thing."

"I'm afraid to say that I do. I dare say I provoked a bit of it when I was Saffron Courtney's age."

"And yet, while she seems to have made a tremendous impression upon society in the past year or two, I have not heard a single bad word about her, aside, perhaps, from the disappointment of the mothers whose sons have failed to win her heart."

"Yes," mused Lady Diana, thoughtfully, "one hasn't heard the slightest suggestion of a love-affair, which is unusual, with a girl that attractive."

"She is very young, you know, only just nineteen."

"True, but even so . . ."

"Perhaps she simply can't find a man who's good enough for her. In my experience, women—and I apologize again for my impertinence—do like to be able to admire and even look up to the men they love."

"Well, we certainly like to look up to them in the purely literal sense. I can't bear a man to be shorter than me, and that must limit her choices, being such a tall girl."

"I don't believe she will give her heart, or anything else, to any man who isn't as remarkable as she is. And that, I fear, may be hard to find."

"Why, Mr. Brown, I had no idea you were so sentimental. I do believe you have a little *tendresse* for Saffron Courtney."

"An old man's affection, perhaps. Though I should add that it's purely a matter of speculation. I haven't actually met the girl."

"Well, we really must do something about that!"

Yes, thought Mr. Brown, *I really must.*

———

Saffron's parents, for she regarded Harriet as a true mother figure now, stayed on until September when they accompanied her as she went up to Oxford to begin her new life as an undergraduate. It was a perfect early autumn day with which to start the Michaelmas Term. There was still a hint of warmth in the sun that shone from a cloudless sky and the City of Dreaming Spires was looking at its best. Ancient buildings that had seen countless generations of students come and go looked down on all the young freshmen, their faces filled with excitement and ambition, but also the nervousness and uncertainty of newcomers to whom everything is unfamiliar as they made their way across their college quads, looking for the staircases on which their new rooms would be found.

"I so envy you," Harriet said. "To have the chance to come to a place like this, and study with some of the world's finest minds . . . It's the most wonderful opportunity that anyone could have."

"I'm proud of you," Leon told Saffron, as he and Harriet were taking their leave. "You said you were going to come here. You worked damn hard, and you jolly well did it. Well done. Now you have to make the best of it because I'll tell you this: if you leave Oxford and you haven't done yourself or the university justice you will regret it for the rest of your life."

Her father was right, Saffron knew it. But still, there were times in her first few weeks when she really did wonder if an Oxford education was all that it was cracked up to be, for women at any rate. The female dons who ran Lady Margaret hall seemed to be obsessed with the dangers posed to their students by the uncontrollable urges of their male peers. The hours during which young men were allowed into the college were strictly limited to the afternoon and early evening and it was even considered unsuitable for young ladies to be seen walking with men unless they were both pushing their bicycles.

Saffron considered herself to be an intelligent girl but she simply could not see the logic of that instruction. "It's so that you can always have your bicycle between yourself and him," one nervous-looking girl explained over their first dinner in college. "That way it's a barrier between you and him."

"Hmm, I see . . ." said Saffron who had walked down countless streets and over all manner of landscapes with a great many male friends, some of whom were obviously smitten with her, without feeling the need to protect herself with a wheeled vehicle of any kind. And then, because the other girl looked so earnest, and so fearful of the opposite sex, Saffron couldn't resist adding, "I find that once men have seen me shoot, they don't give me any trouble at all."

"Oh," squeaked the other girl, nervously, and sat there, unable to eat for a good couple of minutes as she tried to come to terms with the entirely unfamiliar species of female sitting next to her. Another girl piped up, "My big sister's at Somerville. She has a spiffing trick she uses if she's in a taxi and a chap tries to get too fresh with her. She looks out for a chestnut seller and asks the cabbie to stop. Then she says to the chap, "Would you mind terribly getting me some hot chestnuts?" Of course, he can hardly say no. So he buys the chestnuts and then they drive on and the next time he leans over and tries to kiss her, she just pops a burning hot chestnut in his mouth. And then what can he do?!"

Saffy was fascinated by the idea of men as strange, hostile creatures to be fought off at all costs. She enjoyed male company and traditionally male pursuits and had always felt able to match any man as she had once matched small boys. Of course, she also loved looking pretty and dancing with a handsome beau in his white tie and tails. As tall and relatively strong as she was, there was nothing like being in the arms of a man she liked who was taller and much stronger still. She had kissed numerous men and been pursued by many more. But still she had not given herself completely to any of them.

It was not that she was a prude, or had a mystical regard for her own virginity, or was saving herself for her husband. It certainly wasn't because she lacked an appetite for sex, that much she knew for sure. It was simply that she knew that she could not be truly happy unless she could find a man who was her match, and more. She never wanted to have to hold back, for fear that her husband could not cope with her intelligence, or her independence, or her money, or any of the other blessings she possessed that could be burdens too. It was, she often thought, a great unfairness that all the things that made it harder for her to find a man would make it much easier to find a girl, if she were a man. A male student who was the handsome, wealthy heir to a Kenyan estate would have girls queuing all down the High Street and would happily work his way through those that took his fancy.

For her, though, it was different. She was like the dominant lioness in the pack, who would mate only with the alpha male. He was waiting for her somewhere, Saffron just knew it. But until she found him, she would just have to be patient, even if there were times when every inch of her body and every deep, primal instinct cried out, "I want a man!"

———

"My darling, you need a wife," Athala von Meerbach said to her son Gerhard one afternoon as they walked along a path through the woods at the Schloss Meerbach.

He groaned in frustration and annoyance. "Not you too, Mother! Konrad is forever telling me that it is my duty as a good German and Party member to find a nice, Aryan wife and start producing the soldiers and mothers of the future. I always tell him that I haven't yet found the right Aryan . . . and it's true. I haven't."

"I'm not surprised if you insist on having affairs with girls like that little blonde thing, the baker's daughter?"

"Her name was Jana, mother." To Gerhard's surprise, his fling with two young women had turned into an affair, of a sort, with one of them. He had never truly loved Jana, but she had been good company, out of bed as well as in it, and they had spent a pleasant enough year together. She had always known that she had no long-term future with Gerhard and, in the end, had left him to marry a nice young detective in the Berlin Criminal Police. Gerhard had hardly been broken-hearted, exactly, but he had missed her and his big bed had suddenly seemed emptier without her.

"Her father was a perfectly respectable tradesman," he went on. "You seem to forget that we live in a socialist country now. The idea that one class is superior to any other is no longer acceptable."

"Politicians come and politicians go, but a great family goes on forever."

"The Reich will last a thousand years. The Führer said so. Our family had better get used to it."

Athala looked at her son. She did not say anything. No one ever said anything that might be interpreted as criticism of the

Führer or his government. The risk of being overheard and reported was too great, even for a dowager countess in the grounds of her own family's castle. But her look let Gerhard know that she wasn't standing for that sort of nonsense from him.

"Look, Ma," he said, softening his voice, "the truth is that I just don't feel it would be right for me to marry anyone at the moment. I have my work to do for Herr Speer, and most of my spare time is taken up with my duties as a Luftwaffe reservist. How could I give a wife the time that she needs? How could she ever get to know the real me?"

That was as close as Gerhard dared come to stating the truth, which was that he was living a lie. Any woman who entered into marriage believing that the man she loved was really the one she saw in front of her—with his Party badge, his work planning the Führer's new Berlin and his devoted service to the country's armed forces—would be marrying that lie. That was simply not fair to her. He would not ask any woman to be his wife on the basis of a great deceit.

Athala stopped, took his hand and looked up into his eyes. "I understand, my darling. But you are a good man, a kind man, a generous man. That is the real you and any woman would be glad to have a husband with those qualities. God rest your father's soul, but he had none of those things."

"Perhaps. But he had power, and energy and complete self-confidence. A man can go a very long way if he doesn't spend too much time worrying about anyone else's feelings."

"Maybe . . . but you are not such a man, and I am glad of it. Now, listen, I have arranged a dinner on Saturday night, nothing special, just a dozen guests. I have asked the von Schöndorfs to come. They have a very pretty daughter, Francesca. Come to think of it, I'm sure you've met her . . ."

Gerhard laughed, "My God, Mother, I remember Chessi, she's just a little girl! You can't go marrying me off to a baby."

"She was a little girl. But she isn't any more, just as you are no longer a shy little schoolboy or a teenager covered in pimples.

She is nineteen, I believe, and quite sophisticated for her age. The von Schöndorfs sent her to be educated in England. She knew some very smart people there. You might be surprised."

Gerhard sighed. "Very well, then. Sit Chessi next to me at supper. I promise to be nice to her, but I absolutely do not promise to go down on one knee and marry her."

"Well, just meet her. You never know, you might find that you like her more than you expect."

———

"Do I have to go to dinner at the Meerbachs?" wailed Chessi von Schöndorf. "Konrad is a brute and his poor wife just sits there looking pregnant and downtrodden."

She was sitting in her bed with a breakfast tray on her lap. Her mother was perched on the end of the bed, occasionally reaching over to steal one of the grapes that lay in a little bowl on the tray.

"There is another son . . ." the Countess von Schöndorf replied, letting the words hang in the air for a second before she added, "and he doesn't have any kind of wife at all."

"If he's anything like his brother, he will only want to talk about two things: how Meerbach engines are better than any other engines on earth and how the Führer is better than any other leader on earth."

"Shh!" her mother hissed. "When will you learn you are not in England now. You cannot say the first thing that comes into your head!"

"All right, I'm sorry . . . but we're in my room. There's no one listening here."

"How do you know? Now, for your information, you have actually met Gerhard, when you were a little girl."

"I don't remember him."

"No matter, the point is, he is not at all boring. He works as an architect and in his spare time he is a fighter pilot in the Luftwaffe."

The look on Chessi's face told her mother that her attitude

might be changing. She decided to press home her advantage while she could, "So he is creative and also dashing and brave."

"Is he handsome?"

"Ahh," said the Countess, "that you will have to decide for yourself."

Chessi thought for a moment, "I suppose I could wear the Norman Hartnell dress—you know, the one that Saffy bought me."

"It still bothers me, that she spent so much. You should not have let her. It's not fair."

"But she wanted to, Mutti! She said it was her way of repaying me for all the times she has stayed with us. And it is a very lovely dress . . ."

"Yes, it is, and you do look adorable wearing it. No man could possibly resist you."

"Of course not!" Chessi smiled. "But if he is a Meerbach, even a Meerbach who is a pilot and an architect and a great scientist, and heaven knows what else, then I will certainly be able to resist him."

———

That Saturday evening, Athala von Meerbach waved her younger son over to her and said, "Gerhard, do meet the Count and Countess von Schöndorf."

"It's my great pleasure," he said. "How good of you to come. I have very happy memories of visiting your home when I was a boy."

"And this is their daughter, Francesca . . ."

Gerhard cast his eyes upon the girl who was being served up to him as marriage-bait and could not believe what he saw. The little brat with her hair in pigtails and freckles across her nose had turned into a ravishing blonde goddess who was to Jana what Botticelli's Venus was to a cartoon strip. He had always thought that the Schöndorfs were as poor as church mice, but her dress was fit for a Hollywood movie star: a shoulderless satin evening gown in palest pink that cupped her full breasts—Gerhard had to make a conscious effort not to stare at them—corseted her tiny waist and then tumbled in a waterfall of glossy fabric to the floor.

Mein Gott! Gerhard thought to himself. Then he gathered his senses, took Francesca's hand and kissed it as he said, "It is an absolute pleasure to meet you, *Komtesse*. You know, when my mother told me that you were coming here tonight, I said, "But she's only a little girl!"

The von Schöndorfs laughed politely and Gerhard continued. "But my mother said, "You silly boy! Francesca is a grown-up now, and she is very pretty."

Francesca appeared a little embarrassed at that, though her parents looked at her with indulgent pride.

"Mother, you were entirely mistaken," said Gerhard, and for a moment, exactly as he had intended, the harshness of his tone alarmed the others. He waited a second, and then, before anyone could protest, he added, "Francesca is not just pretty. She is absolutely ravishing."

———

Francesca gripped her mother's arm tight. The gesture might have appeared to be one of embarrassment: a girl taken aback by a man's compliment. In actual fact, it was simply a matter of necessity. Francesca was afraid that if she did not hold on to something, immediately, her legs might simply give way.

She had watched Gerhard as his mother gestured to him across the drawing room where the guests had gathered for pre-dinner drinks. He had been talking to a woman who looked a good few years older than him. He was dressed in white tie and tails, but the way he stood, one hand in his trouser pocket, his weight shifted onto his right hip with his left leg slightly out to one side, made his formal evening wear seem as relaxed as if he had just strolled down to dinner in a comfortable old jacket and a pair of slacks. He had smiled at his mother and politely bid the woman goodbye and as he strolled across the room, greeting a couple of the other guests on the way, the woman he had been talking to had followed him with her eyes, as if unable to tear them away from him.

I don't blame you! Chessi thought. Gerhard von Meerbach was the best-looking man she had ever met and when he walked up to her and her parents she realized that the attraction lay in the combination of very different qualities within him. He carried himself with the cool confidence of the daring aviator, with that tall, lean figure and the dark blond hair that fell over one eyebrow, so that it was all she could do not to reach up and push it back. But his eyes and his mouth, when one was close enough to study them—and oh, how she studied them!—had a look of sensitivity and perceptiveness about them that belied the devil-may-care first impression. This was a man who saw, and felt. And he was also, it suddenly struck Chessi, a man who was wounded. There was pain in him. She could not say precisely how she knew that, but she was sure of it. And suddenly there was nothing in all the world she wanted more than the chance to make that pain go away.

In the distance she heard a gong sound. "Ah," said Gerhard, "time to go in to dinner. Francesca, will you do me the great honor of walking in with me?"

He held out his arm and she took it. They walked into the dining room past many an admiring eye, for they made such a splendid couple. And behind them their two mothers looked at one another and exchanged a private smile, as if to say, "Mission accomplished!"

———

Mr. Brown had very few, if any close friends: he did not allow himself the luxury of the shared revelations of one's true self upon which real friendship is based. But the great many people who counted him among his acquaintances would have been surprised to discover that this quiet gentleman, so understated in his manner, so disinclined to make flamboyant gestures or grand entrances, so utterly un-theatrical in every way, did in fact consider himself a sort of impresario. He was, after all, in the business of spotting, unearthing, grooming and then exploiting talent. He scoured the country for brilliant young people: the cleverest, toughest, best-looking or even those who were like him, exceptionally good at fading into the background. He took note of the way that other people regarded them, researched their characters and opinions and then auditioned them, just as a Broadway or Hollywood producer might to see whether they would be right for the parts he had in mind for them.

The difference, however, between Mr. Brown and those other professional talent-spotters was that his subjects were unaware of his interest until a very late stage in the process, and, should they eventually choose to be recruited, gave their performances in absolute secrecy. Eva Barry, a clever, exceptionally beautiful girl from a humble home in Northumbria had been one of Mr. Brown's finds and had served both him, and her country with exceptional dedication, self-sacrifice and courage. Now, a quarter of a century after she had gone to work for him, Mr. Brown was on a train to Oxford to see whether Eva's daughter might prove equally useful.

He knew perfectly well that Saffron Courtney would be very unlikely to sacrifice her virtue for her country in the way that her mother had done. Eva had been dirt-poor, desperate and sufficiently motivated by the desire for revenge that she was prepared to prostitute herself to Count Otto von Meerbach, the man who had destroyed her father, if it helped destroy von Meerbach in his turn. From all that Mr. Brown had gathered about Saffron, her situation was infinitely different. She was blessed by wealth as well as brilliance. Her mother's death had been a tragic twist of fate, for which no individual could be held to blame. Her father was alive and well and his relationship with Saffron was in many ways the keystone of her young life.

That did not, however, mean that she might not be useful one day, and that day might well come in months rather than years. Once again, Hitler had dared the rest of Europe to stop him as he announced his determination to send his troops into Czechoslovakia. Once again, he had got away with his effrontery. Neville Chamberlain, who had taken Balfour's place as Prime Minister a year earlier, had gone with the French premier Édouard Daladier to meet Hitler and his crony, the Italian dictator Mussolini, in Munich. Chamberlain and Daladier had given away the freedom of the Czechs in the hope of preserving what Chamberlain had described as, "Peace with honor. Peace in our time."

Chamberlain's political rival Winston Churchill had retorted, "You were given the choice between war and dishonor. You chose dishonor and you will have war." But the people were just grateful for any shred of hope that war might be averted. As one newsreel, showing footage of Chamberlain's car travelling down roads lined with cheering, waving citizens of the German Reich, had intoned, "Let no man say that too high a price has been paid for the peace of the world until he has searched his soul and found himself willing to risk war and the lives of those nearest and dearest to him, and until he has attempted to add up the total price that might have had to be paid in death and destruction."

There's no "might" about it, Mr. Brown had thought, watching the newsreel himself, for he enjoyed an occasional visit to his local picture-house. *There will be war. The only issue is when.*

With that in mind, and being also aware of the eternal truth that all wars are started by the old but fought by the young, Mr. Brown was on the lookout for the fresh blood his service would require once hostilities began. And from everything he'd heard, Saffron Courtney might be just what he was looking for.

———

As a crowd of undergrads spilled out of the Oxford University Department of Economics, a small group stopped by the line of bicycles propped up against the wall outside. A young man called out to one of the very few women emerging from the lecture on the subject of "Marshall and Pigou's Neoclassical Paradigm': "What ho, Courtney! Will I be seeing you at the library this afternoon?"

Saffron stopped and smiled at her friend Quentin Edery. Although he might be putting on the voice and mannerisms of a real-life Bertie Wooster, Edery was in fact a fiercely intelligent grammar schoolboy from a modest home in the West Midlands town of Dudley. He had won a scholarship to New College and made no secret of his ambition one day to be the Chancellor of the Excheckr in a Labour government.

"I'm sorry but I can't," Saffron replied. "Manners wants to talk to me about my essay. He suggested we discuss it over tea and crumpets."

"Hmm . . . that sounds fishy. You'd better watch out. When a man offers a girl a hot, buttered crumpet, it's a sure prelude to a pass."

Saffron laughed. "I hardly think Manners is going to make a pass at me. I don't think I'm his type at all."

"Fair point. He's not a ladies' man, it must be said. In which case I think he's going to make a last desperate bid to shake you out of your absurd, outdated belief in the future of capitalism and put you on the socialist road to righteousness."

"I think that's closer to the mark. My essay took issue with Keynes and suggested that economic growth would be stimulated more effectively if governments made it easier for private companies to find credit, rather than wasting resources on inefficient public expenditure."

"My God, Courtney, there are times when I realize that behind that lovely façade there lurks the mind of a robber baron, whose only desire is to grind the noses of the poor even further into the dirt."

"And you, darling Quentin, just want to be a Soviet Commissar, telling the people what's good for them. But since I have actually seen how jobs can be saved and wages increased if fundamentally sound companies can be saved from going under during an economic collapse, by the simple expedient of providing access to credit, allowing them to keep trading until they can flourish again under their own steam, I think the poor would be better off under my system."

"Good luck persuading Manners of that. He worships the ground on which John Maynard Keynes treads. Anyway, must be off . . ."

Saffron watched her friend pedal off down the road and thought about how strange it was that one could like someone so much and disagree with them so fundamentally. Quentin Edery wanted to create an entirely new society, one in which people like her would no longer enjoy the privileges of wealth and possession and ordinary men and women, like the people he grew up with, would have their fair share of the prosperity they worked to create. In principle, Saffron could hardly argue with that proposition: she could hardly say that she believed in unfair shares. But she was African at heart, used to a world of predators and prey, in which life was an eternal contest for survival and the strongest always came out on top. So as much as she liked the idea of everyone living in peace, sharing everything equally, she simply couldn't believe it could ever work in practice. Her ideals, therefore, were aimed at working with the grain of human nature, accepting man as the competitive, but also fallible animal that he was, and making the best of what was sometimes bound to be a bad business.

She was rehearsing this argument in her mind, wondering how she could persuade Dr. Jeremy Manners, the brilliant don who was supervising her Economics course, as she walked from New College Lane into the college itself, past the porter's lodge and into the Front Quad. Dusk was settling on the city and the lights in the college chapel were on, illuminating the medieval stained glass windows like a series of brightly colored lanterns as Saffron followed the path around the oval lawn in the center of the quad until she came to an arch at the far end. She passed under it and entered into Garden Quad, so called because it was open on one side and looked onto the gardens that were one of the glories of Oxford. Had this been a summer's afternoon, she might have looked down from the windows of Dr. Manners onto the great expanse of lawn (on which, unlike the one in the Front Quad, students like Saffron were allowed to walk), the tree-topped mound that stood at one corner of the garden and the ancient city walls that enclosed the entire space, with magnificent herbaceous borders at their base that provided a blaze of color when their shrubs and flowers were all in bloom.

This, however, was not the season for flowers. This was the time of chilly, wet afternoons and the single thing that drove Saffron most quickly down the path and up the stairs to the second-floor rooms was the thought of a hot fire, a steaming cup of tea and, yes, a freshly toasted crumpet.

She knocked on the heavy oak door and heard her tutor's voice call, "Come!"

She walked into a large room, lined with bookshelves and strewn, on every possible surface, with more books, both open and closed, assorted journals and academic papers, sheets of foolscap covered in students' handwriting or Manners's own typing, and framed pictures of Manners himself, with friends, his academic peers and the occasional politician who had sought his advice on economic policy.

Manners himself was a tall, quite bulky man in his early forties, with an unruly shock of ginger hair, fading to gray at his temples. He was wearing a pair of baggy tweed trousers and an Aran sweater, beneath which a shirt and tie were just visible.

"Ah, Saffron, how good of you to join us," Manners said, and it was only then that Saffron noticed that there was another man in the room, sitting so quietly in one of the armchairs

Manners had arranged around the fire that he barely seemed present at all. He was small and slightly built, dressed in a perfectly tailored charcoal gray suit, a stiff collared white shirt and a plain, dark blue tie, and was, to judge by his silver hair and the lines on his face, well into old age. Yet she now realized that he was looking at her with eyes that were still very much alive and somewhat unsettling in the cool, unapologetic frankness with which they were examining her.

Now the man rose to his feet, waving away Manners's offer to assist him as he emerged from the armchair's deep embrace.

"Saffron, this is Mr. Brown. He's an old chum of mine and, I might add, a veritable *éminence grise* of Whitehall. He knows absolutely everyone who matters in government and has done for, what, fifty years, would you say, Brown?"

Mr. Brown gave the merest trace of a half-smile and a barely perceptible shrug, "Oh, I don't know, Manners, but I've been around the place for quite a while, I suppose."

He looked at Saffron. "I'm delighted to meet you, my dear," he said, shaking her hand.

"Sit down, Saffron, please," Manners said. "Can I get you a cup of tea? Crumpet?"

Saffron said yes to both and then Mr. Brown said, "I'm afraid I owe you an apology, Miss Courtney. Manners has invited you here under false pretences. So let me reassure you that there is nothing wrong with your essay."

"I thought it was well argued, interesting use of first-hand evidence—one seldom teaches a student who can support their thesis with a first-hand account of the means by which their own family firm was saved from bankruptcy—and really rather impressive," said Manners. "Of course, I disagreed with every single word, from the opening capital letter to the last full stop. But still, beta double-plus, good work."

"So why am I here?" Saffron asked, looking from one man to the other.

"Mr. Brown particularly asked to meet you," said Manners.

"Would it be rude to ask why?"

Mr. Brown gave another hint of a smile. "Of course not, Miss Courtney. The truth is that His Majesty's Government always has need of the brightest and best of the country's young people. One of my tasks, therefore, is to keep an eye out for those who show particular promise and, though you may not be aware of this, you are much talked about by your elders."

"Really?" said Saffron, somewhat taken aback.

"Oh yes. I have heard tales of everything from your skill on the hunting field to your good taste in clothes. Now, here's Manners complimenting your academic ability. I may say, incidentally, that I cast an eye over your essay. I hope you don't mind. I agree with Manners that it was a nicely written piece, and I also agree with you that the market, not the state, is the driving motor of a successful economy."

"How can a Whitehall man say a thing like that?" Manners asked.

"Precisely because he knows what the other Whitehall men are like, and wouldn't trust most of them to run the proverbial whelk-stall."

Saffron did her best to suppress a giggle at the look of horror on Manners's face and said, "Thank you, Mr. Brown."

"Not at all, my dear. Oh . . . there's one other thing I forgot to mention. Old age is catching up with me, I fear."

"What was that?"

"Simply that I had another reason for wanting to meet you in particular. You see, I used to know your mother, a long time ago. Knew her rather well, in fact, when she first came to town."

———

Good girl! thought Mr. Brown. *You knew exactly what I was talking about, and it caught you completely off-guard, but you recovered in a flash.*

He looked at Manners and realized that he had not noticed anything out of the ordinary, beyond the obvious surprise of an unexpected connection between two people who had never before met one another.

"Good Lord, Brown, you never told me that!" said Manners. "I wouldn't have bothered with all the cloak-and-dagger stuff if I'd known you were an old family friend."

"I wouldn't go quite that far," said Mr. Brown. "But, yes, I knew Eva Barry, as she was called before she married Saffron's father. And a remarkable young woman she was too. She won the Military Medal, you know, Manners, for her bravery in the East African campaign. The War Office had their doubts, being the stuffed shirts they were, but Delamere absolutely insisted on it, said she'd had as much guts as any of the men under her command. Of course, that was a few years after I knew her."

Mr. Brown was addressing his words to Manners, but his attention was all focused on Saffron. He wanted to see how she would react, now that he had made it absolutely plain that he had known Eva in her spying days. And Saffron clearly knew all about those days because she wasn't asking any of the obvious questions that any girl, particularly one who had lost her mother so young, would normally pose to someone who had known her in days gone by.

When we've trained you properly, you'll know not to make those kinds of mistakes, Mr. Brown thought. But that was just a trifling detail. This girl was every inch her mother's daughter. Not only was she just as beautiful, perhaps even more so if such a thing were possible, but she also had the same steely core that Eva had possessed. Mr. Brown could see it in the dark blue eyes that were looking at him now with such cold, implacable fury, though her mouth was smiling sweetly. Saffron knew the whole story, that was obvious, and she had naturally, and correctly, jumped to the conclusion that Mr. Brown had been responsible for what her mother had been obliged to do.

Brown let Manners chat on for a while, asking who wanted their tea-cup refilled or another crumpet on their plate—"More butter? Strawberry jam?"—and then asked Saffron, "Would I be right in thinking you have visited Germany more than once over the course of the past few years?"

"That's right. My closest friend at school was a German girl, Francesca von Schöndorf."

"What did you make of the place?"

Saffron paused for a second and then said, "Well I felt the same way about Germany as Dr. Manners did about my essay. I thought the country was beautiful, it's culture—you know, the architecture, the music, the literature and so on—was magnificent and all the people I ever talked to were charming. But I disagreed with every single word of Nazism from the first capital letter to the last full stop."

Manners burst out laughing and clapped his hands. "Now that deserves an alpha!"

"What makes you say that?" asked Brown.

"Because it's hateful . . . I mean literally filled with hate. The way the Jews are degraded is appalling. And there's a bullying feeling to it: all those huge red banners with swastikas on them, and beastly men swaggering around in fancy uniforms like little tin gods. Every time I went there it got worse."

"Do you think the Germans want a war?"

"No, I'm absolutely certain that the average German is terrified of another war. It's not till you get there that you realize how many more men they lost than we did in the Great War. But it's not a matter of what they want, is it? It's a matter of what Hitler gives them."

"Ah yes, der Führer . . . tell me, what did your hosts think of him? I imagine, with a name like 'von Schöndorf,' they were what we might call upper crust."

"Yes, they were. As for what they thought about Hitler . . ." Saffron cast her mind back and tried to come up with a fair description of how Chessi's parents viewed their leader. "I suppose they feel the way upper-crust people in this country would do if the royal family disappeared and some ghastly little corporal with a funny moustache suddenly set himself up as the country's supreme ruler in their place. They'd be appalled. They'd find it unbelievable. And they'd do their very best to carry on as if he simply didn't exist."

"Plenty of members of the English upper crust are rather sympathetic—too sympathetic, in fact—to Herr Hitler," Brown observed.

"Yes, but only as ruler of Germany. They wouldn't much like it if he was lording it over them."

Mr. Brown was struck by the self-confidence and directness with which Saffron expressed her opinions. He'd expect that of a bright young Oxford man, though not, perhaps, one who was still a fresher. But even the brightest bluestocking, who privately held very forceful opinions, was apt to feel constrained by the rules of ladylike behavior. It wasn't that the Courtney girl was in any way shrill or hectoring. He had asked her straight questions. She had given him straight answers. It was more that it clearly did not occur to her to behave in any other way.

Your mother never had that, he thought. *She was just as beautiful as you, just as brave, just as bright. But she didn't have that inner self-belief, not at first, anyway. That, my dear, is your great privilege.*

He looked at his watch. "My goodness, is that the time? I really must be going. Manners, thank you so much for your hospitality, which is as generous as ever."

"It was my pleasure, sir."

"And Miss Courtney, I greatly enjoyed our conversation. I think you are a young woman to be watched and I would very much appreciate the chance to talk with you again. For example, should you happen to make another trip to Germany, I should be very interested to hear your observations."

"That's very flattering," said Saffron, with a suitably appreciative smile. "I should be delighted to provide them, though I'm sure you already know far more about the place than I ever will."

"Ah, but there's nothing like a fresh pair of eyes . . . Well then, I'll be off. Don't worry Manners, I'll find my own way out."

And with that, Mr. Brown walked out onto the wooden staircase, and as he made his way back down to ground level he thought to himself, *We will have a use for you, Miss Courtney. Oh yes, you will certainly come in handy one day.*

———

Just before the end of term, as she was packing up for Christmas, Saffron received a letter from Chessi von Schöndorf. It was written in her usual chatty style, full of news about her family, and questions about Saffy's life as a student at Oxford. Chessi's big news was that she had been invited to join a group of friends who were going to St.. Moritz for a fortnight, just after Christmas. "Of course the skiing will be wonderful, though I know that is of no interest to you!!" she had written, making Saffron smile, for it was one of the running jokes in their life that in the three years she had visited Chessi and her family, all of whom were put on skis almost as soon as they could walk, Saffy had never really developed any great skill on snow. It baffled them both, for there had never before been a sport that Saffron had not taken to like a natural, but for some reason—they agreed that it must be something to do with her African upbringing—she was, though brave enough to tackle any slope, no more than a competent skier. Chessi had been thrilled to discover that here at last was something at which she outshone her otherwise brilliant friend and Saffron made a deliberate decision to set aside her usual, ferociously competitive nature because it seemed only fair to let Chessi get her share of the limelight for once. But the subject of skiing was soon forgotten because then there came some really interesting news:

"Now, Saffy my darling friend I must tell you the most wonderful news of all—I AM IN LOVE!!!! He is called Gerhard and he comes from a very good family (a very rich family, too, as

Mutti keeps telling me!). He is an architect by profession, but also in his spare time he is in the Luftwaffe and he flies fighter planes. So he is an artist AND he is a brave warrior AND he is tall, and handsome, like a film star, but he has lovely eyes, that are so kind and gentle. Oh Saffy, when he looks at me with those eyes I am in heaven!! So, he will be joining us in St. Moritz, toward the end of our stay and I think that he may propose marriage to me and if he does I will say Yes because I love him so and I want to be with him forever!!"

Saffron could just hear Chessi's voice, filled with giddy happiness, as if she were in the room beside her, and the two of them were giggling with excitement and going into every tiny detail of what he had said and done, and what it all meant. It was such a contrast to the earnestness of her Oxford life, which seemed filled with fascinating but deeply serious debates about important subjects with dons and fellow students, all determined to set the world to right. She wrote back to Chessi, congratulating her on her good fortune, assuring her that she absolutely insisted on being a bridesmaid at her wedding and adding, "I'm off to Scotland for Christmas and New Year with the Ballantynes, which is lovely, but it does mean having to fend off my cousin Rory. Do you remember, I told you about him at Easter? He's an estate manager rather than a brave warrior, but he's quite good-looking I suppose. The thing is, he's perfectly sweet and I do like him, but only in a friendly, family sort of way. I just hope he doesn't start getting fresh after he's drunk too much on Christmas Day. If he makes a pass at me I shall have to slap him in the face and then where will we be?!"

Rory had done his best. He had gone to the trouble of drawing out a family tree on the back of an old roll of wallpaper. On the afternoon of New Year's Day he unfurled his masterpiece on a table in the library and showed Saffron that the two of them were only cousins by marriage, because her great-aunt had married his great-uncle, so there was no blood link and therefore no impediment to their getting married. "Not that I'm proposing, or anything," Rory had added.

"That's just as well," she replied, "because if you were, I would have to say no, and I'd much rather not do that because then we couldn't be such good friends. I think you're a smashing chum, and I love you very much as part of my family, even if we don't have any blood in common. But I'm not in love with you. It's nothing you've done or not done. I just don't feel that way about you, that's all."

"I suppose there's some brainy chap at Oxford you're sweet on, the lucky blighter."

"Don't be silly, of course there isn't! There isn't anyone at all."

"Then maybe I still have a chance."

Saffron didn't reply to that. She simply said, "Come on, let's get back to the drawing room. Tea will have been served by now. Everyone will be wondering where we've got to."

To Saffron's surprise there was a telegram waiting for her on a silver salver. Her first thought was that something awful had happened to her father or Harriet but when she opened it she saw that it had been sent from the Badrutt's Palace Hotel in St. Moritz.

———

HAVING WUNDERBAR TIME STOP HE WILL ARRIVE IN TWO DAYS STOP SO EXCITED STOP WISH YOU WERE HERE LOVE CHESSI

"I've been to St. Moritz, you know," said Rory, when Saffron told him about the message. "Splendid place. I'm proud to say I went down the Cresta Run, which was without doubt the most terrifying thing I've done in my life but hellish good fun. You know that cricket jumper I wear, the one with the burgundy stripes around the collar—that's my St. Moritz Toboggan Club jumper. It proves I've been down the run and jolly proud of it I am too!"

A mischievous smile crossed Saffron's face and her eyes twin-kled with the light of an idea forming in her mind. "Just out of curiosity, how would one get from here to St. Moritz?"

"Ah, well, I can tell you exactly because of course I've done it. One simply takes the midday Flying Scotsman from Edinburgh to King's Cross, getting in at about half-past seven. Then nip across London on the Tube to Victoria and hop on the overnight boat train to Paris. That gets you into the Gare du Nord at nine in the morning . . . I say, I'm not boring you am I, with this recitation?"

"Not at all. Please continue."

"Well then you have to get across Paris, on the Metro this time, of course, to the Gare de Lyon, catch the first train to Zürich, which is another five hours or so. From there you go to a place called Chur, change again, for the final time thank goodness, and that takes you all the way to St. Moritz, arriving just in time for a nice drink before dinner."

"Well that sounds splendid," said Saffron. "Do you think your ma and pa would mind awfully if we set off for Switzerland tomorrow?"

"I'm sorry . . . what did you say?"

"I said I think we should go to St. Moritz. It will be a lovely surprise for Chessi and you can show me the Cresta Run. I think I'd like to try it too."

"But . . . but you can't!"

"Why on earth not?"

"Because you're a girl. Female riders were banned about ten years ago. They're absolutely not allowed."

"All the better," said Saffron. "Now I absolutely insist on going down it."

———

A call to the Edinburgh office of the Thomas Cook travel agency, first thing the following morning, revealed that they could book trains and even hotel rooms in St. Moritz, but it would take a day at the very least to arrange. A little over twenty-four hours later Saffron strode through the door of Thomas Cook with Rory in her wake, paid for and collected two return rail tickets to St. Moritz and was informed that they had been unable to find two rooms at the Palace Hotel but had procured a pair at the Suvretta House. "I am assured that you will find it more than satisfactory, Miss," the lady serving her said, with a pursed-lipped look of a respectable Edinburgh woman who senses something of which she should disapprove, even if she has not yet decided precisely what that might be.

Saffron sent a telegram to Chessi:

———

ON MY WAY SEE YOU SOONEST LOVE SAFFYXX.

She and Rory lunched on the train to London; dined, slept and breakfasted en route to Paris; grabbed a *croque monsieur* and a cup of coffee each at the station café in Lyon and got off the train at St. Moritz to find a member of the hotel staff waiting to meet them.

Saffron ate a hearty supper, went up to bed immediately afterward and slept like a log till half-past eight. She ordered breakfast to be brought to her room and was sitting up in bed, sipping a large cup of hot chocolate and looking out at the wonderful view down the valley toward the frozen lake, when there was a knock on the door.

"Who is it?" Saffron called out.

"Just me," came Rory's muffled voice. "Can I come in?"

"Yes!" replied Saffron, pulling her robe a little tighter over her chest to cover up the faintest hint of cleavage.

"Goodness, aren't you up yet?" Rory said when he saw her still luxuriating in bed. "I thought you'd want to be dashing off to see your chum."

"It's too late for that. I know what Chessi's like when she

gets anywhere near a ski-slope. She'll have been heading for the slopes and absolutely raring to go by eight at the latest. So I'll see her this evening instead, and what I thought was that it would be really fun if I had a story to tell her all about how I went down the Cresta Run."

"You're not still set on that, are you? I was rather hoping you might have gone off the idea."

"Why on earth would I do that? I raided your wardrobe and your pa's for men's clothes. I don't have any other reason to wear them."

"But honestly, Saffy, you could hurt yourself."

"I could just as easily hurt myself skiing, plenty of people do, but you wouldn't try to stop me doing that."

"I know, but no one would blame me if you hurt yourself. But the only way you can go down the Cresta is if I help you do it."

"Oh I wouldn't worry about that," Saffron said. "No one would ever blame you for not being able to persuade me to be sensible. No one can. Just ask my poor father."

"Very well then. This is your funeral and you can't blame me if you break your silly neck. And that being the case I suggest we meet at ten o'clock in the hall. And then I will take you to meet Herr Zuber."

"Ooh, that sounds mysterious, who's he?"

"The man without whom neither you nor anyone else is allowed anywhere near the Cresta Run, no matter how much of a man you might be."

———

Saffron had eaten, showered and allowed herself the indulgence of some particularly pretty underwear. *Just because I have to look like a man on the outside, I'm jolly well going to still feel female on the inside.* She pinned her hair up into a bun and shoved a man's woolly hat down over her head. She was as tall as most men, so that wasn't a problem, and a thick woollen jumper worn beneath a blouson windcheater bulked up her shoulders and hid her pretty but not particularly large breasts. Her face, though, was far from manly, which was normally a very good thing, but not today. She wrapped a scarf around her neck and up over her mouth and covered her big blue eyes and long thick lashes with a pair of dark glasses.

Having done her best to look like a man, she now got to work on acting, moving and sounding like one too. For years, Saffron's height had condemned her to play the man's roles in school plays: she had made a fine Romeo, but she would far rather have been Juliet. But now, quite unexpectedly, that experience was coming in useful. She stood in front of the mirror, stuck her hands in her trouser pockets and slouched. *Men are so lucky to be able to do that!* she thought. *We have to keep our backs straight and our heads up and cross our legs when we sit down. We hardly ever just relax, the way they do. And that reminds me—knees apart when I sit down!*

She practiced her man-walk up and down the room a couple of times, not moving from the hips as women did, but leading with her shoulders. Next item on the agenda was her voice. She had decided to limit the chances of being caught out by keeping her speech to a bare minimum. She lowered her voice as much as she could and tried out a couple of manly grunts, indicating yes, or no, and then a few brief phrases: "Right-ho," "Absolutely," "Got it" and "Can't wait."

I know plenty of men who never say anything more for themselves than that, she thought, and told herself on no account to giggle, squeal or describe anything as either "sweet" or "adorable." She was reasonably sure that she'd be screaming like a banshee once she set off down the run itself, but once she was sliding down the ice at fifty miles an hour, there was absolutely nothing that anyone could do about it until she reached the bottom.

She gave herself one last look in the mirror, gave a manly shrug of her shoulders and set off to find Rory and the mysterious Herr Zuber.

———

Gerhard had also arrived in St. Moritz the previous afternoon, although he had driven the two-hundred-odd kilometers from Schloss Meerbach. Having once pretended that he wanted money to buy a Mercedes, he had acquired a newer model a couple of years ago, a gloriously sleek, bright red two-seater 540K cabriolet, with whitewall tires and pale beige, almost honey-colored leather seats, and never once regretted the decision: the thrill of driving it at the unlimited speeds allowed on the new autobahns was almost a match for being at the controls of a 109. Like Saffron, Gerhard had chosen not to stay at the Palace, although in his case his reasoning had more to do with a sense that he ought not to see Chessi before he proposed to her: it seemed more romantic that way, somehow. He had stopped off at home for a night on the way down from Berlin because it broke his journey very conveniently and he wanted to tell his mother that he was about to propose to Francesca von Schöndorf.

Athala was, as he had expected her to be, delighted by the news. "Oh I'm so happy for you both!" she exclaimed, wrapping her arms around her son. "From the first time I saw the two of you together I thought that you looked so perfect together. She really is such a beautiful creature, and so charming. She will make you a wonderful wife, and you, my boy, must be as good a husband to her."

"Of course, Mother. Why else would I marry her?"

Gerhard had meant it, too. He really did want to be a good husband. His father and older brother might have regarded their marriage vows as an irrelevance that had no effect whatever on their sexual liaisons with other women. But he would be different. He would treat his wife with the respect she deserved. And surely that would not be difficult. Chessi was just as lovely and as sweet-natured as his mother had said and they really did make a fine pair together: everybody said so.

If only he loved her just a little bit more. Oh, he liked her well enough and he never had the slightest trouble in finding her attractive, though he wished she had not been quite such a good Catholic girl or insisted quite so fiercely on remaining a virgin until her wedding night. He was sure that if they had made love then he would no longer be quite so beset by . . . not doubt exactly, more a feeling that he was not quite as swept up in the overwhelming passion that he had always imagined true love would bring.

He had been working very hard, of course, and spending a great deal of his spare time with the Luftwaffe, so there had been very little of his time, or mind to spare for thinking about love. And Chessi, bless her, was so filled with excitement and anticipation, so enraptured the very idea of becoming his wife that she seemed to have enough love to spare for them both. Still, there was a very small, quiet but insistent voice in the back of his mind wondering whether he felt quite as strongly, or as certainly about the whole idea as she did.

Well, it was too late to worry about that now. He was about to offer his hand in marriage to Chessi and what man would not envy the thought of waking up next to her for the rest of his life? Gerhard had made a point of keeping her away from Konrad, not because he had the slightest fear that he would steal Chessi away from him—he might very well try, but she would certainly not respond—but because something about his mere presence would feel like a sort of bile or poison, making everything just that little bit meaner, less joyful than it should be. Once they were married, at the wedding reception, then Konrad could meet Chessi, but not before.

So, tonight he would propose to Chessi and all would be well. Yes, that would surely make all the difference. In the meantime, he intended to spend the day reacquainting himself with another old flame, a mean old bitch he had conquered three years earlier but wanted to master again. By God, she could treat a man badly. But damn her, she was worth the pain!

———

Herr Zuber was an avuncular, gray-haired man, whose family had lived in St. Moritz for as far back as anyone could remember, and who ran a shop in the middle of town that not only supplied normal skiing equipment but also the particular accoutrements required by riders on the Cresta Run. From the top down the complete outfit began with a helmet with flaps that covered one's ears and buckled under the chin. There were pads to protect one's elbows and gloves that resembled a cross between winter mittens and a knight in armor's gauntlets, with a metal plate over the top of the wearer's hands and knuckles to protect them from hard, rough-edged ice. Another pair of pads protected the knees and the whole ensemble was completed with boots tipped with steel toecaps from which protruded two wicked, jagged-edged steel tips.

"They'd come in jolly handy on the dance floor sometimes, what?" joked Rory, to which Saffron responded by nodding and grunting, "Huh!"

She thought her male impersonation had gone rather well, but as she was leaving Herr Zuber said, "May I wish you good luck, Fräulein. I have always admired women who have real courage."

She stopped dead by the doorway and was about to bluster it out but then thought it was wiser to find out now what she'd done wrong. That might stop her being caught out again later.

"How did you know?" she asked.

"So many ways . . . You had to take off your . . . I do not know the word . . ." He pointed at his eyes, "*Sonnenbrille.*"

"Dark glasses," said Saffron.

"*Ach so* . . . And your eyes, ah, no man could have any so beautiful."

"Thank you . . . I'll make sure I keep my dark glasses on all the time."

"Also your hands. You should always your gloves keep on because you have very, ah . . . slender fingers, *sehr hübsch.*"

"What does that mean?" Rory asked.

"Herr Zuber very sweetly said that my fingers were pretty. *Vielen dank.*"

"*Bitte*, you are welcome, Fräulein. But finally I could not help but notice that you were wearing a scent, I do not know its name, but no man would smell this way. Not unless he was, you know, how shall I say? Not a true man?"

"Oh goodness, my Shalimar! I must have put it on this morning after my shower, without even thinking."

"I have a little *toilette* at the back of the shop. There is a basin there. If you shall wash your face the scent will go. Then keep your glasses and your gloves on and maybe you will be able to go down the run. You can tell me all about it when you bring this equipment back. Until then, *viel Glück* . . . good luck!"

Saffron washed around her neck, and behind her ears. Then she put her dark glasses and gloves back on: it was time to get back into character. As she and Rory walked out of the store she was vaguely aware of the presence of a tall man coming the other way, but then the door shut behind her and Rory was sniffing the air and saying, "Can't smell a thing. Excellent. Tally-ho!"

They walked together up the path that ran alongside the Cresta Run. Rory still felt that he had one card left to play in his bid to prevent his cousin from killing herself.

"We won't be going all the way to the very top," he said. "There's a special start for novices halfway up. Everyone uses it for their first few runs. It's actually a rule, now I come to think of it."

"So is prohibiting female riders and I'm not obeying that one, either," she retorted. "Now, you'd better let me know what I can expect to find on my way down."

"All right then," Rory sighed. "The run is about three-quarters of a mile long and it drops rather more than five hundred feet. The average gradient is one-in-eight which is jolly steep,

I can tell you, and the steepest bits are much worse. Look, Saffy, I really don't think it's a good idea to . . ."

"That's enough! I've made up my mind. The best thing you can do now is just to help me. Tell me what I need to do to make it down in one piece."

"Dig your toes in. You should be good at that. Just stick the ends of your boots into the ice and go slowly at first, till you get the hang of it. Don't be embarrassed, or think you look stupid. You'll look a lot more stupid going too fast and then having a crash than getting down to the bottom in one piece at a nice steady pace."

"Would you tell another man that?"

"Yes, actually, I would. And I'd also tell him that the Cresta is full of tricks and surprises. Some of the bends are deliberately made to spit riders out and send them flying off the track, unless they maintain complete control of the sled. Which brings me to the matter of Shuttlecock . . ."

"What's that?"

"The deadliest turn on the course, Cousin Saffron, assuming you get that far. Which you probably won't if you are mad enough to set off from the very top . . ."

Saffron gave Rory a look that a gorgon would have been proud of.

"Very well, then," he conceded, "you start out from the very top, go past Stable Junction and over Church Leap, so called because of the rather picturesque parish church that stands beside the top of the track . . . then round a few more corners, past the beginners' start and onto the Junction Straight. Now, unless you're very careful you may find yourself picking up rather more speed on the straight than you—or any novice, including a man!—can handle. You zoom up and around the right-hander at Rise, crash down on the other side, whizz under Nani's Bridge, take a turn called Battledore and then you're at Shuttlecock, which is the perfect example of the type of corner I was talking about."

"The type that spits you out?"

"Exactly. That's what it's there for, to dispose of riders who are going too fast. It's like a kind of safety-valve, so that they can't come to even more trouble further down. There's even a Shuttlecock Club for people who come off there. They have a club tie and everything.'

"Perhaps I can have a Shuttlecock Club garter belt made for me."

"I wouldn't say that sort of thing while you're in any other chap's hearing."

"By the way," Saffron asked, "what happens if you come off on the wrong side of the track and go flying straight off the mountain?"

Rory shook his head sorrowfully. "Nothing to be done, I'm afraid. There's a special little cemetery, down by the lake, just for people who died on the Cresta Run. Hell of a way to go, what?"

"Yes . . . yes . . . hell of a way," Saffron muttered and this time Rory could see she was genuinely shaken.

"Don't worry," he said. "I was only teasing. There's no cemetery. There are nets at the side of the track, wherever it's near a bad drop, so they catch anyone who crashes. Look," he pointed up the hill, "there's one up there, on that curve, d'you see?"

"You brute!" Saffron exclaimed. "I have a good mind to punch you with my metal gloves. That will teach you not to be so cruel!"

They walked on and Saffron occasionally caught sight of prone figures flashing by in a dark blur, the metal runners of their skeleton sleds rattling furiously against the ice.

"This is the novices' start," Rory said as they passed a group of beginners standing by the side of the track, taking instruction from an old hand.

"Goodbye, novices!" said Saffron, walking up the hill.

———

Finally, they came to the start of the Cresta Run. It wasn't much to look at. A small wooden hut stored the sleds and provided shelter for the timekeeper who recorded all the runs. There was a small iron stove inside to keep him warm and ease the chill for the riders on really cold days. This, however, was perfect alpine weather, with clear blue skies, dazzling sunshine and thick snow on the ground. A group of riders, all in their helmets, gloves, pads and boots, were sitting on a wooden bench facing the top of the run, which was blocked by a plank hinged to a post by the side of the track. A man in a St. Moritz Toboggan Club sweater was standing by the plank, acting as the starter.

No rider could go down the track until the one before had got off it, either because he had made it to the end, or because he was lying in the snow, somewhere to the side. At that point, a signal was sent up to the hut, the starter raised the plank and the next rider set off.

One of the men sitting on the bench seemed to be looking at Rory and Saffron with particular interest as they walked toward him. Saffron felt her skin flush, thinking he must be looking at her, seeing something wrong, but then a grin broke out across the man's face and in an American accent he said, "I got it! You're Ballantyne, right? You were here in '37."

"That's right. And you must be . . ."

"Holland Moritz."

"Of course, Moritz . . . Didn't you like to tell the ladies that ol' Saint Moritz himself had been an ancestor of yours?"

"I might have used that line once or twice," he admitted and Saffron had to make a conscious effort not to look too obviously at his perfect white teeth, his suntanned skin and the twinkle in his black-brown eyes.

"Say, who's your friend?' Moritz asked.

"Oh, this is my cousin, S . . ." he paused for a second, "Stephen Courtney."

"Good to meet you Steve," said Moritz, giving Saffron a hearty handshake.

"You too," she replied doing her best not to wince as the bones in her hand seemed to be crushed by the Moritz's grip.

Just behind him, Saffron could see a man pick up his sled and walk to the start. The plank was lifted. The rider took two or three quick steps then dived forward, holding his sled in front of him and landing on his stomach, his head right up at the front just inches from the ice as he raced off down the track and around the first bend.

"So, you as fast on the run as your cousin?" Moritz asked her.

"Actually, Stephen's a novice. This is his first day on the course."

"Is that so? And you're going from the top?"

Saffron nodded, "Uh-huh."

Moritz whistled in admiration. "Well you've got balls of steel, I'll say that for you."

"Oh yes, Stephen's got balls all right," said Rory.

Saffron nodded and gave another grunt.

"You don't want to talk, I get it. Don't blame you, first time on the run and all. Just get down it and everything will be grand. You'll feel as high as a kite and you'll want to come straight back up here and do it all over again. Uh-oh, time for me to go . . ."

A few seconds later Moritz was running toward the start, going much faster than the previous rider, hurling himself onto the ice and going like a human bullet down the mountain.

"Don't be fooled for one second by that wide-eyed, all-American charm," Rory said. "Holland Moritz is as tough a rider as ever went down the run and he wins practically every event he enters. Damn nice chap though and an absolutely first-rate rider."

"It's my turn next," said Saffron.

"Now, be honest, are you absolutely sure you want to do it?"

Saffron looked at the track. Suddenly it didn't look like a gradient of one-in-six, it looked like a vertical tunnel of ice that would hold her in its icy claws for three-quarters of a mile, beating and battering her, terrifying her for every single second until, if she survived at all, she arrived in a heap at the far end.

She was scared witless.

"Yes," she said, "I'm sure."

"Very well then, don't even try to emulate Mr. Moritz and his flying leap at the start. Walk steadily up to the edge, put the sled down, lower yourself onto it and only at the very end give a gentle push with your standing foot. So long as you are moving, no matter how slowly at the start, the track will do the rest."

"Mr. Courtney, the run is all yours," said the starter.

Saffron picked up one of the sleds and was startled by how light and insubstantial it felt in her hands. The body of the sled was little bigger than a metal tea-tray with a padded top and a pair of steel runners attached to the bottom. This flimsy device was all she had to carry her down the Cresta Run.

"Mr. Courtney . . . ?" the starter asked.

"Just coming," Saffron grunted.

Then she took two steps forward, past the raised plank, bent forward with her arms out in front of her, so that the sled was only a foot or so off the ice, took a final deep breath, lunged forward, felt the sled hit the ice, flung herself down on top of it and then, as the sled tipped over the edge, felt the ice beneath its runners and in an instant she was away.

———

The speed: that was what hit her, overwhelmed her, robbed her of any control over her destiny and filled her with a combination of raw fear and absolute excitement unlike any she had ever experienced. Saffron had ridden horses flat out, pushing them as hard as they could go, and jumping them over obstacles that seemed impossibly high. She had driven trucks at speed across the African savannah, heedless of the potholes or termite mounds that could wreck them at any moment, and taken cars out for spins around the narrow lanes of Devon, where every turn was blind and the fear of collision constant. On holiday with the von Schöndorfs she had insisted on throwing herself however gracelessly down the steepest ski-runs the Bavarian Alps could provide.

But never had she known speed like this.

It was the closeness to the ice that did it. That and the deafening noise of the sled, rattling against the track, which was made all the louder by the way the sound bounced and echoed off the ice walls on either side so that now it seemed as though the sound had penetrated deep into her head, beating at her brains and her skull from within. Saffron was shaken from side to side as if trapped inside a giant cocktail shaker. As the sled hurtled over rises, flew through the air and then crashed down on the far side the air was driven from her body, winding her, making her struggle for every breath and adding to her sense of panic as she hurtled down the hill. She realized now why there might actually be one good reason for keeping women off the run: the pounding of the sled against her breasts was seriously painful. She had told herself that no matter what Rory might say, she wouldn't try to slow herself down. But as she raced down a long, undeviating piece of the course—*Is this the Junction Straight? I don't know where the hell I am!*—she desperately tried to plunge her jagged toecaps into the track surface to make the speed, that terrible, overpowering speed abate just a little bit.

But it didn't seem to work. She just kept going faster. She felt the sled being flung to the right and then she flashed under a low bridge, and straight into another turn. The sled rose up and up the banking, higher than she'd ever gone before, so that Saffron felt certain that she was bound to be thrown right over the edge. She leaned as hard as she dared in the opposite direction, downhill, but it didn't seem to make any difference.

The sled kept going up. She could see over the edge. She braced herself for the inevitable crash but then an invisible hand seemed to grab the sled and fling it back down toward the floor of the run. *I made it!* she told herself and for a fraction of a second she relaxed.

The next thing she knew the sled was running up another bank, and it was going faster than before, and the edge was getting closer, the white of the track so clearly outlined against the great blue expanse of the sky, and this time there was no invisible hand, she was not thrown back down onto the center of the track. This time she was up and over and flying through the air. The sled going one way, her body quite another, and she felt as though she was hanging suspended in the air as if she had the power of flight, but then the earth exerted its pull, she plummeted downwards and landed, with a great white explosion in a pile of soft, fresh snow.

———

Gerhard had been walking up the path toward the start of the Cresta Run when he heard a high-pitched cry of alarm coming from the track to his left. He turned in time to see a sled flying through the air in one direction, while its former rider plummeted to the ground in another. He landed in a snowdrift barely twenty meters from where Gerhard was standing. And lay there, clearly dazed by the impact and the shock of the accident.

Gerhard dashed over and held out a hand. He had studied English at school and picked up some of the slang on his two previous visits to St. Moritz. The only reason he'd come had been to try his luck at the Cresta Run (there were, after all, plenty of mountains much closer to home if all he wanted to do was ski) and it was impossible to do that without conversing with upper-class Englishmen. So, without really thinking, he spoke as they did and said, "Here, let me help you up old man."

The rider took his hand and let Gerhard pull him to his feet. He was a lightly built fellow with surprisingly small hands and . . . Gerhard let go of the man's hand and stood, stock still, unable to speak, hardly able to breathe, looking into the most beautiful eyes he had ever seen. They were almond shaped and colored a blue as deep and pure as the sky up above, fringed by long, thick black lashes. He felt as if he had been hit by some kind of bolt from above and he suddenly realized that this was the feeling, that immediate connection, deep in the heart, between one soul and another.

And he had experienced it with a man.

Gerhard's pulse had been racing just standing looking into those eyes, which had not left his but seemed caught by the same magnetism as his own. But now his heart beat still faster in panic as he thought, *No, it can't be! I'm not a homo! I've had so many women. I can't be . . . can I?*

Finally the man seemed to emerge from his dazed state. He put his hand to his face and then, in a voice that sounded almost as alarmed as Gerhard felt, said, "Dark glasses . . . fell off . . . you seen them?"

Gerhard looked around. The glasses were lying on the snow just a couple of paces away. He picked them up and handed them to their owner who said, "Thank you," in a soft, low voice and smiled shyly at him: shyly and so prettily that Gerhard would have sworn that . . . *No, how can that be? Only men can ride the Cresta Run. It's a rule. And the English are like us Germans. They obey their rules.*

"Well, ah, better find my cousin. He'll be worried. You know, about me falling off," the mysterious rider said. He turned to walk back up the hill.

"I'll come with you," said Gerhard, who suddenly saw a golden opportunity to get to the bottom of the mystery. "It would be sensible to have someone with you after such a shock."

"Second thoughts, I'll wait for him at the bottom."

"Very well . . . by the way, what's your name?"

"Courtney," said the rider, over his shoulder as he walked away. Gerhard watched him go and then, just as he was about to turn back up the hill, the mysterious Mr. Courtney gave a little wiggle, just a quick, utterly feminine swish of the hips, and Gerhard burst out laughing. *Thank God for that!* he thought and continued on his way.

A couple of minutes later he met a wild-eyed Englishman

coming the other way in a state of great alarm. "Have you seen my cousin?" he said. "Chap by the name of Courtney. I think he's crashed, but I don't know where."

"*Ach so* . . . yes I saw Courtney. The crash was at Shuttlecock. But please, do not concern yourself. Courtney is alive and well . . ." Gerhard grinned, "And she is waiting for you at the bottom of the run."

———

Saffron could not help it. She knew it was madness to give the game away, but she had to let him know that she was a girl. She had felt it, just as he had, that sudden overwhelming certainty that she had just met her man, the one she had been waiting for, and it had come as even more of a shock than the crash. She had heard about love at first sight, of course, in songs and films and silly romantic novels. But she had never really believed that it happened in real life. But it had, and of all the rotten luck, she had been pretending to be a man and she had seen the alarm in his eyes as he thought about what that meant, and even if she never saw him ever again, she had to let him know that it was all right to love her. But how were they ever going to meet again?

She was lost in thought, pondering the best way to find one tall, handsome man—no, he was more than handsome: he was a beautiful man—amidst the crowds of tourists at the height of the season in St. Moritz when Rory came racing up behind her.

"There you are! I was so worried. You were going at such a lick, I knew you were going to have a wreck. Thank heavens you're still in one piece."

"I'm perfectly all right," Saffron assured him. "I landed in a great big heap of snow and was rescued by a rather charming German gentleman."

"I think I met him on the way down. Looking rather pleased with himself, I thought. He'd worked out you weren't a man."

"Oh dear," said Saffron, doing her best to sound concerned although her heart was turning cartwheels of delight. "Do you think he'll give the game away to anyone else?"

"Probably. You can't trust a German, that's what I think."

"Oh, don't be ridiculous, Rory. Do you know any Germans?"

"Well no, not personally . . ."

"Well I do and they are delightful. I shall introduce you to my dear friend Chessi von Schöndorf this evening and I promise you that you will think she is perfectly delightful. You never know, she may even have a nice German girlfriend who'll change your mind about her nation."

"I don't want a nice German girl. I want—"

"Ssshh . . ." Saffron put a finger to his lips. "I'll have none of that talk around here. I am going to go to the Palace to leave a message for Chessi, asking where we are all to meet this evening. Then we shall lunch and I don't know about you, but I am going to spend the afternoon making up for the horrors of having to be a beastly man by indulging all my most frivolous female instincts. I shall have a nice, hot, steamy Turkish bath, followed by a massage. Then I will have my hair done and my nails. I might even go shopping for a new dress."

"That seems like an awful lot of trouble to go to just to see another girl."

"In the first place, it's not trouble, it's the most perfect fun. In the second, another girl will appreciate the trouble I've taken more than any man ever would. And in the third . . ." Saffron caught herself just in time. Her third reason was that she was completely certain that she would see him again and she wanted to look her absolute best, because . . . "Oh," she said.

Rory was looking at her in the manner of a man who was completely baffled by whatever was going on in the head of the woman next to him.

"Oh, what?" he asked.

"Sorry?" Saffron said, plainly distracted and not really paying attention.

"Well you were just about to tell me the third reason why all this rigmarole you were planning wasn't really a lot of trouble when you stopped, and then you went "Oh," and I just wondered what that was about."

"Oh . . . nothing. Forget I said a word. You're completely right. I'm a foolish female and I'm sure that whatever you do this afternoon will be a lot more sensible."

Now she sounded put out and Rory could not for the life of him work out what he had done to deserve it.

But of course, Rory hadn't done a thing. He was, indeed, the very last thing on Saffron's mind. She was fully occupied trying to come to terms with a train of thought that had connected a whole series of fragmentary ideas, memories and perceptions floating around in her subconscious and come to a ghastly conclusion.

For the awful feeling had suddenly struck Saffron that she knew who that beautiful German man, the one she was destined to make her own, had been. He was the man that Chessi was expecting to marry. And if he hadn't proposed to her already, then he would do so very soon, quite possibly tonight. *I'm supposed to be her best friend*, she thought. *How can I possibly come between her and the man she loves?*

Saffron thought a little more. *Hold your horses, girl! You don't know that he actually is her man. And you didn't come between them. You literally landed at his feet AND it was a complete accident AND what happened—whatever it was—was completely unintentional. You didn't plan to look into his eyes and fall head over heels for him. It just happened.*

She considered all that she had learned from a single term of Philosophy and concluded: *So that means that you bear no moral responsibility for what may or at not have occurred.*

Ah, but what about what might happen in the future? the Angel on her shoulder asked.

Saffron considered the question and came up with her response. *It's not my decision. It's this man's, whoever he is. If he prefers me, then he shouldn't be with Chessi anyway and she would never have been happy with him. And if he chooses her then I will be extremely cross, but I will have a clear conscience and know that she is perfect for him and I have helped him prove that.*

Which led her to her final verdict: *He's a big boy. He can make up his own mind which one of us he wants.*

That said, she was going to give him every reason to want her. Because, after all, she still didn't know if he really was Chessi's man . . . did she?

———

Chessi and the others had all gone up to the galleried first floor of Chesa Veglia, where four of the little tables with their red, white and blue checked tablecloths had been pressed together to accommodate their party. Gerhard, however, had decided to stay downstairs a little longer and have another drink. "Do you need a little extra courage, old man?" one of the others had said. "I wonder what could possibly make you feel like that?" Everyone had laughed and Chessi had blushed happily because they all knew that this was the night when Gerhard von Meerbach would propose to her and she would of course say, "Yes," because even if she weren't as madly in love as Chessi obviously was, what girl in her right mind would ever turn away a young man as handsome, charming, rich and in every way blessed as him?

So Gerhard stayed downstairs, drank a beer, smoked a cigarette and looked around at all the other wealthy men and their beautiful, pampered women enjoying their evening at the restaurant that the Badrutt family had created inside an old farmhouse. It had opened only three winters earlier but the skill of the conversion had been the way that everything had been designed to create the feeling that people had been eating and drinking here for decades, centuries even. No attempt had been made to disguise the basic structure of the building. In that respect, Gerhard mused, as he cast a professional architect's eye over the place, even his old Modernist tutors at the Bauhaus would have approved. The massive wooden posts that held up the floors of pine planks, dark with age (or simply stained to look that way), were left as they were, undisguised and unadorned. Ceilings were simply the underside of the floorboards of the room above them. Stone walls were either whitewashed or covered with wooden panels decorated with pots of flowers painted onto their surface in a very basic almost childlike style. It created an effect of hearty, rustic simplicity for people who lived very sophisticated, urban lives: *It's a modern version of Marie Antoinette's farmhouse at the palace of Versailles.*

Gerhard's beer glass was empty. He had no reason to stay down here. There was only so much time he could spend looking at the room around him, trying to postpone a proposal which he now knew for certain could never lead to a happy marriage. But he stayed in the hope that she might walk into the room, the woman who had dressed like a man, with her blue eyes he would happily gaze into for all eternity and that cheeky little flick of her rump that had lit a fire of raw lust that he knew would never go out.

It was ridiculous. Why should she come here? There were plenty of other places in St. Moritz to eat, and if she was with the Cresta crowd they would all be at their unofficial clubhouse, the bar of the Kulm Hotel. By now, he imagined, the truth behind her escapade would have got out and all the Englishmen would long ago have forgiven her for breaking the rules and be competing for her attention. But she would never look at any of them the way she had looked at him, Gerhard was sure of it.

Ach, don't be so pathetically sentimental! he told himself. *It was a fleeting moment. It has nothing to do with reality. So grow up, stop believing in daydreams and go and propose to the beautiful girl upstairs, who will make such a wonderful wife.*

Gerhard paid the barman. He picked his packet of cigarettes

up off the counter and got down from his stool. He turned to face the room and was about to walk to the stairs.

And then, as if she had just materialized in the Chesa Veglia, more like a ghost than a living, flesh-and-blood woman, there she was, looking like the heroine of a Russian novel in a black fur coat and hat. Her skin looked very pale and her scarlet-painted lips and blue eyes were bursts of color against that black and white background. Her cousin was talking to the restaurant manager who was pointing upstairs. Meanwhile, she was darting her eyes from side to side, scanning the room, and Gerhard realized at once that she was looking for him. *I must not call out to her or wave. That would only give the game away. We have to find each other's eyes. It has to be a matter of chance, or destiny.*

So he did no more than look in her direction, trying not to make it too obvious, and as he did, he saw her sense his gaze, like an animal catching a predator's scent on the wind. But she did not try to escape, as a hunted animal might. She turned her head and looked back at him. And in that instant, Gerhard knew that his fate was sealed.

———

"If I've understood the restaurant chappie correctly, your friend and her chums are all upstairs and the stairs are just over there so we should be able to find them in a jiffy," said Rory, looking suitably pleased that his efforts had proved successful.

Saffron did not appear to have heard him, which was hardly surprising given the hubbub being generated by all the people thronging the restaurant. Rory decided to try again, but more loudly, slowly and clearly this time, as if speaking to someone who was hard of hearing, tremendously stupid, foreign, or all three. "I say, Saffron dearest . . . your . . . chums . . . are . . . upstairs."

"What? Oh yes, Chessi . . . Well, can you be a darling and go up there by yourself?"

"Why on earth would I want to do that? I don't know a soul up there. She's your friend."

"Oh, Chessi's very easy to spot. Blonde, very pretty and she has a rather splendid bosom. That seems to be the first thing chaps notice about her."

"But what about you? Don't you want to see her? I mean, you've come all this way for the express reason that you want to see your closest girlfriend and now you don't seem to have the slightest interest at all. I'm sorry, Saffy, but what on earth is going on?"

She gave him her most dazzling, ingratiating smile. "Nothing's going on, darling. It's just that by the most extraordinary co-incidence I've spotted the mysterious knight in shining armor who rescued me after my crash this morning. And it really would be jolly rude not to go over and say thank you to him. I'm sure you don't want to hang around twiddling your thumbs while I do that. So why don't you toddle along and introduce yourself, and you can tell Chessi that I'll be along to join you, just as soon as I've said my words of thanks."

"Well, I can just as easily wait down here for you to do that."

"Please don't, there's a dear," said Saffron, with a very heavy hint that Rory heard loud and clear: for whatever reason she didn't want anyone getting in the way when she went to say hello to this man.

"Oh all right," he said. "I know when I'm not wanted."

"Oh, thank you, darling Rory," she said. Then she gave him a peck on the cheek and was off across the room like a hound after a fox.

I should have gone down to Shuttlecock before her run, thought Rory bitterly. *I knew she was going to come off. The girl's never done anything slowly or steadily in her life.*

He sighed with resignation and went off to find the Schöndorf girl and her friends. It wasn't difficult. They were all clustered around a long line of tables and a seriously pretty blonde girl— *By George, she really does have some really cracking boobies!*—was at the head with empty seats to either side of her, clearly in-tended for her husband-to-be and her best friend.

"Ah . . ." said Rory to himself, suddenly wondering whether those two seats were ever to be filled. Oh well, no time to worry about that now. He went over to the girl and said, "Hello, my name's Rory Ballantyne. I'm Saffron Courtney's cousin. She asked me to say that she'll be up in a second."

The girl frowned. "Really? What has detained her?" she asked, in English.

"Oh nothing of any importance really, she just had to say thank you to a chap, a German, actually . . . Frightfully funny story, actually. You see . . ."

Then Rory told the story of Saffron's attempt to defy the rules that banned women and go down the Cresta Run. And though he said so himself, he really thought he told the story jolly well, with lots of amusing little jokes and observations. But he had the horrible feeling that the longer his story went on, the flatter it fell and at the end, instead of the laughter he might reasonably expected at the tale of a girl landing head-first in the snow, and all the questions and requests to tell this bit or that bit of the story again that would normally follow such a splendid yarn, there was nothing but silence.

Chessi said something in German, addressed to the table as a whole, and made as if to get up from the table. Then one of the other Germans, a man, spoke to her in the universal tone of a man letting a woman know that she was being very fool-ish but it did not matter because he would solve her problem. He got up and walked off toward the stairs.

Rory watched the man go down the stairs and a couple of minutes later he saw him come back up again, alone. He walked to the end of the table where Chessi was sitting, glared at Rory as if to suggest that this was all somehow his fault, then got down on his haunches and, with one hand placed consolingly on Chessi's shoulder, spoke to her with quiet, unsmiling earnest-ness. She listened to what he had to say, thanked him politely, though Rory could see that she was fighting back the tears. Then she stood up. Numerous voices were raised from around the table, but she ignored them and stalked off toward the stairs.

Rory was now getting a very strong feeling that his presence at the table was not welcome. Clearly he was being blamed for Saffron's absence as if he had been part of her deception. He would have loved to have had the chance to explain that he was just as much in the dark as anyone else, but this was clearly not the time or place for that conversation. So he got up, gave a polite little bow to the table and took his leave.

When he got to the bottom of the stairs, Rory met Chessi coming the other way. "She is not here," Chessi said, her sweet, doll-like face now radiating barely controlled fury. "She has left and taken the man who is to be my husband with her. Tell her from me that she has one day in which to explain herself, apologize and then leave St. Moritz, so that I and my man may get on with our lives. And if she does not agree to those conditions, then our friendship is at an end."

"Golly, yes, I'll pass that on. Absolutely," said Rory Ballantyne. "Look," he said desperately, feeling almost as hurt as the woman in front of him at Saffron's apparently appalling behavior, "I don't know if it's any consolation, but this sort of thing is in her blood. Her mother was just the same. She ran off with some German chap, von-something, can't remember exactly . . . anyway, he went off to Africa and that's how she met Saffron's pater, my ma's cousin, because he was their white hunter . . ."

The anger on Francesca von Schöndorf's face had faded like mist in the sun. Now something close to a smile was playing around her face. "Tell me," she said. "I hope I am not being too personal, but I sense that maybe Saffron has hurt you, too."

Rory frowned. "Well, yah, she has, rather. I mean, I'm dashed fond of her and so forth, but yes, she rather let me down, actually."

"Then we have something in common. I have to go back to my friends now and try not to be too upset when my girlfriends tell me how sad I am when all the time I know that they will be thrilled because they were jealous of me getting Gerhard von Meerbach and now that I have lost him they will be thinking, "Maybe I have a chance." But tomorrow, maybe, you and I should talk and you can tell me all about Saffron's past, because she has always kept it very secret from me."

"Well, she only told me a few bits and bobs, but there was a lot of family gossip, you know, things people had picked up on the grapevine. I say, did I hear you correctly? Is your fiancé chap called von Meerbach?"

"Yes . . . why?"

"Well, it rather complicates things actually. I mean, I wonder if it would really be a good idea to talk. Not really the act of a gentleman, what? Spilling the beans about a lady?"

"My dear, Rory, do you think that Saffron's actions are those of a lady?" Chessi asked, making his eyes pop as she wiggled her body in such a way as to present her spectacular breasts very close to him, directly in his line of sight.

Rory felt his pulse quicken, his trousers bulge and his brain scramble, all at the same time. "Well no . . . no, I suppose not."

"Then we should certainly talk. Why don't we meet for coffee? Eleven o'clock, in the foyer of the Palace Hotel. Would that suit you?"

"Um . . . well, I don't see why not."

"Splendid! I really cannot tell you how much I am looking forward to our conversation."

————

When Saffron reached him they did not even say hello. He simply told her, "We must go. Now!"

She did not ask him why. She already knew the answer, but she did not want to hear it said. She did not even want him to give her his name. That way she could maintain the pretence of ignorance.

When they got outside he asked, "Where are you staying?"

"The Suvretta House."

He grinned. "Me too. Here, I have my car. We can drive back."

"Ooh," Saffron purred, when she saw the sleek lines of the Mercedes.

"You like cars?" he said, opening the doors for her.

"I like going fast."

"Once again . . . me too." He turned his head to smile at her and his face was so handsome that when he looked away to drive the car she felt as though she had been given a wonderful present at Christmas, only to have it snatched away again.

It took less than five minutes to drive through the snowy streets to the hotel, but it was enough for a feeling to build inside Saffron: a combination of desire, frantic impatience—she had an almost desperate need to feel his arms around her and press her body close to his—and apprehension. It was like standing at the top of the Cresta Run. She knew what was going to happen and there was not the slightest possibility of turning back.

She tried to distract herself by watching him drive. He drove fast, but without any sense that he was showing off, for his every movement was calm, precise, always in total control. He was not even close to the limit of his abilities and that sense of his confidence and assurance was both comforting, for it made her feel entirely safe, but also profoundly attractive. *He will know exactly what he is doing, even when I don't*, she thought, and longed all the more for that moment to come.

Just as they were arriving at the hotel, he said, "I am in Room 424. I will take the stairs. You take the elevator. That way, no one need suspect anything."

He pulled up outside the entrance and a uniformed doorman opened Saffron's door. She got out and waited while he tipped the man and handed over his car keys, trying to seem no more than polite, as she would wait for any male friend. Then they walked into the hotel, not even holding hands.

"Goodnight," he said when they reached the lifts.

"Thank you for a lovely dinner," she replied and got in without even giving him a peck on the cheek. "Fourth floor, please," she said to the operator.

Saffron tried to stay calm and control her breathing, hoping that the young lad with his funny pillbox cap could not tell that her pulse was racing and that the molten heat between her legs was almost more than she could bear.

"Thank you," she said, with a polite, ladylike smile when the lift came to a halt, the operator pulled the metal grating wide and the doors slid open.

She walked slowly and steadily, just in case anyone should be watching, until she got to his room. The door was very slightly ajar. She pushed it open and there he was. He kicked the door closed as he took her in his arms and kissed her, hard, not hesitating for a single second.

Saffron gave a muffled moan as their mouths locked together. His lips and his tongue were strong and assertive, as though they were taking possession of her, and she yielded to him, giving herself without restraint, exploring his body and his face with her hands, taking in the man-smell of him, pressing herself against him and thrilling to the sure sign of his arousal. She had been kissed before, but it had not excited her. She had felt a man's erection before, but just felt amusement, embarrassment or repulsion. She had ridden all her life and did not need to be told about the delicious, tingly, melty feeling of having an animal between her thighs or rubbing her crotch against the saddle.

But this was totally different. This was raw, animal passion and she knew that she had provoked that feeling in him too, and that sense of achievement, of power over him only aroused her all the more.

They had barely got more than a couple of steps into the room, but neither of them could even wait to get to the bed. He shoved her up against the wall and, still kissing her, pulled her

hat from her head and threw it to the floor. She gave a shake
of a head to release her hair and he ran his fingers through it
and then clenched his fist, grabbing a handful. She moved her
head and that pulled at her hair and made it hurt a little so she
tried to shake free, but she didn't want to succeed and he didn't
let her. He held her harder, trapping her and she shuddered as
a shock of pure pleasure shivered through her. Now his other
hand lifted her skirt with practised dexterity. She lifted her
bottom forward away from the wall to make it easier for him
and the higher the fabric rose and the more exposed and utterly
vulnerable she felt, the more excited she became.

She was wearing a pair of French camiknickers in pale peach
silk, trimmed with lace, and now his hand was running over
the soft, slippery fabric, over the hot wetness between her legs
and she pushed herself against his hands, making her hunger
obvious, glorying in her shamelessness, Now his fingers were
inside the elasticated waistband of her knickers, easing them
down over her bottom, running over her skin as they went,
and tugging them over her hips and now she didn't need any
help from his hand because she could let them fall down her
legs to the floor and step out of them, and while she was doing
that, and the kissing was still not stopping and her head was
still caught in his grasp, he was undoing the front of his trousers and she could feel him against her and his fingers sliding
up and down and into her. She felt as though she were being
lifted up and up and up, like a boat riding to the top of a wave,
but never getting there because the wave kept growing and
growing. Except the wave was inside her, that feeling of pleasure building and building, that longing for release. And suddenly he had let go of her hair and his hand had left her crotch,
but she could still feel him there. Now his hands were going
behind her back and around her bottom and he suddenly lifted
her up, so that she had to wrap her arms around his neck to
cling on and he was lifting her, like the wave lifting her and
then bringing her down and he was in her and the heat of him,

the size of him, filling her up from within was like no feeling she had ever known.

She gave a little cry, "Oh!" of surprise and just the tiniest moment of discomfort and he paused for a second and she groaned, imploringly, "Don't stop!"

He thrust even deeper inside her, and then again and again and she couldn't think any more, but was just a mass of sensations, inside her, outside, touch, smell, taste, sound and of course the sight of his own ecstasy on his face. She was utterly helpless and her only desire was for him to consume her, take her, break down the barrier between her body and his until they were just fused together in one being. Now he groaned, a deep, guttural, animal expression of pleasure and the intensity and desperation of his movements increased still further. She knew that he was feeling it too, this unbearable intensity of excitement, and she suddenly realized that she was moaning and screaming and she just didn't care because her entire existence was focused on the joy of this mutual possession, the two of them, and then she reached the top of the wave and the wave crashed down and it was like an explosion, an earthquake, an eruption and she felt him come inside her and knew that he had felt it too. "Oh God . . . oh God . . ." she gasped.

He held her for a moment, his chest heaving as he caught his breath and she felt little spasms of pleasure hitting her like aftershocks, and when he withdrew she pleaded, "Don't go," for the loss of him, the absence of him inside her was almost unbearable.

He tucked himself back into his trousers, then gently pushed a strand of hair away from her face, smiled and said, "Here, let me help you with your coat."

She laughed at the absurdity of it: all that had happened, her life had been changed utterly, forever and she'd not even taken off her coat. He took it and placed it over a chair, then he returned to her and said, "Now let me help you undress."

He undid her dress at the back and when she stepped out of

it he took it and laid it over the coat with that same sense of confident, easy precision with which he'd driven his car. By the time he'd got back she had taken off her bra and was about to remove her suspender belt and stockings when he said, "Wait."

He stepped back and looked at her and although his eyes were entirely frank in the way they ran up and down her body, taking in every detail, Saffron realized that she did not feel in the slightest bit embarrassed, still less ashamed to be examined so freely or to display herself so openly.

He took her in his arms again and said, "Thank you. I wanted to fix you in my mind, every last bit of you, so that in years to come, no matter where I am or how much time goes by, I will always have the memory of you, at this moment. The memory of the most beautiful woman in the world."

Then she slipped out of her stockings, casting glances up at him as he removed his own clothes, and her gaze was as greedy as his as it took in the straighter, harder lines of his body, the breadth of his shoulders and the narrowness of his waist and hips, the way the muscles moved in his torso, his arms and legs and even, with affectionate gratitude, the soft, wrinkled remnant of what had been so hard and smooth. She had never looked at the details of a man's body before, not at any rate from the perspective of a woman who has just experienced that magical fit between the male and female forms. She had never seen a man's forearms and known how the strength of them felt, or seen his buttocks and felt an overwhelming desire to sink her red-painted nails into them as she pulled him ever closer, ever deeper into her.

"I will remember you too," she said as they got into bed. "Always and anywhere, forever."

He nodded, lying on his side, his face almost touching hers, looking at her with an expression of profound gravity, understanding that they were bound together now and that any public vows they might make would only be the formalizing of a bond that had long since become unbreakable. Then he smiled and said, "Do you realize that after all this, we still have not been introduced?"

She giggled, "Nor we have."

"Very well," he said, pushing himself up into a sitting position and holding out his right hand. "It is my very great pleasure to meet you, Fräulein. My name is Gerhard von Meerbach."

––––––––

If he had slapped her in the face, she could not have looked more shocked or more appalled. "I'm . . . I'm Saffron Courtney," she managed to say, her voice barely rising above a whisper. Then she asked, "Did you say, "von Meerbach", like the company that makes engines?"

"Yes, that is my family."

"So you're related to Count von Meerbach?"

"Yes. The present Count is my older brother Konrad. My father was Count before him. Why do you ask? And, please . . . why do you look so unhappy, my darling Saffron? *Liebchen*, what is the matter?"

"Because of all the men in the world to fall in love with, you are the very last I should have chosen. Chessi von Schöndorf is . . . I suppose now that should be "was" . . . my best friend."

Gerhard reached out an arm to touch her shoulder, feeling far more nervous and uncertain trying to reassure her now than when he was stripping her and taking her, ravishing her just a short while earlier. "You cannot blame yourself for that," he said. "You did not even know my name."

"I knew, though . . . I just knew . . ."

He nodded sympathetically. "I understand. I suppose I knew too. But neither of us set out to hurt Francesca. What happened was a matter of fate. If anyone is to blame it was me. I had a choice. I could have ignored what happened this morning and gone ahead with my proposal. If we had met at dinner, I could have been polite, but no more than that. But in truth that was impossible. I had to have you. And if that was the case, how could I be untrue to Chessi even as I was asking her to be my wife? So, as I say, I had a choice to make and I chose you."

Saffron smiled, but it was a sad, ironic smile that struck fear into Gerhard's heart. "So that's another thing we have in common: our logic. I told myself it was up to you to choose and if all we had to worry about was that choice, then I could live with that. If the price of having you was losing Chessi, I would pay it. It would make me sad, but I wouldn't think twice. But that isn't our problem, is it?"

Gerhard frowned in bafflement. "I don't know . . . I don't understand. What are you trying to tell me?"

"So the name "Courtney" means nothing to you?"

"No, should it?"

"How about Eva von Wellberg?"

"No . . . who is she?"

"She was my mother. She was also your father's mistress. She married my father, Leon Courtney . . . after . . . after . . ."

"After what?"

"After he killed Count Otto von Meerbach by shooting him through the chest with a hunting rifle at point-blank range."

Saffron had maintained her composure up to that point, but that broke it and she burst into desperate sobs and he could only catch occasional words and phrases as she tried to speak through the tears. "How can we? . . . Oh God, of all the people . . . so cruel, so unfair . . . How can we possibly love each other now . . . ?"

Gerhard held her and calmed her, and the very fact that he did that, rather than throwing her out of his bed, seemed to ease her distress a little.

"I was only very small when my father died, so I hardly knew him," he told her. "But I know how much he hurt my mother, and I know what kind of a man my brother is, and everyone says how much he takes after our father, so . . . It's strange, but this does not seem to upset me as much as it does you. I'm not sure why that is. It seems wrong somehow, and yet that is how I feel . . . Hold on a moment . . ."

Gerhard reached for the phone by the bed and asked the operator to be put through to room service. He ordered a cold supper for two to be brought up to Room 424: a selection of cold meats and chicken, smoked salmon, bread and butter, a little cheese, some grapes and, because this no longer seemed an occasion for champagne, a bottle of Riesling: "An Auslese," Gerhard said, specifying the bold, honeyed wine made from the ripest and thus the richest tasting grapes. "The best you have, please. And also a bottle of cognac and some Perrier. We will need an ice-bucket for the wine, of course."

Then he turned back to Saffron and said, "We have much to talk about and a lot more love to make. We will need to keep our strength up. Now, you have a long and complicated story to tell me, that is obvious. So start from the beginning, tell me everything, and when you have finished, then we will decide what to do next."

And so she told it all, from her grandfather's ruin to the Zeppelin crash on a mountainside in Kenya and its consequences, while Gerhard listened intently, only interrupting occasionally to make sure that he had understood her correctly. She was less than halfway through her tale, with her mother on the way to Germany to seduce the man who had ruined her father, when supper arrived. Gerhard was struck by Saffron's self-possession at being found in bed by the waiter. She had wrapped a cotton bathrobe around her to preserve her decency and talked to the waiter in confident, almost fluent German about all the various items on the trolley, specifying which ones she wanted on her plate with that combination of ease, good manners but unspoken assumption of command that marked someone used from birth to dealing with staff. *This girl can barely be twenty, maybe less, but if she became the mistress of a great house tomorrow, she would be able to run it and everyone would accept her as their mistress.*

The waiter opened the wine and poured out the first two glasses then disappeared, cheered by a suitably generous tip. They each took their glasses and tapped them together. "To you," Gerhard said. "Now, eat, and then tell me more of your story."

He grinned at the relish with which Saffron demolished the substantial plate of food that the waiter had prepared for her. Clearly this was not the kind of girl who spent hours talking about her diet and lived off nothing but lettuce leaves and water.

She saw him looking at her as she set about a chicken leg like a lioness consuming her dead prey and grinned: "I had no idea how much of an appetite one can work up by making love." She put the leg down, stripped bare of its meat and took another drink of wine. "Or a thirst."

"Now you must tell me the rest of your story, like Scheherazade and the Sultan, and I will feed you grapes from time to time, just to encourage you."

And so she kept talking and every so often he would pop a grape between her lips, or simply kiss them himself, and somehow the telling of this tale of treachery, theft, infidelity, betrayal and killing seemed to bring them together, rather than driving them apart. Finally Saffron said, "My father hid the five million marks at the bottom of a pool, halfway up the mountain where the Zeppelin landed. After the war he and my mother went back there . . ." she smiled, "and I went there, too, in a way, because my mother was already pregnant with me. They recovered the gold and my father used some of it to buy our estate in Kenya . . . Oh, I'd love to take you there one day. It's so beautiful, rolling hills with wonderful views of mountains in the distance . . ."

"That sounds like our estate in Bavaria," he said.

"Does your estate have lions, and cheetahs, and rhinos, and hippos, and zebras, and giraffes, and . . ."

He laughed. "Is this an estate or a zoo?"

"It's Africa," she said, quite seriously. "And if you want to know me truly, never forget this. I may be a subject of His Majesty the King, and I may study at Oxford and have cousins all over England and Scotland. But I am not really English at all. I am African."

A mischievous grin crossed Gerhard's face. "There was something I was going to say. Something very important about us, and our love, and our future . . . But the way you said that, "I am African," was so . . . what is that new word you English have? . . . Ah yes, so sexy that I am afraid, my darling, that I am obliged to seduce you all over again."

"Are you sure that's a good idea?"

"Yes . . ." he said, taking the robe off her, without the slightest resistance on her part, and laying her down on the bed. "I want to explore you, like Dr. Livingstone and Mr. Stanley exploring Africa . . ." He gave her a little kiss on the lips, but then his head moved down her body, following his right hand as it ran down her breastbone and then around each of her breasts in turn. They were not large, but they were pretty and in proportion to the sleekness of the rest of her; the long, flowing lines of a body that was naturally athletic, gifted with speed and strength but still entirely feminine.

Her nipples were a delicate shade of coral pink and they were standing up for him as proudly as little guardsmen on parade. "Here for example," he whispered, taking her left nipple between his finger and thumb, squeezing it slowly, gently, just to the point where she gave a little gasp and arched her back, and then he ran the palm of one hand over that same nipple touching it as faintly, delicately as he possibly could while his other hand squeezed her right nipple so that she was engulfed by two totally different feelings at one and the same time. Then, still working her right breast with his hand, he lowered his head over her left breast and started playing with it with his lips and tongue and teeth: sometimes kissing her skin, sometimes flicking the nipple with his tongue, then very gently biting it, taking infinite care to apply just the right amount of pressure. Her hands were running through his hair and then stroking his back and then, as he brought his head over to her other breast, she moaned and shuddered with pleasure, her fingernails tore at his skin and her buttocks began to writhe as the need for him took hold.

"Now, I must look for the source . . ." he murmured and slid his body down the bed so that his lips and tongue slipped lower and lower until she was crying out, "Oh God . . . oh God . . . please!" He drove into her with all his force, as if he could somehow put his entire body and soul within her, consuming her, feeling like a conqueror, but knowing that she had over-whelmed him absolutely, too

Afterwards, they lay there together until he summoned up the energy to pour some more of the sweet, rich wine and they shared a glass. "Here," he said, "try some of this with it." He passed her a piece of Emmentaler and the combination of the two flavors, the honey wine and the strong salty cheese, was magical.

"My God, that's almost as good as the you-know-what-ing," Saffron said, and now there was nothing in her smile but the absolute happiness, with a slight degree of smugness, of some-one who has just enjoyed a bout of wonderful loving. "Now, tell me your important thing, the one that you were about to explain before we were so delightfully interrupted."

"Ah yes . . . It is really very simple . . . Terrible things hap-pened between our families in the past. Great wrongs were done, on both sides. So now we must decide: do we live in the past and concentrate on old hatred, or do we live in the present and concentrate on our love? If we live in the past, the hatred gets worse, nothing is solved and we are both unhappy. If we live in the present we will be adding happiness to our own lives and, in some tiny little way, to the world. So, I say we should love."

"And I say, I love you, Gerhard von Meerbach." She wrapped her arms around his neck again and kissed him. Then she said, "I love a man called von Meerbach. Good heavens . . . what an utterly extraordinary idea!"

———

They talked and made love all night long. Saffron told Gerhard about her life in Africa: how her mother had died and her father had brought her up alone for almost a decade until he had finally found happiness with Harriet. She described Manyoro: how he and her father considered themselves to be brothers; all the years that he had always been there whenever she needed him; and her own delight when Manyoro had told her that she was no longer his little princess and, "Now I shall call you my queen." When Gerhard heard the heartfelt respect and affection she felt for this black African, he knew that Saffron would have nothing but contempt for the hatred of other races that lay at the heart of Nazism and that their love would have no chance of lasting unless he was completely open about the life he had led for the past five years.

So he told her about his meeting with Heydrich and how the second most powerful man in the SS had united with his brother to force him into a pact with the devil of Nazism. He confessed to all the benefits that he had gained from being seen to be a good Nazi and to the joy he had found as a pilot, alone in the air. "Now I know why people talk about being as free as a bird," he said, "because up there is where I find true freedom."

He recounted his meeting with Hitler and realized that even this English girl, who considered herself an African and despised racial prejudice, was still fascinated by the idea of his personal encounter with a man whose fame was now universal, among those whom he appalled as well as those who adored him. The one part of his story that he did not tell in full was its beginning: his gift to Isidore Solomons. He did not want to sound as though he was making excuses, or portraying himself as better than he was. But Saffron saw at once that something was missing. "How was Heydrich able to make you join the Nazi Party?" she asked. "Surely, even in Germany, you can't force an innocent man who has done nothing wrong to give up everything he stands for and stand up for something he doesn't believe."

"I would not be so sure about that," Gerhard replied. "I imagine that if you come from a land that is truly free, where you can say and think whatever you like without fear, and criticize the government, or have political arguments with your friends over dinner or in a bar, then it is impossible to imagine what losing that freedom is like. In Germany you cannot argue, because you cannot trust the person who argues against you. Even your oldest friend, or your brother, or your child might report your opinions to the secret police. My brother and Heydrich could have labeled me a communist and thrown me in a camp, just for studying architecture at a school that was later banned, even though I have never voted for a communist candidate, or supported communist ideals in my life."

"But there must be trials, surely? You must be able to defend yourself."

"Five years ago, maybe . . . just. Now the judges belong to the Party too and justice is defined by the Party's ideals."

"My God . . . I had no idea. That's awful."

"Yes, it is, but I can only say so because we are not in Germany and you are not a German. Look . . ." he paused, sighed and then said, "There is someone you should meet, someone here in Switzerland. He is, you could say, my own Manyoro. When you talk to him everything will make more sense."

————

Saffron left Gerhard's room just as the first rays of the sun were prizing their way through the gaps between the mountains. She collapsed into her own bed and slept like a log until ten. Three messages had been left for her at the concierge's desk and then slipped beneath her door. Each had been placed inside a hotel envelope, so that she had no idea who had written them, although it wasn't hard to guess. So she took pot luck and opened up one of the envelopes at random. It contained a furious, heartbroken, devastating indictment of her behavior from Chessi von Schöndorf that left Saffron in tears, for she knew how much her friend had adored Gerhard and how utterly crushed and humiliated she must feel at losing him. No matter what finely reasoned, impeccably logical justifications Saffron could dream up to justify what she had done, still the fact remained that someone who had trusted her absolutely had been absolutely let down.

The second note, from Rory, was no less irate.

———

I might, perhaps, begin to understand, if not forgive your actions if you had prostituted yourself for an Englishman, but to throw away your honor on a damned Hun is unspeakably low. Of course, as the whole family knows, your mother did the same thing. Clearly you take after her. I shall remain in St. Moritz for a few days, enjoying the company of the decent, honest chaps from the Tobogganing Club. I will then make my own way home and I expect you to do the same. I dare say you are worried now that I will besmirch your reputation once I return to England by telling people the truth about what you have done. You may rest assured that my lips will be sealed. I have no desire to lower myself into the same gutter as you. I pride myself on being a gentleman. You, however, are no lady.

Saffron felt as though she had been physically attacked. She lay on her bed, defeated, and distraught. In one fell swoop, one moment of reckless passion, she had lost her two closest friends in the world. Chessi had been the first person to show her any kindness on that train to Roedean. Over three Easter holidays she and her family had welcomed her into their home and treated her like one of the family. How could she have repaid such generosity with such selfishness? And poor Rory . . . Saffron knew that his letter must have been motivated as much by his envy of Gerhard and his own frustrated, rejected love for her as by his disapproval of her immorality. *He wouldn't have thought it was so immoral if he'd been in the bed with me last night.* But that didn't make his outrage any less justified or less sincere. She had behaved like a tramp, a slut, a harlot. She had given herself to a man, and done it gladly, wantonly, heedless of the consequences of her actions. And now, for the very first time, the most obvious consequence of all occurred to her: *My God, what if I'm pregnant?*

Saffron was starving hungry, but she could not eat. She was exhausted, but unable to sit still. She had to escape, but she had nowhere to go for once she stepped outside the four walls of her room she would be in enemy territory.

Her only hope was the third note. It must surely have been sent by Gerhard, but her fingers were shaking so much she could barely open the envelope, for if he had rejected her too she would be left with nothing.

————

My darling,

   I have written to Francesca, explaining that I cannot marry her and taking full responsibility for my actions. In the circumstances it is best that I should leave St. Moritz. I am going to Zürich. I would like it very much if you could join me there, so that I can introduce you to my own "Manyoro." He will explain everything. I am thinking of you and my heart is breaking for you because I know how much pain you will be in today. Just know that I love you with all my heart. This is a very difficult day, but you are a good, kind, beautiful person. Do not forget that. I love you with all my heart—G

PS: I will wait for you between 15.00–18.00 at Zürich station. If you miss me there, I will be staying at the Baur au Lac.

Finally, Saffron had a shred of hope. And she also had a plan to follow, something to do, a train to catch. With that renewed sense of purpose came a slight lifting of her spirits. She was a long way from being happy, but the crushing, hopeless despair was beginning to lift from her soul. She ordered breakfast and ate it, all while composing two short notes to Chessi and Rory. Though she made it plain that it had never been her intention to cause pain, she did not attempt to justify what she had done, or make excuses, or pretend that they had no right to be hurt. She simply apologized, in the most straightforward, sincere terms she could find, without even begging their forgiveness for she knew she had no right to ask for that. It was for them to give, in their own time, if they ever so desired. And in the meantime the best thing she could do—the only thing that would justify everything else—was to put her heart and soul into loving Gerhard von Meerbach.

It was only later that a thought struck her. She had promised, well, not promised exactly, but certainly agreed to tell Mr. Brown about her impressions of Germany and its people. Did that mean she had to tell him about Gerhard? She hadn't actually been to Germany again, after all, even if—and here Saffy could not resist a giggle—she did know an awful lot more about at least one of its people.

No, this was her private life. It was none of his business. And with that matter settled, she got on with the rest of her day.

———

Gerhard was waiting on the platform at Zürich when the train from Chur arrived. Saffron had been nervous as the end of her journey drew closer. What if she saw him in the cold light of day, away from the excitement and glamor of St. Moritz, and suddenly realized that she had made the wrong choice? What if she should have ditched him and gone back to Chessi and Rory on her bended knees begging them to take her back? It was not an appealing prospect: begging did not come naturally to Saffron Courtney. Then she smiled to herself as she thought: *Except when I'm begging him to take me, wicked girl that I am!*

That thought sent little tremors through her body, for she had discovered that she could almost re-create the sensation of having Gerhard inside her, simply by thinking about how that had felt. And that delectable reminder of the wonderful night she had spent with her man reassured her that all would be well.

And so it was. Gerhard looked as edible as ever in a long, olive green loden coat, with a scarf draped around his neck with a casual elegance that made her wonder why none of the male students who thronged Oxford in their college scarves ever looked half as dashing. She ran into his arms and from the moment he was holding her again there was nothing else in the world but them, and she would have given up anyone and everyone in order to keep him. "I was wondering if you could possibly be as lovely as I had remembered," he said, echoing her own thoughts. "And here you are, even more beautiful today than you were yesterday. Kiss me."

She looked around and gave a nervous little laugh. "But there are so many people! They'll all see us."

"Let them. Every man will envy me."

And every woman will wish she were in my place, thought Saffron, willingly surrendering to his lips and his tongue and wishing they could just stay there, in that wonderful embrace, forever.

All too soon, he pulled away. "I have booked a room for you at the Baur au Lac . . . If we were in Paris or Nice, we might be able to share a room. But the Swiss are even more orderly than us Germans. They would certainly not approve."

"You never know, I might refuse to share a room with you. I'm a respectable young lady, you know . . ." And then, before he could say anything, she added, "Well, I used to be, anyway."

"One day, if I am very lucky, perhaps I will be able to make you respectable again."

"May I finish university first?" she said. "You needn't worry. There's not a man in all Oxford that could tempt me away from you."

"Ah . . . wouldn't it be nice to be able to make plans? But this world we are in . . . I fear that none of us can plan for anything . . ."

"Don't say that," she said, squeezing his arm with hers to cling to him as tightly as she could. "It frightens me."

"You? . . . Frightened? That is one thing I would never expect from you."

"I'm frightened of losing you. I've always done my best to beat the boys at everything." She looked up at him with an impish smile. "That's why I went down the Cresta Run . . . But I'm still a girl. You know . . . underneath."

"Oh, I know . . . *mein Gott*, how I know! Now, come, my car is waiting to take us back to the Baur. You can drop off your cases and then we have an appointment."

"With your mysterious Manyoro?"

"Exactly!"

––––––––

A short while later, in the car, on the way between the hotel and the meeting Gerhard had arranged, he said, "You know, I have been thinking a lot about something that happened last night . . ."

"Mmm . . . me too!" Saffron purred.

Gerhard laughed. "Not that! Well, not just that, should I say."

"What else, then?"

"The way I reacted when you said that your father had killed my father. I should have been shocked, no? I should have been angry, outraged. It should have been the end of any love or even friendship between us. But instead I felt nothing. That is not normal, surely. So ever since I have been asking myself why that was. I thought maybe it was because I was so young when he died and therefore I do not have memories of him, nothing that would make me miss him and all the things we did together. But no, that cannot be right, because that is exactly what should make me angry: your father robbed me of the memories a son should have of his father; all the times they went hunting or skiing together; all the games they played when the boy was little, even the fights they had when the boy was fifteen or sixteen, rebelling against his old man."

"I know exactly how that feels. That's how it is for me, too, not having my mother. We never did all the things that a mother and her daughter should do. I never learned from her how to be a woman."

"Yes, but your mother was good and kind. I am sure she loved you and always wanted the best for you. But I would never have had those good memories, even if my father had lived. I know that he was a bully. It was bad enough growing up with my brother Konrad. All the time, whenever he could, he tried to push me down, sometimes with words, sometimes with his fists."

"He sounds horrible."

"He thinks that being in the SS—arresting people, torturing them, ruining their lives—is the best job in the world. And for him it is. That is the kind of man he is and the kind of boy he was. But we were only boys, not men, and even though he always used to say that he was the head of the family, he could not control me, or stop me being the person I wanted to be."

"Not then, at any rate . . ."

"No, not then . . . and maybe not now . . . or at least not in the future, I don't know. But my point is, if my father had been alive, he could have controlled me. He and Konrad would have thought the same way. Konrad used to tear up the drawings I made when I was small. He said that only girls played with pencils and paints."

"But that's stupid! Think of all the men who were great artists!"

"Konrad doesn't think. Or not like that, at any rate. But even though he made my life hell, my mother encouraged me and supported me when I said I wanted to be an architect and he could not stop her. But I'm sure my father would have overruled her, and prevented me from studying architecture. I could not have been myself if he had been alive. And so what I have concluded is that by killing my father, your father saved me."

"I see what you mean," Saffron said. "But it's sad that you should think that. Even worse that you might very well be right."

"Mmmm . . ." murmured Gerhard. His eyes were on the road. They were in an area of narrow cobbled streets with tall, old buildings on either side, many of them with cafés or restaurants on the ground floor. Now Gerhard seemed to find what he was looking for, turned sharp right and went down an even more cramped sidestreet that opened onto a little square. "I think we've arrived," he said.

Gerhard parked the car, they got out and he led the way to a café–patisserie called Konditorei Kagan. A handwritten sign in the window beside the entrance said, "Koscheres Essen serviert hier."

"Kosher food served here," Saffron translated, murmuring to herself.

But Gerhard heard her and said, "One used to see signs like that in Germany, you know. All over Berlin there were Jewish bakeries, butchers, delicatessens. But now . . ."

He led the way in. Saffron saw a serving counter to the left of the door, close to the window with tables and chairs beyond it, many occupied with people enjoying coffee and cakes to warm up the cold winter afternoon. A middle-aged man, presumably the proprietor, Kagan himself, was standing behind the counter serving his customers. It was obvious to Saffron, from the way he had a word for everyone as he fetched them their food, or made their coffees, or handed back their change, that these were all regulars. And she could see from the looks being cast in their direction that she and Gerhard were very obviously strangers and that his loden coat, such an obviously German piece of clothing, marked him out all the more clearly.

He approached the counter and spoke to the man behind it. "Herr Kagan?" he asked.

"Yes . . . who is asking?" The suspicion in his voice was palpable.

"My name is von Meerbach. Max said I should ask for him here."

At once, Kagan's attitude was transformed. He leaned forward and clasped Gerhard's hand. "I am honored to meet you, Herr von Meerbach. You are a *mensch*."

Saffron was puzzled. "*Mensch*" was simply the German word for "human being".

"I hope so," said Gerhard, sounding equally bemused.

"*Oi vey iz mir!*" exclaimed Kagan. "Did my old friend never teach you anything? In Yiddish a *mensch* is not just a man, but a man of honor, a good man, someone to admire. You did a fine thing, Herr von Meerbach. You are a *mensch*."

Saffron realized that although Kagan's words had made her smile she was suddenly very close to tears, so moved by hearing Gerhard described in such fine terms.

"And you, Fräulein," Kagan said, turning his attention to her. "Ei-yei-yei, such a *shainer maidel!*"

"I hardly dare ask what that means," Saffron said, hoping that her German grammar and accent weren't too terrible.

"It means that you are a beautiful girl, my dear . . . but not a German girl, I think."

"No, I'm English."

Gerhard looked at her with a little smile, as if to say, "I thought you said you were African?"

And she gave a little shrug of her shoulders that meant, "It's easier just to say "English".

"A handsome German man and a lovely English rose, so obviously in love," Kagan said. "Maybe there is some hope for this sad world, eh?"

"I hope so," agreed Gerhard.

"But I am keeping you and Max will be wondering what has happened. Go through to the back and take the door on the right-hand side. Then up the stairs. You will find Max when you get to the top."

They walked between the tables and Saffron was conscious that they were being appraised in a very different way now. The women in particular were openly curious, wondering what these Gentiles had done to earn such a warm reaction from Kagan, whom they knew to be no friend of the new Nazi Germany.

The unashamed inspection made Saffron smile, so that the moment they were through the door Gerhard asked, "What was so funny?"

"Just that they reminded me of Masai women. They stare at people, men in particular, in just that same way, you know, really having a good look, completely unbothered by all the conventions that say it's rude to stare."

"Ah, my lovely African girl . . . Come on, let's find our man."

———

They climbed the stairs and came to a landing that served as the hall of the apartment where Kagan and his family lived above their shop. But when one of the doors that led off the landing opened, the figure that walked out was not Frau Kagan or any of her children, but a distinguished-looking man who appeared to Saffron to be about the same age as her father. He wore a pinstripe suit, with a waistcoat and stiff collared shirt and tie, and when he saw Gerhard his face broke into a look of absolute delight as he opened his arms and said, "My dear boy . . ."

"Izzy!" Gerhard replied and they hugged and slapped one another's backs.

So he does have a father in his life, after all, Saffron thought.

Gerhard disentangled himself and said, "Izzy, I would like you to meet Miss Saffron Courtney. She is the woman I will love for the rest of my life."

"And who could blame you?"

"Saffron, this is Isidore Solomons, who was for many years my family's lawyer, as his father and grandfather were before him. He is also a true hero."

"*Ach*, please . . ." Isidore rolled his eyes at Saffron and, switching to English, said, "It is my very great pleasure to meet you, Miss Courtney. I am sorry that I could not invite you to my home. I should love you to see it, Gerhard, our circumstances are much improved since you last saw me. But it might not be wise. Even here, in Switzerland, I can feel eyes upon me. But please, come through into the Kagans' sitting room, which they have kindly placed at our disposal. Herr Kagan has made a big pot of coffee and you must try the cakes, Miss Courtney. If there is one thing a Jew cares about it is his food, and I doubt there is a finer baker in Zürich than Yavi Kagan. In fact, I know there is not."

"It sounds as though you and he are close, Herr Solomons," Saffron said.

"Yes, I suppose we are. It has become my habit every morning to stop here on my way to work for a cup of coffee and a couple of Mandelbrot. Look, Kagan has put some out for us this afternoon." He pointed at a small pile of hard biscuits shaped like little slices of bread. "They are flavored with orange, lemon and vanilla and covered in slices of freshly toasted almonds. Dip them in your coffee, Miss Courtney, you will not regret it."

Saffron did as she was told and then took a bite, "Mmm . . . delicious!" To Isidore's evident approval, she polished off the biscuit in her usual brisk style and then asked, "When we came in, Gerhard asked for Max. I can see now why you might not want to use your real name. But is there any reason why you chose Max instead?"

"It's nothing really . . ." Isidore said.

"Nonsense!" Gerhard protested. "The truth is, I chose the name because Izzy won the Blue Max in the war. That is the highest award for gallantry that Germany has to offer. It is like the Victoria Cross for the British."

"Oh . . . goodness," said Saffron, feeling a little overawed.

"I am sure you are not the slightest bit interested in old men telling war stories," Isidore said.

"On the contrary, Herr Solomons . . ."

"Please, call me Izzy."

"May I call you Max? After all, that is how I first knew you."

"You may call me anything you like. And I believe you were about to make what we lawyers would think of as a counter-argument."

"Yes, I was. You see, I was brought up among Masai warriors in Kenya . . ."

"She's an African, Izzy, can't you tell?" Gerhard said, earning himself a playful slap on his leg for his cheek.

"So I was taught that there was no higher praise for a man than to call him a great warrior. I salute you for it."

"Thank you my dear, I shall treasure that compliment," Izzy said. "And now, I dare say you are wondering why Gerhard has brought you here. So I will tell you . . ."

And so it was that Saffron discovered what Gerhard had done, why a Jewish café proprietor in Zürich should call him a *mensch*, and what had made two Nazis so determined to force him to abandon his principles. When the story was over, she got up, walked around to Izzy's chair, said, "Thank you, Max. Thank you from the bottom of my heart," and gave him a little kiss on the cheek.

Then she walked back to where Gerhard was sitting. "Stand up," she said. "I want to hug my man." So she hugged him and told him how proud she was of him and then she giggled and hissed, "Not now, you wicked man!" as she felt the effect that her words were having.

Saffron sat down and for the next while was happy to sit and listen as the men caught up with everything that had happened since they had last met. She loved to see the affection between the two of them and was fascinated by all she heard, wanting to know absolutely every single thing she could possibly learn about this man who had walked away with her heart.

Then Gerhard asked, "Izzy, is it wrong that I love flying so much and that I take pride in being part of the Luftwaffe and having an aircraft as fine and fast and deadly as a 109?"

"Was it wrong for von Richthofen to be proud of being our greatest ace or to love flying his little red Fokker?"

"Well no, but that was different."

"Why?"

"You, of all people know why, Izzy."

"I know two things, Gerhard. I know that I was proud to serve my country, our country. And I know that I hate Hitler and everything he stands for. But as much as Hitler would like to pretend that his Nazi Party and our country are one and the same thing—which is one of the many reasons I despise him, incidentally—he is wrong. Germany will still survive when he and his evil henchmen are gone, and all that I ask of God is that I should be allowed to live to see that day and have my country returned to me. So I say, no, you are not wrong to be proud. But I have a question for you, my boy . . ."

"Go ahead, ask it."

"When you were very young, and had all the arrogance and invincibility of the young, you took a crazy risk to help me."

"And I don't regret it, not for an instant."

"I do not doubt that, but here is my question. You are five years older now. You are making a reputation as an architect . . ." Isidore held up his hand to stop Gerhard from interrupting. "I know, it is not in the style of design you would have sought, but still it is there. Also you have a position within your squadron and the Luftwaffe, one in which you take pride. And now, you have met the woman who will be your companion through life, I have no doubt at all about that, if only the fates will allow. So my question to you is this. If you knew another German family, who happened to be Jewish, would you give them, too, five thousand marks to help them escape? For we surely know now, if we did not in '34, that there is no future for them in the Nazi Reich. Would you give them the money, and with it the gift of life?"

Saffron could see that the question had taken Gerhard completely unawares. He wanted to say, "Of course!" She could see him trying to frame the words. But she could also see that his honesty forbade him from saying them. In the end, he shook his head sadly and said, "I don't know . . . I really don't know . . . but I very much fear I would not."

Isidore nodded sympathetically. "I understand, and I do not think any the worse of you. You have done your good deed. If every man in Germany were even half, even a tenth as generous as you, my people would not be in the mortal danger that confronts us today. So all I ask of you Gerhard, is that you carry in your heart the memory of the reckless, but fine young man that you were. Treasure it like a candle that must be kept burning. Do not let the light go out. One day you may have need of it."

Saffron watched as Isidore's eyes went from her to Gerhard and back again and they seemed to her to be filled with a sorrow so profound that she could hardly bear to look at him: the sorrow of an entire people, an echo of persecution and suffering that stretched back into the mists of time.

"Do you remember that poem I read you, the one that said the center could not hold: "The blood-dimmed tide is loosed and everywhere the ceremony of innocence is drowned"?"

"Yeats," Saffron said, quietly.

"Indeed . . . My children, that time is upon us. I can feel it coming. That evil barbarian will not be satisfied until he has engulfed the whole world in war and death. I fear for us all, and I fear for you, the young whom the old will sacrifice, just as they sacrificed my generation. I want to see you together, living in peace, with your children running around, playing happily between you. I want to be there, with my silver hair and my walking stick, smiling to see life being created and love being shared.

"And so I say to you both now, as I once said to you, Gerhard: whatever happens, for God's sake stay alive."

———

It was pure chance that Mr. Brown discovered that Saffron had been in St. Moritz, and when he did the information did not come from an intelligence officer or secret agent, but simply from a snippet of gossip, overheard at a wedding reception. He had been threading his way through the mass of people thronging the reception rooms of a country house in Wiltshire when he caught a young, female voice saying, "Did you hear what Saffy Courtney got up to in St. Moritz this year? It was too, too wicked."

Mr. Brown stopped and adjusted his posture to be able to see one of the bridesmaids talking to a girlfriend.

"Oh do tell!" said the girlfriend, leaning in expectantly.

"Well, first she insisted on going down the Cresta Run, which is strictly chaps-only."

"Golly, how daring!"

"I think it's rather show-offy, myself. And she came flying off, which rather serves her right."

The bridesmaid's friend gave an appreciative giggle at the thought of the famously, and, to her mind, rather annoyingly beautiful Saffron Courtney making a fool of herself.

"But that wasn't the really wicked thing she did . . ."

"Oh, my dear, what did she do?"

"She ran off with a German! Stole him from his fiancée, right under her nose, and spent the night with him. And she'd never even clapped eyes on him before!"

"No! How awful!" the friend gasped, wondering why she never had adventures like that.

"I know! Poor Rory Ballantyne, who'd taken her to St. Moritz and smuggled her onto the Cresta, much against his own better judgement, was absolutely furious, apparently. They've been on absolute nonspeaking terms ever since."

"Dear Rory . . . he's so sweet."

"A bit dull, though . . . but terribly sweet."

A week or so later, Mr. Brown made sure that he just happened to be in Oxford during the last week of Hilary term (why they did not call it the Spring, Lent or Easter term, like everyone else, Mr. Brown—who was a Cambridge man—could not imagine) and invited Saffron Courtney to a spot of lunch at the Randolph Hotel.

"I thought it would be nice to catch up," he said. "Did you go anywhere jolly for Christmas?"

"I was up in Scotland with my cousins, the Ballantynes," Saffron said. She paused fractionally and Mr. Brown could tell that she was trying to decide how much he did or did not know. "Then I went skiing in St. Moritz. It was a complete spur-of-the-moment sort of thing."

"Did you have a nice time?"

"I did actually, yes." Saffron leaned over to him and stage-whispered, "You mustn't tell anyone, but I did something that is totally *verboten*. I had a bash at the Cresta Run."

"Ah yes, I gather women are not allowed."

"No, I had to dress up as a man. I'm not sure I was very convincing."

Mr. Brown smiled amiably. Then, like a poker player making his opening bet, he asked, "Did you learn anything interesting while you were there?"

She looked him right in the eye, didn't miss a beat, and like an opponent seeing the bet and raising it said, "Yes, actually, I did. I met a rather interesting man."

"Really? Did he say anything that might interest me?"

"Yes . . . He was a Jew . . ."

Saffron left the sentence hanging just long enough to make Mr. Brown wonder if she had slept with a German Jew, and then continued by telling him the story of a lawyer who had been a hero in the Great War but been forced to flee the country he had served so valiantly. She told the story very well, so that it was as moving as it was genuinely informative. And while she was rather vague about exactly how and where she had met this gentleman, whose name she said she had sworn not to reveal, it was plain that her tale was true. But she said not one word that even hinted at a lover, let alone a German one.

Mr. Brown left the meal in high spirits. He had rarely seen information withheld so effortlessly, and such a good cover story put in its place. The girl was an absolute natural.

———

Saffron and Gerhard met one more time, that Easter, when he found an excuse to visit Paris. The plans that Speer had drawn up for the new Berlin, guided by his Führer's fantasies, were very strongly based on the drawings of an eighteenth-century architect called Étienne-Louis Boullée. His works were collected at the Bibliothèque National in the French capital and, having assured Speer that a direct study of the old master's work would greatly assist his own endeavors, and promised that he would meet all the expenses himself, Gerhard was given permission to pay the Boullée archive a personal visit. He booked a quiet room at the Ritz, spent many delightful hours in bed with Saffron, had their photograph taken in front of the Eiffel Tower—both smiling at the camera and locked in a passionate embrace—and even, having kissed Saffron goodbye at the Gare du Nord, managed one exhausted day in the Bibliothèque before returning to Berlin.

While they were in Paris, Gerhard and Saffron talked for

longer than either of them would have wanted about the war they both felt certain was coming. They agreed that they had each of them an obligation to do their bit for their country. They also agreed that they would never say a word about any detail of their service to the other. If they did, and were intercepted, that would lead to suspicions of espionage or treachery. Furthermore, if either of them knew what the other was doing, and had any idea of the danger they were in, it would be impossible to bear. And finally, their love depended on being able to forget their nations' political and military differences and see one another as individuals. All they really needed to know was that they were still alive and still in love.

Gerhard had worked out a way by which they could communicate. In order to protect her and the other people involved, the only information he gave her was Isidore Solomons' office address in Zürich. All he wanted from her in return was an address in England to which Izzy could safely write. She provided her Aunt Penny's house in Tite Street.

"You don't mind, do you?" Saffron asked, a few nights later when she and Penny were having dinner in a little Italian restaurant in the backstreets of Chelsea, between the King's Road and the river.

"That depends on your answer to three questions," Penny replied.

"Well then you'd better ask me them."

"Very well. First: do you know that you love him?"

"Oh, absolutely, from the bottom of my heart," Saffron replied and Penny knew at once that she was telling the truth.

"Second: are you sure that he loves you?"

"Absolutely, without a doubt."

"And thirdly: is he a good man?"

"Oh yes, he truly is," Saffron assured Penny and then told her the story of Isidore Solomons, and described the way they had been received at Herr Kagan's café in Zürich. By the end of the story, both women were in tears and Aunt Penny's co-operation and absolute discretion were assured.

When she went back to Oxford for the summer term, Saffron volunteered for the local branch of the Mechanised Transport Corps, a voluntary organization founded in the '14–'18 war to provide trained female driver–mechanics to the armed services, so that men could be freed for duties on the front line. Leon and Harriet came over to London for the month of June, as they had done before, and as they ate their strawberries and cream at Wimbledon and took in the Summer Show at the Royal Academy, they were all three painfully aware of the sense that twenty years of peace were drawing to a close.

"When war does break out, I'm going to leave Oxford," Saffron told Leon. "I want to do my bit."

"But there's no need to do that right away. You won't be called up. Finish your studies and then if, God forbid, the bloody war still isn't over you can decide how best to serve your country."

"But what's the point of staying at Oxford when it's half empty and all the boys one knows have gone to war? It would be miserable. I can do my bit, even if it is only driving a car or a lorry or something and then go back there afterward. Oxford will still be Oxford, no matter what happens in the war."

Leon could see there was no budging her and for all that he wanted to keep his baby girl safe, he admired her courage and determination. So rather than fight her, he decided to redirect her, for the thing he feared above all was for Saffron to be stuck in London when the bombs started falling. For if there was one thing all the military experts seemed to agree on it was that modern bombers could inflict death and destruction on a scale never before seen in time of war.

Saffron had not been home to Kenya for a year and went back to Africa with Leon and Harriet. On the way they stopped off in Cairo, staying with Grandma at the old Courtney family home in the Garden City. For a couple of days after their arrival in the city, Saffron could not help but notice that her father seemed to be unusually busy and secretive. But finally, he came clean.

"I dare say you've been wondering what I've been up to," he said to Saffron as they were having a drink before dinner.

"I have rather, yes," she replied.

"As have I," Harriet interjected. She looked at Saffron, "He's not said a word to me either."

"Well, I'm in the fortunate position of having a bit of influence in this city. Courtney Trading will be a major asset to the war effort, if and when the show begins, what with our oil, ships and whatnot. So I've been able to pull a few strings. It turns out that the army has just appointed a new General Officer Commanding the British and Empire troops in Egypt. He's Major General Henry Maitland Wilson, who's known to one and all as Jumbo, for reasons that will become apparent when you meet him. Anyway, he's just arrived in Cairo, barely knows a soul and is in need of a driver. I said I'd be happy to show him the ropes, introduce him to everyone, get him set up at the Sporting Club and so forth. And in return, all I asked was the chance to provide him with a trained MTC girl to chauffeur him around: my own dear daughter in fact. So, how does that sound?"

"Interesting . . ." said Saffron, in the skeptical tone of someone waiting to hear what the catch is.

"Oh, it's more than interesting, darling," said Harriet. "Any girl would jump at the chance to drive a general."

"Of course, he wants to meet you," Leon added, "Make sure you're presentable, know how to drive, aren't some silly little thing who won't be able to deal with him. I assured him he need have no concerns. So we're meeting him for lunch at the club on Saturday. If all goes well I thought I'd invite him duck-shooting in the Delta. I'm sure he'll be all the happier once he's seen you shoot."

"Well, it does sound like a tremendous opportunity. But what if there isn't a war?"

"Then you go back to university. But I'll be honest with you, Saffy, I think there will be. I think Hitler wants to get his paws on Poland. He has to move before the weather turns bad, and when he does I can't see how we can let him occupy another country without the slightest protest."

Leon had only one demand to make of Saffron, and Jumbo Wilson, which he raised over lunch at the Gezira Sporting Club.

"I think it's important for Saffron to have some means of self-defense. I've taken the liberty of procuring a little Beretta 418 pistol. It's an ideal lady's gun: small, very light and fits very neatly into a handbag."

"I do assure you, Mr. Courtney, I have no intention of taking your daughter into battle, or danger of any kind, if I can possibly avoid it," said the general, who was just as tall and stout as his name suggested.

"I'm absolutely sure you don't, General. But I have fought a war in Africa and it's not like Europe. The front lines aren't drawn nice and neatly on the map. You never know when or where you might suddenly run into trouble."

"Do you have any idea how to shoot a gun, Miss Courtney?" the major general asked.

"I have a fair bit of experience, yes sir."

"Tell you what, General," said Leon, "why don't you come duck-hunting with us in the Delta? We'll put a party together, make a day of it."

Jumbo came shooting. Saffron picked him up from his quarters and drove him out to the lake where the shoot would take place. Her driving was perfectly competent and her shooting was exceptional, at least the match of any man there.

"I would be happy to make you my driver and consent to you being armed, though I would be grateful if you kept quiet about our agreement. You are both civilian and female and on both grounds should not be carrying a gun about your person."

"Not a word," said Saffron, "I assure you."

The following morning she reported for work. Leon and Harriet returned to Kenya delighted by the thought that Saffron was unquestionably doing her bit for her country, but in a way that minimized the actual danger to herself, should hostilities begin.

Less than a month later, Hitler invaded Poland. The Second World War had begun.

———

The Christmas season of 1939 was a joyous time in Germany. Poland had been conquered with the loss of fewer than twenty thousand men killed or wounded. After the horrors of trench warfare on the Western Front in the First War, when so many men had been slaughtered with so little to show for their passing, the *blitzkrieg* of the new conflict offered a painless military victory to go along with all the conquests Hitler had already made without a gun being fired. The Reich now straddled the heart of Europe, from the French border in the west to the Russian in the east, and there were many who hoped that the Führer would be satisfied with what he had achieved. Germany's pride and status had been triumphantly restored. Why not now take time to enjoy this new position as one of the great global powers?

The ballrooms and dining halls of Bavaria's aristocratic palaces and castles were filled with happy revellers in that holiday season. Gerhard von Meerbach was still based in Poland and could not get home leave for Christmas or the New Year. But for Konrad, who divided his time between Heydrich's headquarters in Berlin and the Meerbach Motor Works, it was no trouble at all to attend a number of the most prominent social events, though his freedom to do as he pleased was constrained by the presence of his wife Trudi. This was, of course, frustrating, but it was important to be seen with his wife in public.

It reinforced his image as a good family man, which was important within the Party.

At one such occasion, shortly before Christmas, he happened to have been separated temporarily from Trudi, who had gone to gossip with a little cluster of her female friends. The hostess of the party took his arm and led him a few paces toward another guest who found herself without company, a blonde, whom Konrad reckoned was at least a decade younger than himself. She was a pretty little thing all right, with a more than satisfactory pair of breasts displayed by her ballgown like a pair of peaches in a bowl. She looked at him with distinct interest: that black uniform working its usual magic. *By God, I wonder if I've time to have her before that dumb bitch Trudi notices I'm missing?* Konrad asked himself.

"Chessi, may I introduce Count von Meerbach?"

The woman seemed to tense up, as if the name were not welcome, and then hostess suddenly remembered why, realized she had made a terrible *faux pas* but had no option but to continue: "Count von Meerbach, this is Countess Francesca von Schöndorf."

Konrad had noticed the blonde's unease, too, for if there was one thing that his increasing experience in the business of interrogation had taught him it was the ability to spot signs of tension or discomfort in the person opposite. *So this is the girl Gerhard discarded*, he thought. *He must have been out of his mind!*

Konrad clicked his heels, bowed and said, "I am enchanted to meet you, Countess. And I hope you will allow me, as the head of the von Meerbach family, to offer you my most sincere apologies for the appalling and unforgiveable conduct of my brother toward you. And may I say that he was not only an unmannered oaf, but also a blind fool to have treated a woman as beautiful as you as stupidly as he did."

———

Chessi was not about to let a second member of the same family flatter her into losing her wits, but Count von Meerbach's words deserved a polite response and so she said, "Thank you, that is very kind."

"Well I can see that you two have a lot to talk about," said their hostess, who was clearly desperate to extract herself as quickly as possible. "Ah! There are Fritz and Amélie Thyssen. Please excuse me while I say hello."

Chessi saw the tightening of von Meerbach's mouth at the mention of Thyssen's name. The industrialist, a strong supporter of the Nazi Party in the early days, had fallen out with the Führer over the government's hostility toward the Catholic Church and the obsession with making rearmament the focus of Germany's industrial efforts. As an SS officer and the head of a company whose engines helped power the German war effort, von Meerbach was bound to disapprove.

As she waited for him to turn his attention back to her and make the next move in the conversation, she examined the man in front of her. *So this is the infamous Konrad! If only you knew the things your brother said about you!* He was not at all as handsome or elegant as Gerd and had none of the sensitivity or finesse of his younger brother. But though he had crude features and a peasant's body—stocky, thick-limbed, like a carthorse rather than an Arab stallion—there was an unmistakable aura of power around Konrad von Meerbach that Gerd did not possess. Here was a man who would take what he wanted and crush anyone who got in his way. She had no doubt that he was a bully and a bastard. But that could be made to work to her advantage. Because if Konrad's feelings toward Gerhard were as negative as Gerhard's toward him, well then, that animosity could yet be used effectively.

"I dare say you know that my brother and I don't get on," Konrad began, when his attention switched back to Chessi. "I know he parades around, playing the part of the fighter-ace, but that is just a façade, as carefully designed as one of those buildings he likes to draw. I know the real man underneath."

Chessi had an ace to play in this game with von Meerbach and at a party like this, where conversations could be interrupted at any moment, she could not afford to delay it. "Tell me, did Gerhard tell you why, or rather, for whom he broke his word to me?"

Von Meerbach smiled. "Believe me, I am the last person on earth to whom he would confide any matters of the heart."

"Then I will tell you. Some friends of mine and I were on holiday in St. Moritz in January. Gerhard made a special effort to get there to join us for a few days. He was going to make his formal proposal to me, I absolutely know it. But it happened that an old school friend of mine, who knew where I was staying, had taken it into her head to come and join me. I don't know if you are aware of this, Count von Meerbach, but I spent two years of my education in England. That was where I met my friend. So she came all the way from Scotland, where she had spent Christmas, to Switzerland, just to see me, her dearest friend. You understand, of course, that we met in '36, when there was still a friendship between our two nations."

"Of course, Countess," Konrad agreed. "The Führer endeavored up until the final moments before the British declaration of war to find a way to live in peace with Britain and its Empire."

"Quite so . . . The point is, this young Englishwoman came to St. Moritz to see me. But before we had a chance to meet one another she fell at the feet, quite literally, of your brother Gerhard and decided, at once, that she wanted him for herself."

"Was she aware of the connection between you and him?"

"She knew that I was in love, but she swore to me that she had no idea that he was my man. Foolishly, perhaps, I believed her. Had she respected our friendship, withdrawn her claws and given him back to me, I might have been able to forgive her, and Gerhard. But she would not let him go, and he seemed only too happy to be taken."

"So my brother's lover was an Englishwoman?"

"Yes . . . but why do you say "was"? How do you know that he is not still in love with the same Englishwoman?"

Chessi had a friend who was forever going to expensive clinics in her futile attempts to lose weight. Her problem was very simple. She was greedy and ate too much. And while she could just about withstand a week's compulsory starvation, she no sooner stepped out through the clinic's gates than she went back to her old ways. The look that came across Konrad von Meerbach's face when he realized that he was being presented with a means to destroy his brother was very like Chessi's friend's expression when, immediately after her latest cure, she was confronted with a large plate of *späztle* noodles, thickly covered in cheese.

"Do you know the Englishwoman's name?" he asked, practically salivating.

"Yes," said Chessi. The hostess was heading back in their direction, so there was no time to lose. "Her name is Saffron Courtney. She grew up in Kenya where her father has a great estate. Her mother was called Eva. She was the mistress of a very rich and powerful German industrialist before the First War. This industrialist actually died in Africa, at the start of the war. Saffron's father killed him."

Konrad's face had gone pale. His jaw was clenched as tight as a bull mastiff's. The edges of his lips were white with suppressed rage and his voice was thick and hoarse as he asked, "How do you know this? If you are lying to me, or trying to tease me . . . If you are getting back at my family with slurs and slanders . . ."

Chessi suddenly felt very afraid. She could not understand why her story had made Konrad react so strongly. "I promise you, Count, that I am telling you the truth," she insisted, with a plaintive desperation. "I was told the whole story by one of Saffron's cousins. He was in love with her himself. We both felt betrayed. He was only too happy to tell me everything."

Konrad looked at her, jutting his massive head forward, making no attempt to be in the slightest bit polite as he searched her face for any telltale signs of deceit. He nodded. "Yes, I believe you. There is no way you could know these things unless you had learned them in the way you described. Are there more details that you could tell me?"

"Yes."

"But you do not know the name of the German industrialist?"

"No, I . . ." and then it all became obvious. "Oh . . ." she said, thinking, *Why didn't I see it sooner? The von Meerbach boys grew up without a father. Of course, it had to be him!*

"We will talk soon," Konrad said. "We have much to discuss. And I believe our conversation can be to both our mutual advantage."

Rory Ballantyne imagined that storming a pillbox was a rather exciting activity. But somehow the officer standing before him in the classroom of 161 Officer Cadet Training Unit, or the Royal Military College, Sandhurst, as it had been known before the war, was making it as boring as Latin grammar. So it came as a huge relief to him when the class was interrupted by a lance corporal coming in and approaching the instructor.

"Excuse me, sir," the corporal said, "but the adjutant has asked me to fetch Cadet Ballantyne. There's a gentleman here to see him."

"Can't it wait till the end of the class?" the instructor asked.

"I'm sorry, sir, but I'm to bring Cadet Ballantyne at once. The adjutant was most particular."

The instructor gave an irritated, put-upon sigh and said, "Very well then, Ballantyne, off you go."

Rory rose from his desk, looked at a couple of the men in the same row as him and gave a wide-eyed shrug, as if to say, "I haven't got a clue what this is about," and followed the corporal over to the adjutant's office, where he was introduced to a small, elderly gentleman with thinning, snow-white hair, whose name was Mr. Brown.

"Why don't we go for a walk?" Mr. Brown said. "A stroll to Upper Lake, perhaps. How about that?"

"Absolutely, sir," Rory replied. "I think I know the way."

"So do I, dear boy . . . so do I."

And so they went out into the chilly winter air. Mr. Brown

walked slowly, well wrapped up against the cold in a heavy overcoat, scarf and hat, with his hands in leather gloves while Rory walked beside him in his khaki battledress, wishing he could go a bit faster, just to warm up a bit. Finally, when they were on a path well away from the college buildings, where no one could possibly overhear them, Mr. Brown said, "Before we begin, I need to tell you, in the strongest possible terms, that everything we say must remain absolutely confidential. You are to tell no one at all about the content or purpose of our meeting. Do I make myself clear?"

"Yes sir, absolutely," Rory replied.

"When you return to your fellow cadets, tell them that I am an old family friend, who is an official in the War Office. I was visiting the college and asked after you."

"I understand, sir. I'm just not quite sure, what actually is the purpose of our meeting?"

"I'm here to ask you about your cousin, Saffron Courtney."

Rory felt a sudden stab of alarm. "Is she all right? I say, she's not in trouble, is she?"

Mr. Brown chuckled amiably. "Oh no, no . . . nothing like that. No, this is more a matter of assessment. Miss Courtney's name has come up for a possible job and we wish to make sure of her suitability, that's all."

"It sounds rather cloak-and-dagger. There were always rumors in the family that Saffy's mater was a spy before the last war."

"That sounds rather improbable to me. One shouldn't pay too much attention to family rumors. Facts, Ballantyne, that's what I'm after. So . . . I gather that you and Miss Courtney are very close."

"Not as close as we used to be, I'm afraid, sir."

"Oh really, how so?"

And so Rory found himself telling the story of the trip to St. Moritz. And while he honestly didn't want to say anything that would discredit Saffron, for she was still part of the family after all, there was something almost hypnotic about the gentle way that Mr. Brown asked one question after another. He seemed to be able to draw out information without one really noticing how much one was giving away. Then Rory found himself describing how Saffron had insisted on going down the Cresta Run and gone off afterward with a German called von Meerbach.

Mr. Brown's ears had pricked up at that particular name for some reason and he insisted on hearing all the gory details, despite Rory worrying that it really wasn't very gentlemanly of him to be saying all these things about a lady, particularly his own cousin.

"But dash it all," he concluded, "it really wasn't on. I mean, the war hadn't started, obviously, but we were all worried it might be on the way, and if we did fight the Germans would be our enemies again. And there she was going off with a bloody Hun!"

"You sound as though you were quite upset by the whole thing."

"I suppose I was rather cross about it, yes. Wrote Saffy quite a stiff letter, telling her what I thought. Haven't seen her since, if you must know."

"Did you think she might have had Nazi sympathies?"

"Saffy . . . a Nazi?" Rory was incredulous. "God no! I didn't think much of her behavior, still don't, but Saffy's no Hitler-lover. It's just not in her nature. All that marching and goose-stepping—not her kind of thing at all!"

"So why did she fall for a German, do you suppose?"

"Why does any woman fall for a man? He was bloody rich and not bad-looking, I suppose, if you like foreigners. The real question is, why did she not give a damn about him being German?"

"Quite right, Cadet Ballantyne, that is indeed the question. And what would you give as your answer?"

"Oh, that's easy. Saffy didn't give a damn because she just

doesn't give a damn. She's not like other girls . . . that's what's so special about her. She just does whatever she wants and to hell with the consequences. Women aren't supposed to go down the Cresta Run, but that didn't stop Saffy. English girls aren't supposed to love Germans, but . . . Well, I don't know if she loves him, but you get my drift."

"I do indeed."

They were standing beside the lake and Rory was looking out across the water. The more he'd talked about Saffron, the less he'd wanted to catch Mr. Brown's eye.

"You care for her very much, don't you, Cadet Ballantyne?"

Now Rory turned his head. He nodded.

"Are you worried that you may have said too much?"

"Yah, I am, rather."

"Don't be. Everything you have said is safe with me. And I agree with you. I, too, think that Saffron Courtney is a very remarkable young woman."

"I'd hate to think I'd said anything that would cause her any harm."

"Rest assured, Ballantyne. I don't for a single second think that your cousin is in any way disloyal to this country. As I said, I'm just collecting information by way of an assessment."

"If you're assessing her, I suppose you know she's a terrific shot and rides like the wind."

"So I've heard."

"It's funny, here I am with all the other cadets, training to be an officer. But if Saffy was a man, she'd be a better soldier than any of us."

"What makes you think she won't still be a better soldier, even as a woman?"

Mr. Brown left the question hanging in the air for a moment and then said, "I think it's time we were getting back, don't you?"

———

The man who had been known to Francis Courtney as Manfred Erhardt was a senior agent of the Abwehr, the German military intelligence service. He was certain that Francis Courtney could be developed as an extremely useful asset, but felt that his value would be all the higher if he had greater influence within his family firm. But it was clear from everything Courtney said that his way was blocked by his brothers, Leon and David. Erhardt considered Leon Courtney less of an immediate issue, since he lived in Kenya and was not involved in the day-to-day running of Courtney Trading. It was David Courtney, the chief executive, who presented the greater impediment to Francis's advance. On the other hand, he was also much more vulnerable than Leon.

Erhardt accordingly sent word to Francis asking for any plans his brother might be making to leave Cairo within the next month or two. Francis made up a story about planning a family party and wanting to know when David would be out of town, so as not to leave him out, and though his brother's secretary was extremely doubtful about the likelihood of the famously anti-social Francis suddenly becoming a party host, she could hardly say no to a Courtney. The information was provided and passed on to Erhardt.

Four weeks later David Courtney paid one of his regular visits to Alexandria, to spend some days at the family's shipping operation based there. While he was there he had a convivial dinner with his brother Dorian and, since it was a lovely night and Alexandria had an atmosphere quite unlike Cairo's—much more relaxed, Mediterranean and open to the idea of romance— David decided to stroll back to his hotel on foot, rather than taking a taxi. Knowing the city well, he took a short-cut that at one point led him down a sidestreet so narrow that it was hardly more than an alley.

He didn't hear or see the man who slipped out of a shadowy doorway, stepped up behind him, grabbed the bottom of his face from behind, so that his jaw was lifted up and back and then slit open his throat from one ear to the other.

David's wallet, watch and even his handmade shoes were all stolen. The city's police chief expressed his profound regret to the Courtney family. Clearly this appalling crime was the work of brigands, but despite the most arduous and exhaustive searches, the culprits had not been tracked down.

So far as Erhardt was concerned the operation had worked perfectly. But then came an unexpected drawback. Having flown up to Cairo for his brother's funeral, Leon Courtney decided to move to the city full time for the foreseeable future, to take over the running of Courtney Trading for himself. He placed Loikot in charge of the cattle at Lusima, left Manyoro to continue as the unofficial leader and law enforcer of the local Masai community and appointed an ambitious young South African, Piet van der Meuwe, to look after the burgeoning agricultural side of the estate, growing everything from green beans to coffee beans. He already had the best lawyers and accountants in Nairobi and so, with his land in safe hands, he and Harriet established themselves in Cairo and Courtney Trading got used to life under its new boss.

On reflection, Erhardt was not too disappointed with the way things had worked out. Francis Courtney was even more convinced that the fates and his family were united against him. And there was, in Manfred Erhardt's considerable experience, nothing quite like bitterness, resentment and a sense of having been betrayed to make a man a traitor himself.

———

Konrad von Meerbach now had three great tasks in his life: to assist Heydrich, to lead the family firm, and to come up with a strong enough case against Gerhard to have him sent without trial to a concentration camp. A series of conversations with Francesca von Schöndorf had provided him with a veritable treasure trove of incriminating gossip, and enough leads to assist him in turning that gossip into genuinely incriminating evidence. He and Francesca celebrated their private alliance with a dinner in Berlin and she willingly accompanied him back to his apartment afterwards. But although her body was even more inviting when naked than it had been when clothed, there was still something unsatisfactory for both of them about the occasion. Gerhard's shadow seemed to hang over the bed, and the more they told themselves that this was their way of getting back at him, the more power it seemed to give him—that he could still matter that much to both of them—and the more hollow their triumph became.

That did not, however, mean that Konrad was going to go easy on his brother. With the infinite patience of a poisonous spider, he set about creating a web in which to snare his prey. He wanted proof that Gerhard and this Courtney woman were still in touch with one another. For with every day that passed, the difficulty of bringing a charge of treachery against his brother grew.

In April 1940, units from the 77th Fighter Wing, including Gerhard's squadron, were tasked with supporting the invasion of Norway. He shot down two Royal Air Force fighters during the campaign. And even if they had been antiquated Gloucester Gladiator biplanes, they still counted toward his tally of kills. One more, and he would be an ace.

That fifth kill was a Wellington bomber, shot down over France during the invasion of France. Two more victims, a Hurricane and Spitfire—and they were anything but antiquated—followed in the hectic weeks that saw the British driven back to the sea and forced to make a humiliating retreat from the beaches of Dunkirk, leaving all their equipment behind them. By then, *Reichsmarschall* Herman Göring, the commander-in-chief of the Luftwaffe himself, had pinned an Iron Cross on Gerhard's chest. With that, and the famous pat on the arm from the Führer himself, Gerhard was acquiring a status that, however undeserved, would make him very hard to bring down.

So Konrad thought: *If I loved a woman who belonged with the enemy, how would I stay in touch with her?* Any man who was away at the war wanted to write to his sweetheart and to receive letters from her. But Gerhard and the Courtney woman—Konrad could not bring himself to think of her as Saffron, for it made her sound too human, as though she might almost be likeable—could not write to one another directly, for there was no communication between the Reich and the British Empire. Nor could she write to him, even indirectly, in English, or he to her in German. After all, there were censors in both countries, intercepting mail coming in and going out and any communication written in an enemy language would immediately set off alarms.

So there had to be an intermediary, who could render communications safe in both directions. One could only reach such an intermediary, and he or she would only be able to pass messages on, if they lived in a neutral country. And this person would have to be capable of writing in both English and German. Furthermore they would have to have a reason why they would go to such trouble, and run a certain degree of risk, in order to help two lovebirds.

Konrad had been lying in bed with a long-limbed, and remarkably flexible member of the chorus line at one of the Berlin vaudeville theaters, relaxing after an energetic bout of lovemaking, when he realized precisely who the intermediary must be. The girl had taken the smile that had crossed his face as a sign that he was happy to be with her, but her satisfaction had been short-lived because he immediately kicked her out into the night. He wanted solitude, peace and quiet in which to think, not the inane prattling of a dim-witted dancing girl.

Within a week, Konrad had set up the surveillance and mail interception operation that, by August, had come across the first communication from the intermediary to London, though the letter was not sent directly to Saffron but to a relative, Penelope Courtney, who lived in London. At roughly the same time a letter came in from London, though it was almost certainly the reply to a much earlier communication. Letters from Switzerland to Britain, if they got through at all, went on a very long-winded, circuitous route via neutral countries like Portugal or Sweden, so these two lovers would be communicating very occasionally and very slowly. But if they were in love that would be enough to keep the fires burning in their hearts.

There was just one problem. No matter how hard the German agents assigned to the case tried, they could not establish the next link in the chain: from the intermediary to Gerhard. Somehow the letters were being smuggled in and out of the Reich in such a way that the chain was not visible. So then Konrad considered the other end of that chain. Someone in Germany must act as the final link to Gerhard, just as this Penelope Courtney woman did to Gerhard's bitch.

Another man, whose character was formed very differently to Konrad's and who did not live in a system like Nazism might have hesitated before coming to the conclusion that he did. And they would then have felt a great deal less willing than him to institute a second program of mail interception to prove that their hunch had been correct. But Konrad was not such a man. He had his hunch, he acted upon it and he was proved correct. He then discovered that the first individual he had uncovered, the one who operated from neutral ground, was involved in a multi-faith organization. Its aim was to assist and resettle families, in particular children, who had suffered as a result of various Nazi policies, and one of its other leading members was a Catholic priest. And with that discovery, the last link in the chain fell into place.

———

Konrad's web had been spun. Gerhard was trapped, though he did not know it. But then an unexpected problem arose.

"I really don't think it would be wise to have your brother arrested," Heydrich said, one evening in late August, after Konrad had presented him with his findings. "He is a decorated fighter-ace currently engaged in combat operations. If we were to seize him, the fuss would go all the way to the top. Then we would have *Reichsmarschall* Göring fighting with *Reichsführer*

Himmler over a man whose crime is that he fucked the wrong woman. Sooner or later, they would both wonder why the hell they were bothering, and then they would both turn their fire on me. At that point, believe me, I would step aside and let the full weight of their joint fury fall on you.

"I am sorry, Konrad, but this little family feud of yours is really not worth the trouble it will cause. We have a war to win: a war against the international Jewish conspiracy. We will only achieve total victory when we have wiped the entire race from the face of the earth. Concentrate on that task, if you please, not your brother's sex life."

"Yes, sir," Konrad said, but inside he was thinking, *That is what you say now. But if I can find just one word, in one letter, that gives away the slightest shred of sensitive military information, then I will change your mind, and Himmler's and Göring's too.*

Just then the air-raid sirens began to wail. Heydrich remained as glacially calm as ever behind his desk. Konrad felt equally unperturbed. It must be some kind of practice drill. Göring himself had assured the German people that no British bomber would ever be able to reach the Ruhr, on the western edge of the Reich, closest to England. Berlin was five hundred kilometers to the east of the Ruhr, and thus that much further away from the British Isles. There was no need to be alarmed.

Then the phone rang on Heydrich's desk. Konrad could not hear what the man on the other end of the line was saying, but his tone was certainly very agitated. Heydrich listened quietly, with no more than the occasional, "Are you sure?" and "I see." Finally he said, "Very well, I will inform my staff accordingly." Then he put down the phone and looked at Konrad. "It appears I misjudged the situation—this is not a mere drill. Approximately fifty RAF bombers are on a course that will take them directly to Berlin. They are expected to be over the city within the next ten minutes. It seems that we are under attack."

There was heavy cloud over the city that night. The British

bombers could not find their way to the heart of the city. Two
people were slightly injured when a bomb fell close to the
wooden summer house in the garden of their home in Rosenthal,
a suburb to the north of the city. The rest of the bombs fell
harmlessly on farmland, hitting crops and livestock, rather than
buildings and people. A joke ran round the city: "The British
can't defeat us in battle. So now they are trying to starve us
out."

But the Führer was not amused. Göring was deeply embarrassed. Revenge would have to be taken against Britain's cities
and London in particular and every single Luftwaffe pilot would
be required to assist in the campaign. If ever there had been
any hope in persuading anyone to have a fighter-ace removed
from the front line, that time was past.

So now Konrad had to find another way to destroy his
brother.

————

"Steady, now, boys. Eyes open, total concentration. Tommy
will be saying hello soon . . ." The voice of his squadron captain, Dieter Rolf, crackled in Gerhard von Meerbach's earpiece.
Five thousand meters below them the River Thames ran like a
ribbon of silver, gleaming in the afternoon sun, right into the
heart of London. Gerhard did his best, as always, to try not
to think about Saffron. Just before the war began she had
written to him saying that her father wanted her to go home.
He presumed that she meant back to Africa. But perhaps he
was wrong. Or perhaps she had not been able to get there and
was now stuck in Britain for the duration of the war. Gerhard
still assumed that England would eventually fall just as Poland,
France, the Low Countries, Denmark and Norway had done.
There were times when he would lie in his bed and imagine
him, a conqueror, finding Saffron again and . . . what then?

She would be a traitor in the eyes of her people if she con-
sorted with one of their occupiers.

Gerhard could not bear the thought that he would never hold

her in his arms again, never lie with her and make love. He thought of the scent of her hair; the sound of her laughter, and the moans when they made love; the light that flickered deep in the sapphire pools of her eyes; the way she arched her back when he entered her; the feel of her breasts when his hands were cupped around them; the line of her hips, the swell of her buttocks and the swoop into her slender waist; the hot, wet grip of her pussy around him and . . .

Enough, man! Keep your mind on your job!

Between the Messerschmitts and the river were fifty Dornier 17 bombers flying in perfect formation at low altitude, their pilots ignoring the distraction of the anti-aircraft batteries whose shells were already exploding like black pom-poms in the air around them and heading inexorably toward their target.

It wasn't hard to spot. Up ahead the smoke was rising from the London Docks. The route up the Thames had become so familiar that Gerhard's 109 could practically have flown there without his assistance, but he questioned the change of strategy. The original policy of attacking RAF Fighter Command's airfields had been working perfectly. The RAF was losing so many planes, in the air and on the ground, that he could not believe they could possibly replace them. Even more importantly their experienced pilots were being killed and replaced by beginners who had scarcely learned to fly a trainer aircraft, let alone survive in aerial combat against hardened veterans. True the Royal Air Force was now using Spitfires and Hurricanes that were a match for the German 109s, but even so, the boys in the Luftwaffe fighter wings had felt confident of victory.

But then that damn bomb fell on Berlin: one bomb in a damned summer house. And suddenly everything changed. Sure, it was good for the German people to see newsreel footage of London on fire. But it was also good for the Royal Air Force. They had been given time to regroup, to fill in the bomb craters in their runways, repair their aircraft and give their pilots more training and more rest. Even within the past two or three weeks it had become possible to tell the difference. The English were fighting fit again, and they had brought in some friends to help them, a squadron of Polish flyers, all veterans of the invasion, and all willing to do anything to get their own back on the hated Germans.

So now Gerhard settled into the rhythm that any fighter pilot who wished to stay alive had to maintain: his eyes constantly flicking across the sky, searching for the enemy aircraft he knew must be on their way. But where were they coming from? The fighter squadrons on both sides were playing a game of hide-and-seek, using the scattered clouds for shelter, but also knowing that, as long as they could not be seen, neither could they see: in the end they had to come out into the sun. And it was as Gerhard's flight of four planes, with him in the leading position, emerged from the clouds that another voice clamored in his earphones. "Enemy at six o'clock, low! Hurricanes! Looks like a single squadron coming in from the city, heading straight for the bombers."

"I see them!" Gerhard responded, for the Hurricanes showed clearly as black silhouettes against the dazzling river. The 109s peeled away, one flight after another in a perfect sequence born of endless repetition, and soon it was Gerhard's turn as he banked right and then dived at full speed, reaching almost six hundred kilometers an hour as he rocketed toward the Hurricanes below. The roar of air against his cockpit was almost enough to drown out the engine as the numbers on the altimeter rotated as quickly as the fruit on a slot machine, unable to keep up with the velocity of his descent.

Gerhard felt the dizzy sensation as his heart struggled against immense gravitational forces to pump blood up to his brain. It was all too easy to black out in a full dive and just keep plummeting all the way down to the ground and certain death. But if he pulled up too soon, that would simply expose the belly of his aircraft to the enemies' guns. He just had to keep going, down and down, aiming for a Hurricane that he had picked out as his prey, hoping that they wouldn't see him until it was too late, throttling back toward the end to ease the speed, so as not to overshoot the target.

He was almost there, so close he could see the head of the Hurricane's pilot inside his cockpit. He flattened the dive then wrapped his fingers around the firing grip, and flicked down the trigger that operated his two machine guns. On top of the grip there was a button that fired the canon. *Now!* Gerhard squeezed the trigger with his index finger and pressed on the button with his thumb, feeling the airframe shudder as the guns all fired.

And at that precise moment the alarm must have been sounded for the Hurricanes suddenly scattered like a flock of starlings menaced by predatory hawks, some climbing, others diving, yet more twisting and corkscrewing to the side. The pilot Gerhard had aimed at heaved on his joystick and hauled his plane into a steep climb . . . Right into Gerhard's path.

He banked hard right and for a fraction of a second that seemed to drag on for an age he could do nothing but pray as the 109 twisted onto its side, the wings almost vertical as they skimmed past the Hurricane.

Gerhard was fighting for control of his aircraft now and at that moment of vulnerability he became the prey for suddenly his left wing was peppered with bullet holes, right up by the fuselage, just centimeters away from his leg. He looked around to see where the fire was coming from, looked in his mirror, couldn't see anything and then he heard his wingman, Berti Schrumpp, shouting, "He's behind you, Meerbach, right behind you!"

Gerhard reacted just as his earlier target had done, he pulled back on the joystick and as the nose of his plane came up he felt another burst of bullets hit the fuselage from behind, just behind his cockpit. *Two close misses! He won't miss a third time.* Gerhard climbed, almost vertically, in the reverse of his earlier dive. Now the gravity that had impelled him down so fast was pushing against his climb, slowing the plane so that it was on the verge of stalling. One second before that could happen, Gerhard applied the rudder to full yaw, turning it around so that it rolled off the top of its climb and came right back down the way it had come, picking up speed again and, in theory, bringing it right back onto the pursuing enemy plane.

Except that the Hurricane wasn't there any longer. In the pell-mell chaos of the mass dogfight it had itself been engaged by a 109 and been forced to take evasive action. All across the sky, as the bombers continued on their droning, unvarying path to their target, the fighters were turning, diving, firing, missing.

But some were hitting. A sudden explosion of dazzling orange and gold erupted from the engine of one of the Dorniers, which fell away to one side, trailing a plume of smoke. "For God's sake, get out!" Gerhard shouted, as if anyone could possibly hear. He looked for a further second or two for any sign of parachutes, but that was all the time he could spare, for there was danger all around him, and also targets, too.

There was a cry of triumph over the squadron radio as someone hit a Hurricane and then, as if some celestial referee had blown a full-time whistle, the dogfight was over. There was only a certain amount of time and fuel that they could afford to expend if they were to make it back to France in one piece. There was a plaintive cry of complaint, "Now that bastard will be able to get away. I'd have finished him off if I'd had a few more seconds."

"And his friend might have finished off you." That was Rolf talking. "The bomber boys got through, that's what matters. Now let's bring them safely home."

———

Heydrich was right. Konrad was kept so busy in the final months of 1940 that he had no time to plot his brother's downfall. In mid-November he was in Warsaw, acting as his master's eyes and ears as the final touches were put to the ghetto where the city's four hundred thousand Jews were imprisoned.

"As you can see, the walls are almost complete," said Ludwig Fischer, the Governor of Warsaw, proudly as he and Konrad were driven along Okapowa, the street that formed one side of the ghetto. "None of those filthy Yids will ever get out. Not until we decide to take them out."

"Well they can't stay here forever, that's for sure," Konrad agreed, as the car turned left onto Jerusalem Avenue. "But at least you are only wasting a small portion of the city on them. I counted only twenty city blocks from one end of the wall back there to the other."

"That's right. I am proud to say that we have managed to fit one-third of the city's population into one fortieth of its total area."

"Very impressive. How did you do that?"

"It is simply a matter of the efficient utilization of space," Fischer explained. "There are approximately twenty-seven thousand apartments within the ghetto, so that gives us fifteen Jews per apartment, which works out at six or seven of them for each room of each apartment. So yes, they must all lie very close together at night, but they will not mind this, I assure you."

"Why not?"

"Because we do not intend to waste heating fuel on Jews in wintertime. So if they all lie together like sardines in a tin, then they will keep each other warm, even if they have no coal for their fires!"

Konrad laughed heartily at this splendid witticism. "I shall be sure to tell *Obergruppenführer* Heydrich you said that, he will be greatly amused. But, to be serious, I imagine the numbers will in any case lessen through natural attrition."

"Of course. The combination of forced labor, minimal rations and cold will swiftly weed out the weaker members of the population. But I hear that you are already working on other ways to do that."

"Ah, have you had a visit from the Kaiser's Coffee Company van?"

Fischer's face lit up like a child being promised a trip to the circus. "No, but I am very keen to see it."

"You should. It is operated by a *kommando* led by a fellow called Lange. The van is airtight and it is equipped with a canister of carbon monoxide gas, which, as you may know, is odorless but deadly poisonous. We have been testing it on imbeciles, inmates of mental asylums and so forth as part of the euthanasia program. It's very important to rid the population of these defective individuals who are using up resources that could be put to better use elsewhere."

""Useless eaters," as they say."

"Exactly."

The question of "useless eaters' became an even greater part of Konrad's life in the New Year as Heydrich was placed in charge of the SS planning for the occupation of Russia. An invasion was planned for the spring and the SS would have a vital role, following in the army's footsteps and dealing with the necessary task of cleansing the entire population of Jews and Bolsheviks and that required an immense amount of organization.

"One cannot just walk into Russia and say, "Let's kill all the commies and the Israelites," Heydrich would say. "It requires planning. Where will we find these people. How will we kill them? What will we do with the bodies? How will we persuade our men to slaughter defenseless women and children? This is vital work. It has to be given an immense amount of thought."

Konrad was happy to oblige. It was fascinating, thrilling work. To be in at the start of an empire's creation was a privilege granted to few men. So Konrad was in a good mood as he took his regular morning shower, shortly after waking at five thirty as he always did these days. As he soaped his body he sang a French song that seemed to be everywhere in Berlin that spring. It was called "J'Attendrai," or "I will wait," and its subject was the pledge that every woman made to her man as he went off to war, that she would wait day and night, waiting forever until he came back.

Then you're screwed if he doesn't come back, aren't you, my little darling, Konrad thought and laughed at the image of the woman growing old while her man lay rotting on some far-flung battlefield. And then he laughed even harder for he had just had another one of his bright ideas. And this one was an absolute beauty.

———

In Zürich, Isidore walked into the Konditorei Kagan as usual, but instead of Yavi Kagan greeting him in the usual fashion, the proprietor beckoned him over, nervously. He leaned over the counter and whispered to Isidore. "There is a man sitting at your table. I told him it was reserved, but he insisted. He said, "It is Herr Solomons that I have come to see." He's there now, a German. I think he is Gestapo or SS. I can smell those bastards."

If Kagan said the man was SS, the chances were he was right. "You can turn round now and walk out if you like," he added.

Isidore shook his head. "No, I've run enough. I'll not be made to run again."

Before he had taken another five steps into the café, Isidore knew who was waiting to see him. "Good morning, Count von Meerbach," he said, taking his normal chair, directly opposite Konrad.

"Good morning to you, Solomons," Konrad said. "You look very well. You've put on a little weight since I last saw you. Good to know you're eating well. And it suits you, gives you a certain substance. Who wants a lawyer who can't afford a decent meal, eh? My compliments to your tailor. He cuts a fine suit. Must have cost you a pretty penny, eh? Have you paid my brother back his five thousand marks? If not, perhaps you could pay me. It was my money, after all."

"As I understand it, the money came from the Meerbach trust,"

Isidore said. "I, of all people, know the terms of the trust, since I helped draft them, and the money that your brother chose to give me, rather than loan me—he was very insistent on that point—came to him as a beneficiary of the trust. There is, therefore, no sense at all in which that money was yours. So I have no obligation whatever to give it, or any portion of it to you."

Konrad smiled, "That's my clever little Jew-boy. Your kind have always got an argument for holding on to your money."

"You forget yourself. This is not Germany. You have no power over me here."

"Oh really, is that what you think?"

"No, it is what I know to be the law."

"There are all kinds of law, Solomons. For example, there is also the law of the jungle in which the weak are crushed by the strong, so that inferior species are driven to extinction while the powerful thrive and spread across more and more territory."

"Thank you for the lecture in natural selection. Now, tell me what you want, get it over and done with and then we can both go on with our day."

"I want you to write two letters, one to my brother and the other to his English bitch lover."

"I'm sorry, but I am unaware of anyone who answers that description, so how could I possibly write to them?"

"The same way you always do, Solomons. Ah, good, I can see from your face that we are making a little progress here. And here is your brother Yid with your Jew-bread and kosher coffee."

Kagan bridled at that, but Isidore put a hand on his arm and said, "Ignore him, Herr Kagan. He's not worth the trouble."

"If you say so, Herr Solomons, but he should count himself lucky that you were here to restrain me."

Isidore looked at Konrad: "You were going to tell me the purpose of this meeting . . ."

"It's very simple. I know that you operate a kind of post office for my brother and his lover, who is English, meaning that both of them are consorting with the enemy, an offense for which my brother could be court-martialed and shot. That's the law, by the way, Solomons. I dare say she could be executed as a traitor too, if the English were ever given reason to believe that a young woman who acts as the driver for a general—I dare say you did not know that—was writing letters to an officer in the Luftwaffe."

"What do you mean, "a kind of post office"?

"I mean that you receive letters from England written by a Frau Penelope Courtney, who is the aunt of Fräulein Saffron Courtney, Gerhard's lover. These letters appear to be from the older Courtney woman to you, but their content has in fact been composed by the niece and is intended for my brother's eyes. You then copy the key lines of the letter you have received onto a new document which you give by hand to Father Weiss, when you meet for the meetings of your inter-faith committee. He then sends it to his fellow priest Father Bauer who passes it on to my mother, who then incorporates what you have written into her letters to my brother. Then the whole process is repeated, in reverse, when my brother replies to Fräulein Courtney." Konrad sighed. "So many people risking their necks, just so two traitors can each betray their countries. Why would anyone do such a thing?"

"Because they understand that these are two good young people, in love with one another, and that love is a precious thing, and all the more so in a world filled with men like you, who spread hatred and death wherever you go."

"I will spread death to Zürich, unless you do exactly as I say. I will have you killed and your wife and children smuggled back over the border to Germany, where they belong, so that they can be dealt with just like any other Jews. I will have my mother and her priest arrested for treason and my brother too. I will make sure that the English discover what Fräulein Courtney has been doing and have the evidence required to convict her. I will do all this, and gladly too, unless you do exactly what I say."

Isidore looked at Konrad, frowning in puzzlement as he examined his face. "What happened to you, Konnie?" he asked. "I can remember when you were a little boy, letting you ride on my shoulders around the garden. I remember you playing in the sunshine with my younger brothers and sisters, with my cousins, all of you happy—some Christians, some Jews but all little German children. When did you become this . . . this monstrous perversion of a human being? I know you want me to fear you. I know that is what makes you feel strong. But I do not fear you. I pity you. You are doomed. Your soul is forsaken. May God have mercy for what you have become."

For a moment, barely a second, Isidore thought he had penetrated the thick walls Konrad von Meerbach had built around whatever fear or pain it was that now motivated him. But then the Nazi mask that Konrad now wore returned like a portcullis slamming down to block a castle gate. "God does not exist," he said. "You Jews of all people should know that, for no true God would ever let his chosen people be abused the way that we have abused you. And believe me, what has happened so far is as nothing compared to what is to come. There will be horrors that you cannot even imagine. So now, remember what will happen if you dare to defy my demands."

"Which are?"

"You will write two letters: one to my brother, the other to Fräulein Courtney, exactly as if you were passing on genuine messages from them."

"What are these letters to say?"

Then Konrad told him, and Isidore understood what it must have been like for Dr. Faustus, having to make his deals with the devil.

————

Victory! At last, after endless months of nothing but bad news, the British army, with considerable help from its Imperial allies, had an enemy on the run. And as driver to General Jumbo

Wilson, Saffron felt like a spectator with the best seats in the stadium.

It had all begun with Mussolini's declaration of war against Britain and France on 10 June 1940, a decision he had postponed until the German army was practically at the gates of Paris and he was sure of coming in on the winning side. The Italians had an empire in Africa that included Ethiopia, Somalia and Libya, which shared a long land border with Egypt.

In September, the Italians launched an offensive into Egypt and advanced about fifty miles to the port of Sidi Barrani before a lack of supplies, modern equipment and enthusiasm brought them to a halt. The British regrouped and in early December launched a counter-offensive, codenamed Operation Compass. It was a stunning success. Within two days they had recaptured Sidi Barrani and taken forty thousand Italian prisoners for the loss of just six hundred men.

Jumbo Wilson was in jubilant mood and Saffron found her boss delightful company as she drove the khaki Humber saloon that contained the general and his closest aides around Cairo, or up the coast road toward Sidi Barrani and beyond as he paid visits to the forward command posts of the Indian, Australian and British divisions leading the charge back toward the Libyan border.

The Italian XXIII Corps under the command of Lieutenant General Annibale "Electric Beard" Bergonzoli—so called because of his mighty, silver whiskers, topped by a flamboyant mustache—dug in at the town of Bardia. They turned the place into a veritable fortress ringed by an eighteen-mile-long anti-tank ditch that was peppered with strongpoints, armed with anti-tank guns and machine guns and positioned so that it was impossible for the enemy to attack anywhere without coming under fire from at least two different points. Almost one hundred and thirty tanks, ready to move at any moment to wherever the fighting was fiercest, underpinned Bardia's impregnability.

Mussolini placed great faith in his general. He wrote to Bergonzoli, praising him as an old and intrepid soldier and declaring, "I am certain that "Electric Beard" and his brave soldiers will stand at whatever cost, faithful to the last."

Bergonzoli assured *Il Duce* that he need have no doubt of the outcome of the battle: "In Bardia we are and here we stay."

The Allies had other ideas. The British 7th Armored Division, who had given themselves the soon-to-be legendary nickname "The Desert Rats", swung round behind Bardia to cut off any Italian retreat. On 3 January 1941, the Australian 6th Division went into the attack against the stronghold. By the time night fell, two days later, Bardia, and another forty thousand Italians were in Allied hands.

It was now, as the Australians pressed on toward the port of Tobruk, that Jumbo Wilson decided to pay a visit to the field headquarters of Major General Richard O'Connor, who had been given command of Operation Compass.

As Leon had predicted at lunch with Jumbo, Harriet and Saffron almost eighteen months earlier, warfare in Africa was very different to a European campaign. On the Western Front during the First War, the front lines that ran between a myriad French towns and villages had faced one another with immobile, near-impregnable certainty. In the emptiness of the Western Desert, where the local population consisted of little more than scorpions, vipers and thick clouds of flies, the battle moved at such a dizzying pace that there hardly was a front line at all. In this sea of sand the fighting took on some of the characteristics of naval warfare, where half the trick lay in just finding your enemy.

Or your friends, come to that.

———

"How was your day?" Harriet asked after Saffron arrived home from work one day.

"Unexciting," Saffy replied. "Just a couple of errands in town and an awful lot of waiting in between."

"Poor girl. Why don't I make you a nice cup of tea? That should raise your spirits. Oh, by the way, a boy came round from the company with a telegram for you."

"A telegram? That's unexpected."

"Good news I hope," Harriet said, handing Saffron the message.

"Fingers crossed," said Saffy, who was smiling as she opened the telegram.

Then the smile vanished, the blood drained from her face, the telegram slipped from her fingers and she stood white-faced and absolutely silent for several seconds before she broke down into convulsive sobs.

Harriet rushed to her side and took her arm. "Come with me," she said gently and guided Saffron to a chair, where she sat, bent over, still crying helplessly.

Harriet walked back to where the telegram lay abandoned on the floor. She wondered whether it was wrong to read it but then reasoned that if she knew what had happened she wouldn't have to make Saffron even more unhappy by asking.

———

GERRY SHOT DOWN MISSING PRESUMED DEAD STOP SO SO SORRY PENNY

Oh you poor, dear girl, thought Harriet. And then, *You kept him very quiet. I wonder why.*

"Would you like to talk about him?" she asked. "You never know, it might help."

Saffron shook her head. "I can't. I can't ever say a word about him."

"Oh, I'm sure that's not true."

"It is!" Saffron insisted and turned her desperate eyes toward Harriet. "You don't understand, Father would be devastated if he ever found out about him."

"Surely not? He would be terribly sad for you, but he wouldn't be angry just because you were in love. You're perfectly old enough for that sort of thing."

"It's who I was in love with—his family, where he came from. Please can we stop talking about this? I . . . I can't say another word. Really I can't."

"I understand. If you change your mind, you can talk to me whenever you want. And if you don't change your mind, well, I understand that, too."

"Thank you," said Saffron.

She kissed Harriet and took herself to her bedroom. She slept not a wink that night. She lay there for hours, obsessively running through every last moment she had spent with Gerhard. Remembering her first sight of him, the first smell of his body, the first time they had made love and she had taken possession of him, inside her, making him hers alone. She took out all the letters from her bag and read them again and again, though she already knew them all by heart. She realized that her stock of memories was pitifully small. They had spent so little time together. She had been robbed of so many years of love. How lucky Harriet was! She still had her man. Even if he could not see her, they could hold one another, talk to one another, share their lives. They had a future. She did not.

Saffron brooded on the emptiness of the years ahead. Perhaps she could find a husband. He might even be a man for whom she might feel affection, companionship, the sort of love that arose from friendship and perhaps having children together. But they would not be Gerhard's children. She would never feel the immediate, instinctive, animal passion that told her that he was her man, above all others. And what was the point of a life without that?

It was dawn and in the distance, across the river, the calls to prayer were ringing out from the city's mosques when a thought suddenly struck her, very clearly, like a form of revelation. She realized that she was now blessed with a peculiar kind of freedom. If she had no future, then it did not matter what she did now, in the present, for any consequences of her actions were essentially irrelevant: she was lost anyway. So she could do precisely whatever she liked.

————

"Which way do you want me to go, sir?" Saffron asked as the Humber came to a point, twenty miles inside the Libyan border, where the tank tracks that had served as a road for the past half-hour split in two directions. She could feel the tension in the car. In the desert they might just as easily bump into a hostile unit as a friendly one, so every turning became a gamble, with life and death as its stakes.

The constant stress was making the men around her edgy and short-tempered. But she actually preferred this sort of situation to a normal drive. The level of concentration was so high that she had no spare mental capacity left to waste thinking about Gerhard. And if she died, she didn't really care.

Just so long as I take a few of them with me.

"Left," said the eager young staff officer, Captain Wright, who was sitting in the front passenger seat. "I'm pretty sure it's left."

"Pretty sure?" barked Jumbo Wilson from the rear of the car. "That's not good enough. You should know the way as a matter of certainty."

"Well, sir, the last message I received said that the field headquarters had been established eight miles southwest of Bardia, in a wadi," Wright replied and then added helpfully, "That's a dried-up riverbed, sir."

"I know what a wadi is, Wright. I've seen enough of them."

"Quite so, sir. So, anyway, the map shows a wadi about two miles up ahead, to the left. Once we reach the wadi and follow it for another mile or so I'm confident we will reach O'Connor's HQ."

"Let us hope your confidence is justified. Take the left-hand fork, Miss Courtney. Drive on."

"Yes, sir," Saffron said.

A couple of minutes later she heard Jumbo's voice again. "For pity's sake man, could you please stop wriggling around like a man with ants in his pants. What on earth is the matter?"

"Bit of a bad tummy, sir," came the strained voice of the other staff man in the car, Major Morgan. "I'm rather in need of relief."

Jumbo sighed. Sounding more like a parent talking to a fidgeting child than one senior officer addressing another, he said, "Hang on till we reach this blasted wadi and see if you can find a spot to do your business there. Best to get it dealt with before we reach O'Connor, I suppose."

———

"*Mamma mia!* I thought you said you were a mechanic!"

Matteo Frescobaldi, a tough, bullet-headed sergeant from the Blackshirt Division, battle-hardened from service in the Spanish Civil War and the conquest of Ethiopia, was standing by the open hood of a battered army truck and he was not impressed by what he was seeing.

"I am, Sarge!" protested the oil-stained figure standing in front of him, wiping his black-stained hands on his filthy battledress uniform. "But we're stuck in the middle of a godforsaken desert with no tools, no spares, at the bottom of a river that doesn't have any water."

Frescobaldi grinned at the man's cheek and gave him a friendly pat on the face. "Very funny," he said. "But there are eight of us, and only five, at most can fit in that . . ." He pointed toward the elegant lines of the Fiat 2800 staff car that he had appropriated, just as the supposedly impregnable fortress of Bardia was falling apart around his ears. "You will be one of the three we leave behind unless you get that truck working."

"You won't leave the truck. How else will you move the loot?"

They had sneaked out of the town on the night before it fell, taking the safe that contained the cash entrusted to General Bergonzoli to help fund his campaign. Or at least they thought that was what it contained. They had not been able to open it yet.

"You are quite right," Frescobaldi growled. "I will have to move the loot. In which case, you fix the truck or I leave five behind." He glanced down at the Breda machine gun that was, as usual, cradled in his arms like a much-loved baby. "Dead or alive, I don't care."

Just then they heard the sound of an engine—a car rather than a tank—coming toward them. Frescobaldi raced to the top of the low ridge behind which he had concealed his men and their vehicles. He grinned at what he saw, then he went back down to their position.

"Forget about the truck," he said. "We have another way of getting out of here."

* * *

Just up ahead, to one side of the stony, bone-dry bed of the wadi, stood a small clump of desiccated gray thorn bushes. Saffron slowed the car down and said, "Might that be a good spot, sir? For Major Morgan, I mean."

"Yes, that'll do. Stop her," Jumbo replied.

She brought the car to a halt. Morgan hopped out and scuttled toward the thorn bushes.

"I hope he's all right, sir," said Saffron. "He'd better watch out for snakes, underneath the bush."

Captain Wright was just suppressing a laugh when the shooting started. Suddenly the walls of the wadi were echoing to the percussive chatter of a light machine gun, the dusty earth around Major Morgan was bursting with the impact of bullets and the major was dashing back toward the Humber, followed by the gunfire. He was fifteen yards from the car when something seemed to pick him up and throw him forward. He lay on the ground, a red stain spreading through the back of his khaki shirt.

"Get him, Wright!" shouted Wilson. "Courtney, get this car turned around."

Wright leaped out and ran, bent double toward Morgan, drawing the fire toward himself. With the door still open,

Saffron slammed her foot to the floor and the car leaped forward,
then a couple of seconds later she wrenched on the handbrake,
turned the wheel hard and the car slewed round, virtually on
the spot, throwing a cloud of dust into the air that acted as a
temporary smokescreen as she raced back the way she had come.

The Italians were still firing and there was a hammering on
the back of the car as a burst of rounds hit the trunk.

Saffron stopped the car for just long enough to allow Wright
to bundle Morgan into the back seat, screaming in pain, and
then she was off again.

Behind them the firing ceased, but Morgan's cries of distress
were louder than ever and the smell of diarrhea filled the car
as he voided his bowels. Saffron looked in the mirror. There
was nothing behind her. She turned all her attention back to
the wadi. It was littered with stones, rocks and even a few
sizeable boulders, left by the receding waters of the river that
had once run down it. On the way in she had taken it very
slowly and carefully, all too aware of the perils of damaging
the car out here in the middle of nowhere.

Now she was driving a little faster. Then she took another
look in the mirror and sped up again.

"There's a car behind us!" she shouted.

Wright twisted the mirror so that he could see out of it.
"Looks like an Italian staff car. There's a chap leaning out of
his window holding a gun. Duck sir, duck!"

The machine gun fired again, but the bullets passed harmlessly wide: the chances of hitting a fast moving car up ahead
from the window of another vehicle when both were driving
over uneven ground were meager in the extreme.

That did not stop Wright pulling out his Enfield No. 2 service
revolver, winding down his window and firing off three rounds
back at the Italians.

"Don't waste your ammunition, man!" Jumbo shouted.

They had passed over a relatively flat stretch of riverbed but now the ground was getting rougher again. Saffron found that she was not frightened by the gunfire, for her whole mind was taken up with the task of finding the best speed. Too slow and they would be caught by their pursuers. Too fast and they could hit a rock and become sitting ducks.

"What's happening behind us?" she asked.

"The chap with the gun is waving his arm around—typical Italian. Think he wants his driver to go faster."

Saffron increased her speed a little, but not to the point where she felt out of control. Let the other man drive like an idiot. They would soon see who survived the longest.

"They're getting closer, sir!" Wright yelled. "For God's sake, Courtney, can't you go faster?"

"Leave the girl alone," Jumbo said. He twisted round in the passenger seat and then ducked as the machine gun spat fire again and the rear window shattered as it was hit by a round. Saffron felt a shower of glass particles against her back, but she was unhurt.

"Time for suppressing fire, I think," said Jumbo and, with Morgan still holding his hands to the front of his shirt in a desperate attempt to staunch the flow of blood, the general turned until he had one knee on the passenger seat and was leaning on the back of the seat, facing backward. He and Wright fired several times. A couple of rounds hit the chasing car, but to no obvious effect, though the man with the machine gun was forced to duck back inside the vehicle.

The Italians were gaining on the Humber with every second. As the range narrowed, Jumbo Wilson fired a shot that hit the pursuers' windscreen.

"Good shot, sir!" Wright shouted as the Italians veered to one side before the driver regained control and took up a new course, running parallel to the Humber but slightly to the left, on the passenger's side.

"I've got a better shot now," said Wright, for the new course exposed the flank of the Italian car, and, by the same token, the side of the Humber too. He took careful aim at the man with the machine gun, heedless of the fire that was coming from it, and pulled the trigger.

It clicked.

The gun was empty.

"Damn!" Wright exclaimed. "Do you have any spare ammunition, sir?" he asked.

"No," Jumbo admitted. "Didn't anticipate a need for it."

"Me neither."

The Italians had been blessed with a stroke of luck. The side of the wadi onto which they'd been forced was smoother. Now they were gaining fast. Their hood was level with the back of the Humber, with a gap of barely fifteen feet between the sides of the two cars. But now it seemed that the man with the machine gun had the same problem as the British soldiers. He had run out of bullets. Glancing across, Saffron could see him bend down, evidently scrabbling around on the floor of the car for now she could see the driver beyond him.

"Would you open the glove compartment please, sir?" she asked.

"I'm sorry?" Wright asked.

"Open the damn glove compartment!" Saffron snapped.

"Do as she says, Wright," said Jumbo, beginning to grasp what she was up to.

"Now pull out my shoulder bag and open it."

"A gun!" Wright exclaimed. "What a stroke of luck!"

"Hand it to me please, sir." Saffron glanced at the Italian car. The man still hadn't reloaded his machine gun but it could only be a matter of time.

"Do it!" Jumbo commanded.

Saffron took a last look through the windscreen. There was a short patch of relatively clear ground up ahead.

"Take the wheel, please, sir. Just keep it straight. Don't move it."

Wright leaned over to hold the wheel. Saffron rested her right arm on his shoulder, aimed through the open passenger window of the Italian car and fired four rounds in quick succession.

"Thank you sir," she said. "I'll take the wheel again now."

———

Frescobaldi knew he had another magazine. He had thrown a bunch of them into the car as they all leaped in to chase the British. But as he scrabbled around the footwell, with the car bouncing up and down like a whore's bedsprings, he couldn't find the damn thing.

When the four shots came they were so much quieter than the clatter of his Breda that he barely heard them above the noise of the engine, the wind and the crashing of the car against the rough ground. But then he saw his driver jerk back in his seat as two rounds hit his head.

The wheel slewed as the dead man lost his grip. The car swerved off course, ran at full speed for a further fifty meters, with every man inside it shouting out in panic, and smashed into the side of a massive boulder, twice the height of a man.

The car burst into flames. Frescobaldi pushed at the door beside him with all his strength but the frame was buckled and the door would not budge and as the fire took hold of him Frescobaldi wished he had one last round in his gun.

For then he would be able to use it on himself.

———

Major Mason was dead by the time that they finally reached Major General O'Connor's headquarters. As his body was pulled from the car, O'Connor approached his visitor and said, "Good heavens, Jumbo. You look like you got yourself into a bit of a scrape."

"Yes," Wilson agreed. He looked over toward the car. Saffron was sitting on the ground, exhausted, her hands wrapped round a much needed cup of strong, sweet tea. "It was that slip of a girl over there who got us out of it, you know. She put four rounds into a man, cool as a cucumber, never seen anything like it. Tell me, Dick, do you suppose it is technically possible to mention a female civilian in dispatches?"

"Not sure, to be honest. I dare say no one's even considered the possibility."

"Seems only right, somehow. She'd probably be picking up a medal if she were a soldier and a man."

There were men in both the British High Commission and the military headquarters in Cairo whose jobs involved the filing of discreet reports to units in London that did not officially exist. Mr. Brown had asked these operatives to keep him posted on any interesting news about Saffron Courtney. Her exploits in the desert certainly qualified as that and Mr. Brown devoured the reports of the incident with great interest. Saffron's ability to keep her head when others were panicking, and her willingness to shoot an enemy dead impressed but did not surprise him. She was, after all, known to be a good shot and any girl who willingly threw herself down the Cresta Run clearly had an appetite for danger.

Moreover, from the first time he met her, something about Saffron had given Mr. Brown the impression that she might possess a character trait that was surprisingly rare in the population at large: the ability to kill another human being at close range, face to face. In times of peace, such an ability was not to be encouraged. But when the nation was at war it became an essential commodity.

That Saffron could kill when her own life was in danger had now been established.

But can you kill in cold blood?

That was what Mr. Brown now wanted to know.

General Archibald Wavell, the British commander-in-chief in the Middle East, was in ultimate control of every British,

Imperial and Allied soldier, sailor and airman in North Africa, the Eastern Mediterranean and the Middle East, including Palestine, Iraq and Iran. In February 1941 yet another country fell into his sphere of influence and he summoned Jumbo Wilson to his office in Cairo to discuss it.

Wavell was not a small man. He had a strong, square jaw and, though his hair was gray, his eyebrows and mustache were still dark. He had lost his left eye fighting at Ypres in the First War, but his right was still sharp enough. He was, in short, as imposing as his rank suggested, but still he was dwarfed by the height and bulk of Jumbo Wilson.

Wavell was Wilson's boss. On the other hand, Wilson was two years his senior in age. More significantly they were both very senior officers and so when they met in private they cast the formalities of rank aside and talked as old friends.

"I've got a job for you Jumbo," Wavell began. "Think there's a promotion in it, full general, if you play your cards right."

"That certainly sounds interesting. What's the score?"

"As you know, the Greeks have done a terrific job against the Italians in Albania, given them a hell of a bloody nose. Now Mussolini's gone bleating to his big brother in Berlin, asking Hitler for help, and it seems he's about to oblige. The Greeks are convinced there'll be German invasion in the spring and have asked for our help."

"I hope we've said that we're awfully sorry but we're rather busy at the moment. So no can do, but we wish you the very best of British luck."

Wavell winced in discomfort at what he was about to say. "Not exactly. A view has been taken that Greece is now our only ally left standing in Europe so we can't just stand by and watch them fall beneath the jackboot, too. So we're sending the First Armored Brigade, the first New Zealand Division, the sixth and seventh Australian Divisions and the Polish Brigade to Greece, and I want you to be in charge of the whole show over there."

Wilson said nothing.

"You don't seem overwhelmed with enthusiasm," his commander-in-chief observed.

"Well, I'm very grateful for the job, Archie, of course I am. Appreciate you placing your trust in me and so forth."

"You've earned it."

"But, for pity's sake . . . Sending so many of our best units off to Greece, undermining our forces here, it's just madness. Surely those fools in Whitehall can see that."

Wavell sighed. "I'm afraid it's more the fool in Downing Street that's the problem. Winston's determined to open up a Balkan Front and he sees Greece as the place to do it. It's not just a matter of keeping Greece out of German hands. He's also got it into his head that we can use air bases in Greece to bomb the Romanian oilfields and cut off Germany's best source of fuel."

"A Balkan Front?" Wilson repeated incredulously. "God almighty, you think he'd have learned his lesson at Gallipoli. Someone has to talk some sense into him, or we'll have another disaster as bad as that one on our hands."

"I don't disagree with you, but the Prime Minister must have what the Prime Minister wants."

There are times when a man continues to plead his case, even when he knows that the effort is futile, simply because he cannot quite believe that anyone could be so foolish as to disregard it. Major General Wilson was now such a man. "But it's obvious, surely, that we've got our hands full here in the desert, particularly now that the Germans have joined the party. We're not just facing a bunch of Italians any more. Rommel's a damn good general—he proved that with the 7th Panzers in France. What's more his troops are tough, battle-hardened and, above all, used to winning. But they're not invincible. Not if we hit him with everything we've got. He'll have the devil of a time keeping his army supplied, for one thing. Every gallon of fuel for his tanks, every drop of water, every bullet will have to be brought hundreds of miles along the coast road by truck. We can beat him, Archie, you know we can, but only if we have all the men and equipment we need for the job."

Wavell knew that he was sending Wilson on a fool's mission. He also knew that, having sent him, his own chances of defeating Rommel would be greatly reduced. And both men knew that they were now likely to be held responsible for defeats in campaigns that could not have been won. But in the meantime, Wavell had his own orders to obey and that meant packing Wilson off to Greece.

"I agree with you, Jumbo, honestly I do," Wavell said. "We have a terrific chance here in the desert to send the Germans packing and show that we can actually go up against them in the field and win. But Winston has decided that Greece is the new priority. He's like a child in a toyshop . . . "I want that one!" "No, I want that one!" And he must have his way, whether we like it or not."

"So what's the plan?"

"There'll be troop convoys leaving Alex for Piraeus every three days, starting from the first week in March. The Navy will provide escorts, of course. Meanwhile John D'Albiac is heading up the RAF side of things. Once his chaps are set up in southern Greece they'll be able to provide air cover, too, if needs be."

Wilson frowned thoughtfully. "That's less than a month from now. I'm going to need to be on the ground with my staff by the time the first men get off their troopships."

"I agree."

"Then I'd better get started."

"Good man," Wavell said. "And Jumbo . . ."

"Yes?"

"Don't you worry. Whatever happens over there, I'll make damn sure it's not held against you."

———

A number of Luftwaffe fighter wings were withdrawn from their bases on the Channel coast at the New Year of 1941 and sent to Poland to start intensive training. They were never told exactly what they were training for, but it was perfectly obvious from the huge build-up of forces just behind the easternmost border of the Reich, army as well as air force, that an invasion of Russia was on the way. But then, just when it seemed that they might at any moment receive the orders that would send them into action against the Ivans, they were suddenly sent in another direction.

"This is strictly between you and me, but I've heard we're off on a jaunt to the Balkans and Greece," Dieter Rolf told Gerhard, one evening in the officers' mess. "It appears our Italian friends have got themselves into trouble and we've got to pull them out of it."

"Won't that hold up the, ah . . . the other big push?" Gerhard asked—for security's sake it was best not to say the word "Russia".

"It may well do. But that's not our problem, is it? We'll be flying over the Parthenon in a month or two."

"Wonder if we'll be able to take some leave in the Greek islands? That would be nice."

"I'll say . . . Oh, by the way, I've got a letter for you from home."

Gerhard took it. He waited until after dinner, barely able to suppress a smile as he thought of the joy he would feel when he read Saffy's letter. Then he raced back to his bedroom, slammed the door behind him, ripped open the envelope and ten seconds later collapsed onto the bed.

He didn't know how long he spent sitting on the edge of his mattress, head in his hands, sobbing helplessly. At one point, he heard the door open, a couple of footsteps into the room and then Schrumpp saying, "Sorry, old man, didn't mean to disturb you." At some point in the night he fell asleep and had terrible dreams in which Saffron appeared, except that he could never see her face, or get any closer to her, no matter how hard he tried.

The following morning Gerhard walked into the mess. He couldn't face eating breakfast, but he very badly needed coffee to jolt his brain back to life. He didn't say anything and nor did anyone say anything to him. They were all used to the constant presence of death. For all the Luftwaffe's triumphs, the squadron had lost almost half its original complement of pilots over the past eighteen months of war, and many of those who had survived had lost brothers and friends who were serving in other areas of the Wehrmacht, or family members killed in air raids and accidents at home.

It was best not to dwell on these things. Best to let a man come to terms with his loss and then carry on as normal. There would be time enough for mourning when the war was over. So Gerhard said not a word. But his heart was broken and his soul scarred.

Saffron had been his love, his hope, his redemption. Without her, those things were gone. And without them, what was left of him at all?

———

Wilson was hard at work, planning, executing and supervising the movement of more than three full divisions of troops, with the prospect of more to come if the fighting became as serious as expected. Saffron found herself shuttling up to Alexandria and back as her boss and his senior staff officers met with their naval equivalents. In between those trips there was an endless round of visits to all the units that would be involved in Operation Lustre, as the expedition to Greece had been titled, more meetings with Wavell and more trips to Alexandria.

Wilson himself was due to fly from Cairo to Athens in the final days of February. Less than a week before his planned departure date, Saffron still didn't know if she would be accompanying him. Finally she plucked up the courage to ask.

"Been thinking about that myself," Wilson said. "No denying

you might come in handy. I can always get a chap to drive me, but you know my ways, what to say, when not to say anything, all that kind of thing. Don't want to have to train someone else. So my conclusion is yes, you will come. But I'm not letting you anywhere near the fighting."

"But sir . . ."

"No "but sirs" about it, young lady. This is going to be hard, bloody fighting and the front line is no place for a woman, even if she can shoot straight. Once the balloon goes up, I'll be packing you off to Athens. You can make yourself useful there. And if things go badly and Jerry puts us on the back foot, I want you taking the first available aircraft or ship back to Alex."

"Yes sir," said Saffron, grudgingly.

"That's an order."

"Yes, sir."

———

There was a war on, an Empire to defend and the myth of British invincibility to uphold, so the English language newspapers always did their best to find the most positive possible interpretation of any bad news from the front. But even so, Leon could see that the Greek campaign was going badly and his fears were magnified a thousand-fold by the knowledge that Saffron was over there, doubtless perilously close to the fighting and in danger of capture, injury or even—though he made a conscious effort to avoid brooding on this possibility—death. Late one evening, barely a week after the first German forces had crossed the Greek border, Leon found himself summoned to General Wavell's Cairo headquarters. As one of the leading English businessmen in Egypt, with interests across Wavell's sphere of command, Leon had crossed paths with him once or twice at social events, but they had never had any professional dealings with one another. But here was one of the general's staff officers calling up at half-past ten to inform Leon that a car was on the way to pick him up, making it politely, but very firmly clear that this was an order, not an invitation, and adding, "It would be a great help if you knew where all your ships were at the moment, so if you need to call anyone to find out, I advise you to do so right away."

Leon didn't need to ask. He held regular morning and evening meetings to check on the whereabouts of Courtney Trading's fleet of six oil tankers and a dozen merchantmen of various sizes. Thus far, they had not lost a single vessel, unlike vessels on the North Atlantic run, whose every move was tracked by wolf packs of German U-boats. For the sake of the men who crewed his ships, quite apart from the state of his company bank balance, Leon intended to keep it that way if he possibly could.

Wavell sometimes preferred to wear civilian clothes when working late and so, on this chilly April night, Leon found the C-in-C sitting at his desk in a checked jacket and a white-spotted burgundy silk scarf, neatly tucked into a dark blue woollen jumper. The desk was covered in papers, but still there was evidence of a neat, ordered mind in the row of pens and pencils neatly lined up in easy reach to Wavell's right, and the blotter, ashtray and glass paperweights distributed as carefully as divisions on a battle-plan.

"Ah, Courtney, good of you to come at such short notice," said Wavell, removing a pair of tortoiseshell reading glasses as he stood to greet his guest.

They shook hands and Wavell indicated that Leon should sit down on a leather-backed chair that had been placed opposite the desk.

"It's late and I'm sure you'd rather be at home in bed, so I'll get straight to the point. What I am about to discuss with you is a matter of grave importance and absolute secrecy. I trust I can count on you to respect that."

"Absolutely."

"Good man. Now, I dare say you've been following events in Greece."

"Yes. Reading between the lines of the newspaper reports, one gets the impression that things are not going well."

"That is putting it very mildly indeed, Courtney. Between you and me, the situation is disastrous. The Greeks had most of their army up in Albania, to the northwest, fighting the Italians, and the rest to the northeast, on the Bulgarian border. Field Marshal List sent the German 12th Army charging right between them, smashed the entire front to pieces in a matter of hours, typical *blitzkrieg* stuff. Now half of their forces have swung west to trap the Greeks on the Albanian front. The other half's swung southeast, cutting off the Greeks on the Bulgarian front, and raced to the sea at Thessalonica. We begged the Greeks to mount an orderly retreat from Albania before they were completely cut off, but they simply refused to give a single inch of it back to the Italians. So now they're being pounded by a couple of crack SS divisions and they'll have to surrender within days, possibly even hours."

"What about our chaps?" Leon asked. "I admit, I have a personal interest. My daughter Saffron is General Wilson's driver."

"Hmm . . . can't be easy for you. My boy's a subaltern in the Black Watch. One worries, can't help it. I'm sure Jumbo will do his very best to get her out in one piece, but I must tell you, it's not looking good. We're falling back in as orderly a fashion as possible, but we're having to leave supply dumps—rations, petrol, even ammunition—and now Jerry's using our materiel to supply the troops attacking us."

"Will we be able to get our chaps out of the country? It sounds like we're on the way to another Dunkirk."

"Quite so. I fear the resemblance will extend to all the tanks and artillery pieces abandoned by the roadside as we run to the sea. You know, we hadn't even finished putting our chaps on the ground when the German offensive began. Some units have been getting off their ships and re-embarking before the tide has even turned because there's simply no point trying to get them to the front."

"How long do we have?"

"A couple of weeks, at most. We might still be putting up some kind of a fight by the first week of May, but it could equally well be all over by then. That's why I need you to help me with the greatest possible urgency."

"Of course, General, what can I do?"

Wavell took a cigarette from a silver box on his desk, which he then offered to Leon, who declined. He lit the cigarette and smoked it for a few seconds while he composed his thoughts.

"One of the less, ah, publicized issues raised by Herr Hitler's acts of conquest concerns the gold reserves of the nations he seizes. To be frank, neither we nor the governments of the countries concerned have had much luck keeping that gold out of Nazi hands. We don't want to make the same mistake with Greece. Our aim is to get it out of the country, across the Med, through the Suez Canal and down to South Africa before the Germans even know it's gone."

"You'll have a hard time doing that if the Germans are moving as fast as you suggest."

"Agreed. The chances of completing the entire journey before they reach Athens are very small. But if we could at least get it through the Canal, I would feel very confident of reaching Durban and from there taking it by train to Johannesburg."

"And you want me to supply the ship that carries it."

"Precisely."

"Might I ask why you aren't entrusting the job to a naval vessel rather than a merchantman?"

"We are desperately stretched, Courtney, I'm sure I don't need to tell you that. I simply cannot spare a single destroyer, or even a frigate to undertake a mission that would take it thousands of miles away from the front. But just as importantly, I want to do this on the QT. The Germans do their damnedest to keep track

of all our warships, just as we try to do of theirs. A single merchantman, on the other hand, is a much less visible proposition."

"I see. And how large would this cargo be?"

Wavell took a last pull on his cigarette, stubbed it out and
said, "I am led to believe that the Greek reserves weigh somewhere in the region of one hundred and thirty tons. A ton of
gold is currently worth around four hundred thousand pounds
sterling, making the value of the reserves rather more than fifty
million pounds."

Leon gave a long soft whistle. "That would buy Hitler a lot
of new tanks."

"About five thousand, and all their spares as well," Wavell
replied.

"I take it that if you can't spare a destroyer to carry the gold
then you certainly won't spare one to escort the ship that does."

"Even if I could, I wouldn't. It would rather give the game
away, don't you think?"

"In that case I insist that my men have the ability to defend
themselves. They'll need anti-aircraft guns in particular."

"Again, I would argue that the less one does to draw attention
the better. We haven't got time to mount any Bofors guns, let
alone train your chaps to use them."

"Let me be blunt, General. I am willing to send one of my
ships to pick up that gold. I'll even give you the best I've got
available. She's the *Star of Khartoum*, so called because my late
father ran supplies into Khartoum when General Gordon was
under siege there, back in '85. Seems apt that she should be
doing this job now, and she's well-suited for it, too, because
she's only a couple of years old, built to my specifications at
the Swan Hunter yard on Tyneside and powered by a Parsons
Marine Steam Turbine engine producing ten thousand ship
horsepower. She can get from Athens to Alex doing twenty
knots all the way, and that's allowing for all the ballast she's
going to have to carry."

"Why carry extra weight?" Wavell asked. "Surely you want her to be as light as possible?"

"No, you don't, not if, as you say, the whole point is to be inconspicuous. If the *Star*'s only got a hundred-odd tons of gold in her holds she'll be riding awfully high in the water and any snoop hanging around the waterfront is going to ask himself why a ship flying the Red Duster is leaving Greece with nothing aboard when we have so much kit and so many people who need extracting."

"Fair enough. When can you leave?"

"Just one moment. I have two conditions. The first is that I am not sending my men into harm's way without at least some means of defending themselves. Manning a Bofors may be beyond them, but there's no reason they can't fire a machine gun. The Navy mount Vickers point-fives in groups of four as short-range anti-aircraft defense. I'll have six of those mounts, if you please."

"Well, I'll have to have a word with Admiral Cunningham and see—"

"The only words you have to have with Cunningham are, 'That's. An. Order.' I'm sure he'll take the point."

"I'm sorry, Mr. Courtney, but I really don't take kindly to being spoken to in this way."

"And I don't like the idea of informing the families of good, brave men that their sons and husbands have died because they had no means of defending themselves against attack. There's fifty million in gold sitting in a vault in Athens. If you put the guns on the dock at Alex by 08.00 tomorrow, I'll have the *Star of Khartoum* on her way by midnight and into the dock at Piraeus forty-eight hours after that. I'm assuming the Germans won't have got there by then, of course."

Wavell seemed to hesitate.

"Fifty million pounds," Leon repeated. "Worth the loan of a few Vickers guns, I'd say."

"Very well, you will have your guns. Now, you said you had two conditions. What is the second?"

"It's not a condition, so much as a piece of information. I'm going to Greece on my ship."

"There's really no need. Arrangements are already being made for the gold to be brought to the dockside and loaded."

"Damn your gold, General. I'm going there for my daughter."

Wavell looked at him. "Mr. Courtney, I must advise you, in the strongest possible terms, not to do that. You could be placing yourself and your daughter in very grave danger indeed."

"I understand, General. But my daughter is already in danger and I would feel a very great deal happier if I could do my bit to get her out of it."

"It is possible, you know, that you might be making her position worse, rather than better. I quite understand a father's desire to help his child, particularly a female one. But you should ask yourself why you are doing this. Is it really for her sake, or for yours?"

"Are you officially advising me not to go?"

"Yes, Mr. Courtney, I am."

"Well, I note that advice, but I must tell you that I reject it."

Wavell shrugged, and for a moment Leon caught a sign of the profound mental exhaustion, the accumulated burden of so many life-and-death situations carried out in such stressful circumstances that accompanied his level of command.

"Very well then, I have done my bit to help you. Now you must go and do your bit to save your girl."

———

"I'm sorry, Leon, but you can't have the *Star*," Francis Courtney protested. He looked at the other men around the table at the morning shipping review, looking for signs of support. "She'll be fully laden with finest quality Egyptian cotton, bound for Bombay, there to be made into bed-linen fit for a Maharajah."

"Good, then I won't have to worry about ballast. Anwar . . ." Leon looked at Courtney Trading's shipping manager. "Please tell the chaps at the dock to clear the Number Two hold, just for'ard of the engine room. And assemble every maintenance man, welder and fitter we've got by the ship. Any minute now a convoy of trucks is going to turn up, laden with machine guns, courtesy of the Royal Navy, and we need to get them positioned. I'll be driving up to Alex as soon as this meeting is finished and will supervise the job when I get there."

"Yes, Mr. Leon."

"Good man. I'll tell you where I want them mounted before I leave here, so they can get down to work right away."

Francis wasn't giving up. "This is outrageous! We can't go around arming our ships like a bunch of pirates."

"Since that is precisely how our forefathers made their fortunes in the first place, I really can't see the problem. I have agreed with General Wavell to send the *Star* to Greece. I will discuss the matter further with you in private, but for now all I will say is that I am satisfied that we will be giving sufficient assistance to the war effort to justify the risk involved."

"That is a practically new ship and you know as well as I do that if she is damaged or sunk, the compensation we will receive will not come anywhere near covering the cost of replacing her."

"I am well aware of that, Frank."

"Well then this is gross irresponsibility and I must protest as both a shareholder and director of the company."

"I really don't think we should be having this argument in public, Frank. So let me just say this. If Hitler should win the war, then it really won't matter what our balance sheet looks like, will it?"

"I don't see why not. Herr Hitler has always made his respect for the British Empire plain. I am sure he would see no reason to wreck its economy or harm its commercial interests. Of course, he would want to bring our activities into line with his economic policies, as any leader does, but . . ."

"That's defeatist talk, Frank, and I won't have it. Gentlemen, our meeting is at an end. As the chairman and leading share-holder, I am ordering the *Star of Khartoum* to sail for Athens at the soonest opportunity. This meeting is at an end. Frank, I'd like a word with you. In private."

Leon waited until the others had left the room, furious that he had given Frank the opportunity to speak as he had: reports of it would be all over the company by the end of the day, demoralizing the majority of workers who were loyal to the Allied cause and encouraging those few, and Leon knew there must be some, who secretly hoped for Nazi victory.

Finally the door closed behind the last man to leave and Leon turned on his brother. "How dare you? How dare you come up with your ghastly pro-Nazi propaganda in front of other members of staff? Anyone listening to that might have thought you wanted the Germans to win this blasted war . . . Maybe you do . . . well . . . do you?"

"No, no, of course not . . . far from it," Frank blustered. "It's no secret that I'm disappointed that we have entered into what I believe to be an entirely unnecessary conflict. We allowed ourselves to become ensnared in Polish attempts to provoke Berlin and declared war at a time when there was no threat whatever to British or Imperial interests. It was a grave mistake in my view and is causing us to waste the Empire's human and material resources on war, when they would be far better served in peaceful trade and economic activity. And I cannot for the life of me see why anyone would think that opinion was unpatriotic."

"You are, I suppose, entitled to your view on government policy. The freedom to express contrary views is one of the things we're fighting for. Not much of it in Germany, I fancy. But now that the war is here, and we have to win it, we all have a duty to do whatever we can to help the war effort, and that includes you."

"How in God's name is sending one cargo vessel to Greece going to help the war effort?"

"I'm afraid I am not at liberty to tell you that. I gave my

word to General Wavell that I would not discuss any of the details of the voyage or its mission."

"You're sending our fastest ship to a country that is rapidly being overrun—"

"There's no reason to suppose that."

"Oh, don't be ridiculous, Leon. I can read Arabic and believe me the Arab papers don't pussyfoot around bad news the way the English ones do. The Germans have us on the run, again. So Wavell wants you to get something or someone out of there before they march into Athens. I think I have a right to know what it is that you're putting in one of our ships."

"Ask Wavell, why don't you? He can decide if he wants to tell you. Meanwhile I will be going to Greece with the *Star*, so you will be in charge while I'm gone."

Francis's face suddenly brightened.

"Yes, I thought you'd like that," Leon said. "But it's purely a question of day-to-day management. No major decisions are to be made without my specific approval. And if I hear you have been expressing even the slightest lack of faith in our eventual victory, by God I'll horsewhip you out of the building."

"I shall ignore that threat and the slander behind it. Neither does you any credit whatever, Leon."

The phone at the head of the boardroom table by Leon's chair rang. He walked over and picked it up. It was Anwar: "The guns have arrived at the dockside, Mr. Leon. I am told there are six trucks carrying the guns and another two with ammunition and mounting equipment. If you could please tell me where the guns are to be placed, I will make sure the work begins at once. I am told the Navy has also supplied men to assist the fitting of the guns and also a dozen men to fire them. They insist that this is better than having untrained seamen who must, in any case, attend to their own duties."

Leon could see the sense in that, and appreciated the generosity of the offer. Wavell must have made it clear to Cunningham that total cooperation was required. "Very well," he said, "I want all the Navy men dressed in exactly the same clothes as our chaps. Can't have them standing out. As for the positioning of the guns, it's very simple. One set should be mounted in the bows, and another in the stern. The remaining four go up on the top deck, above the bridge, one on each corner."

"So that they form a square around the funnel?"

"Exactly."

"It will be done as you instruct. And Mr. Leon, I wish you a safe voyage."

"Thank you, Anwar."

"Will Miss Saffron be returning with you from Greece?"

"I sincerely hope so."

"Then may God the all-powerful and all-merciful watch over her on her journey."

————

Within the hour, Leon was on his way to Alexandria. At lunchtime, Francis informed his secretary that he would be out for an hour or so.

"Lunching at the club, are you, sir?" she asked.

"Something like that, haven't decided exactly where yet."

"Very well."

But the moment he left the Courtney Trading office, he did not head for any of the agreeable clubs and restaurants which the leading members of the British community in Cairo patronized. Instead he went to the Old City, into the backstreets where few white faces were seen, bound for the restaurant where he could leave a coded message for Hassan al-Banna. Its contents would be transmitted to Berlin by methods Francis was more than happy not to know. He assumed that the forward listening stations of the Afrika Korps could pick up a transmission from Cairo, sent at a particular time on a specific frequency, and then pass the message on to Berlin. But that was really not his problem.

————

Leon was very nearly as good as his word. The *Star of Khartoum* cast off from the Alexandria docks at ten minutes past midnight. Once the captain, Jerry McAloon, a tough Ulsterman, pickled by sun, salt and alcohol, had seen the ship into open water and checked that a full blackout was being observed, he sat down with Leon and the Navy sub-lieutenant in charge of the gunners. His name was Jamie Randolph, his chin looked as though it had never had need of a razor and he seemed barely old enough to order a round of drinks in a pub, let alone command men in battle. But Leon remembered his own early days in the King's African Rifles and realized he had been no older when he took charge of his first platoon.

"Let me get one thing straight, Randolph," McAloon growled. "I don't like mixing merchant sailors with Navy men. Leads to trouble in my experience. But I'll have no fighting on this ship. Do I make myself clear?"

"Perfectly, sir," Randolph replied, looking the skipper in the eye and not flinching in the slightest.

"I know I can control my men. What I want to know is, can you control yours?"

"I'd be a poor officer if I couldn't. If there is any disorder on board, it won't come from my men."

McAloon looked at the youngster with the first glimmers of respect.

"Make sure that it doesn't," he said.

———

As the *Star of Khartoum* was cutting through the waters of the eastern Mediterranean, bound for Piraeus, a young woman working in a building near the Buckinghamshire village of Bletchley, some fifty miles northwest of London—a building whose very existence was as closely kept a secret as Britain possessed—finished her translation of the decoded German signal to which she had been assigned. She took the English version of the text to her supervisor. He read it and at once understood the significance of the signal's contents, for he had been briefed to expect something like it and to call a number in Whitehall if and when it came through.

The man on the other end of the line listened with interest to the contents of the signal before saying, "That's excellent work. Well done." He then turned to a colleague, a much older man, and said, "They know."

"Already? That's very fast."

"Well, let me clarify that. To be precise they know enough to be able to work out the rest for themselves."

"Do they have the name of the ship?"

"Yes."

The older man sighed. "Then I pity the poor souls aboard it."

―――――

A year after he and his comrades had followed an invincible army through the Low Countries and northern France, Gerhard von Meerbach found himself doing exactly the same, though this time through Yugoslavia and Greece. It was incredible how little the British or their allies seemed to have learned, how unprepared they were for the decisiveness of the Wehrmacht's offences. Once again, enemy armies were outflanked, encircled and forced to surrender, or to run from the closing noose as fast as their legs and wheels could carry them.

In the air, the story was just the same. When the Luftwaffe had taken on the RAF in the skies over England, Gerhard had felt for the very first time that he was in a battle of equals. But here in Greece, the British flyers were hopelessly outnumbered and forced to operate from inadequate airfields without the central organization that had made them so effective in the summer of 1940. The campaign barely seemed to have begun before it was over and yet another vast expanse of sky belonged to the Stukas and the 109s.

The other pilots were jubilant at the ease of their victory, but Gerhard took no pleasure from it. They flew every day across clear blue skies, but without Saffron the sun had gone from his life and the world around him was dark.

"Cheer up, Meerbach," said Schrumpp after they'd come back from yet another successful mission. "You got another kill today. You should be strutting around like the cock of the walk, not moping about like a miserable old woman. What's got into you?"

Gerhard did his best to smile. "*Ach,* it's just too easy. I prefer to have more of a challenge."

"Well I prefer to shoot down the enemy with as little trouble as possible." Schrumpp grinned. "But then again, I'm just a builder's son from Frankfurt. I dare say you Bavarian aristocrats have different standards, eh?"

"Precisely." Gerhard raised his head, looked down his nose at Schrumpp and in his most lordly tones said, "Now run along and get me some schnapps, there's a good man."

"Oh yes, sir, absolutely sir!" Schrumpp said, bowing and scraping.

"Well go on then, get a move on!"

Gerhard managed to maintain the pretence of good humor as Schrumpp laughed and went off to the bar. But as soon as his friend had gone a few paces he slumped down into a battered armchair.

Ah, Schrumpp, what a decent, innocent, good man you are, he thought. *I don't want the enemy to be a challenge. I want them to be good enough to kill me.*

———

"Courtney! . . . Driver Courtney!"

Saffron opened her eyes to see a harassed-looking man in a crumpled linen suit, the top button of his shirt undone and his tie askew, trying to force his way through the crowds of people in the foyer of the British Embassy. Every Briton in Greece was trying to leave the country and they all seemed to think that the route out led through the embassy, as if its harassed staff could somehow produce tickets for aircraft, when none were flying, or ships, when all civilian passenger ships had long since sailed away. They weren't the only ones hoping for a miracle. There were Jews, some of whom had already been forced to flee once from other conquered countries; artists, writers and intellectuals who knew they would be marked men under the Nazis; citizens of other Empire nations who looked to the mother country for help in their hour of need. All had congregated at the embassy. And there was no help that could be given to any of them at all.

That the Germans had been victorious did not take anyone by surprise. From the moment he had first sent his troops into the Rhineland, five years earlier, Hitler had never once faced an opponent he could not defeat. But even now the speed and inexorability of *blitzkrieg* warfare took people by surprise. Just eighteen days had passed since the first German soldier crossed the Greek border and now the war was almost over. Trucks filled with exhausted, filthy, demoralized Allied troops, many of them bloodied or bandaged, had been spotted heading for Porto Rafti, fifteen miles east of Athens itself, en route to the naval ships waiting to carry them back to Alexandria. They had to leave from there, people said, because the city's main port at Piraeus had been all but immobilized by German bombing.

How long would it be before the Germans marched through the streets of Athens? No more than a day, surely: two at the most. Saffron had been given orders to get out, and Wilson had repeated them when he paid Athens a flying visit to confer with the King of Greece and confess that his country was lost. She had been assured by some of the diplomats that her best way out was to leave with them, under cover of diplomatic immunity, after the Germans had arrived. "Dress up in civvies and we'll say you're one of the secretaries," a young diplomat had told her. "Even the Nazis can't touch anyone who works for the embassy."

Saffron had decided to count on that and not worry about even trying to find another way out, for there was none. And even if there were, she had no time to spare to find it. She had been working flat out, driving diplomats and other British worthies to and fro across the city, or just helping deal with the chaos at the embassy, making endless cups of tea for all the people crowded into the halls, corridors and even outside in the garden.

"Driver Courtney!" the man in the linen suit called again.

Saffron rubbed the fatigue from her eyes, got to her feet and called out, "Yes, sir," waving as she did so.

The man saw her and forced his way through the crowd toward her. "There you are!" he said. "Got another taxi ride for you. Off to the Bank of Greece again, usual two passengers. Dare say your old Humber can drive itself there by now!"

"I should think it can," she agreed, for she had indeed been making regular visits to and from the spanking new Central Building on Panepistimiou Street over the past few days, always taking the same two men. One was a thin, balding, mustachioed fellow by the name of Watkins who said, in his fussy little voice, that he was a Bank of England official, though what he was doing in Athens was hard for Saffron to imagine. The other was a much tougher, smoother, more dangerous, and clearly (in his own eyes at least) more seductive figure called John Swift, who said he was a Second Secretary at the embassy.

"Watkins doesn't speak Greek," Swift had explained, on their first drive down. "It's all Greek to him, what?"

"Actually, I do have a little Ancient Greek," Watkins protested, "though that sadly doesn't seem to be much use in the present century."

"So I'm here to be his liaison with his opposite numbers at the Bank of Greece, make sure everyone has the right end of the stick."

"I see," said Saffron, whose own impression was that Swift carried himself a lot more like a military man than a diplomat.

He might be Watkins's translator, she thought. *I bet he's also his bodyguard. But why on earth would a meek little man like that need a bodyguard? Who would ever want to hurt him?*

She had slung her ever-present bag with its vital contents of wallet, gun and letters from Gerhard over her shoulder, gone to get the Humber and was standing beside it on the pavement outside the embassy when her two passengers appeared. They seemed more than usually preoccupied and got into the back of the car without a word. She closed the passenger door behind them and drove off. As the Germans approached ever closer to the city, the Greeks seemed to have vanished from sight. Almost everyone had retreated into their own homes, waiting with their families for the moment when the first of their conquerors appeared on the streets of their capital city. Though there was plenty of petrol for military vehicles, for huge supplies of fuel, food and ammunition had accompanied the Allied expeditionary force, in anticipation of a lengthy campaign, the civilian garages had long since run dry, so the journey to the bank had become a very swift one, particularly at this time of the evening, for it was past seven and the sun was starting to go down.

This time, though, was different. She passed two trucks, then a third and a fourth all going the same way as her. Three were military, one Greek and two British. The fourth was civilian, with the name of the firm that owned it written in Greek script on its sides. But all four were big vehicles, capable of carrying heavy loads, and they were heading in the same direction as her, past the National Gardens, cutting the corner of Syntagma Square and then heading down Panepistimiou Street itself. Parked to the side of the road, by the National Library building, there was a British armored car with a turret-mounted heavy machine gun and just beyond it two army trucks, surrounded by soldiers smoking, chatting and doing what Saffron had long since realized was what all soldiers do for most of the time: waiting for something to happen.

But by now the trucks that had been driving alongside her were slowing as military policemen were flagging them down and guiding them to the side of the road, each taking its turn in a line that began just outside the National Library, ran for a hundred yards or so up the road and came back down the other side toward the entrance to the bank itself. All along the way there were more police beside the parked trucks, sitting astride motorbikes.

Now Saffron herself was ordered to halt. She wound down her window as a policeman wearing a British uniform approached and asked to see her papers. She handed them over and added, "I'm driving these two gentlemen to the bank. They are expected."

Swift got out of the back of the car, approached the policeman and led him off to one side. Whatever he said must have worked because less than a minute later he returned to the car and said, "It's all sorted, Miss Courtney. You can drive on."

Sure enough the policeman was waving them through. Saffron followed the line of trucks, made a U-turn at the top of the road and came back down the other side, parking just ahead of another armored car, which was itself positioned in front of the first truck in line.

"Wait for us here. This shouldn't take long," Swift said as he and Watkins got out. It occurred to Saffron that Swift always did the talking for both of them, and that wasn't, she decided, because Watkins was naturally shy and retiring. It was because Swift was the man in charge.

Unless the weather was pouring wet Saffron had long since acquired the habit of waiting outside her car, rather than in. On a hot day in Athens, the rays of the midday sun were actually less brutal in the open air than being roasted inside a motorized tin can. So she stepped onto the pavement and looked around.

The entrance of the bank resembled a modern take on an

ancient Greek temple. It was all very clean, very simple: a white marble portico enclosed three high doorways, split by two classical columns. Normally the doors were closed, but this evening they were wide open and a stream of soldiers were coming out of two of the doors, pushing hand-trolleys laden with small wooden crates down the short flight of steps and then taking them along the pavement toward the trucks where other soldiers loaded them aboard. Then the empty trolleys were being taken back into the bank through the third door.

"Hey, Miss!" Saffron looked round to see the commander of the armored car, a sergeant, whose body was now poking up out of the turret. Now he clambered out, jumped down to the ground and walked toward her.

"Planning on staying here long, love?" he asked.

"Just until the gentlemen I'm driving have finished their meeting, Sergeant. They told me it wouldn't be long."

"Well you can't stay here, you're blocking the way and we're going to be on the move. Park up ahead, in that sidestreet. Right on the corner is fine, just so long as you're not causing an obstruction."

"Well, I'm sure I'd hate to do that."

The sergeant grinned. "You can obstruct me any time, love!" he said and she laughed, because the impish cheek in his eyes was a nice change from the fear, fatigue and panic she had seen in so many faces for so many days.

She got back in the car and did as he had asked. A couple of minutes later, the sergeant disappeared back into his turret and the armored car started up and slowly rolled down the street, past where Saffron was parked, followed by the leading trucks. About a dozen must have gone by before the line came to a halt. There were two trucks blocking the end of her street, but if she looked through the gap between them she could see the far end of the line, on the other side of the road, start to move.

The process was repeated half a dozen more times over the

course of the following two and a half hours. The sun went down and in the blackout the only illumination came from the dimmed torches of military policemen, guiding the men with the trolleys to the trucks they were loading, like ushers showing cinema-goers to their seats. Finally she could see the process was complete. Just as the final trucks were rolling slowly past her, followed by the army vehicles bringing up the rear, there was a tap on her window. It was Swift.

"I'd be very grateful if you could get us to the front of the column, please, Miss Courtney. Don't be afraid to drive on the wrong side of the road. We'll be going to Piraeus, incidentally. We need to be the first to arrive."

Saffron knew better than to ask why they were going to the port, or what was in the trucks. But the question was superfluous anyway. When a country that is about to be conquered empties the vaults of its central bank and sends them off to the nearest ship, it wasn't too hard to guess what those trucks might be carrying.

———

The chestnut trees along the Landwehr Canal were just coming into leaf opposite the headquarters of the Abwehr, a long, five-story, gray granite building with a red tiled roof that Hitler's spies shared with the *Oberkommando der Wehrmacht*, or OKW, the supreme high command of all his armed forces. The room where coded transmissions from agents working in the field were decrypted was on the fourth floor and looked out at the chestnuts through windows decorated with curtains and flounced valances that seemed more in keeping with an apartment's parlor than an intelligence agency's nerve centre. But it was here that the transmission from Cairo, passing on the information that the British had sent a merchant vessel named the *Star of Khartoum* to Greece to collect a valuable, highly classified cargo, was eventually decrypted. It had not been assigned a high priority. The Abwehr's masters at the OKW needed hourly updates about the status of the Allied forces

facing them on the battlefield in Greece. The suicide of the
Greek Prime Minister Koryzis, brought on by his shame at his
nation's collapse, had affected planning for the political administration of Germany's latest dominion. And even more important than either of those was the intelligence being gathered
in preparation for the imminent invasion of Russia and the
destruction of Soviet communism, the only cause that was even
close to being as dear to the Führer as the annihilation of the
Jews.

All that being the case, the *Star of Khartoum* was already
docked in the bombed-out remnants of the port of Piraeus by
the time that its potential significance was explained to Admiral
Canaris, the head of the Abwehr, at a meeting with three of his
senior subordinates. Canaris was a gentlemanly figure who
seemed out of place among the cold-blooded careerists, Nazi
ideologues and, as he was himself coming to realize, bloodthirsty
psychopaths who populated the higher echelons of the Reich.
But he had been a brilliant, daring junior naval officer in his
youth and now he was a cunning, sophisticated spymaster in
his middle age. One thing he was not, however, was impetuous.

"So, we know that this ship is sailing for Greece," he said,
having heard the contents of the signal from Cairo. "We know
that it is bringing a cargo of great value back to the British in
Egypt. The question remains, however: what precisely is the
cargo?" He held up a hand to forestall the words that might be
about to be spoken by any of the other three men around the
table. "And let me be the first to say, before anyone else does,
that it is very unlikely to be olive oil, retsina or Greek cheese."

The others produced the degree of laughter required of a
boss's witticism and one of them dryly inquired, "Do they have
anything else to offer?"

"Gold, of course," said a second man, somewhat impatiently,
for he was serious by nature and did not approve of tomfoolery
at work. "What else could it be? They are hoping to get the

gold out of Greece before we can seize it and we must strain every sinew to stop them."

"A very reasonable point, Hümmel," said Canaris. "I would say that there is at least a seventy-five percent chance, maybe even a ninety percent chance that you are right. But there is in my estimation one other cargo that the British might wish to take from Greece before we can take it back to Berlin: antiquities. They already have the Elgin Marbles. I am sure that they would be happier having the rest of the treasures of Ancient Athens under their own safe keeping than made available for inspection by the citizens of the Reich."

"I suppose that might explain why they have only sent a cargo ship," said Hümmel, conceding the point to a degree at any rate. "I must confess I have been asking myself: if I wanted to transport six hundred million Reichsmarks in gold, would I really just send a single cargo ship? Surely I would load it aboard my mightiest battleship, with more smaller warships around it, and make it impossible for the gold to be lost."

"Also reasonable," Canaris agreed. "But now I shall argue against myself. Consider the position of General Wavell and Admiral Cunningham. The expedition to Greece has turned out to be the disaster they must have feared, wasting men and equipment that would have been much better used in North Africa. What is their number one priority now: saving the gold? No. All their resources must be focused on a single task: getting as many of their men back to Egypt as they possibly can. And so where will they put Cunningham's cruisers and destroyers? Surely alongside the troopships. The gold they must now move in a very different way, as inconspicuously as possible. So they choose one small cargo vessel, for we surely will not pay attention to that when there are so many other more important targets for us to look at."

"Excuse me, sir," said the fourth Abwehr officer at the table, "but I do not quite understand what difference it makes what this British ship is carrying. Let us just sink the damn thing and let them worry about what they have lost."

"It matters, Friedlander, because we Germans are proud of being the most cultured race on earth. We did not bomb Paris before we captured it, for to do so would be an insult to the very European civilization we exist to defend. If we sank a boat containing priceless treasures of antiquity, we would be handing the Allies a propaganda coup. "Look at these Nazi barbarians!" they would say. "See how they treat the master-pieces of classical art." Goebbels would not be happy at having to counter that. Nor would all the professors and museum keepers who have made Berlin the world center of study into the antiquities.

"No, first we must beg General List please to speed up his advance to reach Piraeus before this ship leaves. If we capture the ship and cargo intact, that is the best outcome of all. At the same time we order our agents on the ground to observe the port as closely as possible. When this *Star of Khartoum* arrives, they must not let the ship out of their sight until they have established its cargo. Then if the army does not get there in time we act as follows. If the cargo is nothing more than old statues, we let it sail. Who knows, the way Rommel is going, maybe he will be on the quayside to greet the *Star of Khartoum* when it arrives in Alexandria. If the cargo is gold, we tell the Luftwaffe to sink the ship, at all costs. It would be bad enough for us not to have that gold. But for our enemies to have it would truly be a disaster."

———

General Wavell had done Leon a great favor. At the bottom of one of his dispatches to Jumbo Wilson he had appended a question. "What are whereabouts of your driver, Miss Courtney?" Wilson had countless better things to think about but it did not do to ignore a superior officer's questions, even if he was also a friend, so he replied, "Athens c/o UK Embassy."

This information had been passed on to the *Star of Khartoum*, from which Leon had radioed the embassy shortly after arriving in Piraeus and been told that his daughter had gone to the Bank of Greece, acting as driver for a Bank of England official and his embassy liaison officer. Leon knew what was about to be delivered from the bank. The chances were that the bank man would want to see the cargo safely aboard ship, in which case Saffron would drive him.

Still he had a nervous wait until the army Humber appeared, the only sign of its approach being the slivers of light from its taped-up headlights, and Saffron got out, looking as smart as ever in her uniform, and politely opened the door for her passengers.

Leon waited until she was finished and then called out, "Saffy!"

She started, looked around, peered through the near darkness and then a huge smile crossed her face as she cried, "Daddy!" and ran toward him.

"What on earth are you doing here?" she asked.

"Well, this is my ship, and as my daughter was at its destination, I thought I'd come along for the ride. Now, get aboard, I've got you a cabin for yourself, so you should be very comfortable."

"But I can't. I've got to take Mr. Watkins and Mr. Swift back to Athens."

"No you don't. Wavell himself has given me his personal permission to bring you back to Alex."

"Yes, but—"

"But nothing." Leon looked around and saw a man whose suit and tie did nothing to hide his toughness. This, it was perfectly obvious, was a man who knew how to look after himself. "That Swift?" he asked.

"Yes."

"Hold on a minute."

Leon walked over. "Mr. Swift? My name is Courtney. This is my ship. And your driver is my daughter. I have General

Wavell's permission to take her back to Alex. Do you have any objections?"

"Not at all. I can find the way back to Athens."

"You and your colleague are welcome to come aboard if you need a passage back to Egypt."

"Very kind, but no thanks. We've still got a few loose ends to tidy up and we'll both claim diplomatic immunity. The Germans won't touch us."

"Good luck to you then," said Leon. Then he shook Swift's hand and walked off.

———

"Hell and damnation!" cursed Swift, as he settled into the driver's seat and started up the car. "My orders were to get the Courtney girl out of Athens safe and sound."

"Well that's not going to happen now," said Watkins. "But don't blame yourself, old boy. What could you have done? Old man Courtney wasn't going to take no for an answer and you could hardly tell him to find another ticket home without giving the whole game away."

"I suppose you're right . . ."

"I know I am. In any case, you just have to look at the man to see he'd never even countenance deserting his own ship, and the girl's hardly going to leave her pater in the lurch, is she?"

"I know, but my orders were as clear as bloody crystal: Saffron Courtney gets out safe and sound. God knows why, but someone very high up is keeping an eye out for her."

"I don't blame them. What man wouldn't?"

Swift gave a smile that was more of a grimace. "No, it's not that. I think they have plans for her."

"Well then they're going to have to find new plans. Look, the thing I always tell myself in circumstances like this is: think of the bigger picture. One can't go compromising an entire operation, just for the sake of a single individual, or even a hundred individuals."

"I feel bad for her though. She was a damned good girl, that one."

"Oh yes, she was a cracker. But think of the bigger picture."

———

A German asset in Athens, whose cover was that of a left-wing Romanian journalist forced into exile in Greece, duly made his way to Piraeus. The one functioning wharf was ringed with armed guards. But the piles of rubble and the hollowed-out shells of warehouses and customs buildings that now littered the site provided plenty of cover and the blackout was a gift to anyone wishing to pass by undetected. So he had little trouble in getting to within fifty meters of the ship. What he saw was men handling shallow wooden boxes, no larger than the boxes of fruit one would find on a market stall. Whatever was in these boxes was a very great deal heavier than apples or peaches, however, for it was apparent in the way the men were carrying them off the trucks lined up along the quay and onto pallets that were then winched aboard the ship that this was hard, back-breaking work.

He made his way back to his attic apartment, pulled out a suitcase from underneath his bed and extracted his portable Enigma coding machine. Having translated his dispatch into meaningless and, so far as he knew, unbreakable gibberish, he used the radio hidden in his wardrobe to send it.

This time the men in the decrypting room in the building on Tirpitzufer wasted no time in dealing with the message. The news that the British were trying to take the Greek gold reserves out of the country was passed immediately to both the OKW and the Führer's office at the Reich Chancellery. Prompted by Göring's personal insistence that the Luftwaffe would deal with the issue, his most senior planners responded that there was not time to organize a night-raid on Piraeus of a size large enough to provide any likelihood of hitting a single, relatively small target in a blacked-out area.

They did, however, propose that a close watch should be kept on the target vessel so that its precise departure time could be reported. Sunrise would be at 07.32. By that point a Junkers Ju 86 P-2 reconnaissance aircraft, capable of flying at altitudes higher than any Allied aircraft could reach, with a sixteen-hundred-kilometer range that would enable it to sweep a huge area of the Aegean, would be in the air, ready to find the gold-ship. There were, the planners believed, only two courses the *Star of Khartoum* could possibly plot en route to Alexandria. Both began by sailing south, but then one veered to the west of Crete, through the Antikythera Straits, and the other turned toward the Kaso Straits to the east. The target vessel, however, would only have been steaming for a few hours by the time the Ju 86 began its sweeps of the area, so the two possible courses would not yet have diverged greatly. One spotter plane would therefore be sufficient to find the ship and lead a formation of Stuka dive-bombers and their fighter escorts straight to it. This was just as well, since the Luftwaffe only had a single Ju 86 in the Balkan theater of operations, but there was no need to tell the Führer that.

"The gold will not reach Alexandria, my Führer," Göring assured Hitler. "You have my word on that."

"You gave me, and the German people your word that not a single bomb would ever fall on the Ruhr. You did not keep it that time, Herman. Why should I believe you now?"

"Because by this time tomorrow we will know that all the gold in Greece is sitting at the bottom of the sea."

———

The agent who had sent the Abwehr news of the *Star of Khartoum*'s cargo was ordered back to the docks to report on its departure. It was three in the morning in Berlin when the message came in. The *Star* had left at shortly after two. The quarry was on the run. The hounds would soon be after it.

The men of Gerhard's squadron were roused from their beds

before first light and informed of a vital mission: a precision attack on a small target at the very outermost limits of their range.

Squadron Captain Rolf briefed them on their task. "The target is a British ship, carrying a strategically important cargo and, before you ask, no I don't know any more than that. But the orders have come from the very top, Göring himself has taken a personal interest, so it must be damned important.

"This ship will be almost five hundred kilometers to the southwest by the time we reach it. We'll be carrying droptanks with extra fuel, but even so, we'll have to be very careful. As for the Stukas, those lads will have to lean out of their cockpits and flap their arms because even with extra tanks they'll be flying on fumes by the time they're even halfway back. Our job, as always, is to escort our slow, fat friends, but once we get to the ship, we don't anticipate any RAF presence in the area, and they don't have any escort vessels there, so we can attack the ship ourselves. If we maintain a steady stream of strafing runs that will draw enemy fire, if there is any, away from the Stukas and let them drop their bombs right down the funnel.

"This strikes me as a tricky little assignment. On the face of it, the target is a sitting duck, all alone, bobbing up and down on the pond. But you never know, the duck may fight back, and it is, in any case, a very long way away and we have to be very conscious indeed of our fuel levels. So don't waste a drop doing anything you don't have to because I want all of you and your planes back here safe and sound in the evening when I read out the message of congratulations from Berlin."

Gerhard felt oddly cheerful as he climbed into his 109 and went through his routine of pre-flight checks. This mission felt like a pleasant change, an interesting technical exercise with an important target at the end of it.

"You seem very cheerful this morning, sir," one of the ground crew working on his plane observed.

"You're right, I am in a good mood," Gerhard replied. "It is a beautiful morning, not a cloud in the sky and I'm going to be up there soon myself."

———

The Ju 86 tasked with finding the *Star of Khartoum* had flown over what remained of the Allied ground forces and aircraft in Greece at an altitude of thirteen thousand meters, one and a half times the elevation of Mount Everest, so far above the earth that no one had the slightest notion of its passing. Now, as Homer's rosy-fingered dawn spread its rays across the wine-dark waters of the Aegean, the pilot brought the aircraft down to a mere six thousand meters, at which point he and his two crew felt they could cover a wide area of sea in a single pass, but would still be able to see a solitary vessel on the water.

Their cabin was pressurised, making the Ju 86 infinitely more comfortable than most military aircraft, and a Thermos flask of coffee was chasing any lingering, early morning bleariness from their systems.

For three hours they swept back and forth across the Aegean like an airborne pendulum that lengthened its string with every swing. But although they encountered plenty of troopships fleeing across the water and even received a few desultory rounds of anti-aircraft fire from the destroyers escorting the defeated, retreating army, there was no sign at all of anything that matched the description they'd been given of the *Star of Khartoum*.

"It has to be here," muttered the pilot. "I'm going to go back the way we came, flying the same pattern but in the opposite direction. Maybe if we come at everything from a different angle, we'll spot something we missed before."

"We didn't miss anything," the navigator argued.

"We must have done. We're almost two hundred and fifty kilometers southeast of Piraeus. That ship has been in the water for no more than nine hours. It would have to be doing almost thirty kilometers an hour to have gone any further than this. It's a cargo steamer, for hell's sake, not a torpedo boat."

"It's a steamer carrying a precious cargo and I bet the skipper and all his men are shit-scared. All alone on the water, no escort . . . I know what I'd do if I were them: run the boilers right up to the red zone and beyond and, if they burst, too bad. I tell you what else I'd do—stay away from all the other ships. They're going to attract attention. What do you bet the Italians have got submarines waiting for them? All the troopships we saw were heading to the west of Crete. I say we fly southeast and look for a ship going like a bat out of hell for the Kaso Straits."

"I call that a waste of time," the pilot insisted.

"Listen, we have nothing to lose. If we don't find that shitting boat we are going to get our arses kicked black and blue. We've got to fly back the way we came anyway, or we won't be able to get back to base, so if it is there, like you say, we'll spot it. But just in case it isn't, and while there's still plenty of fuel in the tanks, let's just try to see whether we can complete our mission successfully, eh Captain?"

"*Ja*, you're right, we have nothing to lose but our sore arses. Give me a bearing for the Kaso Straits."

Ten minutes later, they had just begun to start having their doubts when a cry of "I can see it! God in heaven, I see it!" burst into their headsets from the third member of the crew, who was perched in the plane's glazed nose with a perfect view in all directions.

And sure enough, about three kilometers to the south, steaming flat out at very nearly forty kilometers an hour, there was the *Star of Khartoum*.

———

The sea was clearer than any Saffron had ever seen, the crystal water shading from a deep, purple-black to the purest blues and turquoises she could imagine. The islands, so sudden and sharp, emerging from the water like the tips of drowned church spires, were a mosaic of white houses and white mills and black olive trees against the dusty, khaki earth. She would have loved to explore them with Gerhard one day. But there was nothing to be gained in letting her mind dwell on that. She was on a ship that was fleeing for its life and she did not have her lover beside her, but a bunch of sailors manning the machine-gun emplacements, bragging to one another about all the things they planned to do when they got back to Alex—the drinks they would consume, the tarts they'd screw—occasionally saying, "Sorry, Miss," when their language became too explicit.

If only you knew . . . Saffron thought. She wondered how many of the boys around her, for they were none of them yet true men, had even kissed a woman properly, let alone made love to one. Yet she had given every inch of her body to Gerhard, and taken every bit of him in return and her hips squirmed a little at the wetness those thoughts induced.

"Gorgeous day, isn't it?" an upper-class voice said over Saffron's right shoulder. She turned, looked over the top of her dark glasses and saw Jamie Randolph coming toward her. *Speaking of virgins . . .*

"Yes, pity to waste it on a war."

"Well, we seemed to have sneaked away without anyone knowing. With any luck we'll have a smooth passage back to Alex. I know it sounds silly, but I'm almost sorry. I was rather hoping my chaps might get a spot of real action. It's all very well training for hours on end, but none of us have actually been under fire, as it were."

"Then count yourselves lucky," she said and the tone of her voice made Randolph frown as he said, "I say, do you mean that you have?"

"Yes. Only once . . . but it wasn't something I'd choose to repeat."

"Well I should think not. Hardly the sort of thing a woman should have to endure. But as I was saying—"

"Wait a second," Saffron interrupted him. She screwed up

her eyes as she looked up to the sky behind the stern of the ship. "We have company."

"Where?" said Randolph.

"Off to the northwest, at high altitude. Follow the line of the wake, then go a bit to the right and look up. Do you see it?"

Randolph did as he was told, pulling the peak of his cap down over his eyes to shade them from the glare. "Hang on . . . can't see anything . . ."

Saffron stood beside him and pointed up into the sky to guide him. By now the two lads on the nearest Vickers battery had caught on to what was happening and were peering at the heavens too.

"I see it, Miss!" one of them said. "Look sir, just where the young lady was saying . . ."

"Got it," said Randolph. "Hang on . . . back in a jiffy . . ."

He disappeared off across the deck and down the ladder to the bridge. A minute later he was back bearing a pair of binoculars. He looked through them and his lips gave a little wince of frustration. "It's an aircraft all right, but I have no idea what it is. Doesn't look like anything I've ever seen before, not even on those diagrams one has to memorize. You know, the silhouettes of enemy aircraft."

"Can I have a look?" Saffron asked.

Randolph handed the binoculars over, conscious of the fact that this absurdly pretty girl, whom he'd approached in the hope of a bit of social conversation, maybe even mild flirtation, had turned out to have more battle experience than he or any of his men.

"I've seen that before," Saffron said, and now she was the one with a puzzled, frustrated look on her face, "but I can't for the life of me remember where or when. Not in the war, though, I'm almost sure it was before this all started."

She looked again. "Got it! I know this sounds silly, but I flew in a plane just like that once. I think it was a flight from Cologne to Munich . . . a girlfriend from school lived in that part of the world. I'm sure that's a German plane. But what on earth would an airliner be doing out here?"

"I think I can answer that," said Randolph, thrilled to have something he knew that she didn't. "After the last war, the Jerries weren't allowed to have bombers, Treaty of Versailles and all that. So they designed airliners that could be converted to be bombers. Typical underhand sort of trick those bloody Nazis go in for."

"Do you want me to take a pop at it, sir? Let 'em know we've spotted 'em?" the gunner asked.

"No, we'd only be wasting ammunition and I fear we're going to need every round we've got. Excuse me, Miss Courtney . . ." he cleared his throat. "Listen here, men. Jerry knows where we are. If he sent a plane all this way to find us, then it's because he thinks we've got something worth chasing on board."

"I should think 'e bloody does, sir, seeing as 'ow we've got the contents of the Bank of bleedin' Greece down there in the 'old."

"Well, I can't say quite what we've got, but I dare say you're right, Bowyer. The point is, they'll be coming after us. More aircraft, I imagine. If they're flying all the way from Greece, they'll be at the very outside limits of their range, so they won't hang around for long. We've got to make sure that while they're here, they don't get a decent shot at us. That means keeping clear heads and firing concerted bursts at specific targets, not just blazing away and hoping for the best. Now, check your guns, make sure they're all working. Tin hats on. Let's put on a damn good show, shall we? See if we can't impress Miss Courtney."

"Tell you what, sir, she don't 'alf impress us!"

"Perhaps you would like to accompany me to the bridge, Miss Courtney," Randolph said, "and leave these ruffians to do their worst? I'd better let the captain know we're expecting company. And then, if you don't mind, I will leave you. Need to pass the word to the chaps in the bow and the stern. Good to know that our presence here isn't being wasted, eh? That's the main thing. We've got something to do."

———

There was no point in changing course or trying to hide the ship somewhere among the islands. As long as the Germans had that plane, with its huge, triangular wings like black sails in the sky, circling high overhead, watching their every move, there was no possibility of escape. And so Captain McAloon took the complete opposite course of action. He had the radio operator send out their course, speed and position, along with the message that they were anticipating an imminent attack from the air. That way, with any luck, if the ship went down, any survivors might stand a chance of being picked up.

Saffron had been given a helmet and a lifejacket. She pinned up her hair and put the tin hat on top. There was still no sign of any more enemy aircraft in the sky so while she still had time she went to the ship's kitchen and asked the cook for some greaseproof paper, which she wrapped around her package of letters and photographs and over the barrel of her gun. Then she smeared a thick layer of lard over both wrappings to make them more waterproof. The cook also gave her a ball of twine which she wound like a cocoon around her bag. Then she slung the bag across her body and put the lifejacket on top. If she was going to die, there wasn't a lot she could do about it. But if she was going in the water, then she wasn't going to lose her most precious possessions.

Her preparations complete, she went back up to the bridge. Her father was there, talking to the captain, making plans for what they would do with the Courtney Trading fleet when they could finally get back to being a normal peaceful business again. "I wouldn't listen to a word my father says, Captain," Saffron said, going up to them and allowing herself the brief indulgence of wrapping her arm around her father's tall, solid, comforting form. "He knows perfectly well that when this ghastly war is over, I will be taking control of everything."

"I wouldn't be so sure of that, young lady," said her father, pretending to be cross. Then he squeezed her tight and kissed the top of her head, just as he had done when she was a little girl and she had exactly the same feeling that she had done then: that as long as her daddy was beside her, like a wall protecting her from any harm the world might throw at them, nothing could possibly go wrong.

Then Jamie Randolph walked down the ladder to the side of the bridge, came in and said, "They're on their way: Stukas, with an escort of Messerschmitt fighters. I estimate they'll be here in a couple of minutes. Better sound the alarm."

McAloon sounded two long blasts on the ship's horn and all over the vessel men snapped into action. Down in the engine room, the turbines were revved still higher and further beyond their limits to squeeze the last little bit of speed from them, for the faster they were moving the harder, surely, they would be to hit.

Men who had been assigned to fire parties took their positions, as did those who had the carpentry or welding skills to be able to make emergency repairs. Leon had taken the precaution of recruiting the firm's best medical officer for the trip and he was ready in the sick bay with a couple of orderlies. A silence fell over the ship as men retreated into their own thoughts, their own fears, their own love for all the people they had left behind and might never see again.

And then, like a breaking storm, the first Stukas hurled themselves at the ship and the battle began.

———

Saffron had heard the scream of diving Stukas on cinema newsreels enough times. It was the sound of the *blitzkrieg*, the sound of the Nazis crushing everyone in their path. But nothing had prepared her for the sheer volume and almost physical aggression of that banshee shriek, rising in pitch and volume, the sound echoing around the bridge as the first three planes dived down toward their prey, rising to a shrieking, hysterical climax just before the Stukas released their bombs, one after another, no more than a few seconds apart, flattened out their dives and rose again into the sky.

For the first few minutes, this was a battle she heard, more than saw. The frantic chatter of the Vickers guns, desperately trying to fend their attackers off; then the roar of the German fighter planes and the hammer of their cannons as they made their runs, trying to silence the guns on the *Star of Khartoum* so that the Stukas could finish off their prey at their leisure; the roar of Captain McAloon's voice as he shouted out the commands that sent the helm spinning this way and that as he tried to make the ship dodge and swerve in a bid to make the dive-bombers miss.

And it worked. The first three bombs all missed, sending up huge geysers of seawater that crashed down like waves onto the *Star*'s decks but did no serious harm. But still some damage was being done. The fire crews had been sent to put out a blaze ignited by one of the Messerschmitts' incendiary rounds in the afterdeck house by the stern of the vessel. The rear battery had been mounted on the deck house roof. The blaze had to be extinguished before they were forced to abandon the guns.

Then Randolph reappeared in the cabin. His face was white with shock and pain and his left arm hung, bloodied, limp and useless at his side.

"Three of my lads are down. One of the gun batteries is out of action. The guns work, just don't have anyone to man them. Can you spare me anyone, Captain?"

McAloon didn't even acknowledge that he had heard Randolph. It was very likely that he hadn't. The cacophony of battle was deafening and the captain was at the very limit of his powers, just trying to keep his ship moving forward.

But Saffron heard. "We'll do it," she shouted back. She looked at Leon. "Come on, let's go!"

He paused for a moment, as if about to tell her to stay under cover, but then he nodded and followed her out.

"The guns fire in two pairs, one gunner for each!" Randolph shouted as he led them up the ladder, finding it hard to keep his balance with only one hand to hold the rails. "Don't worry about ammo, they're self-loading. There are two hand-wheels. One makes the gun mounting rotate. The other controls the elevation of the guns. You'll get the hang of it."

Coming up behind Randolph, Saffron put her dark glasses back on, feeling that the gesture was oddly frivolous but knowing that she would be able to see much more clearly if she was not screwing up her eyes against the glare of the midday sun off the glittering sea. They reached the top deck. Two hours ago, when Saffron had been sunning herself and watching the view, it had seemed like a lovely, airy place to be. Now she felt utterly exposed, with nothing to protect her from the bullets and bombs as she dashed across the deck, following Randolph to the silenced gun battery. There was a dead man lying on the deck at the base of the guns and another semi-upright, his feet on the ground but his torso draped across one of the drum-shaped magazines that contained the ammunition. Saffron recognized the sailor who had said that she impressed him. Half his skull was missing and brain matter was dribbling down the remains of his face and onto the top of the magazine.

Randolph did his best to make himself heard as a Messerschmitt roared across the bows, aiming for the guns there. "You'll have to move them!"

Her father took the one who was standing, heaving him out of the way. Saffron grabbed the lying man under both armpits and dragged him backwards so that she had room to get past him and stand behind the guns.

The 109 that had strafed the bows came back for a second

run. Somehow the men behind the guns down there had survived the first run and they were still firing as the pilot swooped down and came in at them again, so low over the water that he was firing directly at the gunners, and they at him, like duellists with banks of machine guns, rather than single pistols to fight with. And then one of the gunners was hit, his body jerked by a series of impacts in lightning-fast succession that drove him backwards, with the back of his lifejacket disintegrating in a bloody mess as the bullets went straight through him. He took one step back, then a second and finally a third before he fell, his legs bent under him, his arms flung out to either side, his dead eyes looking up at the German fighter as its racing shadow passed across his corpse.

"Try your wheel!" shouted Leon.

Saffron reached down to the wheel. It was about a foot wide, mounted horizontally atop a steel rod, with a vertical handle for her to grip. She rotated the handle clockwise and saw the barrels of the guns point up: counterclockwise and they came back down.

"My turn!" Leon said and he got the feel for the identical control that made the guns rotate. They each had a gunsight, fixed parallel to the guns, with an eyepiece and a round sight, criss-crossed with aiming wires about two feet beyond it.

"Ready to give it a go?" Leon asked.

Saffron nodded.

"Right. The bow is twelve o'clock. To the left is nine, to the right is three, to the stern is six. OK?"

"Yes!"

Overhead the Stukas were circling, waiting for the fighters to finish their job. Another of the 109s began his run, determined to finish off the bow battery, coming in from the opposite direction to the previous plane.

And the guns in the bow were pointing the wrong way. Saffron and Leon saw it at the same time, the sole surviving gunner dashing round to his dead comrade's position, frantically turning the abandoned wheel so that he could bring the guns round to bear on the incoming plane.

But he wasn't moving fast enough.

"Three o'clock, low!" Leon yelled.

He put all his strength into turning his wheel as fast as possible but the guns seemed to move with agonizing slowness. Saffron was working her wheel anti-clockwise, bringing the guns down until the end of the sight was pointing barely twenty feet above the bow deck.

The 109 raced toward the *Star of Khartoum*, closer and closer.

"Wait!" shouted Leon.

The plane was speeding over the waves, its guns firing.

"Wait!"

The man by the Vickers flung himself to the deck as the bullets ricocheted off the steel deck and the bow rails.

The plane was so close Saffron could actually see the leather helmet and goggles of the pilot in his cockpit.

"Fire!"

The hammering of the four guns battered Saffron's eardrums, but then, in the blink of an eye, the plane was past them, keeping low for a couple of seconds and rising up into the sky as it climbed and banked and prepared to come back in again.

"Keep that elevation. Don't think we were far off him. I'll bring us round for the next go," Leon said as the guns tracked back across the bows.

While they had been occupied at the front of the boat, another plane had been attacking the stern. Suddenly, behind them they heard an explosion. Saffron turned and saw that the entire stern section of the ship was ablaze. She could not see the afterdeck house at all for all the smoke. But then she spotted a figure emerge from the inferno, apparently walking in the air. She realized he must be on the deck house roof, which meant that he was one of the gunners. And he was ablaze, a walking torch, his arms waving, beating at his body in a futile attempt to keep the fire at bay. He stumbled and fell to his feet and then the flames engulfed him as they gathered him into their white-hot embrace.

"Saffron! Saffron!"

She heard her father's voice as if from a great distance and turned to see the 109 coming in for another run. The bow gunner was curled up on the deck, his arms wrapped around his head, his nerve broken by the repeated assaults.

Saffron forgot about him. She looked through her sights, imagining she was out on a shoot and that the Messerschmitt was really a pheasant or a duck and that she shouldn't find this metal bird any harder to kill than the real one.

Leon had been thinking much the same thing. Having turned his guns toward the attacking aircraft, he now planned to bring them back again, moving ahead of the 109's course, knowing that its speed would bring it into his sights and that the motion of the guns would throw the hail of half-inch rounds in a wider arc, like the pellets from a shotgun, increasing their chances that some at least would hit.

The plane came in.

Once again they waited.

And then, when she judged the moment right, without waiting for an order, Saffron fired.

Gerhard was impressed. The first three Stukas had gone in expecting an easy kill, but the British had made this harder than any of them had expected. The *Star of Khartoum* was surprisingly fast and agile, moving through the water more like a warship than a normal cargo vessel and she had sharp teeth with those machine-gun nests. So the 109s had gone to work, knowing they had to act fast to neutralize the guns, for every few seconds spent over the target cost the Stukas another kilometer of range.

Schrumpp had gone in first to take out the guns in the bow and almost finished the job. Now it was Gerhard's privilege to apply the coup de grace. His first run peppered the area around

the guns and sent the one remaining man there diving from
his post. Now he intended to put a few of the shells from the
20mm cannon mounted in the nose into the guns themselves,
disabling them and possibly even setting off their own ammunition.

He pulled on the joystick and climbed, turned, came over
the top of the arch he was creating in the sky and now he was
racing back down again, feeling the pressure of the dive force
him back into his seat before he flattened out and came in again.
He positioned the nose of the plane absolutely in line with the
bow guns and fired the cannon and the machine guns in his
wings, seeing the tracer bullets home in on the target. Gerhard
saw the entire gun battery ahead of him rocking with the impact
of his rounds. There was fire coming in at him from the upper
deck of the ship to his right. He looked toward it and saw a
figure behind one of the machine-gun nests. It should have
been a man. But in a fraction of a second he saw black hair,
dark glasses, a woman . . . a ghost.

And then the plane was hit.

Gerhard felt the punch of heavy machine-gun bullets smashing into his wings.

All his other thoughts vanished as his entire concentration
was focused on the here and now. First question: was he all
right? He looked down and saw no blood. His limbs were all
working. He was unhurt.

He was past the ship now, climbing again and his controls
seemed to be functioning and then he heard Schrumpp's voice
in his ear: "You're on fire, Meerbach! Your right drop tank!"

He looked down at the wing and saw the flames blazing from
the tank. He didn't think twice. The tank had to go before the
fire spread to the wing itself. Gerhard pressed the release button.
Nothing happened. He pressed again. Still the tank remained
fixed to its position, the flames now growing. If it got any worse
there was a danger the whole tank could blow.

Gerhard suddenly felt a clawing fear in his guts. He wasn't

at a high enough altitude to bail out, but if the plane hit the sea he was a dead man. And all of a sudden his indifference to death, his loss of interest in life had disappeared. His natural survival instincts would not be suppressed. He desperately wanted to live.

Bu the damn tank still wouldn't release.

In a final desperate act he started working his flaps at random, shaking one wing and then the other up and down. He could see flames now licking along the edge the wing. He threw his plane into every contortion he could think of, veering from left to right and then climbing into a vertical ascent, praying that the force of gravity would rip the tank from its moorings, still waggling his wings as he rose.

The rate of ascent slowed as the propeller steadily lost its battle with gravity. He was almost at stall speed. But Gerhard did not pull out of the ascent. He forced the plane to claw its way higher. Any second now the tank would blow, or the plane would stall. Either option would kill him.

I mustn't die. I refuse to die!

And yet he was going to die.

But then he felt a jolt, and the plane lightened as the tank finally broke free, and it was the drop tank that fell into the Aegean and Gerhard who pulled out of the ascent into a controlled dive, letting the wind over his wings blow out the last lingering flames before he flattened out.

But now there was a problem. About twenty percent of his remaining fuel had just disappeared into the depths.

"Everything all right?" That was Rolf.

"I think so," Gerhard replied. "There doesn't appear to be any damage to the controls, engine's running fine. Fuel is my only issue."

"Then don't waste another drop. Head for home. Take it nice and easy. And good luck."

"No, it's all right, I want to see this through," said Gerhard and banked his 109 to circle over the stricken vessel. By his rough calculation he had enough fuel to carry him three hundred kilometers.

His base, however, was almost four hundred kilometers away.

His only hope was to begin his return journey immediately and yet something inside him, that same instinct that had so recently demanded that he should live, was now telling him to stay. It was madness. He had to go. And yet he stayed, and even as the Messerschmitts finished their attack runs and then peeled away toward the Greek mainland, and the last of the Stukas dropped their bombs, Gerhard remained over the smoking, sinking *Star of Khartoum*.

———

"Got him!" Saffron grinned exultantly as she saw the flame burst from the German fighter as it flashed past her. She watched the pilot's desperate attempts to get rid of the burning tank that could at any second destroy him and followed his ascent, still frantically shaking his wings. When the tank finally plummeted to the sea she felt cheated, deprived of the kill she deserved, and when she saw the pilot start circling over the ship, like a spectator wanting to see the end of the game, she was seized by a bitter, helpless anger.

But there was no time to think about that any more. The other 109s were coming in from all sides now, aiming for the deck on which she and her father stood, trying to take them out of the battle, just as they'd dealt with the guns fore and aft. Two more of the machine-gun batteries went down: one more man killed, three too injured to fight on. Saffron heard the angry mosquito sound of bullets fizzing through the air around her and the clamor as they hit the wood and metal around her but she and her father remained miraculously untouched.

Then the fighters had gone, disappeared up into the sky again, and for a second there was nothing but the noise of the ship's engines, the sea against the hulls, the cries of the wounded and the shouts of the men still fighting the fire in the after deck house.

She dared to ask herself: *Is that it?*

And then she heard the answer in the wail of the first Stuka. She looked up and saw it falling through the air, at one and the same time utterly modern and horribly primitive: a shrieking steel pterodactyl coming to kill them, screaming its glee at the prospect of her death.

Leon wheeled the guns round to face the monster. Saffron brought them up to full elevation and they fired a long burst but saw no evidence that they'd hit the target. And now a second Stuka was peeling off the formation and then a third, and it was clear that they were all going to attack now and it suddenly became very plain to Saffron that some of them might miss, and one or two might even be hit, but one would get through. But there was nothing to be done but to keep firing, fighting back as the first bomb went wide, and then the second.

The third bomb hit. Saffron watched its bulbous black form drop from the Stuka and head straight for the afterdeck. It landed. It buried itself in the planking.

But it did not explode.

The relief was so intense, the release of tension so absolute that it was almost exhausting. But then another Stuka was coming in and the fear and adrenaline energized Saffron again and she fired and thought she saw her tracer bullets ripping into the Stuka and sure enough the cockpit was smashed to pieces and the engine had burst into flame. But the siren was still wailing and the Stuka was still diving.

And it was heading straight for the top deck.

Saffron hurled herself toward the ladder, but did not bother climbing down it. She just jumped for the small patch of deck at the bottom of the ladder, next to the bridge and as her feet hit the planking and she stumbled and fell to the ground the Stuka hit the *Star of Khartoum* and the whole world seemed to explode around her.

The blast blew out the windows of the bridge and if Saffron had not fallen when she hit the deck she would have been killed by a thousand flying shards of razor-sharp glass. She blacked out for a moment and when she came to the ship was on fire. It took her a few seconds to get her bearings and work out what had happened. The Stuka had hit the upper deck on the far side of the ship from where she had ended up, so she had been sheltered from the worst of the blast. And as soon as she understood that, the next thought hit her. *Daddy!*

She clambered back up the twisted, buckled frame of the ladder and when she got to the top was met with a scene of total devastation. The funnel that had stood in the middle of the deck had been almost totally destroyed. Only a jagged stump remained, belching oily black smoke. The remnants of the Stuka were embedded in the side of the main deck house, with the tail, which was somehow still intact, sticking up at an angle. Three of the gun mountings were lying scattered around the deck. The fourth had disappeared completely.

But where was her father?

Saffron looked around, trying to make anything out through the choking smoke. Then she saw him. He was facedown on the deck, pulling himself forward, one leg struggling for purchase while the other dragged along, motionless beside it. Beyond him, just visible through the smoke, there was a slick red train of blood smeared across the deck.

Leon looked up. His face was ashen as he struggled to prop himself up on one elbow. He reached an arm toward her and mouthed, "Saffy!"

She put a hand over her nose to give her some feeble protection against the smoke and ran to her father. He had collapsed back down onto the deck and rolled onto his back, barely conscious, his gray cheeks and forehead wet with sweat, gritting his teeth, his features contorted into rictus of pain. And now Saffron saw the source of his torture, for his right trouser-leg had been torn open, the flesh beneath it shredded as though some wild animal had been tearing at it with crimson teeth and claws, and right at the heart of the terrible wound, standing proud of the rest, were the broken, splintered, jagged-edged remains of Leon's thigh-bone.

Saffron felt the sickness rising in her gorge and the tears springing to her eyes. *No! You can't be weak! Not now!* she told herself. So she bent down over him and said, "Don't worry, Daddy, I'm here."

Then she grabbed him under the armpits and, with her back to the ladder, started heaving back toward it. The two ends of her father's broken bone rubbed together and he could not help himself: he screamed in pain. Saffron forced herself to be deaf to his agony. She just pulled all the harder.

The *Star of Khartoum* was mortally wounded, that much was obvious, but the Stukas' orders had been to destroy it, so two more of the planes dived down and one missed, for the smoke was so thick that the target was hard to see. But the other hit, at virtually the same spot as the unexploded bomb. But this one went off and that finished the job.

The ship was sinking fast. Its fate was sealed and meanwhile the Stukas were past the safe limits of their fuel consumption. Their commander gave the order to return to base and they headed back, accompanied by their faithful fighter escorts. The second bomb had killed everyone by the stern of the boat and caused terrible damage in the engine room too. Barely anyone on the ship was still left alive. But the lad by the bow gun had come unscathed through the whole inferno, just as Saffron had done. He saw her up on the top deck trying to drag her father to safety and helped her get him down the ladder and then another to the lifeboat deck. A couple more survivors, including the ship's doctor, had gathered there and were struggling to get at least one lifeboat into the water before the *Star of Khartoum* went down.

They made it, just, and were able to row about fifty yards from the ship before it finally gave up the ghost, split in two and sank.

The doctor did his best to tend to Leon. He had grabbed his medical bag before running for the lifeboat, reasoning that he might have wounded survivors to deal with, and was at least able to pour some disinfectant on the open wound and give him enough morphine to ease his suffering a little.

Then Saffron heard the drone of an airplane engine. In all the chaos and the noise she had not realized that there was still one solitary German fighter up there, the one she had hit, still circling above them.

"What's he doing?" she asked, to no one in particular.

The doctor looked up, saw the 109 and muttered, "Bloody vulture." Then he shook his fist and shouted a string of foul-mouthed curses at the sky. "I do apologize," he said to Saffron, reverting to his normal, civilized self. "Doesn't make a blind bit of difference, but at least one feels a bit better."

Then one of the other survivors, Bowyer, the ship's rating whom Saffron could remember bantering with Captain McAloon before the battle said, "Uh-oh, doc, I think the bugger heard you. Look out, he's coming our way."

————

What am I doing here? Why am I wasting fuel for no good reason?

Now that the adrenaline of combat had dissipated, Gerhard felt that bleak, depressive emptiness return. His mind went back to the vision he had seen, the delusion of a woman where no woman could be. His mind was playing tricks on him. Fate was taunting him. Slowly the emptiness inside him filled with acrid, vengeful bile. He wanted to lash out at any target he could find, just so someone else could feel as bad as he did.

Gerhard banked his plane into a turn that took it around the pathetic little lifeboat that contained the last few survivors from the sunken ship. As he dived out of the sun, flattening out just a few feet above the sea, he knew that he was betraying every principle he had, wilfully casting aside any shreds of decency and honor that he still possessed and joining his brother and all the black-hearted bastards like him in the legion of the damned. And he didn't care.

The lifeboat was rushing ever closer. He could see the people in it pathetically waving their fists. One quick blast from the 109's guns would obliterate that tiny boat and every man inside it. Gerhard's finger tightened around the trigger.

And then he saw the ghost again. Black hair. Black dark glasses.

His first instinct was to fire, and keep firing until the ghost was blown out of his mind's eye for good.

But a millisecond later something told him, "No, don't," and then he flashed over the lifeboat without firing, soared up into the sky, looped around and swooped down into another dive, back the way he had just come.

"Go on then, you Nazi bastard! If you want to kill us, here we are! Just get on with it!"

Bowyer's voice was near hysterical with desperation. The pilot was toying with them, taunting them. He could kill them whenever he wanted. So why didn't he?

"Here he comes again," said Saffron. Faced with certain death, she found that she was blessed by an unexpected sense of calmness. Everything was going to be all right. She was going to be with Gerhard again, where there was no war to keep them apart, and everything would be all right.

She kept her eyes fixed on the plane and stood to greet it, standing quite still, offering herself as a sacrifice.

The ghost was her! Gerhard knew it was impossible, and yet that figure standing so tall in the hull of the lifeboat, shaking out her hair, looking straight at him . . . that was Saffron. He knew it as sure as he knew his own self. *She's alive! My God, it's true, she's alive.*

He slowed the plane down until it was as close to stalling

speed as he dared go, then he slid back the canopy of his cockpit, feeling the wind rushing at his face like the breath of life itself. As he flew over the lifeboat, Gerhard waved. He could have sworn he saw her smile.

Then he was past the lifeboat and now he really couldn't make another fly-past. His fuel status had been critical before he had decided to remain over the ship. Now it was disastrous.

Gerhard didn't care. Saffron Courtney was still alive. Love and hope came surging back into his heart. So what if his 109 had no fuel? He didn't even need a plane. He could fly back to Greece all by himself, on the wings of joy itself.

*   *   *

"Good Lord," the doctor said, "what an extraordinary thing to do. Do you suppose he was saying, "Well played?" You know, for putting up such a good fight?"

"Jerry don't say things like that, doc," Bowyer said. "Not 'is style at all. Nah, I reckon it was more like taunting us. Unless . . ." A sly, cheeky grin crossed his face. "Well, if you don't mind me saying, Miss . . ."

Saffron didn't even hear him. She was still trying to come to terms with what she had seen, or thought she had seen in the cockpit of the passing plane. She didn't know whether to whoop with joy, or cry bitter tears at the endless cruelties of fate.

"Miss . . . ?" Bowyer repeated.

Saffron forced herself to pay attention to the people around her. "What is it?" she asked.

"I was saying you looked such a picture, standing there, like a proper film star or summink . . . I reckon our Kraut chum took one look at you and thought even he couldn't go shooting a girl like that. I mean, what a waste, eh?"

"It certainly would take a very bad man indeed to shoot an unarmed young woman in cold blood," the doctor agreed.

Saffron had not said a word. But then the thought struck her that she had not been unarmed, not when it mattered. *I hit that plane with my guns. And if it was Gerhard's plane . . . No, it was, I'm sure it was, why else would he have waved at me? . . . Oh God I almost killed him. And I'd never have known what I'd done, or how close he had been. And if I had killed him . . .*

And then she broke down in tears, and the doctor put his arm around her shoulder and said, "There-there, my dear. It's all right. We have all had the most terrible experience and you have behaved quite remarkably. But it's over now. We shall soon be rescued, I'm quite sure of that. Everything is going to be all right. Just you wait and see . . ."

* * *

It was early evening before a Royal Navy motor torpedo boat, sent from Crete in response to Captain McAloon's signals, finally found them. As Leon was being hauled aboard, the doctor took Saffron to one side and said, "Your father is very badly wounded. Provided the wound does not get infected he should live, but whether he'll ever walk again is another matter."

Saffron did not reply. She was too physically and emotionally drained by the battle and its aftermath to formulate any words. A sailor helped her aboard the torpedo boat and she was given a cup of tea, that standard British cure-all for any disaster, great or small. As the brew worked its magic, Saffron opened up her bag and gave a rueful shake of the head. After all the precautions she had taken and all the hell she had been through, those carefully wrapped and greased possessions had never even had a single drop of water on them. She took out one of her precious photos of Gerhard and hunched over it, so that she could look at him without anyone else knowing. It was wonderful to think that he was still alive.

But then Saffron shook her head again and put her petty treasures away as she reminded herself of all that had been lost.

The pride of the Courtney Trading fleet had been sunk. Many good men had lost their lives, and it had all been for nothing. Greece's gold was lying on the sea floor hundreds of feet beneath them and no one was ever going to find it again.

Gerhard ran out of fuel about ten kilometers north of Athens, still a hundred shy of his base. By then, though, he had risen slowly and steadily to an altitude of seven thousand meters. When the engine cut out he just let the plane glide, remembering his first glider flights over Bavaria, savoring the absolute peace and quiet after all the clamor of battle, letting his mind relish the image of Saffron, standing so proudly, so bravely and so, so beautifully in that boat, staring death in the eye, and not realizing she was actually looking at love.

Mein Gott! If I had pressed that trigger . . . But I didn't, and that's all that matters now.

He felt quite calm as his inexorable descent continued. All he needed was a reasonably straight stretch of road, even a flat field would do, though there weren't many of those in the rocky, mountainous Greek countryside. For weeks now they had been looking at maps of Greece as they were briefed for one mission or another and he knew that there was a highway that ran parallel to the coast. He looked down from his cockpit and sure enough there it was, with exactly the kind of straight he needed about ten kilometers up ahead.

The Messerschmitt came down over an advancing formation of tanks and men, skimmed the last couple of trucks with millimeters to spare and landed on an empty patch of tarmac. It came to a halt another couple of hundred meters down the road, slewed diagonally across the tarmac.

Gerhard got out of the cockpit, undid his lifejacket and the silk scarf round his neck, then took a packet of cigarettes out of his jacket. Smoking cigarettes, he had discovered, was as inevitable a part of going to war as bad food and bullets. Up ahead he saw another mass of men and armor coming toward him. An open staff car detached itself from the column and raced toward him and an officer got out. Gerhard saw the shoulder tabs of an *Oberst*, a full colonel, on his uniform. He slid down from the plane, threw his cigarette away and snapped to attention.

"What the hell do you think you are doing here?" the colonel asked.

"I was on a mission, *Herr Oberst*. My aircraft was hit and I lost a lot of fuel. I could not return to my base and so I landed on this road, instead."

"Well you're blocking the way. I've got to get an entire division to the outskirts of Athens by nightfall. So I order you to move your machine."

"I'm very sorry, sir, but I am unable to do that. As I say, I have no fuel. If some can be found and your men back up a little bit, I should be able to take off without too much trouble."

"Back up? We haven't backed up for the Tommies. Why the hell should we retreat for you?"

"Alternatively, sir, the land on either side of the road is quite flat. It should be no trouble for your armored vehicles and trucks to go around the aircraft."

"I hope this mission of yours was worth it," the colonel said, grumpily.

"Oh yes sir," said Gerhard, as a triumphant smile crossed his face. "We sank a British vessel that was carrying a cargo of great strategic importance. The mission was ordered by *Reichsmarschall* Göring himself. He will be very pleased by its success."

The colonel took the point. This cocky fly-boy, with his kills painted on the side of his aircraft and his Iron Cross around his neck, was protected by Göring himself.

"I will have my radio operator order some aviation fuel to be brought here as soon as possible. I expect you to leave here as soon as you have been refuelled."

"Of course, *Herr Oberst*, that will be my pleasure."

But until that time, Gerhard thought. *I will sit on my plane, smoke my cigarettes, and think about the girl I love.*

All in all, this had been one of the better days on which to be at war.

————

Visiting time at the hospital was restricted to set hours in the morning and afternoon. In the fortnight since he had been brought back from Crete to Egypt, Harriet had tried to spend every minute that she was allowed by Leon's bedside, but she was also conscious of the need to prepare their house for his eventual homecoming. The surgeon who had operated on Leon's leg was confident now that it would be saved. But it would be several months before he could even think of walking and even then there was still a possibility that he might be confined to a wheelchair. In either case Harriet would have to make the house easier for him to navigate, and do it before he left the hospital, for she feared he would be too proud to admit he needed help when he finally did come home. So it was that one morning she was at home, rather than the hospital, talking to an architect about replacing steps with ramps and adding hand-rails to help Leon guide himself, at least in the early days, before he acclimatized. Saffron, however, had taken her place and was sitting at her father's bedside when there was a knock on the door.

"Shall I see who that is?" she said.

Leon nodded.

She went to the door and opened it to find a fresh-faced, bespectacled man in an army captain's uniform. He didn't seem to Saffron's eyes to be more than three or four years older than she was.

"Oh," he said, when confronted by a beautiful young woman in a summery cotton frock, looking at him with limpid, dark blue eyes.

"Can I help?" she asked, since the captain seemed incapable of making any further conversation.

"Ah, yes, absolutely, of course . . . My name's Carstairs, Military Intelligence. Just wondered if I could have a word with Mr. Courtney. I have some information that I have been asked to pass on to him."

"Then by all means come in, Captain Carstairs."

He advanced a few paces into the room and stood at the end of the bed while Saffron closed the door behind him.

"Excuse me, Mr. Courtney," Carstairs said, "but what I have to say is rather hush-hush. It concerns the sinking of the *Star of Khartoum*. For your ears only, as it were."

"May I ask you a question, Carstairs?" Leon asked.

"By all means, sir."

"Have you ever been in action? I don't just mean: have you served in a campaign, back at headquarters? I'm talking about the rough stuff, the sharp end, where people get killed."

"Ah, no sir, I can't say that I have. I'm more of a desk-wallah. Analysis of intelligence is my game."

"Have you analyzed a newspaper lately?"

"I'm sorry, sir, I'm not quite with you."

"Well, there have been a few stories in the Cairo press about my daughter's actions on the *Star of Khartoum*, fighting off the Luftwaffe. People are saying she deserves a medal. So if you have anything to say about that voyage, then you can say it to her as well, or not at all. Do I make myself clear?"

"Yes sir, absolutely. Might I ask you, Miss Courtney, may I count on your absolute discretion?"

"Of course."

"Very well then. My message is this . . . You may have become aware that the cargo loaded aboard the *Star of Khartoum* was . . . how can I put this? Of unusual value, let us say."

"I am," Leon agreed.

"And I dare say that the knowledge that this cargo has been lost added considerably to the, ah, distress that you might have felt at the sinking of your ship and so many members of its crew . . . and, of course, your own personal injury, sir."

"You might say that, yes."

"It may even made you wonder whether it was all worthwhile," Carstairs said, and the silence that followed confirmed
his supposition. He cleared his throat and spoke again. "What
I have to say may, I hope, reassure you that you have, in fact,
made a much greater contribution to the war effort than you
know. You see, the thing is, the cargo you believe was on the
Star of Khartoum was, in fact, ah . . . elsewhere."

"What do you mean?" Saffron exclaimed.

"I mean that your ship was a decoy. The real cargo was on
another vessel and has now reached its destination safely, every
ounce of it."

"But that makes it worse, not better. All those men were
sacrificed for nothing!"

"No," Leon corrected her. "It means that the *Star* was risked,
and eventually sunk so that the real cargo could get through.
That was an entirely worthwhile mission. My only question to
you, Carstairs, is, how did you know that the Germans would
take the bait?"

"Well, we left a few clues for them: for example, all those
trucks lining up outside the Bank of Greece where prying eyes
could see them. In reality, the transfer was made several nights
earlier, much more discreetly. And even more importantly, perhaps, we had reason to believe there could be a leak from our
end, either here in Cairo, or at the harbor in Alexandria, or
even from the vessel itself."

"You mean a spy in our midst?" Leon asked.

"Something like that, yes."

"One of our own people?"

"Possibly, or someone else with a reason to support the Nazi
cause. There are plenty of nationalists, Jewish as well as Muslim,
who want to see the back of us and their enemy's enemy is
their friend."

"Jews supporting Hitler?" said Saffron. "That hardly seems

likely. I've been to Germany, Captain. I know what life is like for Jews there."

"But not for Jews here, Miss Courtney. Most of them are perfectly friendly to us, but there are some Zionists who want us out of the whole region, Palestine in particular, but Egypt too. Of course, they hate the Muslim radicals even more than they hate us and the feeling is entirely mutual. So if or when we ever leave, they will merrily start slaughtering one another. But for now, we are their common enemy."

"Well, I wish you luck in finding your man, Carstairs," Leon said. "If there is anything I can do, just let me know. You can count on my co-operation."

"Thank you, sir. That's very good to know. Good day, Mr. Courtney, I wish you a speedy recovery."

"Let me show you out, Captain," said Saffron and she followed Carstairs to the door and watched him make his way back out into the corridor.

An Egyptian cleaner was busy mopping the linoleum floor. Saffron paid him no attention as she went back into Leon's room.

———

Leon was tired. He had no energy to spare so he got straight to the point. "I think your uncle Francis is the spy. He knew about the shipment, and even though I didn't tell him, in so many words, what we were putting on board that ship, he knew enough to be able to give someone else the means to find out the details."

"Do you really think he'd do that?"

"I wish I could say, "No." But the truth is, I think he's bitter enough and angry enough to betray his family and his country. And we all know what he thinks about fascism, he's never made any secret about that."

"But what does he have to be angry about? You saved the company and made him a lot of money."

"That almost makes it worse, I think. When someone gets into that frame of mind, they stop looking at things fairly. And if you do something decent that just makes them better off, they almost resent you all the more. Frank needs me to be the villain in the warped fantasy that goes on in his head. If I don't play that role then he has to go to even greater lengths to invent reasons why I am, despite all appearances doing him down."

"What a terrible way to live one's life."

"Absolutely. But once a person gets stuck in that rut it's almost impossible to drag them out of it unless they really want to change their attitude themselves. In the meantime, we have a second problem. Not only do I suspect that Frank is the spy, I also wonder whether Carstairs wasn't tipping me off that his mob know that it's him."

"What would be the good of that? What can we do about it?"

"I wish I knew. If I was still in one piece I'd go round and confront him, knock the truth out of him if needs be."

"And then what? It wouldn't look very good for us—as a family or a firm—if one of the Courtney brothers turned out to be a Nazi spy."

"It wouldn't look very good for anyone. I suppose that I could give him a choice: go into exile somewhere like Morocco or Spain—a neutral country where he can't cause any trouble—or I could hand him over to the authorities and let him be tried for treason. It's a hanging offense, after all. I'd imagine even Frank would be prepared to toe the line to save his neck."

"But you can't do that. Not for the time being, anyway."

"Don't remind me."

"Maybe I could, though, or Harriet. Or, I know, how about Uncle Dorian or Grandma? Would he listen to them?"

"We can't involve them without telling them exactly what we were doing in Athens, and that's not on. I wish I had my strength back. I swear I'd find the nearest bus and push my darling brother under it."

"I think it's probably just as well that you can't do that," Saffron said. "Now, get some rest. The important thing is for you to get well again. And if the worst comes to the worst, and Uncle Francis is exposed as a spy, and the scandal ruins Courtney Trading, you will still have Lusima and Harriet and me, and we will all be perfectly fine."

"Yes, that's true. But what about Dorian and Grandma and my sisters?"

"They can all come and live at Lusima too. We're hardly short of space!"

"Darling Saffron," Leon said, squeezing her hand, "what a lovely, kind, splendid daughter you are."

"You're very sweet, but this daughter is going to be strict with you. Harriet will be here to see you later, but in the meantime, you must get some rest."

She kissed her father's forehead, said goodbye and left the room.

Outside in the corridor she noticed that the cleaner had disappeared even though she could see very clearly from the marked, bone-dry state of much of the linoleum that he had only done a small portion of his work. *If Harriet ran this place they'd never dare behave like that*, Saffron thought, and was smiling to herself as she followed the signs to the exit.

———

The moment Saffron had gone back into her father's room, having said farewell to Captain Carstairs, the cleaner who had been wiping down the corridor floor picked up his mop and pail and scuttled away down the corridor toward the stairs. Two minutes later he was coming out of the hospital's staff exit and heading for the Old City. He had news for Hassan al-Banna and the sooner he heard it the better.

Two hours later, a message was on its way, via a forward listening post of the Afrika Korps to Berlin.

———

When Saffron arrived home, Harriet asked her how her father was.

"He was on rather good form, I thought, but he became a little tired so I told him to get some rest before you come to see him."

"Did he do as he was told?"

"He did, actually. I think he was feeling co-operative toward me. He said I was a lovely, kind, splendid daughter, which was very sweet of him."

"Well that's just what you are," said Harriet.

"Do you mind if I pour myself a drink?" Saffron asked. "I rather fancy a nice, cold G'n'T."

"My dear girl, you don't have to ask me permission. You're a grown woman. Just be a darling and make me one too. And don't be stingy with the gin!"

Saffron took her glass out onto the terrace, which looked across the garden toward the Nile. She thought about everything that she had heard at the hospital, and what her father said about Uncle Francis. It appalled her to think of all the death and destruction his betrayal had caused, and it shamed her, too. For he was a Courtney, just as she was, and his actions shamed the whole family.

Perhaps it's right that he should be exposed. Perhaps we deserve to have our names dragged through the mud along with his.

But then Saffron told herself that she had not done anything to be ashamed of, and nor had her father. Why should they be tarred by Francis's brush? And what good would come of having the story of his treachery made public? No one would benefit except for those who wanted Britain and its Empire to fall. So the fewer people who knew what he had done, the better.

But he can't just get away with it, he just can't!

Saffron sipped her drink. She ran the problem through in her mind. Then the solution suddenly presented itself, like the answer to a complex equation. She ran back over her reasoning to see if she could find a flaw, but there was none. The answer was correct.

And now Saffron knew exactly what had to be done.

———

"Is the mint tea to your taste?" asked Hassan al-Banna.

"It'll do," replied Francis Courtney gracelessly.

"Perhaps a little more sugar would improve it."

"Possibly." Francis gave an impatient sigh. "Look, I'm not hear to prattle about mint tea and spoons of sugar. You wanted to see me. I'd like to know why."

Al-Banna shook his head, regretfully. Allah was all-knowing and all-wise. There had to be a reason why He had sent this oafish, ill-mannered, ungrateful infidel into his life. But there were times when it was hard to know what that reason might be. *Perhaps He just wants to try my patience.* Yes, that might be it.

"Our mutual friends are not happy. You misled them about the *Star of Khartoum.*"

"What do you mean I misled them? I told them where it was going, what cargo it was picking up and where it was then going to sail. Then they sank it, which was the aim of the exercise. I'm the one who should be unhappy. They were meant to get rid of my brother and that little brat of his. But the two of them are still alive. What have they got to say about that, then . . . eh? Eh?!"

"They have more important things to concern them than the life or death of two insignificant individuals."

"So what does concern them, then?"

"The gold was not on the ship."

"So where was it then?"

"Our friends do not know. But if I were you, Mr. Courtney, I would make it my business to find out. If you could tell them where it really is, they may be less inclined to suspect that you deliberately misled them."

"I did no such thing! I told them what I knew, what my own damn brother had told me. He's the one who misled you, if anyone did. Not me."

"I do not believe so. There is no evidence to suggest that your brother is connected to British Intelligence. I think he was the first dupe. I think they used him to be their decoy. He told you because he wanted to persuade you that it was vital to send the *Star of Khartoum* to Greece. The question is: did British Intelligence know that you would pass the information on to us? If they did, then you have been compromised and your position is, hmm . . ." Hassan searched for the right word. "Vulnerable . . . yes. You are very vulnerable."

"You mean they're going to do me in?" asked Francis, his face suddenly ashen. A dribble of sweat ran down his temple. "But I have done nothing wrong. It's not fair!"

"Only the English are foolish enough to believe that life should be fair. The situation is perfectly reasonable, however. You have caused our friends a great deal of trouble, all of which was wasted. Now you owe them. If you can find out where the British have taken the Greek gold reserves, and prove that your information is correct, then there will not be a problem. If you cannot . . ." he shrugged. "Allah is just. You will receive precisely what you deserve."

Francis was almost weeping from fear, and anger and a furious sense of self-pity. He had done everything he could to help the cause. He had passed on information that he believed to be both true and of vital significance. How was he to know that Leon was lying to him? And Leon had been lying, knowingly and deliberately misleading him, he was sure of that.

He stopped off at the Sporting Club for a couple of whiskies on the way home and then walked, only somewhat the worse the wear, the short distance to his flat, in a smart new block between the club and the river. He opened the door, threw his jacket and hat onto the end of the sofa and went to pour himself another drink.

The doorbell rang. Frank frowned. "Who in Hades wants to see me at this time of night?" he muttered to himself and then felt a stab of fear as the thought struck him: *Have the bloody Germans sent someone to do me in?*

No, that wasn't possible. He had been warned of what would happen, but given a chance to make amends. And as long as they thought he could find the gold's real location, he was more use alive than dead.

He took a deep breath, as much to sober himself up as anything else, and opened the door.

Then he saw who it was and barked, "What the bloody hell are you doing here?"

———

"Hello Uncle Francis," said Saffron, "aren't you going to let me in?"

"Oh, yes, I suppose I must. Come on then."

Saffron stepped through the door, noticing the bitter twist to her uncle's mouth as she walked by him. The front door of the apartment opened onto a wide hall that had been expensively decorated, with marble tiles on the floor, walls papered in a deep, rich, oriental red and a modern, black lacquer console table with a matching mirror above it, against the wall to one side. Francis led her through to the drawing room at the end of the hall. The far wall was almost entirely comprised of glass doors that opened onto a balcony, with a spectacular view across the Nile toward the Old City.

"I adore your flat, Uncle Francis," Saffron said. "I've often wondered what it was like. When was it you moved in?"

"Summer of '39, just before the balloon went up. Typical bad luck, I could have got it for half the price, more like a quarter actually, if I'd waited another three months."

"Isn't it nice, the way the company's success has made life

so much nicer for everyone? Dorian's studio in Alex is divine."

"I played my part, you know. It wasn't just your blessed father."

"Oh I know. You brought in all that German business. It's so sad that all had to end. I say, you couldn't get me a drink, could you?"

"Oh, yes, of course. Forgot my manners," Francis blustered. "I don't have many people over, if truth be told. Hardly anyone in fact. A chap forgets how to be a decent host after a while, if he doesn't keep his hand in. Do you drink? Alcohol, I mean?"

"Yes, of course I do," Saffron giggled. "I'm quite grown-up, you know, almost twenty-two."

"Are you really? Good Lord, how time flies. So, what's your poison?"

For a second, Saffron caught a flash of the man Francis Courtney used to be and might have still been had he not chosen to live in bitterness, rather than hope; accentuating all the ills done to him, rather than the kindnesses; suspecting the motives of others, rather than trusting in the common decency.

"Could you make me a martini?"

"Don't see why not. I'm a whisky man myself."

Saffron found herself a chair and placed her shoulder bag open on the cushion next to her, while Francis made her cocktail. It was cold and strong with just the faintest suggestion of vermouth. "Mmm," she said, "that's perfect. You should open your own bar, Uncle Francis, call it Courtney's Bar and Grill."

Francis had sat down. His glass, which he had refilled after making Saffron's martini, was already empty.

"I say, Uncle, you need a refill. Don't get up, I'll get it for you."

She took his glass, walked across to the drinks cabinet, refilled it and put it down on the side table next to Francis's chair, just next to a marble table lamp shaped like a classical column. Then she walked over to the windows, opened one up and stood there, leaning against the frame. "Your view is quite breathtaking," she said. "Makes me think of that song . . ." She hummed the first bars of "You Belong to Me": "See the pyramids along the Nile . . ."

Come on! Saffron thought as she tried to remember the second line. *Get out of that chair. You have to be standing up!*

"Do come and look, Uncle Francis, one of the restaurant boats is going by. There are people dancing on the deck. Listen! Can you hear the music?"

Francis downed his glass and got unsteadily to his feet. "I see 'em go by all the time, but if you insist . . ."

Saffron waited till he was standing by her, almost as close as a lover might be, and then she said, "So, Uncle Francis, why did you betray us to the Germans?"

———

"I did no such thing!" Francis protested. He suddenly became aware that he was drunk. He couldn't think straight, couldn't work out how to get out of a hole that seemed to be getting deeper and deeper, the longer the night went on.

"Yes you did!" the girl snapped. She'd dropped the sweet-little-niece act now and there was a tough, aggressive pitch to her voice as she went on, "You told them your brother was sailing to Piraeus . . . Your own brother! The man who saved you from going bust. The man whose money enabled you to buy this ridiculous gin palace where you can live, all alone, no one coming round, boo-hoo-hoo."

"I earned the money that bought this place! I did! Not him!"

"If you did, it was only because you sold yourself to the Nazis. Admit it, you work for them. You told them where the *Star of Khartoum* was bound, didn't you?"

She stabbed a red-painted fingernail at his chest to emphasize the point.

"You told them it was picking up the Greek gold, didn't you?"

She poked him again, harder this time.

"Stop doing that!"

"Oh, don't you like it when a girl shows you up? Well I can't say that I care what you do or don't like. My father, your brother, is lying in a hospital with his leg smashed to bits. He may never walk again . . . because of you."

Damn it, she jabbed me again! Francis thought. "I said, stop it!" he barked, getting properly angry. He took a step toward her, making it threatening, expecting her to back away.

Saffron stood her ground.

"I'm not scared of you. I've been to war, actual fighting, the kind you've never seen. I've been put up for the George Medal, you know, for extreme gallantry in the face of enemy fire. They came at us time and time again, you know, the Germans . . . the ones who somehow seemed to know exactly where we were . . . who picked the *Star of Khartoum* out from all the other ships desperately steaming away from Greece, trying to get back to Alex . . . And it was all . . ."

Stab!

"Because . . ."

Stab!

"Of you!"

She poked her hand at him again, but this time he batted it away.

Saffron slapped him hard across the face, jerking his head and making him feel dizzy as he stumbled back from the force of the blow.

————

Christ! Have I hit him too hard? Saffron thought. Her uncle seemed dazed, lost. *No, come on, you can't give up now! You mustn't!*

And then the anger in him cut through his incapacity and adrenaline sharpened his wits and gave him a little new strength.

"I'll get you for that, you little bitch!" he snarled. And he came at her, punching at her, aiming for her pretty face, wanting to smash it, driving her back into the room.

Saffron put her arms up to defend her head and winced as his blows bruised her flesh and thudded against her bones.

"Yes!" Francis shouted, punctuating his words with his fists. "I told the Germans everything! I wanted you dead! Both of you!"

Then, without warning, Francis changed his point of attack and aimed a short, hard punch beneath Saffron's raised elbows so that it thudded into her solar plexus. She gasped as the air was driven from her body and as she struggled desperately for breath, she dropped her guard.

"I want you dead!" Francis screamed again and he hit her right in the mouth, splitting her lip and catching her nose as well.

Saffron cried out in pain as the blood streamed from her nostrils and mouth. She stumbled backward, caught the backs of her legs on the side of the sofa and fell backward onto it, landing beside her bag.

She looked up and saw Francis coming toward her. The drinks he had consumed had made his step unsteady, but that was small consolation to Saffron. For now she saw him grab hold of the table lamp that had stood beside his chair. As she scrabbled backward on the sofa, dragging the bag with her, he ripped the plug from its socket, pulled the shade off its mount and grabbed the lamp just below the lightbulb. Now he was brandishing it like a marble club, with its thick, square base acting like the head of a mace.

Francis was completely in the grip of his rage, ranting incoherently as he came toward the sofa. Saffron shoved her right hand into her open bag.

He raised the lamp up above his head. He half twisted his body as he prepared to put all the strength behind the swing that would send the stone column smashing into her skull.

And that was when Saffron pulled her right hand from the bag, grabbed it with her left, raised both hands and, as his eyes widened in horror at the sight of the pistol she was holding, shot Francis Courtney right between the eyes.

———

Saffron took a deep breath and looked around. She had been expecting to have to manufacture a scene to fit the story she wanted to tell. But Uncle Francis had unknowingly played his part to such perfection that no trickery was required. The impact of the bullet at point-blank range had knocked him backward and he had dropped the lamp. But it was lying right next to his body, which would back up her account of what happened. Meanwhile, the blood was still flowing from the punch to her face. She ran her tongue along the backs of her teeth, gingerly testing them to see if any were loose. None were, and when she put a hankie to her face to mop up some of the blood her nose felt bruised and bleeding but not actually broken. That was a relief. A battered nose gave a man a certain roguish charm but it was not something any young woman would wish to emulate.

Satisfied that all was as it should be, she called the police. Saffron wondered whether to make herself sound like a panicking, hysterical female but decided against it. She was known for keeping her head under fire. She should certainly sound upset at what had happened, but no one would be surprised that she still had her wits about her.

"I wish to report a violent death," she said, when she was put through to the duty officer, who was English, for the police operated in Egypt as they did throughout the Empire, with native junior ranks under British command.

"It's my uncle. We had an argument," Saffron explained. "He was very drunk and he lost his temper. It was awful . . . he attacked me and he . . . he punched me in the face. Then he tried to kill me, with a marble lampstand and I, I . . . well, I shot him. And I think he's dead."

"Stay there, Miss, we'll be round in a jiffy. Don't touch or move anything. Where is the body?"

"In the drawing room."

"Then I suggest you go into the kitchen and wait there. I strongly advise you not to try to leave the premises, Miss.

Otherwise I'll have to put out a warrant for your arrest and we wouldn't want that, would we now?"

Saffron did as she was told. She half-expected to hear one of the neighbors hammering on the door, wondering what was going on. But the block had been built with its occupants' privacy in mind, so the walls were thick. And there had only been a single shot. Anyone who had heard it, Saffron concluded, might well not have known what the sound was and would probably wait to see if there were any other noises before doing anything. So when there finally was a knocking on the door, it was the police. Saffron, who had checked her appearance in the hall mirror before answering the door, had been startled but also gratified to discover that her throbbing, hurting face looked even worse than it felt.

There were four of them: a plainclothes detective, two uniformed constables and a photographer. "My name is Detective Sergeant Ralph Riley," the plainclothes man said. "Could you give me your name and address, please, Miss?"

Saffron did as Riley asked and showed him her identity card by way of confirmation. He ordered the two constables to stand guard outside and take the names of any inquisitive neighbors who might come by to have a look. He told Saffron to sit down at the kitchen table and wait for a few minutes. Then he and the photographer went into the drawing room to examine the crime scene. Ten minutes or so later, Riley reappeared, sat down opposite her and asked her to give her account.

"I came round to see if I could persuade Uncle Francis to come and visit my father, who's in hospital," she said. "Daddy and I were on a ship that was sunk in the Aegean and he was badly wounded and it's just awful that his own brother hasn't been to see him. Well, my uncle became very cross. I think he resented my father because of a business deal between them, even though he had done very well out of it. And I think he was quite drunk, too. He had two full tumblers of whisky, very quickly, one after the other while I was here, and I got the impression he'd already had quite a bit to drink by the time I arrived."

Riley looked up from his notebook. "Hang on, I've just realized . . . I thought your name sounded familiar . . . Saffron Courtney, of course, you're the young woman that's been in the paper. You're up for a medal."

He sounded as though he was just about to ask her to sign her name in his notebook and inscribe it to his wife.

"That's right," Saffron replied.

"Well, I never, you really have been out of the frying pan and into the fire, haven't you?"

"I suppose I have, yes."

"Now, the crime scene all looks quite straightforward. You have clearly suffered a blow to the face. When we've finished our chat I'll have the photographer take some pictures of you to confirm that fact. And unless there was a third person here that you haven't been telling us about . . ."

He looked at Saffron.

"No, we were alone in the flat," she said. "My uncle doesn't have any live-in staff and he made a point of saying that he saw very few people here."

"I'm sure the neighbors can confirm the truth or otherwise of those statements. But it certainly seems as though your uncle hit you. There are blood spatters on his right hand and the cuff of his jacket. And I dare say we will find your uncle's finger-prints all over that lamp that you say he was intending to use as a weapon against you. There is only one thing, however, that puzzles me, Miss Courtney." The detective looked at Saffron and now there was nothing remotely starry-eyed about him as he said, "Why would a young woman paying a social visit to her uncle just happen to have a Beretta 418 pistol about her person?"

"Because I always carry it, Sergeant."

"Why would that be, then?"

"Force of habit I suppose. I used to be Major General Wilson's driver. I had to take him right up to the battlefield. We MTC girls are civilians, of course, so we aren't armed. But my father felt I should have some means of defending myself, just in case of trouble and General Wilson . . . well, I shouldn't really say this, because I don't want to get him in hot water . . ."

"I wouldn't worry, Miss. He is a general, after all."

"Well, he said he would turn a blind eye, provided that I could prove to him that I knew how to handle a gun, which I could. I grew up in Kenya, you see, so I was used to shooting, so that wasn't a problem. He also insisted that I had to keep my gun out of sight. So my father got me the Beretta, because it could just be popped in my shoulder bag, and it's been with me ever since."

"Have you had reason to use it before? In anger, I mean . . ."

"Yes. During Operation Compass, at the beginning of this year, we ran into an Italian patrol and had to shoot our way out."

"Have you shot a man before, Miss?"

Saffron suddenly found her composure beginning to break, and this time there was nothing feigned about it at all. She bit her bottom lip and then said, "Yes, I have . . . That's how I knew what to do . . . but . . . but it's a horrible thing to have to shoot another human being . . . and he was my uncle, my own family . . ."

She started crying and pulled her bloodstained handkerchief out of her bag.

"I'm very sorry, Miss Courtney, but I will need that handkerchief. Evidence," Riley said. He got up from his seat and fetched a tea towel that had been hanging on a rail in front of the cooker. "There you go."

"Thank you. It just hit me . . . what had happened. My uncle wasn't a nice man, Sergeant. But I wouldn't want . . . I wouldn't want all this."

"I'm sure you wouldn't. I'll just ask the photographer to take your picture and then one of my men will drive you home. I must ask you to stay in Cairo. Are you expecting any orders to go anywhere, by any chance?"

"No, I'm on extended leave."

"Then spend it here, if you don't mind, until I say otherwise."

––––––

The following day, Leon told Harriet to hire the finest criminal lawyer in Cairo, Joseph Azerad, to handle Saffron's case.

"Have no fear, Mr. Courtney, I will make sure that there is no case to handle," Azerad said.

Leon had already informed him of Frank's admiration for Oswald Mosley. Azerad immediately called the head of the Cairo police and stated in no uncertain terms that it would be an outrage if a brave young woman who had served her nation with distinction and whose face was battered by the fists of an evil brute should be blamed for what was clearly an act of self-defense.

He also got in touch with contacts who worked on the newsdesks of the *Gazette* and the *Mail* and informed them that the famously beautiful and heroic Saffron Courtney had been forced to defend herself from an assault from her uncle, a known fascist sympathizer. He told the man from the *Gazette* that if he went to the Sporting Club he would soon find plenty of people willing to confirm Francis Courtney's status as a long-time Mosley supporter, and he gave the man from the *Mail* the address of the doctor who was examining Saffron's wounds and the time of her appointment.

Saffron, who had been forewarned, looked right into the camera, while raising a hand as if to protect herself from its intrusion. Her face had swollen considerably since the point at which the police had photographed her and was now covered with vivid bruises. No one who saw the pictures could possibly doubt that she had been assaulted, and another set of bruises on her forearms proved that she had tried to defend herself against her uncle's attacks before his fists eventually broke through.

By the end of the day it was clear that Francis had been holding the lampstand, close to the light fixture, supporting Saffron's testimony that he had been trying to hit her with the base, while the angle at which the .418 caliber bullet had entered his skull supported her claim that she had been helpless on the sofa, firing up at him as he advanced upon her.

By the end of the week the case had been dropped. Saffron received a telegram from Jumbo.

———

HEARD ABOUT EVENTS IN CAIRO STOP THINK YOU NEED A CHANGE OF SCENERY STOP COME TO JERUSALEM STOP BY ORDER WILSON

As Saffron packed her bags, Mr. Brown was reading a detailed account of the shooting. And by the time he reached the last sentence he knew that he should fly to Cairo.

It took several weeks to arrange the journey, but he was eventually able to obtain a berth on an RAF Liberator bomber carrying a pair of senior officers who'd been transferred to the North African front. The pilot headed across the Bay of Biscay and then on a course over neutral Portugal before coming into land at Gibraltar. The following day he flew south over Morocco before turning east across the Sahara, to the south of the warzone in the Western Desert, before hitting the Nile, which he used as the guide to take him back up to Cairo.

When Mr. Brown disembarked, he allowed himself a day's rest, for it had been a long, hazardous and tiring journey. Then he went to the High Commission and made some discreet inquiries. Having discovered what he needed to know, he boarded a train that would take him to El Kantara in northeast Egypt, from which a sleeper service ran to Haifa, on the Mediterranean coast of Palestine. Once there, he changed trains for a final time en route to Jerusalem.

He really had gone to a very great deal of trouble. Now he was about to discover whether it had all been worthwhile.

* * *

"It's very simple, Courtney," Jumbo said, soon after she had arrived at the British army headquarters that occupied one wing of the magnificent King David Hotel in Jerusalem.

He led her up to the map of the Eastern Mediterranean and Middle East. "Here's Cairo," he said, pointing to its location toward the bottom-right of the map. "Don't need to tell you that, what? And just to the east of Cairo, here's the Suez Canal, the gateway to India, the Far East and Australasia. If we were ever to lose control of the Canal, that would be curtains for the Empire. So, Rommel's charging along the coast road toward Cairo from the west, and getting rather too close for comfort. The Jerries have occupied Greece and Crete, meaning that they're now just a short hop across the Eastern Med from Crete to Alex."

"But they could never get an invasion force past the Royal Navy, surely sir?"

"You're quite right, my girl. But look up here."

He pointed his swagger stick at the territories of Lebanon and Syria, directly north of where they now were in Palestine. "After the last war, we took control of Palestine and Transjordan and the French got their sticky mitts on Syria and Lebanon. Now those mandates are under Vichy control."

"And the Vichy government is extremely sympathetic to the Germans."

"And so . . . ?" Jumbo asked, exactly like one of Saffron's Oxford tutors leading her through an academic argument.

"May I ask a question, sir?"

"Fire away."

"What forces do the Vichy French have in the region?"

"About forty-five thousand French, Lebanese and Syrian troops, the best part of a hundred tanks, three hundred aircraft and a modest naval force: couple of destroyers and three submarines. What does that tell you?"

Saffron stepped up to the map, looked at it for a few seconds and then said, "If they were feeling daring the Germans could put men ashore at, say, Sidon, here, south of Beirut. Or they could go further north, up by the Turkish border, if they wanted to stay away from our fleet. In either case, they would land on friendly soil and link up with the Vichy forces. Then they could either go eastwards, toward the oilfields of Iraq and Iran. Or they could strike south and if they broke through our forces here in Palestine, they would then advance on Cairo and the Canal and catch us in a pincer movement: them from the north and Rommel from the west."

"Oxford girl, aren't you?"

"Yes, sir."

"Ever considered going to Staff College instead? By God, I wish the young men under my command had half your grasp of military strategy. Might I ask what you would do in my shoes?"

"Yes sir. I would attack, as fast and as hard as possible before the Germans have a chance to do anything."

"And that is precisely what I have been ordered to do. They're calling it Operation Exporter. We're hitting the French hard with a mixed bunch of our own chaps, as well as Indians, Australians, and even Free French."

"Will they fight their own countrymen?"

"Apparently they can't wait to get at 'em. Hate them all the more for being turncoats. Anyway we're hitting them from all sides, marching on Beirut and Damascus as well as securing all the major oil pipelines and ports. I'll be running the show from here, of course, but you know me, I like to see what's going on at the sharp end, so there'll be a fair amount of dashing about. Think you're up to it?"

"Absolutely, sir. Can't wait."

"That's the spirit! And I can assure you of one thing, Courtney. This time we are going to win."

*   *   *

Wilson was as good as his word. The disasters of Greece were followed by a series of triumphs in the Levant. It took just over a month to rout the Vichy French, destroying most of their aircraft and ships in the process. By 12 July, Saffron was in the old Crusader port of Acre where Jumbo was sitting down to talks with his French counterpart General Henri Dentz and a gaggle of pompous, but utterly ineffectual Vichy bureaucrats in the officers' mess of the Sidney Smith barracks. By ten that night they had agreed a ceasefire. Another day and a half of talks led to the signing of a treaty that handed over absolute control of all the French territory in Syria and Lebanon to the British. The armistice treaty was dated 14 July. It was Bastille Day, the French national day, an occasion for patriotism and pride. But on this occasion the dateline to an abject surrender.

A similar Allied campaign had defeated nationalist rebels in Iraq, securing the country's oilfields, and plans were afoot to do the same in Iran. A great swathe of the Middle East was now secure in Allied hands. In the desert a sort of stalemate had been reached. General Wavell had failed in an attempt to push Rommel back across the desert and relieve the siege of Tobruk, and been sacked as a result. But Rommel's lines of communication were stretched so tight, and his supplies of fuel, food and water had to make such a long and perilous journey across the desert to reach his army that he was finding it hard to make any more progress.

But all of this was now just a sideshow. A new conflict had begun, one that made every other campaign in the war so far seem like a mere skirmish. Hitler had reneged on his peace treaty with Stalin and flung the full might of his war machine at the Soviet Union in Operation Barbarossa, the most massive military operation in the entire history of warfare.

The carnage on the Eastern Front had begun.

* * *

"You know, Meerbach, I think you might be right after all," said Schrumpp one still, sunlit summer evening, as they stood outside the tent, pitched beside an airfield in the midst of the endless wheat fields of the Ukraine that served as an officers' mess. "Even I'm getting bored with killing the Ivans in their decrepit old planes. It almost makes me nostalgic for the days of Spitfires and Hurricanes. If you shot one of them down it felt like a real achievement."

Gerhard grinned, "We'll make a proper gentleman of you yet!"

The squadron had ceased operations for the day, but now the drone of airplane engines could be heard, coming from the southwest.

"Can't be one of ours," said Schrumpp. "Sounds like a Tante Ju."

"Must be someone important, then," said Gerhard, for only the most senior officers and Party officials were transported around the front on one of Junkers Ju 52 airliners that had been requisitioned by the Wehrmacht for wartime service.

"Do you think we should make ourselves look a bit more like proper German officers?" asked Schrumpp, rubbing a hand over his unshaved chin.

"I wouldn't bother, they're probably not here for us."

The tri-engined plane landed, came rolling to a halt and an open Mercedes staff car suddenly appeared from behind the control tower—or what still remained of the tower after the retreating Russians had tried to destroy it—and sped across the parched brown grass to meet the new arrivals.

"Here we go," said Schrumpp as the fuselage door was opened and a crewman placed a short stepladder beneath it. Two men emerged from the plane: one in uniform and the other in a smart suit and tie, carrying a briefcase.

"What's an *SS-brigadeführer* doing here?" Gerhard wondered aloud.

Schrumpp shrugged. "It's very strange. You hardly ever saw them in France or Greece, but now the whole place is crawling with them. I was talking about it to Rolf the other day. He says there's a new kind of SS unit. They're calling them Task Forces— and wherever we go they're right behind."

"So what's their task?"

"Search me. But if it's the SS then it's probably to do with the Jews. Maybe they've come to plan those new homelands they're always going on about. I mean, that's the plan, isn't it? Ship the Yids out of the Reich and dump them all out here. You'd think we had enough on our hands conquering Russia without worrying about them too. *Ach*, the hell with it! Come on, old man, let's go and find another beer . . ."

Gerhard walked back into the tent, no longer paying attention as Schrumpp got the drinks, handed Gerhard his glass and then became caught up in another conversation with some other pilots. Gerhard winced every time Schrumpp or one of the other men in the squadron referred to "Yids" or "Hebrews," but at the ripe old age of thirty, he was a grizzled veteran compared to most of them. They'd been stuffed full of Nazi propaganda since they were schoolboys. They didn't know any better. But still, Schrumpp was right, this campaign was different.

When they invaded France, no one suggested that the French were an inferior race. That would have been absurd. But from the moment that they had first been told what Barbarossa was really about, the campaign had been presented as a war between races: noble German Aryans against sub-human Slavs and Jews. The propaganda films were filled with images of ugly, hook-nosed, shifty-looking men who embodied every stereotype of the evil, untrustworthy, endlessly conspiring Jew. And though the words were never said out loud, the tone of all the Party language was unmistakably destructive. These were people who did not just need to be beaten, or even enslaved. They were to be destroyed.

Gerhard could not begin to imagine what that actually meant. How could one wipe an entire race from the earth? It was inconceivable. But he did know that he could not bear to live in any world in which such thoughts could even be expressed as a nation's governing principles. Nor could he see how he and Saffron could ever be united, or be able to live in peace together in such a world. Of course one could not consort with one's enemies in wartime, that was normal. But it seemed to Gerhard that in the event of Nazi victory, the defeated peoples would always be enemies, to be degraded, exploited and enslaved. They were certainly not to be loved, let alone married.

So what am I to do?

Gerhard had always considered that he was not fighting for Hitler, but for Germany. There was no dishonor in serving one's country—his country. But was there a difference any more between Nazism and Germany? And if there wasn't, what in God's name was a decent man to do?

Saffron was lying by the pool at the King David Hotel, wearing a white two-piece swimsuit, reading *Rebecca* and sipping from a glass of beer, which she had sat in an ice-bucket to keep it suitably cold. The beer was making her drowsy, so she put the book down on the tiles beside her lounger and lay back. This was her first day of leave after weeks of frantic activity. An afternoon snooze seemed like the absolute height of self-indulgent luxury.

She was just on the verge of dropping off when she heard a familiar voice say, "Hello Saffron. Not quite Oxford in November, is it?"

Saffron pulled herself up to a sitting position, gave a sharp little shake of the head to wake herself up, then lifted her hand to shade her eyes so that she could see as she said, "Good afternoon, Mr. Brown. I hope you haven't come all this way on my account."

He gave one of his enigmatic smiles and said, "Do you mind?" as he lowered himself to perch on the end of the lounger next to hers. He looked at her in that disconcertingly direct way of his. There was nothing sexual or threatening in his gaze, but it made her feel uneasy nonetheless.

"By all means," she said, steeling herself to keep her wits about her.

Mr. Brown was as dapper as always. He had exchanged the dark, woollen suit he habitually wore in England for a pale beige linen one, but he still wore a stiff collar and tie in defiance of the heat. He replaced the Panama hat that he had politely removed to address her and sat, quite contentedly, saying nothing.

Saffron looked around. Her light cotton kaftan was lying bundled up behind her bag. "Do you mind if I put some more clothes on?"

"By all means do," Mr. Brown said, still looking at her.

"Would you please avert your gaze?"

"Of course, how rude of me."

Saffron picked up the kaftan, which she had bought on a trip to Grandma's favorite market stall in Cairo, and pulled it over her head. Then she reached into her bag, found her powder compact and checked her face in its mirror. She pushed a few stray strands of hair back under the headband she was wearing and then applied her lipstick. There was quite nothing like that essential splash of warpaint to make her ready for a verbal battle.

Mr. Brown meanwhile had spotted a waiter. He waved him over. "Some tea, please, lapsang souchong if you have it, Earl Gray if you don't. No milk, no sugar, but I would like a few slices of lemon. Thank you."

He turned back to Saffron. "I heard about that business with your uncle,' he said, without the slightest preamble. "Very impressive."

"Really . . . why?"

"Well, I knew that you had a certain mental toughness that could, when properly trained, be used for this sort of work. And you've twice shown admirable courage and composure in battle. But I hadn't thought you capable of planning, executing and then extracting yourself from a cold-blooded murder quite so effectively, entirely on your own."

"It wasn't murder, it was self-defence. I was attacked," Saffron said, as calmly as she could manage, though her pulse had started racing at the very mention of the word "murder".

"You see, that proves my point. I have just accused you of a capital crime and you look me right in the eye, calm as you like and deny it."

"I didn't enjoy killing him, you know."

"I should hope not. That would make you a psychopath and I wouldn't want that. Psychopaths are unreliable. They always put their own compulsions ahead of their duty. But enough amateur psychology . . . You did us a great favor. We've known for a very long time that your uncle was cultivating a number of extremely undesirable friends. It was all just about tolerable before the war, but not once the balloon went up. Your uncle was a full-blown traitor. We rather think that he had your uncle David assassinated."

"I thought he was killed by thieves."

"Or his death was just made to look like a robbery. Anyway, as I'm sure you have already worked out for yourself, we couldn't have allowed dear Uncle Frank to be exposed. There was thus only one way of dealing with the situation and you took it."

"My father doesn't know," Saffron said, feeling surprised at how easy it was to talk to Mr. Brown about this terrible thing that she'd done. "He believed my story. I'd like it to stay that way."

"Of course . . . But speaking of your father, did he tell you about me?"

"Yes. He said that you'd turned my mother into a spy. And then he told me what she'd had to do."

"Hmm . . ." Mr. Brown considered that information. And then his face lit up and he exclaimed, "Ah! The tea has arrived, excellent!"

The waiter pulled up a side table, placed the teapot upon it and was about to pour it into a cup when Mr. Brown held up a hand. "No, please, I prefer to do it myself."

The man frowned. Saffron spoke a few words of Arabic, accompanied by gestures that evidently got the point across. "Ah," said the waiter, "very good." He went on his way and Mr. Brown fussed for a while, getting his tea exactly as he wanted it. "What languages do you have?" he asked as he was busying himself, not looking at Saffron this time.

"Of the African languages I'm fluent in Swahili, competent in Masai, and have a smattering of Afrikaans and Arabic, though I can't read or write Arabic script. In German I could read a newspaper and conduct a conversation but I certainly wouldn't pass as a native."

"Not yet," Mr. Brown said. "But your mother managed it."

"Do you want me to do the same thing she did? Is that why you're here? Because I won't do it, you know."

"I've never for a moment thought that you would. I'm here about a rather different line of work." He sipped some tea thoughtfully, clearly concentrating all his attention on his tastebuds, gave a contented little grunt of approval and went on. "About a year ago Mr. Dalton, the Minister of Economic Warfare, authorized the formation of an outfit that was officially labeled the Joint Technical Board. It was a name one could put in funding proposals or stick on office doors without anyone knowing or caring what on earth it was."

"Because it's so boring."

"Quite so, but some of its small but growing number of members have a more accurate name for it. They call it the Ministry of Ungentlemanly Warfare."

Saffron laughed. "That sounds like more fun."

"I'm glad you think so. Now let me tell you the truth about Mr. Dalton's private army. Its actual name is the Special Operations Executive. Its purpose is to insert agents into Occupied Europe, to liaise with local resistance groups, establish spy networks, conduct reconnaissance on enemy positions and operations, carry out acts of sabotage and, in a few, particular cases, kill evil men whose deaths will save a great many innocent lives."

"And you think I would be suited to that task."

"I know you would. The missions that S.O.E. operatives undertake will be hazardous in the extreme. The chances of being caught, tortured by the Gestapo and then sent to a concentration camp, or simply shot, will be so high as to approach certainty. My job, therefore, is to recruit some of the most intellectually and physically gifted young men and women our nation possesses so that they can be trained to give their lives for their country. I do this because I know that the missions they undertake will be of supreme importance and that their lives will not be wasted, their sacrifice will not be in vain."

"Are you trying to appeal to my idealism?" Saffron asked. "I am not sure I have a tremendous amount of that."

"No, I'm appealing to your decency. I think you are a fundamentally decent person, Miss Courtney."

"I can think of at least one person who'd disagree." Saffron said the words with a bitter flippancy, not expecting them to be understood. She had underestimated Mr. Brown.

"You mean Fräulein von Schöndorf?"

Saffron saw at once what he meant by that. "How did you know?" she asked. "How could you possibly know?"

"You might not believe this, but I was at a wedding when I

caught wind of what you really got up to in St. Moritz. Two silly young women were gossiping about you and the man I later discovered was Gerhard von Meerbach."

"And now you wish to use it against me?"

"That's a rather harsh way of putting it. But the fact remains, you have had, and I believe are almost certainly still managing to conduct in some form, a liaison with the scion of one of the great German industrial dynasties, whose brother is a senior officer in the Nazi Schutzstaffel, or SS."

"I'm quite aware of Konrad von Meerbach's rank and his politics. And I'm sure you know that you could make life very difficult indeed for me. So I suspect, Mr. Brown, that you came here thinking that if you couldn't sweet-talk me into joining this Ungentlemanly Warfare show of yours, then a bit of blackmail might have to do the job. But you're too late. You can't use Gerhard von Meerbach as a weapon against me. He's dead."

———

Ha! That took you unawares, didn't it?

Saffron had to admit it had surprised her as well. She hadn't planned to use the false report of Gerhard's death as any kind of tactical gambit, but then it had struck her: *If Gerhard is dead, then Brown can't use him against me.*

She picked up her bag. "We had a way of communicating with one another. It was long and tortuous and took forever, but it worked. That's how I found out about this . . ."

She held out the telegram for Mr. Brown to read. "You see, he's gone. We saw each other for a few days in Switzerland at the start of '39, and a few more in Paris at Easter. We were doing nothing wrong, we loved each other very much and if this vile, beastly war had not come along, we would have married one another. But now he's dead, so it's over. *Kaput.*"

"Miss Courtney, I really am most awfully sorry," said Mr. Brown.

"Don't be. You didn't actually blackmail me and you certainly didn't kill Gerhard. Now, about the job offer that you were about to make . . . I accept. I want to be useful, just as my mother was in the last war. I'm very grateful to General Wilson for letting me be his driver, but I know I can do more than that. I believe I've proved that to your satisfaction, too."

"Indeed you have, Miss Courtney."

"Then you can count me in. I just have one request."

"Go ahead."

"Before I sign on the dotted line, I'd like to go home, to Kenya. If I'm going to risk my neck, there's someone I absolutely have to talk to first."

———

Gerhard was over Kiev on the way back from a mission, crossing the Dnieper River at a height of no more than three hundred meters, descending all the time as they approached the abandoned Russian air base that had become their new home.

Something caught Gerhard's eye as he passed over an area of open land on the edge of the city itself. He could have sworn he saw a long line of women, all stark naked, with armed, uniformed men on either side of them, and then a long trench with something in the bottom of it. *Was that a pile of bodies? Can't have been. Surely . . . can it?*

When he landed, Gerhard asked a couple of the other pilots if they'd seen it.

"Not me, skipper," said Willi Kempen. "Maybe it had something to do with that SS Task Force that arrived a few days ago. I heard there were posters up telling all the Yids to assemble by the cemetery at eight this morning. They're supposed to bring money, paper, warm clothing—sounds like they're being sent away somewhere."

"I heard an army major arguing with one of those SS bastards a couple of days ago," said Schrumpp.

"Whoa, Berti, watch your tongue! Don't you know our noble squadron captain's brother is in the SS?"

"True," said Gerhard. "But he's also a total bastard."

When the laughter died down, Schrumpp got back to his story. "So, this major was saying, "Who's going to do all the work if you kill all my Jews? I need carpenters to mend carts, mechanics for my trucks. How am I going to supply the boys up at the front if I can't fix my damn trucks?"

"What did the SS man say to that?" asked Gerhard.

"He said he didn't give a shit about carts or trucks. His unit had orders to kill every last Yid in Kiev and that was the end of it. "If you don't like it, send a letter of complaint to *Reichsführer* Himmler." Those were his exact words."

Later that afternoon, Gerhard took a long hard look at the maps of the locality. The area he had flown over was marked as Babi Yar. He fixed its exact position relative to the airfield in his mind, then went to Rolf and asked permission to make a quick test flight. "I just want to check the flaps on my starboard wing. The controls felt a little stiff this morning. If there is a problem, I can have the ground crew fix it in time for tomorrow's mission."

"Why bother? You could fly without any flaps at all and the Ivans still couldn't shoot you down!"

Gerhard said nothing.

"Oh, all right, go ahead," said Rolf. "But make it quick. We can't just go burning fuel for no reason."

Gerhard went up in the plane. He put on a little aerobatics display for the benefit of anyone watching from the ground: not to show off his skills, but simply because that's what he would do if he were testing the handling of his plane. Gerhard pulled out of his final dive and leveled out at less than a hundred meters, then he eased back the throttle until his airspeed was barely one hundred and eighty kilometers per hour: as low as he could go without stalling. So he was able to get a very clear view of what was happening down below. He realized that the trench he had seen was actually part of a natural ravine. It was filled with dead bodies, presumably of Jews, piled so high now that they were almost spilling over the top. Gerhard saw naked men and women being led up to the edge of the pit where they stood in a long line. Then he saw SS men—one for every Jew—put pistols to their heads, fire and blow them into the ravine with the force of the bullet smashing into their skulls.

Gerhard made three passes over the area. On the third he gave a little waggle of his wings, just to make it seem as though he were congratulating the killers below on the fine job they were doing of exterminating Ukrainian Jewry. Then he headed back to base.

"Flaps all right then, sir?" the mechanic asked when he clambered out of the cockpit.

Gerhard nodded, just about managed to say, "Fine," and forced a tight, bitter smile.

Then he returned to the barrack-house where he was billeted, went straight to the bathroom and vomited his guts out into the basin. When his stomach was entirely empty, he rinsed out his mouth and proceeded to the officers' mess where he became joylessly, but determinedly blind drunk, sitting alone, waving the other pilots away.

They let him be. Plenty of men had reason to numb themselves with alcohol these days. It was just one of those things and no one thought any the worse of them. So Gerhard emptied the bottle and as he did he realized that what he had seen at Babi Yar, though it was happening far from the Reich, out of sight of its people, was the true face of the Nazi empire, the true faith that would one day be worshipped in that vast, impossible hall he had labored over for so long. This was the darkness in Hitler's soul brought out into the light, let loose upon the world.

Izzy was wrong. There was no distinction between Nazism and Germany any more. There was no possible way that any man with a conscience could say that he was fighting for German honor and pride, because that belonged to Hitler now. The Führer had been proved triumphantly correct. They were all his slaves, his soldiers, his people to dispose of as he pleased.

The following morning, Gerhard sat on the runway, waiting to take off on their latest mission, praying that the pills they all took to keep themselves alert would kick in before he fell asleep at the controls of his plane. He had lain awake all night without the slightest hint of sleep, and in the darkness he had made a resolution: *I would rather be dead than live in Adolf Hitler's world. And there cannot be any hope for me or for Saffron or for our love as long as he is alive. So therefore I must dedicate myself to destroying him and all his cohorts. From now on, that will be my greatest purpose in life.*

Now dawn was breaking and nothing had changed. Gerhard von Meerbach had dedicated his life to freeing Germany, and the world, from the death-grip of Nazism. He had no idea how to do it, or who would be his allies. He just knew it had to be done. And with that grim thought in his mind, he lined up on the runway, pointed the Messerschmitt's nose to the east, and flew up and away into the first golden rays of the rising sun.

————

Saffron had been walking since before dawn, watching the mountain as it emerged from the darkness, separating itself from the great escarpment of the Rift Valley behind it, glowing in the golden light of the sunrise on its flanks and then revealing itself in all its majesty as the mist on its upper reaches cleared. Fuel was so strictly rationed that she could not have driven all the way from the Courtney residence, and flying was out of the question. But Saffron was glad of the full day's walk that had taken her to within five miles of the mountain, and the night she had spent under the stars. With every step she took and every breath of Kenyan air that entered her lungs she felt more at home. For the first few hours she had passed through farmland and plantations, stopping occasionally to talk to the workers. Saffron discovered that her command of the

Swahili and Masai languages came back to her in an instant, as did her memory of the names and faces of people that she met. Many were men and women she had known since her earliest girlhood and they greeted her like a long-lost daughter while Manyoro stood to one side, beaming as proudly as any father at the good impression she made.

Saffron loved the huge smiles, the ready laughter and the unrestrained emotions that she encountered along her way. That wonderful African warmth was such a stark contrast to the insipid, buttoned-up, joyless personalities of so many of the people she'd met in England. She didn't even mind when all the older women insisted on asking whether she had a husband yet and, if, so how many sons she had given him. Invariably they were shocked to discover that she was still single and childless. Saffron explained, again and again, that she would love to have babies, but there was a war on and she was too busy serving her country to have time for marriage and motherhood.

At this, Manyoro would shake his head in a great display of bafflement and sorrow and agree with all the wise Masai woman that there was, indeed, no limit to the foolishness of headstrong girls. But he would, he promised them, have a good, strong word with his niece and remind her where her true duties lay.

He had insisted on accompanying Saffron. "You are my brother's daughter, little princess. You are going to see my mother. Of course I must come with you to keep you safe. No man or beast will dare to trouble you when I walk at your side."

For her part, Saffron was only too happy to have Manyoro's company. She was proud of her independence and knew that she was as capable as any man of fighting her way out of trouble, or taking the hardest of all possible decisions and living with the consequences. Still, it was wonderful to feel protected and secure in the company of a father figure she loved, and whose love for her was as warm and reassuring as a cozy fire on a cold winter's day.

She knew, too, that while the deeds to the Lusima estate might declare it to be the property of Leon Courtney, and the revenues from its farms might end up in his bank account, Manyoro was indeed the king of all he surveyed. He was greeted by all the estate staff and their families with the profound respect due to a monarch and he responded with a suitably regal air of a man who loved all his people but was still, nonetheless, their master.

He was not, however, an entirely contented king. "Can you believe that I offered my services to the King's African rifles and was rejected on the grounds that I was too old. Ha! Look at me, am I not still a mighty warrior?"

"You are, indeed, the very mightiest of warriors, Uncle Manyoro," Saffron agreed, with a suitably serious look on her face, for he was indeed a fine figure of a man, for all that he must now be the best part of seventy, at the very least. "It is a scandal and an outrage that these fools turned their back on you. But then, my father never made any secret of his contempt for his regiment's senior officers, as you well know."

Manyoro nodded. "That is very true. And he had reason to feel aggrieved for they were lying jackals who betrayed him with lies and injustice."

"Then you should not take this personally. These men are not worthy of you. In any case, your people would suffer if you went away to war. They need you. And we need the food that they grow here and the meat of the cattle that they raise and herd. Believe me, Uncle, my people are hungry. They are attacked on all sides. They need all that you can give them. So you, and all the people of the Lusima estate, are doing the King and the Empire a very great service."

"I can see that you tell the truth, princess," Manyoro said, "and I thank you for it. I know that your mother looks down on you now and her heart swells with pride to see her daughter grown to such a fine, brave woman. And I know that my mother will be filled with joy to see you again, for you are as a granddaughter to her, too."

As the sun rose toward its zenith, Saffron walked with Manyoro up the mountain path, passing through the cloud-line that marked the point at which the dry, savannah vegetation of the lower slopes, the grass and umbrella acacia trees gave way to the lush montane forests that were constantly watered by mists and rain. As they came closer to the summit, Saffron could feel the delight bubbling up through Manyoro like clear spring water through black basalt rock as he approached his birthplace, his truest home.

Then they surmounted the very last, steepest portion of the climb and stepped onto the tabletop plateau and the mountain's summit. Now the cries of delight were all for Manyoro. Little children scampered around his feet and he greeted them all by name for these were his great-grandchildren and he took huge pride that there were so many of them, and all so healthy and well-fed. Saffron had been here before, to be introduced to Lusima Mama, but it had been before she went away to Roedean, so she could only have been eleven or twelve, at the most: too young to fully comprehend the significance of the occasion, or appreciate the true stature of the elderly lady she was meeting.

Now, though, she was a grown woman. And so, as Manyoro led her through the trees to the shady spot where his mother now liked to spend her days, enthroned in the chair cut from the stump of a once-mighty hardwood tree, she felt awestruck by the vision that greeted her.

Lusima Mama was now so ancient that she seemed to have gone beyond any mundane embodiment of old age. She did not rise to greet Saffron, but lifted her hand so that her visitor might take it, and tilted her head so that her cheek could be kissed. Saffron placed the most delicate of touches of her lips against Lusima Mama's skin and it felt warm and dry and as fine as the most delicate, gossamer silk. The bones of her fingers seemed so light and fragile in Saffron's strong hands that she feared she might snap them with the slightest pressure. And though her limbs were still long and straight and the bone structure of her face retained its exquisite elegance, Lusima Mama's presence seemed less physical than ethereal, more like an elven queen from an African fairy tale than a mere mortal human.

As Manyoro discreetly slipped away, leaving the women to their business, his mother smiled and shifted her body to make room on the seat. "Come, sit beside me, my child."

Saffron did as she was told. She said nothing. Every ounce of intuition that she possessed told her that it would be best to allow Lusima Mama to lead the conversation. She let herself be examined by dark eyes that had lost none of their insight until Lusima Mama smiled and said, "You are a daughter worthy of your parents. You have the beauty and courage of your mother, and the strength and fighting spirit of your father. I should like to meet the one you love so much. He must truly be a man among men."

Saffron knew from her father's stories about the first time he met Lusima Mama that she had an unsettling habit of already knowing everything before one had said a word, but still she could not stop herself from gasping. "How . . . how did you know?"

Lusima Mama laughed. "I have the power to see things that others can't. But I had no need of them to tell that you were in love. And no man could win the love of a young lioness like you unless he was truly worthy of possessing it."

"Thank you, Mama," said Saffron, speaking with a formality she felt that so venerable a woman deserved. "You are as kind as you are wise. I'm sure I do not deserve such generous compliments. And of course you are right. I am in love and he is a good, and strong, and handsome man."

"And he pleases you, too, does he not?"

Saffron found herself blushing like a schoolgirl. "Yes," she said, trying hard not to giggle. "Like a lion."

"But now you and he have been parted by the war, and find yourself on different sides of the battle as your tribe fights his."

"Yes, and I don't know what to do. I feel I should serve my country. But I don't want to die . . . Not because I'm frightened. I just have to be alive for his sake. So I'm torn."

Lusima Mama shook her head. "No, you are not torn. Your head may be filled with different ideas, but your soul knows what it must do. And, once again, I need no trance, or powers of divination to see this. It is obvious. You must be fit for your man, just as he is fit for you. But how could you be worthy of him if you took the coward's path? Remember, child, that the lion is the hunter of the pride. You are a hunter too. That is your nature and you must not deny it. Now, give me your hand again."

This time it was Lusima Mama who took Saffron's hand in hers. She stroked the skin between Saffron's knuckles and her wrist. "I have not done this for many years," she murmured. "I have known that I only had the strength for one last journey and that I would know when it was time . . ."

"But Mama . . ." Saffron protested.

"Hush, child, you are the light in my son M'Bogo's life. I do this for both your sakes . . ."

Lusima Mama's eyes close and she fell quiet. The silence stretched out for what seemed like an eternity and then her eyes were wide open, rolled back so far that only their whites were visible. As her divination began she rocked back and forth as if moving to the rhythm of another world and when she spoke her voice was not that of an elderly lady, but was a low, gravelly monotone that sounded more male than female.

"You will walk alongside death, but you will live . . . I can see you, but I cannot see the lion. He is there, but he cannot be recognized. You will look for him, but if he is ever found, it will only be when you have ceased your search, and if you see him you will not know him, for he will be nameless and unknown, and if your eyes fall upon his face they will not see it for they will not know it to be his. And if he is alive, it will be as if he were dead. And yet . . . and yet . . . you must keep searching, for if he is to be saved, only you can save him."

The voice that was not Lusima Mama's voice fell silent, her body became inert once again and then, as if waking from a dream, she shook herself, blinked several times, fixed her eyes upon Saffron and smiled.

"Now you know all that can be known, my child," Lusima Mama said.

———

"I will not see her again, or not in this life at least," said Manyoro, as he and Saffron walked back down the mountain path.

"No, that can't be right," said Saffron, who could not bear the idea that she might have hastened Lusima Mama's passing.

"It is not a matter of right or wrong. It is just life, which ends when it must end. Mama wanted you to know that what came to pass today was always going to happen. It is not so much that she will go because you came, but that she lived until you arrived."

Saffron nodded, knowing that Manyoro's words seemed true to her, even inevitable, in a way she could not quite explain.

"I hope you learned what you needed to know," he said.

"Yes," Saffron replied. "I learned that my love and I were made for one another. I know that our destiny is to be together. I know that this destiny can only be fulfilled if I make it so. And I will make it so, Manyoro. I swear to you . . . I will."